Katy Watson grew up in North Wales, as part of a family of folk singers, storytellers and murder-mystery addicts. An avid reader and notebook collector, her dream was to combine the two hobbies by becoming an author and, after spending her teenage years reading paperback Christies on rainy Welsh caravan holidays, it seemed inevitable that one day she'd try writing her own crime novel.

It took her eight years of writing professionally – and over forty-five non-murderous books for children, teens and adults – to write her first murder mystery, *The Three Dahlias*, and now she's started she never wants to stop! *A Very Lively Murder* is the second adventure for her amateur sleuths, Rosalind, Caro and Posy, and Katy is already hard at work on their next case.

T0053753

KATY WATSON

A VERY LIVELY MURDER

CONSTABLE

CONSTABLE

First published in Great Britain in 2023 by Constable
This paperback edition published in 2024 by Constable

1 3 5 7 9 10 8 6 4 2

A CIP catalogue record for this book
is available from the British Library.

ISBN: 978-1-40871-647-2

Typeset in Adobe Garamond by Hewer Text UK Ltd, Edinburgh
Printed and bound in Great Britain by Clays Ltd, Elcograf S.p.A.

Papers used by Constable are from well-managed forests and other responsible sources.

Constable
An imprint of
Little, Brown Book Group
Carmelite House
50 Victoria Embankment
London EC4Y 0DZ

An Hachette UK Company
www.hachette.co.uk

www.littlebrown.co.uk

To my family, for instilling in me a love of (fictional) murder that spans time and space, from a medieval monk in Shrewsbury to the Orient Express in the 30s to Cabot Cove in the 80s, and far beyond.

Cast List for *The Lady Detective* Movie:

Posy Starling – *playing Dahlia Lively*
Kit Lewis – *playing DI Johnnie Swain*
Nina Novak – *playing Bess, Dahlia's maid and sidekick*
Dominic Laugharne – *playing Dahlia's Uncle Francis*
Keira Reynolds-Yang – *playing Francis's second wife*
Tristan Haworth – *playing Dahlia's ex-fiancé, Charles*
Rosalind King – *playing Dahlia's Great Aunt Hermione*
Gabriel Perez – *playing Dahlia's cousin, Bertie*
Scarlett Young – *playing Bertie's wife, Rose*
Moira Gardiner – *playing Francis's neighbour*
Bennett Gracy – *playing Francis's old friend from India*

Notable Crew Members:

Anton Martinez – *Director*
Libby McKinley – *Writer*
Brigette Laugharne – *Casting Director*

With thanks to:

Rhian Hassan – *Manager of Ty Gwyn, for the filming location*
Owain and Rebecca Morgan, and their daughter, Seren – *Owners of Saith Seren Inn, for providing cast accommodation*
Caro Hooper – *ex-Dahlia Lively (Note from director: What is she doing here anyway?!)*

Chapter One

'Look at them all, Johnnie,' Dahlia said, gazing around the gathering with disdain. 'Any one of them could have killed the old beggar then poured themselves a cup of tea afterwards, perfectly certain that they'd only done what was right and proper, under the circumstances.'

Dahlia Lively *in* **All the World's a Stage**
By Lettice Davenport, 1938

Posy

Posy Starling gazed out of the window at the glitter of snowflakes starting to fall from the leaden January sky. The clouds were so low that the tips of the Welsh mountains surrounding the house were hidden and, even though it was only mid-afternoon, it felt as if night was falling fast.

She felt a million miles away from London, in time, as well as place. Perhaps it was the weather – or more likely the grandeur and feel of the Art Deco mansion she stood in.

With one last look at the fattening flakes, Posy turned back to the room behind her. It was dominated by a large mahogany dining table with high-backed chairs, and by the immense crystal chandelier that hung above it, sparkling in the light from the cheering fire that roared in the large fireplace. Over the mantelpiece hung a large

I

oil painting of the house itself, showing how it would look in the summer months.

Tŷ Gwyn lived up to its name – the White House – as it shone in the sunshine of the painted landscape, with its curved windows reflecting brighter still above matching balconies. Posy hadn't had a chance to explore the whole house, yet, but just from that painting, and her impressions as she'd arrived through the wrought-iron gates, she thought this place had to be bigger than Aldermere. More luxurious, too, if the glimpses of the rooms she'd passed were representative. There was nothing shabby or faded about Tŷ Gwyn.

Everything here was both shiny and new-looking, but also of the perfect vintage for the shooting of a Dahlia Lively film. As if they'd travelled back in time to the actual 1930s, rather than bother trying to recreate it with antiques.

It would be perfect for the movie.

Posy just hoped she could live up to her surroundings.

Because right now, she didn't feel shiny or new. She felt the weight of her past, her experiences, hanging heavy around her shoulders as the occupants of the room all sized each other up. This was the first time the cast of the new movie had been all together in the same place, ahead of filming beginning next week. Today, they would do a full table read of the script, and start to get a feel for each other as actors.

She just hoped the other cast members wouldn't let their preconceptions of her as a person get in the way.

The wind howling outside the walls, rattling the window frames and screaming down the chimney didn't seem to disturb any of her new co-workers, many of whom were already chatting like old friends. Probably most of them were, she realised. Brigette, their casting director, had assembled a cast comprised of big names, familiar faces and a few up-and-comers. Posy wasn't entirely sure where she fitted into that mix, and hadn't really wanted to ask. But the chances were, most people in this room had worked together on some show or film before, except her. They had history.

She had a past. And that, she'd learned over the years, wasn't at all the same thing.

Posy glanced down at the table. A name card with *Dahlia Lively* written in perfect black calligraphy denoted her place, beside a stack of bound paper.

The Lady Detective – Shooting Script.

Inside that script lay her professional future. Her place here. After all the months of setbacks – and the occasional curse – it was finally time for the movie that was going to rebuild her career to start filming.

She looked along the table and spotted one of the few members of the cast she did already know. Rosalind King, the first actor ever to play Dahlia Lively, in the original 1980s movies, was back on set to play a different part, this time – Dahlia's Great-Aunt Hermione, the last murder victim in the film.

Rosalind shifted to look at her, a small smile on her face. And in that moment, Posy ventured she could read her co-star's mind perfectly.

Look at them all. You don't need to worry about what they think. None of them *solved a murder last summer, did they?*

She might not have acting history with the rest of the cast, but she *did* have history with Rosalind. That was something. She wasn't alone here. She belonged.

That was what she needed to remember.

Unfortunately, her brain had other ideas.

The delight of seeing Rosalind King on screen again is dimmed only by the realisation that, even as a Lady Of A Certain Age, King still projects more Dahlia Lively spirit in her limited scenes than Starling manages in the full hundred and eight minutes.

Posy clenched her jaw as the mental review ran, unchecked, in her mind. She'd thought she'd rid herself of her inner critic – the one who always sounded like her Uncle Sol, famous film reviewer and her godfather – but apparently he was back with a vengeance now filming was starting.

Just what she needed.

At least Caro Hooper wasn't in the movie, too. After starring as Dahlia Lively for thirteen years on TV, she was by far the most synonymous with the character. For Posy to attempt to play the Lady Detective on screen next to *two* Dahlias would just be too much.

Still, it did seem strange to be back in another large country home with Rosalind, but without Caro and her encyclopaedic knowledge of all things Dahlia.

Posy's gaze slid across the room to Kit Lewis. Her only other friend on set, he would be playing DI Johnnie Swain in their revival – having weathered the initial outcry from certain quarters that the role should have gone to yet another white actor, just like the last two to play the part. He stood near the fireplace, the flames behind the grille making his dark eyes flicker amber.

She'd seen Kit since they'd left Aldermere last summer, although not as often as either of them would have liked. He was a hot commodity these days, and had had two other projects to finish up or promote before heading to Wales to film *The Lady Detective*.

The rest of the cast were all new faces to her – albeit many of them familiar from the big screen. She'd googled those she didn't know the moment she'd got the cast list. Now, she watched them each in turn, connecting names with faces and faces with films or shows. Caro's

4

words, from her good-luck phone call the night before, echoed in her mind.

Remember, kiddo, you're the star there. You're *Dahlia. And that means you're the boss, whatever that director of yours thinks.* You're *the one who needs to pull the team together, to encourage them when you've been filming in the rain for three days straight, or when craft services have run out of the good sandwiches. You go in there and show them that you're a team player all right – but that it's* your *team, okay?*

Posy wasn't sure how well that would go down with some of the big stars present. But Caro was right; she had to try. And remembering everybody's name would be a good start.

She tested herself now, as she leaned against the back of her chair and observed them all.

There, talking softly to Kit, was Nina Novak, the Croatian-British actor playing Dahlia's maid and sidekick, Bess. This was her first film role, as far as Posy had been able to tell, although she'd done quite a bit on stage. Nina fidgeted with her long, dark hair as it hung in a braid over her shoulder. She'd definitely need to befriend Nina; if this movie went well, they could be working together on any number of sequels. Bess had appeared in most of the Dahlia Lively books, serving as Dahlia's sidekick and someone to whom she could explain her theories.

With them was Tristan Haworth – another one of the actors she'd needed to Google, although she'd instantly recognised a handful of shows she must have seen him in. He was playing Charles, the man Dahlia's Uncle Francis hoped she'd marry – and to whom Dahlia had no intention of shackling herself.

Tall and lean, with short, pale hair and striking blue eyes, Tristan definitely looked like the classic British aristocratic type Dahlia's uncle *would* want her to marry, Posy decided. Brigette had done well finding him.

Tristan said something that made Kit throw his head back with laughter, and even the nervy Nina Novak smile and giggle up at him. The satisfaction on Tristan's face told Posy that he was going to be the joker on set, although the slow smile he gave her when he caught her watching suggested he might be the cast flirt, too. The idea made the nerves in her stomach kick up a gear, as she thought about how all the personalities on set needed to work together perfectly to avoid issues among the cast. Something that was even more important than usual on such an isolated shoot.

She could almost hear Caro murmuring beside her. *A worse flirt than Kit? Kiddo, you* are *in trouble.*

Maybe she did wish Caro was there, after all. Life was a lot more fun with Caro Hooper around. And at least it would be one voice out of her head . . .

Posy broke away from looking at Tristan, and turned to look down the other end of the room. Over by the window that framed the view across the river, Keira Reynolds-Yang had just arrived and fallen immediately into discussion with Bennett Gracy, Moira Gardiner and Dominic Laugharne. None of *them* had required any internet searches, of course. The last three were old establishment actors, famous in Britain and Hollywood alike for their long, distinguished careers. Bennett and Moira were just there for the day, to participate in the table read. Their scenes were few, and involved filming away from Tŷ Gwyn, so Anton had scheduled them separately. At least that was two big egos not to have to worry about on set.

Dominic, of course, would be playing her Uncle Francis. In recent years, that seemed to be his preferred sort of role – dominant patriarch types, of varying eras and styles. He had to be in his sixties now, but he retained the good looks that had made him a star in the first place, while the years added an authority that suited him. Recently, he'd been playing the corrupt billionaire CEO of a family business in a long-running TV series where he yelled at people and then arranged to have them made bankrupt or worse.

Prior to that, Posy recalled, he'd had a spell in the wilderness not unlike her own – although his had been due to his behaviour around his young, female co-stars. The TV role could have been a step down from his previous movie stardom, but after a few years of being blacklisted, she suspected he'd had to take it. And actually, it now seemed to have his star back on the rise.

From what she'd read of the script, Dominic would mostly be red-faced and blustering in this movie, while she got to be cool and cutting. Posy was quite looking forward to that.

Despite being decades younger than the three big name actors she stood with, Keira was just as famous in her way – for her social media follower count, her modelling career, her newly burgeoning movie career, her ex-boyfriends . . . and most of all, her parents.

She'd be playing Dominic's younger – *much* younger – second wife. Posy wondered how Keira felt about that thirty-plus-year age gap, under the circumstances.

The final two cast members, Scarlett Young and Gabriel Perez, had joined Rosalind at the table, sitting either side of her. Gabriel was playing Dahlia's cousin, Bertie, with Scarlett his wife, Rose. There was at least a ten-year age gap between them, too, Posy guessed – with Gabriel in his mid-thirties, and Scarlett only twenty-two, according to her profiles. He had a fairly established line in support-ing roles in Hollywood while she had, until very recently, been appearing in a well-known British soap opera.

Posy didn't know either of them personally, although she was almost sure she and Gabriel had met at an awards ceremony or simi-lar over in the States. Given how Swiss-cheesed her memories from those days were, perhaps she'd better hope that *he* didn't remember the encounter, just in case.

Outside in the hallway, raised voices caught her attention. Posy shifted slightly behind her chair, so she had a direct line of sight into the entrance hall as Anton, their director, and Brigette came into view.

'I'm just saying—' Brigette was cut off by Anton before anyone could learn *what* she was just saying. He was, by all accounts, a brilliant director – but in Posy's experience, not the most patient of men.

'And *I'm* saying that if you don't like it you can— Yes? What is it?' he snapped at someone standing just out of view. Posy leaned forward, and caught the edge of the bright pink hijab that Rhian, the manager of Tŷ Gwyn, was wearing.

She spoke too softly to be heard at a distance, but as Anton turned to give her his full attention, Brigette threw up her hands and turned away, only to be intercepted by Keira, who had slipped out of the room, presumably also intrigued by the drama in the hall.

'I say it *has* to be Moira.' Bennett's American accent cut across the room, his voice projecting just enough for everyone else to pause their conversations and listen, as Posy was sure he'd intended. It certainly caught her attention.

'Oh, no, really,' Moira demurred, but there was a glow of pride about her that spoke of a well-appreciated compliment.

'I'm sure it does,' Tristan said, moving to merge their small groups of chatter into one larger one. 'But what, exactly, has to be Moira?'

'Why, the murderer, of course,' Dominic replied, with a dramatic waggle of the eyebrows to accompany his 'I was in the RSC, don't you know' delivery. 'It's *always* the most famous guest star in these things, isn't it?'

Ah, that explained Moira's glow. And the slightly sour expression on Rosalind's face.

For such a classic novel, Posy would have thought the question of whodunnit was easily answered. But of course this was a reboot, and Hollywood seemed to have a thing for rewriting the rules on endings recently. It was entirely possible that Anton would follow suit and change the murderer for his version of *The Lady Detective*.

She was pretty sure it wouldn't be Moira, though. Her character of Uncle Francis's neighbour was barely in it – and scheduled to die in the opening scenes. Posy was looking forward to filming those. She got to burst into the room and derail Kit's investigation by announcing that 'Only an idiot would think this was suicide. You're not an idiot, are you, Detective Inspector?'

That was going to be fun.

Posy looked up as Keira slipped back into the room. Out in the hall, she saw Anton and Rhian still in conversation – the former's expression growing more impatient by the second. Behind them, Brigette held her phone to her ear and, frowning, opened the door to the room opposite and stepped inside, closing it tight behind her.

'Don't fancy the "most famous guest star" title for yourself, Dom?' Gabriel joked. 'We've all heard the rumours.' A slight pause, just enough for Dominic's smile to tighten. 'About this year's awards, I mean.'

'Ah, but Dominic *can't* be the murderer – he's the victim,' Kit pointed out. As a Dahlia fan himself, he'd know exactly who was supposed to commit the crimes – and who suffered them. 'Same goes for Moira, and for our illustrious Rosalind King.' He shot a fond smile towards the head of the table at that, and Posy noticed that Moira's glow had dimmed a little. 'So who does that leave?'

'I'd think perhaps they'd want to go for a . . . fresher take, for the new movie,' Keira said. 'Fame doesn't mean what it used to, does it?' Her voice was sweet, but Posy could hear the poison in her words all the same, as she smiled at Scarlett, who looked away.

A tension that hadn't been there earlier pulled the air in the room tight, until Posy longed to open a window.

'I'd think the solution to the argument was fairly self-explanatory,' Rosalind said, raising one eyebrow the way she had on the big screen as Dahlia. Something Posy had been practising in the mirror for four months and *still* couldn't get right.

When Rosalind didn't continue, Posy realised that her friend had given her the opening to fix this. To lead, the way Caro told her she needed to. Posy suspected that Rosalind might have got a call last night, too.

They'd all been given scripts before today, of course, but not the finished article – and if hers was anything to go by, they'd all been missing the important, final scenes where the killer was unmasked.

Was the killer the one Lettice Davenport had written? Or had Libby McKinley, their latest writer – who just happened also to be Lettice's granddaughter – twisted the ending to fit her own story?

Posy picked up the script in front of her to find out – just as several others did the same.

'Like I said: Moira.' Bennett snapped his script closed. 'She must have faked her death.' Posy frowned. That couldn't be right.

'Mine says it's the uncle's second wife,' Tristan corrected him. 'That's Keira.'

'And mine says it's you, Bennett. The uncle's friend from India.' Kit shrugged and dropped his script back onto the table. 'How about yours, Posy?'

'I've got cousin Bertie and his wife,' she replied. 'Gabriel and Scarlett.'

'And mine claims Charles did it,' Rosalind said. 'Which I suspect means we're being played with. Correct, Anton?'

Posy looked up to find the director standing in the doorway, amusement twisting his lips into a smile. 'Not *played* with, Rosalind. I wouldn't dream of such a thing.' Rosalind raised that eyebrow again. 'It's simply that we cannot risk our chosen ending leaking to the public before the movie is released. A large part of our publicity campaign is going to hang on the idea that we're recreating Dahlia Lively for the twenty-first century, and that means anything can happen. After all, why would people want to come and see a murder mystery where they already know for certain who the murderer is? So we'll be filming five possible endings, so that no one can be sure which is the real one!'

A murmur raced around the room at that, although whether it was in appreciation for the tactic, or because of the extra work and time involved, Posy wasn't sure. Knowing Anton, she wasn't surprised at the publicity gimmick. Something to make a big deal about in the press – and something else for people to talk about that wasn't the curse that seemed to have haunted the movie last summer.

'Now, if we're all here, why don't we get started?' Anton made his way to his chair, in the centre of one of the long sides of the oval table, then stopped. 'Where did Brigette go? She was with us in the hallway, before that Rhian woman side-tracked me with more of her bloody questions.'

Dominic laughed. 'Story of my marriage to the woman, Anton. Whenever I thought we were ready to leave to get somewhere on time, there was always something else she needed to do first.' Posy waited for the 'and that's why I divorced her' punchline, but it never came. She remembered the last interview she'd read with Dominic, maybe six months ago now, where he talked about their power couple heyday in the nineties and noughties, and how Brigette would always be the love of his life.

Obviously, she'd felt differently, Posy concluded.

'She ducked into the room over there to take a phone call.' Keira waved towards the still closed door. 'We were having the *loveliest* catch up when her phone buzzed, so of course I left her to it and came in here.' She smiled around her. Posy got the strangest feeling they were supposed to be grateful for her presence.

'Well, Brigette said she wanted to be here for the read through, but if she's too busy sulking—' Anton started, but Keira jumped to her feet and interrupted him.

'I'll go and find her.' Keira flashed that too-sweet smile back at the director, and darted for the door. 'Won't be a moment.'

They all sat there in the strange stillness of the falling snow, waiting for her to return. Over the table, the candle bulbs in the ornate chandelier flickered for a moment.

'That's strange.' Keira reappeared in the doorway. 'The door won't open.'

Anton stalked out into the hallway and glared at Rhian, who hovered just outside. 'Is it stuck? Or do these doors just lock themselves, now?'

One by one, the rest of the cast also migrated into the hallway.

'I'd imagine Brigette might have locked herself in there to keep people like Keira out while she had a private conversation,' Rosalind, who'd come up beside her, murmured in Posy's ear. 'I know I would.'

Posy attempted a smile, but the knot that had suddenly formed in her chest wouldn't allow for it.

Something about this didn't feel right.

Rhian knocked on the door, then, when no response was forthcoming, tried the handle.

'You see? Locked,' Keira said, triumphantly, as Rhian reached for the heavy keyring that hung at her waist.

'I'll see if I can open it.' Rhian slipped the key into the lock and turned it. Posy held her breath as the door swung open and—

Silence.

The room, they could all plainly see, was empty. No sign that Brigette had ever been there at all.

'She must have left already, and the door locked itself.' Rhian bent to pick something up off the floor just inside the room, then pushed the door fully open. 'Sometimes they do that. Would you like me to look for her?'

Anton shook his head, sharply. 'No need. If she wanted to be here, she would be. Now, let's get started. If we could all get *back* into the dining room and take our seats?'

Posy did as she was told, a frown furrowing her brow. She'd been sure that Brigette had gone into that room, too. She'd had a view of it the whole time, and hadn't seen the door open again, or Brigette walk out. But how was that possible?

Perhaps she was mistaken. But from the way Keira kept glancing across the hallway to the study door, she wasn't the only one confused by Brigette's sudden disappearance.

Rosalind was sat at the head of the table once more, already staring down at her script. As she passed on her way to her own seat, Posy leaned in towards her, intending to whisper her thoughts about the mystery to the older Dahlia – but then she saw exactly what Rosalind was staring at.

A postcard, tucked into the pages of her script. One that hadn't been there before.

One that read:

Watch out.

I'm coming for you.

13

Chapter Two

'Well, if you want my opinion – I take it you do *want my opinion, Johnnie?'*

Johnnie sighed. He was past pretending that Dahlia's unusual insights weren't often the key to solving his cases. Even if he'd never admit as much to his superiors. 'Yes. I suppose I do.'

Dahlia smiled her cat-like smile. 'Well, I think it's perfectly obvious who was behind this. Don't you?'

Dahlia Lively *in* **To Catch a Fly**
By **Lettice Davenport, 1970**

Two Weeks Later
Caro

Caro Hooper was balancing on a kitchen stool, trying to reach a rogue Tupperware lid on top of one of the cupboards with her wife's favourite feather duster, when her phone rang. Holding the duster between her teeth, she fished it out of her pocket, pressed speakerphone, then dropped it onto the counter.

'Caro? Caro! Can you hear me? This line is rubbish.' Posy's voice rang perfectly clear.

Caro rolled her eyes, and resumed her retrieval operation. 'I can hear you. Must be all the egos on set messing with the reception at your end.' Not that she didn't wish she was there with them. Her wife, Annie, reckoned Caro's ego could give some of theirs a run for their money. 'What's up?'

'We need you. Can you come up to Wales? We're filming in some old National Trust-type place since Aldermere's up for sale.' Posy's voice caught a little on the word Aldermere. Even Caro paused, the dust bunnies on the top of the kitchen cabinets forgotten. 'It's very grand.'

'I did a god-awful indie film in a swamp of a woods in mid-Wales in the early noughties. Swore I'd never go back.' Although she had to admit, even Wales sounded more fun than the cleaning schedule Annie had stuck to the fridge, and was insisting they follow with relentless attention to detail. 'Unless Anton has suddenly found a part for me in the film . . .'

'Not that I know of,' Posy admitted. 'But Caro, we really do need you. Me and Rosalind.'

'Why on earth would you need me?' Caro asked. An unemployed, forty-something actress who hadn't even been able to nail the 'Mum in a cereal advert' audition she'd been up for last week.

'Give me that thing.' Rosalind's voice sounded in the background, growing louder as she wrestled the phone from Posy's grip. 'Caro Hooper, get yourself to Wales. Now.'

'Hello, Rosalind. How lovely to hear from you. How are things in the middle of nowhere?'

'There's been a murder,' Rosalind said, bluntly. 'Well, possibly an attempted one, anyway.'

'Haven't we done that one already?' Caro asked. All the same, she could feel her pulse kicking up a gear at the idea of another investigation. 'Don't want to get typecast now, do we?' Not that she'd been given the choice so far.

'Yes,' Rosalind replied. 'But this time, we think they're trying to kill me.'

Caro climbed down from her stool and sat on it, staring out of the kitchen window at the bright but cold February day outside. 'Start from the beginning. What happened?'

'There was an ... accident on set,' Rosalind said, cautiously. 'Yesterday. I'm fine, and maybe it really *was* an accident. Only, I've been getting letters.'

Letters. Caro knew what that meant. *Death threats. Accidents. Attempted murder* . . .

'We need you to come and help us figure out what's going on,' Rosalind finished.

She had so many more questions, but Rosalind's cagey tone told her she wasn't going to get answers over the phone. She'd need to go to Wales for those.

'Can't you two solve one little mystery on your own?' Caro asked, even though she was hoping that they'd say no. Everyone wanted to feel needed, didn't they?

What if Annie needs you here? Her better angel sounded in her head, but Caro pushed it away. Annie was finding things to keep her busy, that was all. Spring cleaning. Whoever did spring cleaning in February, anyway? It was still winter out there, whatever the bright blue skies said.

No. Annie would be glad she'd found something else to occupy herself, since it was obvious that the juicy-roles-for-mature-women market had been cornered by the two or three household names who got cast in everything.

Caro loved her wife, more than anything. She knew that Annie loved her too. That didn't change the fact that their relationship had always worked best when they were both following their own passions too – even if that meant time apart.

A bored Caro was a *boring* Caro. And the last thing she wanted was for her wife to get bored of her.

Acting wasn't working for her anymore. And neither was this housewife spring-cleaning malarky.

She needed a new plan. Solving a mystery seemed a perfectly good way to pass the time while she figured out what that was going to be. Even if she had a sneaking suspicion that Rosalind and Posy might be playing up the peril a little bit to make her feel needed.

'We're too caught up in things here,' Rosalind said, after a pause. 'We need an outsider's point of view.'

'You mean you're too busy filming the big movie that's going to make you even richer and more famous.' Just because she wanted the adventure didn't mean she was going to give in easily. 'You need the unemployed Dahlia to come and do the grunt work of the investigation.'

Rosalind didn't deny it, not that Caro had expected her to. 'So you'll come?'

Caro gazed up at the cabinet she'd been cleaning, but found her attention drawn outside the cosy, yellow-walled kitchen again, and through the window. Past the snowdrops Annie had planted by the rosemary bush at the back gate, and the bright blue skies over the roofs of the neighbouring houses.

'I've got some things to finish up here,' she said, as a cloud crossed in front of the weak winter sun, sending shadows scattering. 'But yes, of course I'll come. If you need me.'

'We need you.' Posy's voice was definite; she must have taken the phone back again to hear Caro's answer. 'There's something . . . not right about this film. Maybe several things.'

'Then I'll be there tomorrow,' Caro promised, and went to find her wife to explain why she had to go to Wales for a while.

Driving through the Welsh countryside in her bright red convertible the following afternoon, Caro decided she'd made the right choice in coming. Yes, it would be weird being on set but not in the film – but Rosalind and Posy had *asked* her to come. She had a job to do there, an investigation to perform. It wasn't like she was going to be a spare part. And Posy had sounded . . . worried.

Just being out here in the hills, watching the pale grey clouds roll by overhead in the ice-blue sky, as she tackled twisty corners and unexpected bends, her scarf tucked tight around her throat against the chilly air, made Caro feel freer. Like she was travelling towards something.

Which, of course, she was. In particular, towards Tŷ Gwyn – pronounced *tea g-win*, as far as she could tell from the translation app on her phone, and meaning, imaginatively, the White House in Welsh. Posy had described it as a National Trust-type place but, from Caro's perusal of the website, it appeared to be more of a large, private stately home that was leased for events, such as weddings and parties, and for filming.

A turn in the road gifted her the sight of a glittering lake edged, on the side still in shadow, by frosted ferns. Then the hills gave way to another twisty, narrow road lined with trees on either side and, a mile or so later, one last bend revealed a single-lane bridge over a fast-flowing river. Caro slowed the car to a stop, eyeing the bridge with distrust as she gave way to another vehicle crossing towards her. When the ancient-looking structure survived the passage, Caro decided she'd risk it – although she held her breath while driving across.

On the other side of the bridge sat the village of Glan y Wern, slate roofs shining almost purple in the February sun. She passed several independent shops and cafes, a nice-looking pub on the riverbank and a village green with playground, before she was out the other side again, the road curving and rising before ending abruptly in a small cul-de-sac of palatial new houses.

That wasn't right.

With a frown, she wheeled the car around and headed back along the road, slowly. There – a turning. Well, sort of.

She hauled the steering wheel down and left behind the beauty of actual road markings for the narrow uphill lane that hopefully led to Tŷ Gwyn. It wound its way alongside the riverbank, the ground climbing beneath the convertible's wheels as it sped past a sign that read 'Dark Lane'.

She passed a sprawling building on her right, a much older, traditional one made of reddish stone, and with a large car park to the side and what looked like cottages behind. From the tastefully painted sign that hung above the door, this must be the inn Posy's late-night email had mentioned, which meant she needed to keep going. A few more bends and she should see it . . .

As Tŷ Gwyn came into view, Caro understood immediately why Anton had chosen it as the setting for *The Lady Detective*. It didn't look like Aldermere, exactly – it was whitewashed, as its name suggested, rather than the classic red brick of Lettice Davenport's old home, and it was, if anything, rather grander. More imposing.

Perched on top of the small hill, flanked by more imposing mountains behind, and with a landscape of purple, grey and green surrounding it, Tŷ Gwyn *felt* like the sort of place a murder was meant to happen. Like all of Lettice's best books, it looked as if it had the glamour and the grandeur – with the seedy horror of murder lurking just under the surface.

Maybe that was all this was. Perhaps Rosalind and Posy had just got caught up in the atmosphere of the place – not to mention filming an actual murder mystery – and started seeing killers where there were only cameras.

Except she knew her fellow Dahlias better than that.

She reached the intricate iron gates that barred the driveway while the house was still a little way in the distance, and pulled on her handbrake to wait for the security guy in the hi-vis jacket to lumber over from the guard post set up by the gates. *The Lady Detective* film crew and cast appeared to have taken over the whole place, grounds and all, because she could see trailers, vans and equipment set up on the lawns.

'No non-essential vehicles past the gate,' the security guard said. 'You can park up over there.'

He pointed towards a small number of cars parked neatly on temporary surfaces near the edge of the trees, just above the river. 'Better hope the waters don't rise,' Caro muttered to herself, manoeuvring the convertible into position. As if the lawns and flower beds of Tŷ Gwyn weren't already doomed by having a film crew traipsing in and out with their vans and lighting rigs and trailers for the next few months.

She closed the roof at the press of a button, unwound her scarf, and removed her coat and leather driving gloves. One last check of her lipstick in the mirror and she grabbed her bag before swinging her legs out of the car. She'd gone for a muted Dahlia look for her big entrance, not wanting to draw too much attention to the fact that she *wasn't* actually Dahlia this time around. So, heavy wool trousers, in a wider cut that was currently fashionable enough to find in the shops, but also held hints of Katharine Hepburn. Teamed with a scarlet-red jumper and pearls, she felt suitably armoured to face the cast of the film she wasn't in.

'He won't let you in if you're not on the list.'

Caro turned to find a dark-haired teenage girl loitering near the bushes that separated the road from the riverbank, watching her.

'Won't he?' She pushed the car door shut. 'Whyever not?'

The girl moved closer. 'Because you've got to be on the list to be allowed in. Believe me, I've tried.' Her last sentence sounded so world weary, Caro couldn't help but smile.

'You want to get in there? Where they're filming?' She imagined that a film set would be fascinating to a teenager stuck out here in the middle of nowhere. 'I suppose you want to meet all the stars.'

The girl pulled a disgusted face. 'Them? No, I want to see how the movie is *made*.'

'Really?' Caro asked, in surprise. 'Why?'

'I'm making a documentary, all about them filming here. Since it's basically the only interesting thing to happen in Glan y Wern ever.' She lifted her phone as evidence of her endeavours. 'And because Dahlia Lively is kind of awesome.'

That much they could agree on, even if the girl gave no sign that she realised she was in the presence of Dahlia herself. Well, one of them, anyway. 'Not much of a documentary if you can't get inside though, I suppose.'

'I'll find a way eventually,' she said, with a shrug and the optimism of youth that Caro vaguely remembered having as recently as two years ago. Before the big four-oh.

'I'm sure you will.' Caro held out a hand. 'I'm Caro.'

'Seren.' She took the offered hand and shook it, then looked at Caro with concern. 'Do you want me to show you where all the film lot are staying? They're at my mum and dad's inn, just down the hill.'

Caro favoured her with a wide, Dahlia-like smile. 'Oh, don't you worry about me, kiddo. I'll be fine.' Because she happened to know that Posy had put her on the security list for the day. As long as Anton hadn't spotted her name and taken it off again, she'd be in.

With a last wink in Seren's direction, she sauntered towards the gate and gave the security guard her name. He checked his list, nodded and opened the heavy, wrought-iron gate just enough to let her through.

'How did you do that?' Seren called after her, through the metal whorls of the fence.

Caro shrugged. 'I'm Dahlia Lively. They can't do it without me.'

The buzz of the film set hit Caro the moment she was through the gates, from the hum of chatter as the crew hurried about the place – far more of them than the cast, of course – to the whirr of mechanics being set in motion – tracks for the cameras, or sound equipment being tested. There was a beautifully restored 1930s Bentley parked on the driveway in front of the house, and two stand-ins were leaning against it to allow the lighting and camera crews to get their angles right before the stars came by to shoot later.

Caro skirted around the edge of the drive towards the door, to keep out of their way. The green lawns to the left of Tŷ Gwyn were lost under the muddy tracks and wheels of various catering trucks and vans full of equipment, but Caro could see that under normal circumstances they'd be quite stunning. They were bordered with beds filled with green-leaved plants, and the odd snowdrop just starting to emerge, later here than back home. Beyond the house she glimpsed more formal gardens, perfectly pruned topiary and more lawns, these ones immaculately maintained – and free from the casual destruction of the film crew.

But really, this small corner of tamed nature was dwarfed by the landscape beyond. Those purple-headed mountains she'd sung about in school assemblies, without really imagining what it was like to stand in the shadow of one.

No less imposing, in its way, was the house itself – a sprawling, white, Art Deco-style mansion. It had been built, Caro knew from the website, in the early 1930s. To either side of the entrance, the house stretched out in perfect symmetry, its white frontage curving out into rounded bay windows with arched tops. On the upper floors, gently curved balconies sat outside, and up by the roof the windows themselves were lozenge-shaped, black-edged panes of glass placed in curved patterns between wooden bars.

Caro strolled towards the large, black front door, which stood ajar – but found herself stopped by a young woman in a smart grey suit and a violet hijab.

Since nobody Caro knew of on a film set like this tended to wear suits, she assumed she belonged to the house, rather than the movie.

'Hi there,' she said, brightly. 'Caro Hooper. I'm here to . . .' *Investigate strange goings-on? Find out if someone is trying to kill my friend?* 'See Posy Starling,' she settled on, in the end. Maybe the woman would think she was a reporter, here to interview the star. That could work as a cover story – until someone recognised her. And by someone, she mostly meant Anton. She had a feeling the director might not be as pleased to see her as her friends would be.

'Rhian Hassan.' The woman held out her hand for Caro to take, which she did. 'I'm the manager here at Tŷ Gwyn, on site to assist the film crew with anything they need while they're with us.'

'And make sure they don't destroy anything valuable, right?' Caro joked.

Rhian gave her a small, polite smile, as she stood to let her pass, but didn't answer the question. 'They're about to start filming in the study right now, although I'm not sure exactly where Posy is. The cast have all been assigned trailers, of course, but more often they've taken to using the bedrooms of the house to relax in between filming.' From her tone, Caro gathered Rhian would rather that they didn't.

'I'm sure I'll find her.' Caro headed in with a cheery wave behind her at the house manager.

The entrance hall of Tŷ Gwyn was as grand as the outside. From the richly woven rug covering the flagstones to the glittering chandelier that hung from the double-height ceiling, Caro's overwhelming first impression was 'expensive'.

Period appropriate, dark wood furniture, lamps and other accessories had been placed strategically around the space, still leaving room for the cameras and crew to move around. Caro wondered if they were part of the set or belonged to Tŷ Gwyn itself. The website had promoted itself as offering the perfect 1930s setting for weddings and parties, so either was equally possible.

The proportions of the house already seemed larger than Aldermere – a definite bonus when trying to get both cast and filming equipment into a room. At the far end of the hall, past a couple of doors on either side, was a double staircase – starting from the left and right edges of the hall and curving to meet at a balcony landing on the first floor, all edged in golden balustrades. The dark red and gold carpet running up the centre of the steps, and the gloriously coloured oil portraits and landscape paintings that covered the walls, completed the look.

As she reached the open door of the second room on the left, she paused to peek inside.

This must be the study, since it was clearly set up for filming. As always when shooting in houses rather than on sets, it seemed rather a crush to fit everything in, despite the high ceilings and the large bay window letting in what little light the winter's day outside provided.

The room was packed full of people and equipment, the crew all crammed against the walls, behind the cameras, while Rosalind – aged up rather, Caro thought, and wearing an unflattering sage-green dressing gown – sat behind a solid, wooden Art Deco desk. White screens had been set up to reflect extra light, and the familiar boom mics loomed overhead on their long poles.

Anton bounced on the balls of his feet between two of the cameras, his energy and excitement clear. Caro knew from people who'd worked with him before that his focus on a scene was unshakeable when he was filming. Probably he wouldn't even notice she was here if she stayed out of his line of sight.

His dark hair had grown longer since last summer, and he raked the curls out of his face as he called, 'Action!' and someone snapped the clapperboard in front of the desk. Caro peered around a tall, fair man in costume to watch.

Rosalind slowly raised her head towards the camera nearest the door, a sour look on her face. 'You?' she said, disdainfully, and Caro had to smother a laugh.

Not so very long ago, that was how the eldest Dahlia might have spoken to *her*, if she'd shown up on her film set. How things had changed since last summer, that Rosalind had actually asked her to come because she needed her.

'Why on earth did you ask me to meet you here? At this time of night?' Rosalind continued. Then she shrank back in her seat, her eyes growing wider as she clutched that hideous green dressing gown tighter to her neck.

Ah, this must be the 'flashback to murder' scene so common in murder-mystery movies. There'd always been one in the Dahlia TV show, too. Either a short scene between the investigations showing a further murder committed – without ever showing the murderer, of course, or often, the same scene shown during the big reveal, while Dahlia explained who committed the crime and why, with the camera swinging around to show the culprit as she said their name.

Apparently Anton wasn't straying so far from the traditional format as he'd liked to claim in recent interviews. All that nonsense about five possible endings, and five possible murderers. Anton liked to be seen as innovative and fresh, maybe even a bit of an eccentric. But Caro suspected he just wanted to tell a great story, like the rest of them.

The blonde guy blocking part of Caro's view stepped forward, his arm raised to show the knife he held, and Rosalind opened her mouth to scream. Big reveal, then, Caro guessed, and settled back to watch Rosalind pretend to be stabbed by a prop knife with a retractable blade.

It was the sort of thing that always looked good in the finished cut, but was hard to really sell during filming, when observers standing at just the right angle – one that would never be shown in the movie – could see the blade slipping into the handle.

Caro was keen to see how realistic the great Rosalind King could make it look.

But then Rosalind's scream rang out, too sharp and too real, and the actor stabbing her started swearing, and Caro remembered exactly why she'd been called here in the first place.

Chapter Three

'I like to make myself useful,' Dahlia said.
'You mean you like to meddle,' Johnnie replied.

Dahlia Lively *in* Never Underestimate a Lady
***By* Lettice Davenport, 1930**

Rosalind

They were filming in the study today – filming her murder, of all things. Strange, she hadn't even had a chance to be a suspect yet, but filming chronologically never was very efficient.

Even stranger than filming out of order, though, was watching Posy Starling – child star, screw-up and, more latterly, friend – become Dahlia Lively. She might not feature in today's scene, but Rosalind had been watching her closely on set on previous days, and it still felt odd, hearing Dahlia's lines come out of another actress's mouth. She wasn't sure quite how she'd cope with Posy questioning her as Dahlia, when it came to it.

Rosalind had had it easiest as the first Dahlia, she supposed. There'd been a radio drama or two of the Dahlia Lively mysteries in the sixties, but she had been the first actress to portray the Lady Detective on screen. While Lettice Davenport's books were descriptive enough to give a good feel for the character, Rosalind had been given the leeway to develop Dahlia the way she saw fit.

She'd tried to be faithful to the books, especially after she'd met Letty and her family, incorporating Dahlia's famous solitary raised eyebrow and her stance. The costume department had also paid homage to the original texts, dressing her in wide-legged trousers and silk blouses, or replica cocktail dresses from the thirties.

For years, she had been Dahlia Lively. The one and only.

Until Caro Hooper came along.

By the time the new TV series was made in the mid-noughties, Lettice Davenport was already dead, and most people had forgotten about the original Lady Detective movies. Over thirteen series, Caro became the Dahlia Lively most people would think of, if asked.

Rosalind hadn't minded – at least, she'd told herself she hadn't. After all, her own career had taken off since then, and she herself was known for many more famous roles than Dahlia.

Even if Dahlia would always be the one that stayed with her longest.

But although she'd watched someone else take up the Dahlia mantle before, seeing Posy in full Dahlia regalia for the first time had been something of a shock. Her dark blonde hair was bobbed above her shoulders – although in a far more modern, softer bob than would have been strictly accurate for the time period – and pinned with waves at the front in a nod to the era. The quintessential Dahlia pillar-box-red lipstick stood out starkly against her pale skin, but looked perfectly in character when her lips curved in a mischievous smile. The wide, tan trousers and cream blouse were similar to the ones she and Caro had both worn, yet somehow different, even with the almost identical rope of pearls hanging down practically to her waist and the jewelled loupe dangling from her belt.

Everything was in keeping with the descriptions in the book, but the costume and make-up designers had made it all feel modern, too. Or maybe that was just Posy.

Regardless, she'd grown used to the idea, more or less, over the last couple of weeks of filming. But she wondered how Caro would react, when she arrived, to someone else in her role – even Posy. Rosalind had to admit, the urge to correct Posy's stance, to suggest a different inflection for the line, was still strong even for her – but she held back. *Posy* was Dahlia now, and she was merely a suspect answering questions. Or, today, getting horribly murdered.

Playing the victim was not one of Rosalind's strengths, and neither would she want it to be. Just sitting at an ugly desk in a vile dressing gown waiting to be stabbed? That wasn't acting. That was pure melodrama.

Still, the part was what it was, and today was Great-Aunt Hermione's day to die, so here she sat, grey streaks in her hair and wrinkles emphasised, waiting for whoever was first in line to stab her today.

Because thanks to Anton's ridiculous 'secret ending' plan, there were five different cast members waiting to do her in with the golden dagger. Just perfect.

Keira was first up on the call sheet, if she remembered right, but it was Tristan waiting by the door. 'Where's Keira?' she asked, as Sally the make-up artist touched up her powder.

'Still in the chair,' Sally replied. 'She was late in today, I think.'

Now Rosalind thought about it, she didn't remember seeing Keira on the shuttle transport that ran the cast the five minutes up the hill from their accommodation to Tŷ Gwyn. Not that that was unusual; it was close enough that many of them chose to walk, if it wasn't raining, and especially if they weren't needed for the first scene of the day. A chance for a glimpse of the outside world before the artificial lights took over.

Sally stepped back, out of the camera's sightline, and the assistant director stepped in with the clapperboard, ready for Anton to call for them to start.

Rosalind prepared to sink into the mind of Great-Aunt Hermione. Elderly, frail, but sharp as a tack. Bitter, for reasons to do with a dead husband and a worthless son and grandson. She'd rather have had Dahlia as a grandchild than Francis's son, Bertie, that much was clear from the text. Not that she'd show it. Hermione wasn't the sort to show feelings.

Except she'd have to in this scene. Because today she was going to die. Repeatedly. And the moment she knew that—

Rosalind broke away from the thought, repressing a shudder.

She had to focus on the scene she was here to film. She couldn't let her attention drift to other things. Like hidden notes, with their sinister threats. There were always letters, of course – through her agent or to the film set when she was working. Some pleasant, others . . . not so much. But these ones were something different. They suggested Great Aunt Hermione wasn't the only one destined to die here.

The first one, hidden in her script at the table read, she could almost laugh off as a prank. Posy had been far more concerned about it than she had. Rosalind had preferred to believe it was nothing more than a practical joke. Until the accident a few days ago when, in the crush of people on set in the front parlour, a camera arm had been knocked loose and would have brained her if she hadn't managed to jump out of the way. A move that had her still aching the following day, when she found the letter in her trailer.

A black-edged envelope, with another threatening note. One telling her that she'd been lucky to escape yesterday's close call. That she might not be so lucky the next time.

That was when Posy had insisted it was time to call Caro.

'Action!' Anton's call rang out across the overcrowded room, and Rosalind centred herself.

She was Hermione. That was all.

'You?' she sneered, as the script commanded. She'd repeat it another four times at minimum, she knew, with varying tones depending on the character in front of her. But for Tristan, playing Charles – Dahlia's spurned fiancé – he got all the disdain, and none of the faint respect other suspects might.

Hermione would have no time for a man who couldn't hold onto a woman – even if she also wouldn't have wanted Dahlia to marry him anyway. She was a woman of contradictions.

'Why on earth did you ask me to meet you here? At this time of night?' As Tristan moved forward on her words, raising the knife, Rosalind caught a glimpse of someone behind him, in the doorway. Was that Caro? She couldn't look too closely now, but she hoped it was.

She'd been putting on a brave face for Posy, not that she thought she believed it. But there was something . . . wrong about this place. This shoot.

Whoever had sent that note had to be on set somewhere. And whether they'd sent that camera arm swinging or just taken advantage of the coincidence, they'd made sure to let her know that she was watched. That she was vulnerable.

That she wasn't safe.

Watch out. I'm coming for you. That was what the first note had said.

And now it seemed that they were here. Maybe had been here all along.

Having Caro there to watch her back, to team up with them again to figure out what was going on here at Tŷ Gwyn . . . that would help. The three Dahlias back together.

Rosalind focused again on Tristan as he approached, knife raised, face twisted into a snarl of hatred. A chill settled in her heart at the sight. It looked too real, all of a sudden.

Someone on this film set sent that note.

Her gaze caught on the tip of that gleaming dagger, looking for all the world like it could cut through her breast to her heart and claim her life in an instant. Her scream, when it escaped her mouth, had nothing to do with the cue they'd discussed with Anton in rehearsal. And even she could hear the real terror in it.

This might be some of my best acting ever. The irreverent thought bubbled up amidst the panic.

Because she wasn't acting.

This felt too real.

Tristan placed his forearm against her throat, bracing his hand on the back of the chair so he didn't actually cut off her airways, but she obligingly stopped her scream all the same. Her mouth remained open in silent terror.

He pulled back the knife, and her eyes closed without her bidding as she prepared herself for the clunk against her breastbone as the fake blade retracted.

A heartbeat. Maybe two.

And—

Something crashed against the wood of the desk, a deep thunking noise, as Tristan swore and Anton yelled, 'Cut!'

The arm at her throat was gone. Rosalind opened her eyes to find Tristan a few paces back, eyes wide and hands shaking.

The dagger he'd held was stuck in the wood of the desk, point first.

'It was . . .' Tristan swallowed. 'It was the wrong dagger. Not the prop one. I only just noticed in time. If I hadn't—' He met her gaze with wild and scared eyes.

He'd almost killed her. Because someone here wanted her dead.

Anton stalked towards them, yanking the dagger from the desk and yelling for the prop master to explain what the hell just happened. Tristan had collapsed into the nearest chair, still shaking, and Nina Novak was crouched beside him, Bess's maid cap covering her hair, comforting him.

She'd almost died.

The words seemed almost meaningless in her head. Ridiculous. Impossible.

But the shuddering fear that was working its way through her body, almost to her heart, making her teeth chatter and her knuckles white as she gripped the chair arms . . . that was all too real.

She needed to get out of here. To escape. To survive.

But how, when she didn't know who she could trust?

She was alone.

In an instant, Caro was at her side, with Posy – wearing Dahlia's vintage belted coat – in front of her, both blocking her from view of the rest of the cast and crew as she fell apart.

Because she wasn't alone. She had the other two Dahlias. She had her friends.

And she knew they wouldn't give up until they found who was behind this.

Posy

Posy's hands still shook a little as she made her way out to the front of Tŷ Gwyn. She didn't want to leave Rosalind after her shock, but since they clearly weren't going to be filming any more of the stabbing scenes today, it made sense to take the action outside and film the scenes with the vintage Bentley that had arrived on set earlier that day to rather a lot of excitement. Posy wasn't really up on her antique cars, but she had to admit it was pretty impressive to look at.

She just hoped it was the same to *drive*.

'You okay?' Kit murmured, as they headed outside to take their places.

Posy rubbed her arms through Dahlia's coat, then nodded. 'I just wish I could have stayed with Rosalind.' For two weeks, now, it seemed like she'd been waiting for the other shoe to drop. That first note, left in Rosalind's script, had only been the start of it. And suddenly, Posy was very afraid to see the end.

'She did look shaken up, poor thing.' Kit glanced back towards the door, where Anton was raging at someone inside – probably the prop master, she suspected – about his filming schedule being interrupted by this incompetence. 'At least she has Caro with her.'

'Yeah.' Caro was safe. Caro would take care of her.

And in the meantime, Posy would keep things moving here, so Rosalind could recover without Anton expecting her to act out being stabbed another handful of times.

Really, he might be a great director, but Posy couldn't help but feel that sometimes he got so focused on the project at hand, or even the scene they were filming, that he forgot about the people involved. Everything was camera angles and colours, framing and unexpected vignettes. Not real actors making it happen. They were just their characters to him, puppets for him to move to his own ends.

But then, she'd learned that in Aldermere last summer, hadn't she?

It would be worth it, if the film was the success they were all hoping it would be. As long as Rosalind survived the experience.

As she watched, Caro led Rosalind – now changed out of her Aunt Hermione costume and make-up – towards the gates, out to her own car. She'd brought the red convertible, Posy noted with a grin, rather than Susie, Dahlia's motorcycle and sidecar. Probably for the best, under the circumstances. And when the Welsh rain hit again, at least she could close the roof on the convertible.

Their own car for the afternoon also boasted a soft, fold-down top – a dark grey leather, atop the gleaming cream finish of the car itself. Posy could almost see her reflection perfectly in the paint; dark blonde pin curls, a slash of red lipstick, and wide, lined eyes, all above the pussybow of her silk blouse and the itchy wool of her coat.

Dahlia Lively. That was who she was today. Not Posy Starling.

What would Dahlia do?

Dahlia wouldn't waste time comforting her friend – she'd be too busy finding out who had tried to hurt her, and stopping them from trying again.

Who *could* have swapped the knives on set? Could it really have been an accident, as the prop master had suggested? And if not . . . well. The set was so busy, Posy had to admit that almost anybody could have slipped in and made the swap.

So much for trying to Dahlia her way out of this.

Anton bounded out of the front door, down the steps and across the driveway. 'Let's keep this thing rolling!' he declared excitedly, his previous rage apparently forgotten. He made his way over to one of the cameramen to discuss the next shot, his shoulders rounded as he used intense hand gestures to punctuate his words. The camera operator nodded sagely, clearly used to Anton's brand of direction.

'Posy, later . . .' Kit said, then trailed off.

Posy stopped watching Anton and glanced up at him. 'Hmm? Later?'

'Nothing. Just . . .' Kit's eyes looked troubled, and he looked over every inch of the car, rather than at her. 'There's something I'd like to talk to you about.'

35

'Of course.' Posy checked on their director, who had moved on to a second camera operator – this one in charge of the camera on the track, which would move with the car once she started driving. More fervent gestures. More sage nodding. 'Tell me now, if you like? We're not going to be starting for a while.'

Kit glanced around them at the hustle and bustle of the film set, then dipped his head towards hers. 'It's nothing to worry about. Just that . . . there's someone I need to meet, tomorrow night. So I might be late for the Classic Hollywood fundraiser thing at the inn. Can you cover for me?'

'Of course,' Posy replied. 'But who are you meeting?'

He winced. 'I can't persuade you to let me get away with something vague, like, a friend, can I?'

'Not a chance.'

'Yeah, thought not.' He sighed. 'Okay. So the thing is—'

Just then, Anton finished briefing the crew and, with a loud clap of his hands that seemed to reverberate around the mountains, bounced over towards them, his step light on the gravel of the drive.

'*Later*,' Kit mouthed at her, and she nodded in reply.

From the ferocity of Anton's gaze, Posy knew they were about to get some very detailed instructions on how, exactly, to say two lines, climb into the car and drive out of the gate, and so prepared herself to listen carefully and nod in the appropriate places.

Even if half her mind was still with Rosalind, and another portion wondering what it was Kit wanted to tell her.

After a series of expressive gestures – and a demonstration from another crew member on how to start the car, plus a small practice of actually driving the thing – Anton seemed satisfied that they'd got the gist of what he wanted from them, and they were able to start filming.

'But, Miss Lively, how can you be so sure that they were lying?' Kit said, opening the driver's side door for her.

Posy flashed him a Dahlia smile and climbed into the driver's seat. 'As a general rule, Detective Inspector, I assume that *everyone* is lying to me until they can prove otherwise.'

She let Kit settle into the passenger seat, then pressed the starter pedal on the floor as she'd been shown, and drove towards the now open gates, steadily ignoring the camera on tracks that followed them.

She heard Anton call, 'Cut!' behind them, and obligingly pressed the brake pedal. But she couldn't help wishing she could keep driving – through the gates, down past the inn, through the village and over the bridge – to get her and Kit the hell away from whatever was going on here at Tŷ Gwyn.

Chapter Four

'Where are we going, Miss?' Bess asked, as Dahlia led her through the maze of winding streets and busy feet. 'I thought you wanted to carry on investigating.'

'We are going for tea.' Dahlia's pace never slowed for a second. 'I never investigate on an empty stomach.'

Dahlia Lively *in* **A Very Lively Trip**
By **Lettice Davenport, 1942**

Caro

Caro left Posy to explain to Anton that *clearly* Rosalind wasn't going to be filming anything else today, while she focused on getting her out of costume and away from Tŷ Gwyn. The director didn't seem to have noticed Caro's presence in all the confusion, and she'd quite like to keep it that way for as long as she could.

She bundled Rosalind out of the gates with a cursory wave at the security guard, and helped her into the passenger seat of her convertible, leaving the top up. She felt Rosalind might want the extra protection.

Caro climbed into the driver's seat and slammed the door behind her to shut out the world. She pressed her head back against the headrest as she concentrated on breathing for a moment or two.

'Well,' she said, as they both watched the river below rushing past, skipping over stones and around bends, 'at least we know you were right to call me.'

Rosalind gave a watery chuckle in response to that. 'Admit it. You were bored without us.'

'Very. I suppose . . . it could have been an accident.'

'*Another* accident.'

Yeah, Caro hadn't really believed that, either. She needed to get a look at these threatening letters Rosalind had received. She and Posy were too close to the situation; they needed Caro's outside view to figure out what was going on. Who on set could have swapped that prop knife for a real one? Who would want to?

They needed to find out. And fast. Remembering the look in Tristan's eyes as he'd realised what he'd almost done made her shudder.

She started the engine, swallowing around the lump in her throat. 'You're staying at the inn down the road, yes? Let's head back there.'

The Saith Seren Inn was built of faded reddish-brown stones, no two the same size, and roofed with purple-grey slate tiles. The sign hanging outside had not just the inn's name, but an image of a constellation. Below was a translation of its Welsh name, printed in smaller type. *The Seven Stars.*

To the left side of the building was a large brick archway, which then turned into a low wall that ran around the edge of the property. A small plaque beside it explained that this archway would have been for carriages to pass through, so patrons could stable their horses securely in the buildings behind before heading in for, Caro guessed, flagons of ale, some sort of stew, and perhaps a bed for the night.

Despite its obvious age, the building was immaculately kept – from the window boxes filled with early spring bulbs to the tastefully painted sage-green window frames and door. Wooden tables sat in the courtyard beyond the archway, and on the neatly maintained grass out front, with a view of the river. A cheery light showed through the windows, which warmed Caro on sight. In fact, the only jarring note was a bright yellow skip filled with bricks, half hidden against the trees at the back of the obviously new car park on the right-hand side, where she'd left her car.

However old the inn might be, Caro would bet that someone had spent a lot of money making sure it now appealed to the most modern visitor.

Inside, she was proved correct. In fact, she might have thought she'd walked into one of London's most up-and-coming gastro pubs, if it wasn't for the tasteful, muted artwork of the Welsh flag, surrounded by seven stars, rendered in what appeared to be felted sheep's wool, hanging over the fireplace.

The main bar was a large space, opening up to other, smaller rooms behind. A staircase curled up behind the bar, marked with a slate sign that said, simply, *Rooms*. On the other side of the bar was a passageway with a similar sign that read, *Suites*. The stone walls had been painted white to contrast with the grey of the flagstone floor, and each of the scrubbed wood tables was set with a clipboard menu and a small houseplant. The far wall was taken over by black chalkboard paint, and detailed a menu including 'Welsh Tapas' that Caro found intriguing.

'Drink?' she asked.

Rosalind nodded enthusiastically. 'God yes.'

While Rosalind settled at a cosy table by the fire, Caro approached the bar – lit by a sequence of bare bulbs hanging at different heights from a copper pipe, of course – only to find the teenager from earlier, Seren, sitting on the end barstool.

'I don't suppose you're old enough to serve from the top shelf yet, are you, kiddo?' She looked about fourteen in Caro's estimation, although she had to admit she'd never been great at aging anyone, especially not kids.

Seren looked to the ceiling. 'Mum! Dad!'

The door behind the bar opened, offering a glimpse of the state-of-the-art kitchen behind, and a dark-haired man emerged, drying his hands on a branded bar towel. 'What can I get you?'

'Dad, this is Caro. She's here for the film!' Seren's father looked blank, but the red-haired woman who descended the stairs beside the bar gasped.

'Caro Hooper, right? You were Dahlia Lively on the telly?' She hopped the last couple of steps to reach them.

'I was,' Caro admitted, demurely, enjoying Seren's obvious surprise.

'I've read loads of the books since they announced the movie was filming here,' Seren said. 'And I've seen the old movies. But not any of the TV show because—'

'Because your evil mum won't let you get yet another streaming service, I know.' Rebecca placed a quick kiss on the top of Seren's dark hair. 'But I must have seen most of the episodes. My mum and Gran *loved* that show. Whatever happened to it?'

'Things move on,' Caro said, a little sourly. 'Anyway—'

'Are you in the new movie, then?' Rebecca asked. 'Ooh, they've been keeping that under wraps, haven't they? A surprise cameo, is it?'

'Not exactly.' And not exactly a subject she wanted to get into. 'I'm actually just visiting friends.' She motioned towards Rosalind, sitting by the fire.

'Well, if you're looking for a room, we're pretty full, I'm afraid.' Owain leaned against the bar. Unlike his wife and daughter, he had the classic Welsh accent Caro had been hoping for – a perfect match for the dark hair flopping over his forehead and the soulful brown eyes. 'Anton booked us out.'

'She'll be sharing my suite with me,' Rosalind called, from across the bar. 'Assuming that's all right.'

Rebecca's eyes widened with surprise. Probably thinking that she wouldn't have imagined National Treasure Rosalind King bunking up with a friend. But Caro understood.

She was here to help protect Rosalind. That meant staying close. And getting the lay of the land.

'How many rooms do you have here?' Caro asked. 'Is the whole cast and crew staying?' It didn't look large enough to host the whole mob of people a film set usually involved.

'Most of the crew is at the Travelodge across the river in the next town, but Anton wanted all the main cast here.' Rebecca put the kind of emphasis on the director's first name that told Caro she was more than a little bit starstruck. Seemed like Seren wasn't the only one who thought this movie was the most exciting thing to happen in the village, ever.

'We've got four rooms upstairs, and another eight suites in the converted stables out back, so far,' Rebecca said. 'But we're hoping to get another four ready before the summer, when the weddings start.'

'We're aiming to be the perfect place for guests attending weddings up at Tŷ Gwyn to stay,' Owain explained. 'We only moved back home to take over Saith Seren from my dad a year or so ago, and this summer will be our first big season.'

'Before that, we lived in London,' Seren said, somewhat wistfully, Caro thought. She could hardly blame her. As lovely as the Seven Stars Inn was, it had to be a huge jolt for the teenager to leave the city behind to move to the back of beyond.

'Glan y Wern is a growing hotspot here in North Wales,' Rebecca said. 'We wanted to get in on that early. Now, can I get you a hot drink? Coffee and cake? Or something more alcoholic?'

'Coffee and cake sounds perfect.' She glanced back at Rosalind, who still looked a little pale. 'But if the coffee could be Irish, that would be even better.'

Owain grinned. 'We can do that.'

Rebecca disappeared to the kitchen, presumably in search of cake, while Owain fiddled with the fancy coffee machine on the far end of the bar, leaving Caro to examine her surroundings further.

A glass-fronted set of shelves next to the bar caught her eye, mostly because of their unusual shape. With a frown, she looked closer. Yep, coffin-shaped. In fact, it seemed to be an actual coffin that had been turned into a display unit, of sorts, filled with yellowing letters, the odd horseshoe, a photo of the inn looking rather more like a local boozer, and an old leather bible, among other things.

Owain placed the two Irish coffees on the bar. 'That's our heritage display,' he explained. 'Turns out that my great-great-grandfather, when he inherited the pub from his older brother, was already the local undertaker. So he combined the businesses.'

'Take the hearse down to the church for the service, then back up here for the wake. Makes sense to me.' Caro blew across the surface of her cup, then sipped. Oh, thank God. Decent coffee. That had been a worry.

'I reckon so,' Owain said, with a nod.

Rebecca emerged from the kitchen carrying a tray laden with chocolate cake. 'We found the coffin out back when we were converting the stables into the suites. Owain thought it made an interesting display.'

Caro had to admit, it did that.

'Thanks for these.' She loaded the coffees onto the tray and carried them over to the table by the fire.

'Making friends?' Rosalind asked, as she took her coffee.

Caro shrugged. 'You know me.' Pushing her plate and coffee to one side, she reached into her bag and pulled out her laptop. It was time to get down to the real reason she was here. 'Now, do you want to tell me everything, or do we need to wait for Posy?'

Rosalind tilted her head to the side, thinking. 'Wait for Posy,' she said, finally. 'I don't want to have to go over everything twice, and you know she'll only feel left out otherwise.'

That was true. 'Fine. But I want to at least get a picture of the players here, who could be behind all this.'

'It could be anyone on set – that's hundreds of people. Maybe more.' Rosalind spread her hands. 'The cast, the crew – the third assistant wardrobe person could have it in for me, for all I know.'

'Perhaps,' Caro admitted. 'But we've got to start somewhere. You said you'd been getting notes. Death threats, I assume?' Rosalind nodded. 'Okay. So when did you get the first note?'

'The day of the table read,' Rosalind replied. 'It was tucked inside my script.' Her eyes widened, suddenly. 'But most of the crew weren't on set that day. It was just Anton, Brigette, a few assistants and the cast.'

'*That* narrows things down a bit.' If they assumed that whoever had swapped the knives was the same person who'd sent the notes, it had to be someone who'd been at Tŷ Gwyn on both days. 'In that case, let's start with the people staying here at the Seven Stars with you.'

'The cast.' A shadow passed over Rosalind's face. 'I suppose that makes sense.'

It only took a moment to unlock the laptop and pull up the latest reported cast list and start viewing photos and CVs. Rosalind talked her through who was who, and everything she'd noticed about them so far, but Caro had to admit it didn't add up to much.

Sometime later, the rumble of an engine outside caught her attention and, closing her laptop, she stood, stretched and looked out of the window as a sleek shuttle bus pulled up right outside the front door.

'They're back,' Caro said.

The cast streamed inside, all chattering and laughing together. *This* was what Caro missed most, she decided. Being part of a tight-knit group, almost like a family for the time they were filming. The camaraderie of a shared project, a communal goal beyond the decluttering of the attic.

Oh, that wasn't fair. She and Annie had goals. They just weren't the sort that you could sit down later with your family and watch on a screen.

Maybe she just missed being a part of something bigger than just her, or her marriage, or her home. Something that the world outside cared about too. Something people *noticed*.

She was feeling invisible. That was the problem. And Caro Hooper was not born to be ignored.

'Caro! It's so good to see you!' Posy rushed in first, sweeping into Caro's arms like a long-lost sister. 'Is Rosalind okay?' she added in an undertone. Caro managed a small shrug in answer, and Posy darted to take the third seat at their table, helping herself to some of Rosalind's leftover chocolate cake. But Caro could see her careful, assessing glances under her eyelashes as she spoke softly to their friend.

'You do still realise you are not *actually* in this movie, don't you?' Caro turned towards the familiar, acerbic voice. Anton Martinez, still an up-and-coming director at forty-odd, stood in the doorway, arms folded across his chest, looking amused and faintly pitying.

How was it fair that he was still an emerging talent, while she was over-the-hill, when they were basically the same bloody age?

She forced herself to smile charmingly at him. 'Naturally, dear Anton. As it happens, I'm not actually here for the film.'

His eyebrows shot up, as if he'd forgotten things outside the film still existed. 'Then why *are* you here?' Over at the table, Rosalind was shaking her head discreetly, and Posy's eyes had widened with alarm. Clearly, neither of them had thought up a decent excuse for her presence here. Lucky for them that Caro had had plenty of time to think about it on the drive up.

'A new project I'm working on.' She gestured towards her laptop, still sitting on the table. 'I decided I wanted to tell the story of everything that happened at Aldermere last summer – the *real* story, you understand – and share it with audiences everywhere. So I came here to work because I'll have Rosalind and Posy on hand to help me with my recollections. And Kit and maybe Libby, and even yourself, if it comes to that.'

Was it her imagination, or had Anton turned a little grey? 'You're writing a documentary?'

'Oh, I always find that stories tell more truth than dry facts, somehow, don't you?' she said, sweetly. 'And I do so want to get to the *truth* of everything that happened.'

Caro thought she heard Posy stifle a laugh. Because, of all people, Anton *didn't* want the whole truth to come out about Aldermere. Especially not his part in events.

'I suppose you're imagining that someone will pick up this script and cast the three of you as yourselves in some blockbuster?' Anton barked a laugh. He always did prefer attack to defence, Caro remembered. 'Even if you *could* find someone willing to make it, they'd be more likely to cast *you* as *Rosalind*, Caro dear.'

That stung, not that she'd let it show. Caro clung onto her smile, as she answered. 'That's just one reason I'm not writing a script. I hardly think the film industry could be depended on to reflect our story accurately. So I'm writing a book instead. I already have an agent and a publisher very interested, as it happens.'

All a lie, of course, but a satisfying one, given the way Anton's smirk froze on his face. He had no influence in that world, no way to try and stop her telling whatever *she* decided was the truth. Behind the covers of a book, it didn't matter if the wrinkles were showing, or if forty was far too old to play the love interest of a sixty-five-year-old, for some insane reason.

Actually, why *shouldn't* she write the book? She'd always had a way with words, and the story was just there waiting for her. It would certainly give her a project, and a goal . . .

Once she'd solved whatever was going on at Tŷ Gwyn, and made sure that Rosalind was safe, of course. She still had her priorities.

'Oh, Caro!' Posy got to her feet again suddenly, stalling whatever comeback Anton might have thought of. 'We must show you the lovely walk into the village. Come on.'

'That would be delightful,' Caro lied, as she moved to pack up her laptop. 'Let me just put my things in my room.'

'There aren't any rooms left,' Anton said, sounding triumphant on at least this, small point. 'You can't stay here.'

'Oh, she's sharing with me,' Rosalind said, easily. 'After all, you were so kind as to make sure I had that lovely two-roomed suite with the extra daybed, Anton. Wasn't that convenient?'

'Very convenient.' Anton sounded very weary, as his eyes fluttered closed for an instant. He *definitely* looked older than her, Caro decided. 'Well, far be it from me to stop the Three Dahlias pursuing their art.' He stepped out of the doorway. 'I'll just keep trying to make the best movie I can. If that's all right with Caro.'

'Perfectly fine with me, kiddo.' She patted his arm for good measure as she passed him.

Oh, this was a good day.

Chapter Five

'I don't understand why you're wasting time on such trivial things,'
Lord Acerton said, his cheeks puce with outrage, 'when there's a
murderer out there for you to catch.'

Dahlia didn't look up from the papers she was studying. 'Because
sometimes what seems trivial at first sight, can turn out to be the
thing that matters most, in solving a case.'

Dahlia Lively *in* A Secret to Tell
***By* Lettice Davenport, 1959**

Posy

They waited until they were clear of the inn, and certain that no other cast members were going to decide to join them, before they spoke. Posy used the time to watch Rosalind, looking for signs of the frailty she'd seen in her earlier, on set. But it seemed that the eldest Dahlia had replaced her armour and was ready to face the world.

Which was just as well as, the moment they were out of earshot of Saith Seren, Caro said, 'Right. Tell me everything.'

They crossed the road onto a narrow path that ran along a strip of grass between the tarmac and the trees that lined the river. Rather than turning right, back towards Tŷ Gwyn, Posy led them left, towards the main road.

It didn't take long for them to bring Caro up to speed.

'So that's two death threats—' Caro started, and Posy pulled a face at Rosalind, who sighed.

'Maybe slightly more,' Rosalind admitted. 'There's been a few since I got here – presumably because it's been all over the gossip sites that we're filming here. And not all of them are death *threats*, exactly. More people who think the world would be better if I wasn't in it any more. But they're all different to the first one – the one in the script – and the one I got the day after the first accident.'

'Different how?' Caro asked.

Rosalind shrugged her shoulders under her heavy wool coat. 'They all have different handwriting and postmarks for a start. Plus those writers, well, they seem to think that what happened at Aldermere last summer brought disrepute onto the memory of Lettice Davenport unnecessarily, and that I should have let sleeping dogs lie, so to speak.'

Caro's eyebrows shot up. Posy didn't blame her. The metaphorical dogs those writers talked about hadn't been sleeping. They'd been murdered.

'Maybe I really do need to write that book. Set the record straight,' Caro said.

'I'd appreciate it,' Rosalind replied, drily. 'Not that I think for a moment that the people who sent those letters would believe it.'

They reached an opening into the trees where the path split, beside a shiny red postbox, which was today topped by a crocheted dragon hat – something Posy ascribed to the quirky craft shop in the village and the sign in its window encouraging yarn bombing.

Instead of continuing along the road, Posy led them onto the trail through the woods. 'It's quicker than going all the way to the main road and in that way,' she explained to Caro. 'This path comes out right by the village green.'

She didn't miss the way Caro looked down at her suede boots and sighed.

But she did follow. 'Okay, but those other two notes – the one in the script and the one about the accident. What were they like?'

Posy pulled two pieces of card from her bag, and handed them to her. Caro raised her eyebrows with an unspoken question, and Posy shrugged. 'She wanted to burn them.'

'Destroying evidence, Rosalind?' Caro said, with mock horror.

'I just didn't want to have to look at them anymore,' Rosalind grumbled. 'Used to be, all this stuff went through my agent, and I never had to see it, he just told me not to worry about it. Nowadays anyone can find me if they've got a passing acquaintance with Google. And everyone feels that their thoughts are worthy of being shared. Even when they are clearly wrong about that.'

Was that why she wasn't taking these threats seriously – or hadn't been, until now? Posy supposed in a career as long and illustrious as Rosalind King's, she was bound to have attracted hate as well as adoration. And if she'd got used to those messages meaning nothing . . .

But there was definitely something different about these notes. And from the way Caro was frowning at them, she agreed.

'No postmarks or stamps – these two were hand delivered,' she said. 'Another vote for someone on set being behind this.'

She handed them back to Posy, who tucked them in to her bag.

'So! *Multiple* death threats, an on-set accident with a camera arm that nearly took your head off, another threatening note referencing it – which is when you called me – and then today's incident with the switched dagger.' Caro shook her head. 'I'm grateful you trusted me enough to call me, but I have to ask . . . Have you told the police?'

'I told her to,' Posy said. 'After the first note.'

'I talked to the police last autumn.' Rosalind wrapped her coat a little tighter around her. 'I had a few letters then, too, after everything was in the papers about Aldermere. They took copies, kept them on file or what have you. But the impression I got was that it was par for the course when you're in the news like we were, and there was no reason to think it was anything more.'

'I think we now have reason,' Caro said, flatly. 'You're going to have to talk to them.'

'Let's just see what we can find out first,' Rosalind said. 'I don't want to make a fuss.'

You mean you don't want people talking about how hated you are, Posy thought. Rosalind's reputation as a national treasure had certainly taken a battering after her long-standing affair with her best friend's husband had come out, the previous summer. Posy knew that the last thing she'd want was to give the gossip pages more reasons to rehash it all. And these things always got out, once the authorities were involved. She knew that from her own experiences.

She could empathise with Rosalind hoping that if she just ignored it people might stop talking and it would all go away – God knew she'd felt the same often enough. But there was something about those notes that scared her.

Posy didn't think this was more of the same. And from Caro's frowning expression, neither did she.

They reached the end of the path, where the trees gave way to riverbank and verdant grass, which in turn became pavement, road, shops, pub, houses – the village of Glan y Wern. On first impressions, Posy supposed that Glan y Wern was much like many other villages dotted around the north of Wales. It had a couple of streets that met at a cross, a rickety bridge across the river which – according to signs posted by the church – was due to be replaced that summer, a small school, a handful of old cottages plus some newer builds back off the high street – and rather more craft shops than Posy thought was probably normal.

Hands on hips, Caro turned slowly around to take in the sights. 'Artisan bakery, "The Craft Collective", organic deli, vintage and antiques shop, "The Inspired Pen" bookshop, *another* organic deli – no, wait, vegan deli and cafe . . . Rebecca wasn't kidding about this place getting gentrified, was she? Not a pound shop or an arcade in sight.'

'The pub over there even has some very decent wine,' Rosalind confirmed. 'God knows what Anton paid the location people who found this place, but they earned every penny.'

'Especially with Tŷ Gwyn,' Posy added. The Art Deco mansion was everything Dahlia could have dreamed of.

'And the locals are onside with the film, I suppose?' Caro paused outside a cafe called WelshCakes, and looked longingly at the decidedly non-vegan cream-filled Victoria sponge in the window.

'What are you thinking?' Posy asked. 'You think one of the locals could have it in for Rosalind? There are a few working on set, I suppose . . .'

Caro nodded towards the alleyway between the cafe and the next row of shops. Posy followed her gaze and saw the graffiti, half scrubbed off the wall but still readable. *Locals only*, read one line. Below it, in faded black paint, *Ban second homes*. Considerate of them to put it where it wouldn't mar the picture-perfect appearance of the rest of the village.

'They've been fine as far as I've seen,' Rosalind said. 'I've been stopped for autographs and photos whenever I've visited the village, but that's all.'

Posy nodded. 'Same for me. And we're holding a fundraiser at Saith Seren tomorrow night, raising money for the local school. Most of the disruption is up at Tŷ Gwyn, anyway, which helps.'

'Fundraiser?' Caro asked. 'What sort?'

'It's a Classic Hollywood Night,' Rosalind said. 'Glamour, red lipstick and cocktails. You'll love it.'

'We can borrow you a costume from wardrobe,' Posy added. 'It'll be fun.' As long as Rosalind's anonymous correspondent stayed away.

A camera flash from behind them drew their attention, and Posy's heart sped up instinctively – the automatic churning of guilt and fear hitting her stomach before she could remind herself that she wasn't doing anything wrong. She was out for a walk with her friends, not high or drunk or snogging someone she shouldn't be.

That life was behind her, and she had nothing to fear from the paparazzi. She hoped.

Rosalind and Caro had already turned towards the flash. Posy was amused to note that, from long experience, they both automatically twisted and posed at their best angles before they could have even spotted the guy with the camera.

'The three Dahlias together again!' The photographer across the street lifted his camera. 'Can I get a few proper ones, yeah?'

As they all smiled for the paparazzi camera, Posy considered that the three of them together must be more of a draw than any of them individually. The story of what had happened at Aldermere had made all the front pages for days and, while they'd agreed between themselves not to accept any exposé tell-all interviews, Posy had been asked about the other two Dahlias in every press event she'd done before they started filming.

She'd had a few photos taken since they arrived on set, too – alone, or with Kit or another member of the cast. None posed like this, though – just candid shots that later showed up on websites in all their grainy glory. According to Keira, Scarlett had taken to calling in a local photographer whenever she was heading into the village, to make sure no one forgot she was in the movie, with all the big names present threatening to overshadow her soap successes. In contrast, Gabriel never left the inn without a baseball cap pulled down low over his sunglasses, even when it was raining.

In a place like Glan y Wern, the movie was big news, that much was clear.

Photos done, and after a quick tour of the village, they stopped in at the pub on the river, the Drunken Dragon, for dinner. Rosalind snagged them a corner table by the crackling wood-fired stove, while Caro queued at the bar and Posy found menus, ignoring the curious stares of the locals and the odd camera phone pointed in her direction. At least every local who wanted autographs or selfies had sought them out in the first couple of weeks they were on set, and things were starting to calm down a bit at last.

Once they were all settled at their table, with dinner orders in and glasses in front of them, Caro brought them back to the subject at hand.

'Okay, so, Posy, what happened after we left the set today? Did you see or hear anything that might give us a clue who swapped the knives? And what has Anton had to say about these accidents on set? I can't imagine he'd have let them go without some shouting.'

'The camera-arm thing genuinely could have been an accident,' Rosalind said. 'There've been a few similar things going on generally, in fact, so it could just be an inexperienced crew if the producers have been cutting corners. I don't know. If it hadn't been for the letter I received the next day referencing it, I wouldn't have thought it was anything targeted, I don't think.'

'Had it been reported on social media sites?' Caro asked.

'I don't think so,' Rosalind said. 'Nobody really made a fuss about it. Anton yelled a bit in the moment, but that was all.'

'But he was *raging* today after the thing with the dagger,' Posy said. 'After you guys had gone. Wanting to know who was responsible.'

Mostly for holding up filming, rather than out of concern for Rosalind's safety, but she didn't think her friends needed to know that right now.

Caro tapped her index finger against the table, and frowned. 'Did anyone take fingerprints from the dagger?'

Posy shook her head. 'After Tristan and Anton had held it, I'm not sure there'd have been much left anyway, even if the culprit didn't wipe it or wear gloves or whatever. But . . . should we tell the police about it?' She wasn't sure exactly what they'd say, but still, it felt like they should be doing *something*. Something more than just whispering in corners.

'Nobody got hurt,' Rosalind said, heavily. 'And getting the police involved would only hold things up with the filming.'

Caro turned to Rosalind. 'Tell me exactly what happened on set today. Posy, take notes.'

Posy obediently fished her notebook from her bag and found a pen. It was always so much easier to see the patterns when everything was written down.

'Well, we were filming the scene where Great Aunt Hermione gets murdered,' Rosalind said. 'And because of Anton and Libby's obsession with no one leaking the murderer—'

'But everyone knows the murderer! It's in the book. And the original film. *And* my TV series.' Caro sounded personally affronted at the idea that the culprit might be a mystery.

'We know,' Posy said wearily. Even *she* knew, and she'd never read any of the Dahlia Lively books before last summer. 'But Anton has been hinting that they've changed the ending for the movie. He even had Libby write five different versions of the *J'Accuse* scene at the end, with five different potential murderers.'

'Of course he did,' Caro grumbled under her breath.

'The point is, that meant five different characters had to act out murdering Great Aunt Hermione, one after another, ready for the recreation reveal at the end,' Rosalind went on. 'So they were all on set, ready to take their turn.'

'Had any of them filmed their shot with the dagger before I arrived?' Caro asked.

Rosalind shook her head. 'No. Tristan was first. Actually, it was meant to be Keira, but she was late, so they switched around.'

'So, Tristan went to stab you, but realised just in time that the prop knife wasn't, well, a prop?'

No retractable blade. No escape if he'd actually committed to the scene and plunged it into Rosalind's heart. She wouldn't have even known to try and move out of the way.

Posy shuddered. 'He said he and Gabriel – that's Gabriel Perez, playing cousin Bertie – they'd been playing with the prop one earlier,' Posy said. 'The weight was different. It took him a bit to realise, but at the last moment he stabbed the desk instead.'

'Where did it come from?' Caro wondered aloud.

'Rhian recognised it,' Posy answered. 'It was a ceremonial one that usually lived on a stand on the fireplace in the study, where we were filming. It looked a lot like the prop one. Someone must have just laid out the wrong one by mistake. At least, that's what everyone assumed.'

'Was the whole cast on set today?'

'I think so,' Posy replied. 'We can check the security sheet for the day, though. Nobody gets inside Tŷ Gwyn unless they're on it.'

'What happened to the real prop?'

'It was back on the trolley where it belonged. The prop master couldn't explain it, however much Anton yelled.' Posy swirled her fruit juice around in her glass. 'Said it must have been another screw-up by one of the other crew, probably knocked it off the desk where it was supposed to be when setting up something else, and someone else assumed the other one was the right one. I don't know.'

'Hmm.' Caro sat back in her chair, while Posy looked over her notes. No patterns yet. 'Is there anything else – anything you can think of at all – that's seemed strange about this movie?'

Rosalind shrugged. 'Not that I can think of.'

'Except—' Posy said, and stopped. Was she just seeing mysteries where there weren't any, now? Maybe Rosalind's death threats had made her paranoid.

'Except what?' Caro pressed.

'Brigette. The casting director.' Posy flipped back a few pages in her notebook to the lines she'd scribbled down the day of the table read, just in case.

'She quit, didn't she? I'm sure I read something about that.' Caro leaned forward to try and read Posy's notes upside down. Posy put her arm over them.

'She left, that's for sure,' Rosalind said. 'Everyone heard her and Anton getting into it the day of the table read, and then she just walked out.'

'Next thing we know, there's a post on her Instagram page from Heathrow, saying she's heading back to LA. Since then, it's all been shots of some glorious retreat resort in the desert.' Not that Posy had been checking daily, or anything.

Okay, fine. She had.

Caro's eyebrows furrowed. 'What's so weird about that? I'd think Anton *not* driving crew to quitting would be more unusual.'

'It's the *way* she left,' Posy explained. 'She went into the study opposite to take a call and . . . never came out.'

'Wait. What do you mean, "never came out"?'

'Exactly that.' Posy gave Caro a helpless look. 'I could see the door to the study from where I was sitting in the dining room. She didn't come out. Then, when Keira went to fetch her . . . she was gone.'

'That's impossible,' Caro pointed out.

'We know,' Rosalind said, drily. 'Obviously she must have slipped out when no one was looking, or pretended to go into the room but actually made a run for it when backs were turned. But all the same, it was strange . . .'

'It doesn't sound right,' Caro said, thoughtfully. 'Something else to think about, anyway.'

Posy's shoulders relaxed, as she looked up to see a waitress approaching with what she hoped was their dinner order. Maybe Brigette leaving was nothing. But at least she wasn't the only one worrying about it.

There were *three* Dahlias to puzzle things out now, and that made all the difference.

Rosalind

On their return to the Seven Stars Inn, later that evening, Kit was waiting for Posy in the bar, a hopeful look in his eye.

'That's still going on, then,' Caro murmured near Rosalind's ear as they both waved goodnight.

'Apparently so.' Rosalind wasn't sure exactly what the status of Posy's relationship with Kit was currently – certainly nothing official, and in any photos of the two of them that had been snapped around town there was always a respectable distance between them. But the paparazzi didn't see the way Posy's eyes lit up when Kit walked on set, or how his gaze lingered on her whenever she was in the room.

There was something there. Rosalind just wasn't sure if either of them was brave enough to grasp it and hold on tight enough to make it work.

'Come on,' she said, leaving the younger couple to gaze adoringly at each other at a table by the fire. 'We're too old for this, and it's a long day tomorrow.'

'Speak for yourself,' Caro replied, but she followed all the same.

They nodded to Owain, emerging from the cellars as they passed the bar, and headed for the back door that led out to the suites behind the main building. The stone path across the courtyard was lit up by solar-powered torches, leading the way past a large central raised bed, and keeping the focus on the ferns and grasses planted there rather than the car park over the wall on the right.

Rosalind's suite was one of the first, the others laid out in a horseshoe shape around the courtyard, and she let them in with her keycard.

'It's a nice suite.' Caro dropped to sit on the edge of the daybed under the far window. 'I didn't get a proper look when I dropped my stuff off earlier.'

'It is.' Rosalind glanced around; she'd got so used to the place over the last couple of weeks, she'd almost forgotten how relieved she'd been when she first saw it. Not only did it have two rooms – one with a wonderfully comfortable double bed, the other with the daybed sofa that Caro would sleep on and a low coffee table and armchair – but there was also a mini kitchenette attached that meant she didn't have to eat *all* her meals out, unless she wanted to.

Although, given Owain's cooking, it wouldn't be the worst thing. Keira had told her that the owner of the Seven Stars Inn had been a highly sought-after London chef before he'd moved home, and Rosalind could well believe it.

No, she'd definitely stayed in worse accommodation while filming. All the same, she couldn't help but look forward to the day when this shoot would be over, and she could go home to the London flat she'd bought after her husband died.

Rosalind slipped her coat from her shoulders and hung it up in the well-sized wardrobe beside the vanity unit in the corner of her bedroom. A glance in the three-part angled mirror told her that her beauty sleep was going to have to work overtime that night; her complexion seemed grey and tired, and she looked older than she felt, which was an achievement, given the aches that were settling in to her joints.

She frowned again at the mirror as she spotted something else, back out in the main room.

A small, square piece of card, on the floor by the door. Had that been there when they came in, and they just missed it? Or had someone pushed it under now?

'What is it?' Caro sat up straighter on the daybed as Rosalind crossed the suite and bent to pick up the card. 'Tell me it's not a blackmail threat. We've *definitely* done that one already.'

Rosalind didn't laugh at the reference to their adventure at Aldermere. In fact, she didn't react to it at all, because she was too busy trying not to panic as she read the card in her hand.

Close call today, wasn't it? Maybe next time . . .

Her heart pounding and her head buzzing, Rosalind ripped open the door and peered out at the dimly lit courtyard, hoping to spot whoever might have left it. A figure moved beside the planter, and she lurched towards it, even as Caro took the card from her hand.

'Why not say it to my face, you coward?' Rosalind called.

'Rosa . . .' Caro started, but she ignored her.

She was done being scared. Done being cowed and terrorised.

Whoever was threatening her wouldn't dare attack here, with so many potential witnesses. But if she knew who it was, *then* she could talk to the police.

The figure turned. They'd switched on the torch on their phone, the light so bright Rosalind couldn't make out their features at all.

'Is everything okay, Mrs King?' The voice behind the light was familiar, though, and Rosalind felt her shoulders relax a little. 'It's only me, Seren. I'm sorry if I disturbed you. I was just trying to get some footage of the moon. I want to see how the video function on my phone copes at night.'

She lowered the torch, enough that Rosalind could see her young, concerned face.

'Seren, you didn't see anybody push anything under Rosalind's door just now, did you?' Caro moved out into the courtyard, and Rosalind staggered a couple of steps back into her room, letting her friend shield her from view.

'No, sorry,' Seren said. 'But I was over the other side of the courtyard until just now. And I was kind of focused on the sky. Sorry.'

'That's okay.' Caro's voice was warm, comforting. All the things Rosalind didn't feel. *Nothing to see here*, her friend was saying. 'Don't worry about it.'

Caro still had the death threat in her hand, though, as she shut and bolted the door behind them.

Rosalind dropped to sit in the armchair and realised she was shaking.

'That note *had* to be from someone staying here, who was on set today. That's too close.' Caro took the chair from the dressing table, and shoved it underneath the door handle, something Rosalind had only ever seen people do in movies before now. 'Tomorrow, we need to talk about calling the police.'

'Tomorrow,' Rosalind echoed. *Is another day*, her mind filled in.

She just hoped she lived to see it.

Chapter Six

'Every time I answer one question I have about this case, it only
causes three more to pop up from nowhere.' Dahlia sighed. 'But
there's nothing for it but to keep asking them. Right, kiddo?'

Dahlia Lively *in* **A Secret to Tell**
***By* Lettice Davenport, 1959**

Caro

The winter sun was hazy over the roof of Tŷ Gwyn the following
morning, when Caro returned to the film set with a plan.

Rosalind had snuck out for an early call and, Caro suspected,
because she didn't want to have the conversation about calling the
police again. Caro would have worried more, but Posy was with her
– and had already texted for the full story on what had happened the
night before.

I'll keep an eye on her, Posy had replied, after Caro's account. *You*
find out what the hell is going on around here.

And that was exactly what Caro intended to do.

Posy had made sure her name was on the list at the gate again, so
she got on to the set without any problems. Once there, she knew
that the busy, buzzing nature of the film set meant that she could stay
below the radar, and turn what had been a disappointment into a
superpower.

She'd wanted a part in this movie. Well, any movie, but especially this one. She'd felt left out, isolated. But now, the fact that she wasn't in the movie was an advantage.

Because she wasn't really there, not in an official capacity, she could see and hear far more than she would have as a cast member. More than Posy or Rosalind could.

And that was what would help her solve this case.

So, she wrapped the cashmere scarf Rosalind had bought her for Christmas tighter around her throat, and went to work.

She started by making a short tour past the trailers the cast were using, parked up on the outskirts of the lawns to the east of the house, behind generators and equipment trailers and vans. The aromas floating from craft services were tempting, but Caro forced herself to focus on the task at hand.

She needed to get a feel for who her suspects were, and how they related to each other.

Her research the previous day gave her a good head start on recognising the cast by sight. She spotted Scarlett standing with a runner holding an umbrella over her, even though it wasn't raining, as she sipped from a cup of coffee, already in costume. She saw Kit striding towards his trailer, a few crew members jumping out of his way as he passed.

From outside the hair and make-up trailer she could hear Rosalind and Posy's voices. She considered stopping in to say hi, but the snap in Rosalind's voice told her it probably wasn't the time.

The other cast trailers yielded nothing interesting to overhear, and the skies were growing greyer, so she ducked in through the front door behind someone moving a lighting stand, and explored the house instead.

Inside, Tŷ Gwyn was a hive of activity. The large entrance hall, with its double staircase climbing to the balcony landing, was filled with people shifting equipment, checking lights and angles, and having serious conversations over clipboards.

Caro stuck her head into the large dining room on the right-hand side of the hall where most of the action seemed to be centred. This, she realised, must be where they'd done the table read – and where Rosalind had received the first of her hand-delivered death threats. Today, the dining table in the centre of the room was laden with perfectly styled and delicious-looking food – although Caro knew from experience that most of it would be inedible. The stuff that was already there was for looks, not flavour. The food the stylists would bring out once the cast were ready would be the food to be eaten during the scene.

Across the hall was the door to the study where they'd been filming the previous day – also the room from which Brigette had apparently disappeared. Caro skipped over taped-down wires and dodged camera tracks to check it out. If Posy was right, and Brigette really had disappeared from inside the room, there had to be another way out.

The study had been cleared of all of yesterday's filming paraphernalia, which made searching it easier. Caro set about a methodical check of all the books on the bookcases, paintings and anything else attached to a wall that looked like it might hide or trigger a secret doorway Brigette might have escaped through. The fireplace was another possibility, except it was a real one, with an actual chimney, and she couldn't see any way to make it work.

The dagger that had almost stabbed Rosalind the day before was back on its stand on the mantelpiece. A plaque underneath declared it some sort of commemorative award for someone or another. Caro touched her finger gently to the tip, feeling the indent in her skin. Then she tugged on the stand, hoping to see the whole chimney open into a passageway to another room, but nothing moved.

She sighed, and stepped away. Dahlia never had these problems.

Hands on her hips, she surveyed the room one last time. Desk. Chair. Books. Window seat.

Window seat.

Her blood humming with expectation, she knelt down in front of it and lifted the cushions off, but the seat underneath was solid stone. No escape route or even a hiding place there.

Caro replaced the cushions and sat down, trying to decide what it was about Brigette's disappearance that nagged at her the most. A respected casting director walking out on a movie was unusual, for sure, but if she and Anton really had fallen out over something major it could make sense. Especially since, with the film fully cast, her work was pretty much done anyway.

Out in the main hall, she heard Anton's voice – yelling, then quietening, probably because he'd moved into another room rather than because he'd lowered his tone. By all accounts, he could be rather intense on set.

Time to move on.

Rhian, the house manager, had said that the cast had taken to using the bedrooms to hang out in between scenes sometimes – probably to avoid having to run out to the trailers in the rain, Caro assumed. She slipped out of the study and up the left-hand side of the grand double staircase to see who she could find upstairs.

From the balcony, rooms spanned out from a spacious landing, leading to another picture window at the far end of the house, with two armchairs and a small table placed in it. The first room on the left after the stairs had a closed door, so she paused and listened at it, and heard the familiar, booming tones of Dominic Laugharne as he ran lines – lines that sounded more like Shakespeare than Davenport, which she assumed meant he had an audition coming up soon. His distinctive voice was recognisable anywhere.

Leaving him to his rehearsal, she moved to the next closed door. This, at least, sounded a little more interesting – and she didn't even need to press her ear against the door to hear it.

'I'm not saying that!' a man protested, inside. Caro did a mental inventory of the other male cast members, trying to figure out who it might be. Tristan, who'd saved Rosalind yesterday? Or Gabriel? She'd seen Kit headed for his trailer, so it couldn't be him.

'Certainly sounds like it to me.' A woman's voice, sharp and unforgiving. A lover's tiff, perhaps?

'I just think that . . . I know it matters.' The man sounded more tired than angry, suddenly. 'Of course it matters.'

'But you won't speak up. Just like all the rest of them.'

'Because it won't make any difference. At least, not in the way you're hoping. Trust me, I know. And it might get *me* fired. I need this job, Keira.'

Keira. Keira Reynolds-Yang. Daughter of Patrick Reynolds, producer, and Philippa Yang, designer. Social media sensation turned actress.

Interesting.

'All I'm asking you to do is back me up. And you can't even do that.'

More movement inside the room and Caro stepped hurriedly away from the door to try and at least *pretend* she hadn't been eavesdropping. She should move further away, she knew, to complete the illusion, but she really wanted to see who Keira had been talking to . . .

She only made it a few steps away from the door before Keira came swooping out, her dudgeon – whatever that was – clearly high. Caro hesitated, torn between trying to look around the closing door to see who she'd been talking to and following Keira to see if she needed a friendly ear – when the decision was taken away from her.

'Ms Reynolds-Yang?' A nervous-looking young crew member approached from the stairs, her eyes wide. 'Um, they're ready to start downstairs in the dining room. They're just waiting for you and Mr Perez.'

Keira stalked past without replying and, a moment later, Gabriel Perez followed from the room behind her. 'We'll head right down,' he told the girl – Caro assumed she must be one of Anton's assistant directors, probably the third AD – and smiled, although it looked forced.

She turned to watch them go, only to see another familiar face approaching via the other staircase. 'Libby!'

'Caro? Anton told me you were here! Something about writing a book?' The film's scriptwriter, Libby McKinley, darted forward across the landing and wrapped Caro in an unexpected hug.

'Um, something like that.' Caro wondered how in favour of the fictional book project Libby would be, given how the events at Aldermere had affected her and her family. 'I was just trying to find a quiet place to sit down and start work.' Caro pointedly did not look around her at all the empty rooms with open doors as she said this.

'I'll come with you,' Libby said, linking her arm through Caro's. 'Then you can fill me in on what your book is about.'

'Actually, I had been meaning to talk to you about that,' Caro said, weakly.

They crossed the length of the landing to sit in the picture window overlooking the gardens at the back of the house.

'So, about this book of yours.' Settling into the armchair on the left, Libby raised her eyebrows at her. 'I take it I'm not going to like the subject matter?'

Caro took the other chair, and weighed up her options. Lie to Libby like she had Anton, and risk upsetting her over the book, or admit everything – including the real reason she was at Tŷ Gwyn.

It only took a moment to decide.

'I told Anton I was writing a book about everything that happened at Aldermere last summer because I needed an excuse to be here, with Rosalind and Posy, and I didn't want him thinking I was so desperate that I was just hanging around hoping he'd finally put me in his stupid film.'

'You don't really think the film is stupid.' Libby curled her feet up under her in the chair. 'So why are you really here?'

'Posy and Rosalind called and asked me to come. They say there's something going on here at Tŷ Gwyn. Something . . . worrying.' She bit her lip, trying to decide how much to give away. In the end, she decided that it was secrets that had caused so many of the problems at Aldermere in the first place. 'Rosalind thinks someone wants to kill her.'

Libby's eyes widened, and she clasped her hands tight in her lap. 'Because of the conspiracy theory?'

'The . . . what now?' Rosalind definitely hadn't mentioned anything about a conspiracy theory.

'Oh! I thought you knew. I have a Google alert set up for any mention of, well, Aldermere and all that, so I saw it straight away.' Libby motioned to Caro's laptop bag. 'Does that thing have internet connection? If so, I'll show you.'

It took them a few minutes to get Caro's laptop hooked up to the Tŷ Gwyn wifi – longer than it then took Libby to find the website she was looking for. Then she turned the screen back towards Caro.

Caro read through the webpage twice. Then she said, 'We need to get Rosalind and Posy up here. Now.'

Posy

If there was one scene in *The Lady Detective* that was truly iconic, it had to be the dinner-party scene. The whole cast gathered together for an extensive and elaborate dinner, at the end of which Uncle Francis dropped down dead.

Posy was sure she'd enjoy filming it a lot more if she hadn't already lived a deadly version of it last summer.

But here she was, in a silky blood-red evening dress that matched her lipstick, a rope of pearls hanging around her neck and her hair pinned in perfect waves. Ready to dine.

She sat back in her chair as around her the food stylists faffed with the lavish banquet set out on the table – most of it rendered inedible by the same tricks that made it look so perfect. The food set out on their plates would be real, and probably delicious, but the serving platters in the centre of the table didn't need to be. They just needed to stand up to a long day's filming – which Posy had no doubt this scene would require.

She hoped they didn't have to eat all eleven courses, this time.

At Aldermere, it had been the real thing – eleven tasting courses, followed by coffee and mints and tiny sugared flowers. And then death, for one of them.

She caught Rosalind's eye at the other end of the table, and knew she was remembering the same night. Hoping, as Posy was, that this shoot would have a better – less lethal – ending.

That note pushed under Rosalind's door didn't exactly inspire optimism on that front, though. Even if Rosalind had refused to talk about it all morning.

Somewhere in Tŷ Gwyn, Caro was making her investigations. Posy knew that was important, but it didn't stop her wishing she was there at the dinner table, too. Or even just off camera, offering her support.

Posy looked up to the door and realised that, even if Caro wasn't there, she had someone else standing in the wings, cheering her on.

From just inside the doorway, Kit caught her gaze and sent her a warm, reassuring smile. The sort of smile Posy could feel sinking into her chest. She knew he had to be nervous about his meeting that night, but he'd still made the time to come and support her, knowing how difficult this scene would be for her.

'Good to see you and DI Johnnie getting into character with the moony eyes and longing glances already. How many books does it take them to get together again?' Tristan dropped into the dining chair beside her, and flashed her a quick, friendly smile to show he was joking. 'And I genuinely mean good because – honestly – you looked like you were about to throw up all over this perfectly styled food before he walked in.'

'It's a big scene,' Posy said, tearing her attention away from Kit. 'Important. I was just . . . getting into character.'

'Yes, because Dahlia Lively so often looks like vomiting at the sight of a nicely varnished chicken leg.' Tristan waved an arm over the table. 'Why is all this here, anyway? It's supposed to be a tasting menu, isn't it? Surely they just bring the plates out for each course?'

He had a point, Posy had to admit. There hadn't been platters of food in the centre of the table at Aldermere. 'Maybe it just looks more impressive this way. Uncle Francis is definitely the sort to show off.'

'True.' Tristan picked up a stray bread roll – clearly not intended for eating, as it clunked as he knocked it against the pristine white tablecloth. 'Want me to see if I can land this in the water jug?'

Posy giggled. God, when had she become a giggler? 'No. At least, not unless you want the food stylist who's glaring at you to have an actual heart attack.'

'Good point.' He put the roll down. 'My work here is done, anyway.'

'Your work?' Posy frowned. Wait. Was that even Tristan's seat?

'I made you laugh,' he said, with a gentle smile. 'I wasn't kidding when I said you looked like you were about to throw up. I was just trying to distract you for a bit.'

'It worked,' she said, as he got to his feet. Across the room, Anton was speaking to one of his ADs, looking serious and purposeful. That was usually a sign they were about to start.

Posy sucked in a breath and prepared herself. Everyone else was there, now, ready to take their assigned seats for the scene. Dominic at the head of the table, Gabriel and Keira on her side, Rosalind at the far end, and Tristan and Scarlett opposite. Bennett and Moira were back on set this week, too, taking an empty chair on each side. Posy knew from earlier conversations that this was their last day, though, because they were both due back on a train to London tonight. Which meant they had to nail this last scene before their car came to take them away.

In the book, and script, they all changed seats in between each course. Posy knew that the book had a couple more suspects, since they were all supposed to sit in a different chair for each course, but Libby must have pared them down to keep things simple. Too many suspects on film was even harder than on the page, especially when they all started to look alike.

Anton clapped his hands and drew all their attentions, and Posy made a real effort to focus on the scenes ahead. Libby had condensed the eleven-course meal into two scenes; one of them taking their seats and wondering why Uncle Francis had invited them all to dinner – which they would film first – and one with the fatal coffee at the end, which was the big set piece.

They rehearsed each scene through before filming, the make-up artists darting in to touch up their faces the same way the food stylists fussed over the table in between takes. The first scene went smoothly, even though Posy felt her own tension rising as they got closer to the second.

And then it was time.

'Time for my dramatic exit!' Dominic announced, sounding far too gleeful about the entire experience.

Posy and Rosalind exchanged a look. But there was really nothing to say.

Dominic had refused to rehearse his final death sequence, ending the scene rehearsal just as he was due to start clutching his chest. 'Got to save something for the moment, right?'

Anton wouldn't have let anyone else get away with it, Posy was sure. But then Dominic was a Star, capital S intended. Plus there was a rumour he was putting up a significant chunk of the cash for the movie through his production company, too. In which case she imagined there wasn't much Anton wouldn't let him get away with.

As they all took their seats for the final scene, Posy glanced around the table from face to face, in those moments before Anton called 'Action' and their characters descended to hide them from sight. Already she could see Tristan's smiling face slipping into Charles's sneer, Gabriel's sharp, intelligent gaze dulling into cousin Bertie's uncomprehending eyes. Keira's bored look could be her or her character, really, but Posy was willing to believe she was getting into the role. Scarlett, however, looked exactly as vague as she had since the day Posy had met her, which perfectly suited her part as Bertie's wife, Rose.

Rosalind gave her one last look as herself – a glance filled with knowing and more – and Posy knew they'd get through this. They'd relive that awful moment and this time – *this* time – everyone would live.

Especially Rosalind.

Posy summoned up Dahlia from inside her – early Dahlia, before she had her reputation as the Lady Detective. Before she even knew Johnnie, really. Before she'd solved anything.

When all she had was a dead neighbour she knew hadn't killed herself, and a policeman who wouldn't listen to her. An uncle who wanted to rule her life for her, now her parents were gone, and a great aunt who was on her side as long as what Dahlia wanted was the opposite of what Francis wanted. A cousin who'd never understand her, and an ex-fiancé who'd never appreciate her.

Except that wasn't ever *all* Dahlia had.

She had herself. Her . . . Uncle Sol used to call it 'gumption'. She had that.

And she needed it. She *had* to nail this character, and fast. Some of the biggest Dahlia-defining scenes were coming up for filming over the next few weeks, and she had to get them right or the whole movie would be a washout. She knew Anton was frustrated with her, but something about the character just wouldn't come yet.

She wished she knew where to find her.

For now, Posy straightened her shoulders and searched once more for the character inside, just as the clapperboard slammed shut.

'I'd think that a place like this, you'd have no problems with that, Francis,' Tristan said, swirling his wine glass around as he leaned back in his chair.

'Time was, my boy, it would have been simple.' Dominic cast an accusatory glance at Gabriel, then Posy, as his feckless or disobedient family members. 'But these days . . .'

'I don't know why people want to keep big old houses like this anymore, anyway,' Scarlett said, idly playing with the sugared flower beside her coffee cup. Posy tried not to flinch at the sight. 'Surely a little place in town is much more convenient for the theatre and the clubs and so on.'

The platters in the centre of the table had been cleared now, and the extras dressed as period waiting staff were circling with their silver coffee pots, one arm behind their back as they poured.

Marcus didn't drink coffee. He had that herbal tea.

Posy swallowed and willed the thoughts away.

'The attractions of the city aren't the only things that matter to *some* people,' Rosalind said, in Great Aunt Hermione's acidic voice. She reached for her water glass rather than her filled coffee cup, and Posy couldn't help but notice her hands were shaking.

She's acting. Hermione's supposed to be ten years older, fading. It's symbolising age.

But it wasn't, Posy knew. It was the same terror that was racing through Posy's veins as they remained trapped in this repeating nightmare.

Posy lifted her wine glass to her lips, thankful that there was no actual alcohol in the glass.

'What do *you* think, Dahlia?' Scarlett asked. 'City or country?'

And suddenly everyone around the table was focused on her, waiting for her answer.

Dahlia, Dahlia, Dahlia.

She arched an eyebrow – not perfectly, but maybe Dahlia hadn't perfected that yet, either. She was still becoming, just like Posy was. 'I always find that whenever I'm in the city, I long for the country. But when I'm here, I ache for the town.'

The crisp voice came naturally after the weeks of intensive voice coaching, her own transatlantic accent invisible underneath, she hoped.

At the head of the table, Uncle Francis scoffed loudly and picked up his coffee cup. The sugar flower beside it tumbled onto the table, and he pinched it between two fingers of his other hand before popping it in his mouth. Posy's chest tightened.

Tristan, sitting beside her for this course, leaned closer with Charles's sneer on his face. 'You always did think the grass was greener on the other side of the fence, didn't you, Dahlia?'

'Or just more vibrant whichever side of the fence you *weren't* on, Charles,' she replied, sweetly, revelling in the way his eyes narrowed at the hit.

She had this. Everything was fine.

Then Dominic lurched to his feet with his coffee cup in hand and raised it to the assembled company. 'Well, since you're all here, I have an announcement to make. About this house, as it happens.' He lifted his napkin to blot his glistening forehead, glowing under the lights, and Posy felt her hands clammy against her costume.

It won't happen again. It *couldn't* happen again. The team behind the food here were professionals, highly respected and excellent at their job. No one was allowed on set without being on the list. Nobody could have crept in and poisoned anything. She *knew* that.

But the knowledge did nothing to dispel the fear that whoever was behind the death threats was already here, sitting at this table with her.

I'm having dinner with a potential murderer. Again.

Dominic was still talking. 'Time comes when a man has to make a decision, and I've made it – and don't any of you think you can change my mind, either. What's done is done, and—' He dropped his cup into its saucer, his eyes wide as his hand came up to clutch at his chest.

And it was so like the last time. So exactly like it, that Posy couldn't stop herself jumping to her feet.

'I—' Dominic staggered back into his chair, a little foam at the corner of his mouth now, his white shirt wrinkled and stained under his grasping hand. 'I—'

'Uncle Francis!' Was that in the script? Posy wasn't sure. But it felt right.

She glanced around the table. Rosalind gripped the cloth with white knuckles, while Keira continued to look bored and Scarlett's wide eyes grew wider. Gabriel and Tristan were on their feet now too, rushing to Dominic's chair as his eyes stared blankly upwards, his legs sprawled awkwardly beneath him.

Tristan placed two fingers against his neck, then looked up to face them all with sombre eyes. 'He's . . . dead.'

A beat. A long, unbearable beat.

'And cut!' Anton sounded jubilant. 'Do you know, I think we've got that in one!'

Posy couldn't look away from Dominic's slackened face and vacant eyes. Which meant she saw the moment the muscle jumped in his cheek, and he started to grin.

'See? Didn't want to give it all up too soon. Learned that from one of the greats. Needed it to feel real for you all.' He grabbed the arms of his chair and sat up. 'And it did, didn't it?'

'Very,' Rosalind said, drily. 'Does this mean we're done for the day?'

'We'll do a couple more for good measure, and to make sure we have all the angles,' Anton said. 'But then we can all finish early – and get ready for tonight's Classic Hollywood fundraiser.'

There were a few good-natured groans at that, but Posy wasn't really listening. Instead, she met Rosalind's gaze, and felt her breath start to come more easily again. Everything was going to be fine.

Then she turned and saw Caro standing behind the cameras with bad news in her eyes.

Chapter Seven

'Why did you ask them about the flowers, Miss?' Bess asked, obviously confused by her mistress's change in focus.

'I've learned it's important to ask a good witness *everything*,' Dahlia replied. 'You simply never know what's going to prove useful later on.'

Dahlia Lively *in* Disaster, Death and Dahlia
By Lettice Davenport, 1935

Rosalind

'I don't understand. These people think *I* committed the murders at Aldermere?' Rosalind stared in disbelief at the laptop Caro had set up on the counter in the wardrobe trailer, beside the steamer. 'Why on *earth* would anyone believe that?'

'Because people love a conspiracy theory?' Posy straightened up from reading over Rosalind's shoulder. 'They're always so much more exciting than reality.' She moved away, and Rosalind watched her join Caro in the other half of the trailer – the half that was filled with rails and rails of costumes. Surrounded by a mass of sparkly dresses, three-piece suits, vintage costume jewellery, thirties-style shoes and other accessories, they both appeared in their element.

While she was left wondering what it was about her that made people think she was a murderer.

Maybe she should smile more. Except, why the hell should she?

Rosalind scrolled back to the beginning and read through the whole page again, while Caro and Posy flipped through the relevant section of the costume rails, searching for something for Caro to wear to the Classic Hollywood fundraiser that night.

The website Libby had found was downright bizarre. A forum with countless posts and comments showing that there were whole swathes of the literate British population who genuinely thought Rosalind King – Dahlia Lively herself, once upon a time – was a murderer.

'As far as I can tell, they think that the police were involved in some sort of giant cover-up to save your reputation,' Libby explained as she perched on the countertop behind Rosalind. 'That everything we all said happened at Aldermere was just lies.'

'But why? Why do they think that anyone – let alone the police – would do that for me, if I were an actual murderer?' Rosalind realised she was almost slumped against the counter. She forced herself to stand up straighter again. Posture was important. More important than smiling.

'Because you're a national treasure,' Posy said, with a smile, as she looked up from the rail of dresses. 'The country has faith in you, you're a symbol to them, so you must be protected.'

'Or, more cynically, you're an establishment figure with dirt on other establishment figures, so they have to scratch your back so you'll continue to scratch theirs.' Caro held up a silvery dress with spaghetti straps. 'How about this?'

Rosalind pulled a face, then closed the laptop as Caro hung the dress back in its place. The page with the web forum posts, all decrying a cover-up of epic proportions, disappeared.

'You all know that's rubbish, right?' Rosalind said, looking up at the others. Posy held up a classic black sheath dress, and Caro shook her head.

'You know I'm more Katharine than Audrey, darling,' she said.

'That's true,' Libby agreed. 'I always thought it was weird those two weren't related.'

They were losing focus now, Rosalind realised. She supposed finding Caro the right outfit for the Classic Hollywood fundraiser was probably more fun than finding out who was trying to kill her.

Posy picked out a floor-length, emerald velvet dress with flutter sleeves and a skirt that was tightly fitted to the knee before flaring out. It was definitely far more Caro, even if Rosalind wasn't sure either of the Hepburns would have worn it.

'Of course we know you didn't kill anybody, Rosalind,' Caro said, taking the dress. 'We're very clear on that.'

'But . . . you do know people,' Posy pointed out. 'You've been in the entertainment industry a long time, worked with practically everybody. Like my Uncle Sol . . . You must know a few insider secrets.'

Posy didn't mention her family often, or at all really. Rosalind wondered what had made her bring them up now.

'Are you sure I'm okay to borrow something from here for tonight?' Caro asked, as she ran a hand over the velvet. 'I know you said they'd arranged outfits for all the cast but . . . I'm not actually a cast member.'

'You should be,' Libby muttered. 'Anton wouldn't let me write you in.'

Rosalind saw Caro beam at that information. 'It's fine. I cleared it with Cassandra, the wardrobe supervisor.' Who had sensibly found somewhere else to be so she could deny all knowledge of that conversation later if required. 'Besides, that dress is one of the ones they brought for me to try, but I went with the burgundy instead. Now. Let's get back to the reports of my murderous tendencies, please.'

'The earliest post date on that forum that I could see was last month,' Caro said, as she unzipped the dress and wriggled into it. 'The same time as the first death threat arrived, right?'

Rosalind nodded. 'That sounds about right. You think they're linked?'

'I think they have to be.' Caro turned around, so Posy could zip her up. 'So, what happened *then* to make someone come up with this idea? Why not straight after the summer, when it was in all the papers about what happened at Aldermere? Or in the autumn, when Hugh put the house up for sale?' Lettice Davenport's nephew had been given no choice but to put Aldermere on the market after the murders there the previous summer. Rosalind had to admit she'd been glad to see the back of the place – and Hugh – by the time she left.

Caro had a point about the timing, though. 'Or in two months' time when the trial starts,' Rosalind said. 'You're right. Why *then*?'

'Because we were starting filming,' Posy guessed. 'There were lots of pieces online, and in the papers, about filming starting here. Brought us back into the spotlight, I suppose.'

'That makes sense,' Rosalind agreed. 'For the generic letters, anyway. And for the more specific ones . . . if they're from somebody on set, the timing works for them, too.'

'So, what do we do next?' Posy asked.

'Find Caro some matching shoes, because that dress is perfect,' Libby said.

Caro preened in the mirror. 'It is, rather, isn't it?'

'But you meant about the death threats.' Libby pulled an apologetic face. 'Tell you what, you three decide that, and I'll find the shoes.'

'I think you have to do more of what you've been doing today,' Rosalind told Caro, thinking back over her friend's report of her day. 'Listening in, seeing who seems nervous or angry. We need to figure out who has a problem with me, and they're not going to let that slip in front of me, or even Posy, since she's the star of the film.'

'Everyone had the same opportunity,' Posy agreed. 'So we need to look for the motive. And if the cast think you're disgruntled about not getting a part when Rosalind did, they might talk to you.'

'Will they really buy that?' Libby asked. 'I mean, she is here visiting you, Rosalind.'

Rosalind shared a look and a wry smile with Caro and Posy. 'It doesn't matter. Everyone on this cast knows that however friendly you might be with a co-star or another actor, you can still be jealous of their success and envious of the roles they land.' She hoped that she, Caro and Posy were past that now, but she didn't think it would be a stretch for Caro to inhabit that place again for an evening.

'So. Disgruntled and bitter.' Caro took a pair of shoes from Libby, and slipped them on, gaining a few inches instantly. 'I can do that. I'll work my way around talking to everybody at tonight's fundraiser. Much easier than trying to do it here when they're filming, and maybe a few drinks will loosen a few tongues.'

'Then that's our next step, I suppose,' Posy said. 'It feels weird not to have more to do, after last time, you know? Like there should be more leads to follow up, or people to interrogate.'

'Well, nobody is actually dead this time,' Rosalind pointed out. 'Not yet, anyway. That makes a difference.'

'And there is *something* else we could be doing.' Caro tottered over to the counter in her heels and opened the laptop again, tapping out her password. She turned the computer screen towards the others.

'Ashok Gupta, PI,' Posy read aloud. 'You want to call Ashok?' Rosalind understood the scepticism in her voice. After all, it had been them – not Ashok – who had solved the murders at Aldermere.

'Why not? It says here he specialises in online information gathering. We can get him to find out who started that conspiracy theory about Rosalind.'

'Which might lead us to who is sending these threats,' Posy said, thoughtfully.

Rosalind wasn't sure how she felt about calling in a PI, but she supposed it was better than the actual police.

She *should* call the police. She knew that. But something inside her – a voice telling her it was nothing, really, all part of the job – held her back. Aldermere had just made her paranoid, seeing murderers around every corner.

The accidents on set *could* be accidents. And nobody had been hurt yet. If someone genuinely wanted her dead, surely there were easier ways?

That thought, and the knowledge the news would get out that people genuinely wanted her dead, made her hesitate. She couldn't begin to imagine what that would do for her reputation, if the great British public began a debate on whether her letter writers had a point.

At least a private investigator should be able to keep things private.

'It *could* work. If he'll do it. But what are we going to be doing after tonight, then?' Rosalind asked.

'Well, you two will be busy filming,' Caro pointed out. 'That's what you're actually here for, remember? And, of course, keeping an eye on the rest of the cast, seeing if you can get any hints of anything suspect going on. And I—'

'Caro has a book to write,' Libby interrupted. They all looked at her in surprise.

'I thought the book thing was just to keep Anton off your back, and give you an excuse to be here,' Posy said. 'I didn't realise you were actually going to write it.'

'And I wouldn't have thought that you, of all people, would want her to.' Rosalind studied Libby, trying to figure out her angle. 'Don't you want to write it yourself, if anyone does?'

Libby gave her a wistful smile. 'As much as I'd like to forget everything that happened last summer, it doesn't seem like the world is willing to, does it? And if anyone is going to tell stories about it, I'd want it to be you, Caro. I'm too close to it all. And anyway, you're the ones who solved it. The three of you. You figured it all out. And I trust you to tell it the way it should be told.' She gathered up her bag and moved towards the door. 'But now you've got everything in hand here, I have to get back to London. Good luck with the investigation!'

With a last smile for each of them, Libby headed down the trailer steps, leaving the three Dahlias alone again.

'So. We have a plan,' Caro said. 'I'll call Ashok, get him on the case. You two keep track of your fellow cast members when they're on set, and I'll try to get them all talking back at the inn, so we can find out who has got it in for Rosalind, and why, then stop them. In between writing a book, apparently.'

'Sounds good,' Posy said, grinning.

'Well, you did say you were bored,' Rosalind added, with a smile of her own for the first time since Caro had shown her that blasted website.

A plan might not be a solution, but there was nobody she trusted more to get to the bottom of this than the other two Dahlias.

Caro

Ashok was gratifyingly pleased to hear from her.

'Of course I want to help,' he said, and Caro allowed herself a smug smile in the mirror as she fixed her lipstick, the phone clamped between her ear and her shoulder. 'I'd seen the theories about Rosalind, of course – not that I believed them for a moment.'

'Well, no.' Caro patted the jewel-tipped pins holding her hair back a little more firmly into place. 'You were there. You know what really happened.'

'Exactly! And now we can prove it. Together.'

'Right.' Maybe he was a little *too* pleased to hear from her. This was still a Dahlias investigation, after all.

'Anyway. Can't wait to get started. My standard rates are on my website. Invoices to you?'

Ah, that explained his enthusiasm. He was broke, or at least underemployed. Caro could sympathise with the latter, at least.

She checked to ensure that the bathroom door was still closed, with Rosalind on the other side of it, preparing for the Classic Hollywood Night at the Seven Stars.

'Address them to Rosalind,' Caro told him, before they said their goodbyes and hung up. Rosalind was the one whose life was in danger, and she had a damn sight more money than she or Posy had, anyway.

The bathroom door opened and Rosalind appeared, looking more elegant and put together in her burgundy shot-silk gown than Caro ever expected to in her life. Still, she knew she looked good in the emerald-green velvet Posy had found for her, and besides, if she was playing a bitter second-fiddle role tonight, it wouldn't do to outshine the stars anyway.

'Ashok on board?' Rosalind asked, fluffing up her already perfect white hair in the mirror.

Caro nodded. 'So. Ready to party like it's 1935?'

'Always.'

The first sign that things had changed since they'd returned to their suite, to prepare for the fundraiser that night, was an actual sign. There, set up on the hill behind the inn, was a smaller replica of the iconic Hollywood sign, lit up from below so the letters glowed against the night sky, as a strikingly full blood moon rose over it.

'Almost like the real thing,' Rosalind murmured, pulling her faux fur wrap closer around her shoulders against the winter breeze.

Inside, the Seven Stars had been transformed, its usual hipster chic replaced with a glamour and sparkle not normally seen in small Welsh villages, in Caro's experience. A red carpet ran from the front door through the main bar into the restaurant rooms behind, and the flagstones either side of it had been adorned with golden star stickers featuring the names of classic Hollywood actors – and a few of the current *Lady Detective* cast – providing their very own walk of fame.

The white walls, where there was space, had been turned into cinema screens, with old black and white movies playing silently. The largest dining room, which Caro had been told was normally used for private dining events, had been transformed into a casino, complete with roulette wheel and blackjack table, and croupiers in red waistcoats.

Tables had been moved against the walls to make space for mingling, and black-tied waiters moved among the crowd holding silver trays of canapés. And there *was* a crowd, Caro realised. Most of the village had to be there, all dressed in their finest, with outfits ranging from the twenties all the way through to the sixties in vintage. The men had mostly got away with a classic James Bond or Fred Astaire impersonation – it was always easier for men. The women, however, had gone all out with flapper outfits, wiggle dresses and ballgowns.

'Looks like Glan y Wern is really on board with this event,' she said to Rosalind, as she reached for two champagne glasses from a passing waiter's tray.

'Well, so they should be.' Rosalind took her glass with a nod of thanks. 'We're raising money for their school, or bridge, or something local, anyway.'

'Hmm.' But Caro couldn't forget that graffiti in the village. How did the locals *really* feel about the disruption of having a film crew right next door? Not to mention all the press attention it brought with it.

'Right. If I'm going to be bitter and looking for a sympathetic ear, I'd better not hang around your superstar aura too much.' Caro took a gulp of champagne. 'I'll catch up with you later.'

As she moved through the inn, she clocked who was where, while she decided her plan of action. The problem was knowing where to start. Spotting Gabriel and a blonde woman in a clichéd Marilyn Monroe white dress sitting at a table in the main bar reminded her of the conversation she'd overheard earlier that day, so she headed over to join them.

It wasn't until she'd taken her seat that she realised Marilyn was actually Scarlett in a blonde wig and a lot of red lipstick. 'Great costume,' she told her. 'I almost didn't recognise you.'

Scarlett gave a pleased smile. 'It's nice to make an effort, isn't it? Unlike this one.' She elbowed Gabriel lightly.

'What?' he asked. 'The tux is a classic.'

'And a cop out,' Scarlett replied, before turning back to Caro. 'I *love* your dress, though. So classy.'

Caro looked down at the emerald velvet. 'Isn't it? Of course, it was chosen for Rosalind, so it would be. Rosalind King is never *anything* but classy.' She glanced up under her lashes to catch their reactions.

'Oh, *isn't* she?' Scarlett gushed. 'She's *such* an icon.'

'She is Dahlia, I suppose,' Gabriel said. 'Well, one of three.'

'Oh, but she's *the* Dahlia, really, isn't she? No offence,' Scarlett added quickly.

'Don't worry.' Caro smiled tightly. 'I'm used to it.'

Should she be worried how easy it was to fall into the bitter and jealous persona? She didn't think she'd really felt that way even before getting to know Rosalind properly – at least, she hoped not. Maybe she'd ask Annie when she called home before bed.

She was just weighing up her next leading question or comment when a whirlwind in a tuxedo spun past the table, turned and came back to them.

'Where are they?' Anton raked a hand through his already dishevelled dark – with a hint of silver – curls. 'I specifically said everyone needed to be here for this.'

'Where's who?' Gabriel asked mildly, before taking a sip of his champagne.

'The rest of your illustrious colleagues,' Anton replied. 'By my count we're short at least three.'

Caro scanned the room, performing a quick headcount. Tristan and Keira were at the bar, and she knew Rosalind had headed into the back room to find Posy. But where were Nina, Dominic and Kit?

'Kit gave some of the others a lift into the village earlier,' Scarlett said. 'Tristan and Dominic, I think. Oh, and Nina – she said she wanted to post a letter. I'd have gone too, but they said there wasn't room.'

Given Kit's low-slung sports car with its limited space for passengers, Caro could believe it. That said, it was equally possible they just hadn't wanted Scarlett with them.

'Tristan is back.' Anton gestured towards the bar. 'So where are the others?'

He looked accusingly at Caro, who widened her eyes and shrugged. 'Nothing to do with me. I've been working on my book.'

'In the wardrobe trailer, it seems,' Anton commented, before stalking off again.

'Why is he so bothered about everyone being here?' Caro asked, once he was gone.

Gabriel leaned across the table and lowered his voice. 'Apparently there was a bit of fuss from the locals when it was first announced we'd be filming at Tŷ Gwyn. And then again when we brought all our trucks over that crumbling bridge of theirs. I think this was the producers' way of smoothing things over, raising money for a local cause.'

Caro nodded. That made sense.

Up by the bar, Owain tapped a microphone and waited for the room to calm before launching into an official welcome to everyone, with special reference to the cast – leading to a rather awkward moment when three of them, including the illustrious Dominic Laugharne, weren't there.

'And, anyway, I hope you all have a great evening,' Owain finished, to rather lacklustre applause.

'Excuse me?' Caro looked up to find a man dressed as Charlie Chaplin waiting at her elbow. 'You're Caro Hooper, right? My wife and I were wondering if we could get a photo with you.' He waved towards a woman in an Audrey-esque black shift dress and pearls, standing beside a photo booth set up with a stack of props and accessories.

Caro got to her feet. 'Of course.' Couldn't let the fans down, even if she wasn't really supposed to be there.

'Caro Hooper! It's so exciting to meet you!' The woman clapped her hands together. 'I didn't even know *you'd* be coming here until my niece told me she'd met you. I bet she's been following you around with questions, hasn't she?'

'Your niece?' Caro took a closer look at the woman, with her dark hair and bright eyes. 'Let me guess. Seren?'

'That's right! Oh, I'm so rude.' She held out a hand. 'I'm Bethan. And Seren has been wanting to run away to Hollywood since she was about seven, so this is a dream come true for her. She's so annoyed about missing tonight, but the deal was no kids, so she's getting paid to babysit for my two instead. Still, I reckon she'll be spending all of half-term trying to figure out how to get on set with you all.'

'And good luck to her,' Caro said, imagining how much Anton would hate a teenager on set as well as her. 'So you must be Owain's sister, then?'

Bethan nodded. 'That's right. Our parents ran the pub right up until Dad died last year and left it to the two of us. But I already have the cafe in town – WelshCakes, it's called – and Owain and Rebecca were looking for a change, so they agreed to move back from London and take on this place.'

'Looks like they're doing a good job with it, too,' Caro observed, her gaze running over the packed pub.

'They really are.' Bethan smiled sadly. 'I'm glad of it, too. Dad . . . he loved this pub, but he couldn't see that it needed to move with the times. Now, it has a chance. And, well, I grew up here, listening to the locals telling tall tales about the place – how it's haunted by the ghost of a girl who fell in love with the son of the owner of Tŷ Gwyn, and died of a broken heart when the boy was sent away. Apparently they had a secret meeting place somewhere linking the two properties, and I spent *days* looking for it in the school holidays, but I never found it. Anyway. I'd have hated to see it have to be sold.'

'I can understand that,' Caro replied. 'Now, do you want to hold the plastic Oscar or wear the tiara for this photo?'

One photo turned into four or five for other locals who spotted her, and by the time she made her way back to the table where she'd left her drink, her seat had been taken. Keira was cosied up to Scarlett, while Gabriel had clearly found somewhere else to be as Tristan had taken his chair. Caro sidled up slowly to see if she could hear what they were talking about.

'I'm just saying, we could be already half done with this movie if *somebody* didn't keep screwing up,' Keira was saying to Scarlett, acid dripping from her voice. 'Really. You'd expect a little more from Dahlia Lively, wouldn't you?' Was she talking about Rosalind or Posy, Caro wondered?

'Keira,' Tristan said, gently but with a hint of censure as he looked up at Caro with an apologetic smile. So much for sneaking up. But then, she'd always thought she'd make a better detective than a spy.

'Oh, don't mind me.' Caro reached across to take her drink. 'I know all about the pressure of the film set, and how it can get to you if you're not used to it.'

'Well, TV set, anyway.' Keira's smile was most definitely fake. '*Your* Dahlia never made the big screen, did she?'

'No, my Dahlia just ran for thirteen years and was syndicated around the world,' Caro replied, sweetly. 'And Rosalind's became a classic of the genre on film, of course.' She gestured towards the screen on the wall where, fortuitously, Rosalind's version of *The Lady Detective* was currently playing.

'Oh, Rosalind is a pro,' Keira said dismissively. 'It's her young protégée that's slowing us up.'

Ah. Posy, then.

Caro hadn't been able to watch many of Posy's scenes as Dahlia since she arrived, but she'd seen enough to understand why nobody else at the table was denying Keira's complaints were true.

It had felt strange, watching Posy inhabit the character Caro had spent such a large part of her adult life portraying. While she knew, intellectually, that Dahlia Lively wasn't *hers*, her heart had a hard time keeping up with her brain on that one.

In a contrast to the hideous watercolour floral tea-dresses Anton had dressed her in last summer, the wardrobe department had done a stunning job with Posy's costume as Dahlia. With her dark blonde hair curled and pinned back from her bright red lips and wide eyes, she looked like she might have raided Katharine Hepburn's closet in her heyday.

But for all that she looked the part, it was clear to Caro from what she had seen that Posy was having some trouble actually *playing* it. It seemed to Caro that Posy hadn't quite *become* Dahlia yet. She put on her clothes and her mannerisms, but they didn't fit.

Perhaps she should have a word. Or maybe that would make things worse.

For now, she stuck with defending her friend.

'Posy has been on film sets since before you were born,' Caro pointed out. 'She was basically a star before she was out of nappies.' A bit of an exaggeration, perhaps, but there'd definitely been a baby food advert on Posy's CV.

'Maybe that's why she burned out so young.' Keira swirled the dregs of her champagne around in her glass and Tristan got instantly to his feet to fetch her another one from a passing waiter. He placed it in front of her before turning to the next table and asking to take another chair, which he placed next to his own for Caro.

'Thank you,' she said, sitting down.

'So, Caro, what brought you to this little corner of Wales?' Tristan asked, in a blatant attempt to change the subject.

She couldn't blame him. 'Oh, well, I'm working on a new project. A bit of a new direction.'

Scarlett's eyes widened, and she placed her elbows on the table and, leaning forward, treated them all to an enhanced view of her cleavage in the Marilyn dress. 'Is it true you're writing an exposé about what really happened last summer?'

'I am writing a book, yes,' Caro said. 'But only because I want to tell the true story of events.'

Keira rolled her eyes. 'As if we didn't all read enough about that in the papers last summer.'

'Well, it seems that not everyone was paying proper attention.' Caro switched her gaze from face to face around the table, but none of her three companions seemed to get what she was hinting at. Or if they did, they were hiding it.

The front door crashed open again and Dominic strode in, immaculately dressed in white, rather than black, tie. Arms stretched wide, he waited for the gathered crowd to react to his arrival, then clapped his hands together and announced, 'My friends! It's so good to be here with you all tonight. For those who don't recognise me . . .' he paused for a brief bubble of laughter from his audience, 'I am Dominic Laugharne, and I want to thank you all for welcoming me and my friends here while we make our latest blockbuster. And as a small show of appreciation, I pledge to match all donations made tonight, pound for pound!'

That earned a cheer from the gathered crowd, and many hand-shakes and claps on the back as he made his way through the bar towards where Anton was standing.

But as Caro watched him go, she just wondered who Dominic was trying to win over with his fortune now. Because she was almost certain it wouldn't actually be the locals of Glan y Wern.

Chapter Eight

'Dahlia! You just cannot do this.' Johnnie was breathing hard, his
face red as he stared at her.
Dahlia stared back. 'Watch me.'

Dahlia Lively *in* The Devil in the Details
***By* Lettice Davenport, 1946**

Rosalind

Swept into the party atmosphere of the fundraiser, Rosalind found
herself in high demand for photos at the photo booth – although she
left the props to the locals. Finally, she managed to send the last of
her fans in Caro's direction, and escaped with a small plate of canapés
and a second glass of champagne into the smallest of the private
dining rooms at the back, where *It Happened One Night* was playing
on the wall. Rosalind didn't need the subtitles to know every word to
that one.

She'd hoped for a bit of space and peace to regroup, but only a few
minutes later – before she'd even finished the canapés – Dominic
breezed in and plonked himself down at the table beside her.

'Well, that's *that* done,' he said, helping himself to a mini Welsh
rarebit square from her plate. Thankfully he'd brought his own champagne flute, or they'd have had real problems. 'Thought Anton was
going to blow a gasket – thirty-five text messages I had from him about

being late! Honestly, I thought he was a man who appreciated the artistic temperament. But apparently not when money is involved.'

Rosalind sipped at her champagne. 'Yes, I heard your announcement. Very generous of you.'

Dominic rolled his eyes. 'You don't think it was *my* idea? Just another bit of play acting to get the locals off our backs. I promised Anton I'd do it, but I got held up in the village and he started losing his mind.'

'Was it busy in the village?' Rosalind asked. 'I noticed that a few others aren't back yet, either.' Or rather, she'd heard Anton ranting about it. She had to agree with Dominic; Anton seemed strangely concerned about the few cast members who hadn't made the fundraiser. It made her wonder if there were more problems with the locals than she'd anticipated.

Tŷ Gwyn hadn't been their first choice of location for filming, or even their second. The first had been ruled out by an unfortunate fire the previous year, the second by flooding just before Christmas. Perhaps the hurried search for somewhere new had overlooked something – like local sentiment. She imagined that the last thing Anton needed for a movie people were still claiming was cursed was protestors outside the gates when they were trying to film.

Or any more on-set accidents, for that matter. Could *they* be linked to local outrage, rather than her death threats? It was something to consider, at least. She knew that Anton had tried to hire locally for security, and some of the lower-rung crew positions, as well as extras.

'Don't know what's keeping the others,' Dominic replied with a shrug. 'Didn't see them in the pub, anyway.' Which explained his lateness, and his exuberance, Rosalind supposed. Although why he'd chosen to drink in the village rather than the Seven Stars, or even the privacy of his own room, was a mystery.

Through the opened double doors that led to the next room, Rosalind had a good view of the casino set up for the occasion. Tristan was with Posy at the roulette table, but there was still no sign of Nina or Kit, as far as she could see.

Dominic followed her gaze, and smirked. 'Ah, our illustrious new Dahlia. How is it playing second fiddle to a twenty-something screw-up?'

'Posy is a very talented actress. And a dear friend,' she added, sharply. 'I'm thrilled to be able to spend this time on set with her.' Or, she would be, if she wasn't afraid of being murdered every minute.

'Right, right.' He patted her hand knowingly, and she pulled it away to tuck it in her lap. 'You know you can tell me the real answer, right? You and I . . . we're one and the same. Old school. The last remnants of an industry going to the dogs. It's all political correctness these days, isn't it? Can't even tell a girl she's got a nice arse without being hauled in for a warning.'

Since Rosalind suspected Dominic's method of informing a woman of that fact was by touching the body part in question, she ignored that.

'And why's Caro Hooper here?' Dominic asked, suddenly. 'She's not in the movie too, is she? I know Anton's trying to get all the old fans on board, but that's a step too far, don't you think? Especially after what she did to old Tommy.'

Old Tommy, she assumed, was Thomas, Caro's ex-husband. Caro had set his tie on fire, while he was wearing it, after she discovered he was cheating on her. Rosalind wondered if that was what Dominic meant or if, in his eyes, the greater crime was for Caro not to forgive or ignore Thomas's indiscretions, and instead to go on and get married again, to Annie, and be blissfully happy.

'What about what he did to her?' she asked mildly.

Dominic flapped a hand, dismissing her objections without even coming up with an argument. 'Marriage is marriage. Makes no damn sense to anybody.'

Which may or may not have been true, but did give her the segue she needed to ask Dominic about another topic that had been bothering her.

'I was sad to see that Brigette had walked away from the project,' she said, keeping her gaze focused on the next room, as she saw Nina arrive and join Tristan and Posy at the roulette table. 'I was looking forward to spending some time with her again. Do you know what made her leave?'

Now she risked a glance over at Dominic, in time to see him flinch before answering. 'I gave up asking what makes that woman do anything when she left me.'

'Still, you must have some idea,' she pressed.

'We're divorced, Rosalind,' Dominic said, shortly. 'Part of the joy of breaking up is not having to tell each other everything any more. How much are you telling Hugh Davenport these days, anyway?'

Heat spread up her throat to her cheeks, and Rosalind hoped the light was dim enough that Dominic wouldn't notice. From his smile, he did, though.

Apparently knowing he'd got in a verbal hit brightened his mood, because he drained his champagne glass and said, 'Anyway, Brigette's perfectly safe and happy out in the Californian desert or wherever that retreat she keeps posting Instagram pictures from is. She'll be having a much better time of it than we are, I'm sure.'

That much, Rosalind thought, as Rebecca arrived and urged Dominic to join her in the casino, was probably true.

Posy

Against her expectations, Posy was having fun.

Dressed in a silky, beaded, 1920s flapper-girl dress the costume designer had chosen for her, she felt like a silent movie star – something that felt appropriate for her task for the evening. She wasn't here to make a scene herself, but to listen and react to others.

Someone here was threatening Rosalind, and they were going to find out who.

She saw the other two Dahlias in passing but, as they'd agreed earlier, she kept her distance. Nobody would say anything incriminating around Rosalind herself, after all. And while they probably wouldn't say it in front of Posy either, as long as the champagne was flowing there was a chance someone might let something slip.

Posy sipped at the sparkling elderflower drink Owain had prepared for her, in a champagne flute just like all the others, and laughed at Tristan's attempts at a New York gangster impression as he spun the roulette wheel again.

'Not as good as your Keith Carver,' she informed him. His impression of the handsome, 1990s quiz show host had been eerily accurate.

'You should hear his impression of Bennett Gracy.' Nina approached them with a small smile, still wearing a thick wool coat over her dress. 'He sounds more like Bennett than Bennett does, these days.' Posy had to admit she'd noticed the American actor looking – and sounding – older when they'd filmed the dinner scene the day before.

'I was starting to wonder if you were even coming.' Tristan slipped Nina's coat from her shoulders, and handed it to a waiter to put in the cloakroom area they'd set up for the event.

'It takes time to look this good, you know.' Nina did a small twirl in her navy, drop-waisted evening dress, with a rope of pearls hanging down to her navel.

'You look great,' Posy said, sincerely.

'She's right, you do.' Gabriel appeared from behind them, and handed Nina a champagne flute before kissing her cheek. 'Anton was on the warpath, but now Dominic's made his announcement and the mood of the room seems to have improved, he's happily critiquing some old black-and-white movie with the local film club in the other room.'

'And if he asks, you were here all along anyway,' Tristan added. 'Now, who wants to try blackjack?'

Posy was content to watch the gambling, rather than take part. Eventually, the crowds started to thin out a bit as locals headed home, leaving the hardcore drinkers behind.

Dominic appeared with Rebecca to take on the roulette wheel, and before long Keira wandered through to join them, too. Twenty minutes later, Keira checked her watch, then dropped the last of her chips into the donation box. 'I'm calling it a night.'

'Not staying to try your hand at blackjack with me, Keira?' Dominic called after her.

'To watch you fail to count to twenty-one?' It was her tone, rather than her words, that turned Dominic's ears red, Posy thought. 'No thanks. I can watch you fail anytime I like.'

With a last glare in Dominic's direction, she was gone, the door swinging shut behind her before he came up with a response. Posy had to admit that had been particularly harsh.

'Like she'd have achieved anything if it wasn't for who her parents are,' he muttered, turning towards the blackjack table.

'And on that note,' Nina placed her still half-full glass on the tray of a passing waiter who was clearly trying to clear up behind them, 'goodnight, all.' She followed Keira through the back door that led to the suites, leaving Posy alone with Dominic, Tristan and Gabriel.

The men played a few more hands of blackjack, chips changing hands one way then back again, before Tristan and Gabriel both bowed out. Tristan went to work his charm on Rebecca behind the bar for a few more drinks, while Gabriel heckled Dominic's card choices.

At five to eleven, Owain rang the old-fashioned bell behind the bar and announced that it was closing time – for everyone who wasn't staying at the inn, at least.

Posy yawned. She was just considering calling it a night herself when Caro appeared in the doorway.

'Rosalind's gone to bed,' she announced. 'Just us left then, is it?' She settled into a chair next to Gabriel. Given what Caro had reported overhearing earlier, Posy wasn't entirely surprised. With Rosalind *and* Keira gone, this was the perfect chance to ask those questions.

'Those young things couldn't hack it either,' Dominic replied, with a chuckle that turned into a laugh.

'So, how are you all finding it, filming a Dahlia Lively movie with *two* Dahlia Livelys?' Caro asked, as the tired-looking croupier finally packed up and left, and Tristan returned with more drinks.

'You mean Rosalind and Posy?' Tristan asked, his tone teasing. 'Terrible. They're both so territorial about the role . . .' Posy jabbed him in the ribs. 'I'm joking, I'm joking! The more Dahlias the better, in my opinion. I have to admit, I did wonder how it would go. But the two of them seem to be pretty good friends.'

'And now we've got three of you. Of course, after all the stories about last summer, that's hardly a surprise though, is it?' Gabriel flashed a grin at Caro. 'You lot were like the three musketeers, or something, weren't you?'

'Or something,' Caro replied, drily. 'That's why I came, though, really. For a bit of a reunion. Hadn't seen either of them since Christmas.'

Posy was content to tune out the chatter, especially as Caro leaned in closer towards Gabriel and dropped her voice. The other Dahlia would fill her in on anything she learned in the morning. She was too sleepy to concentrate on eavesdropping anyway.

But then, a short while later, the front door to the pub swung open and Kit appeared – and suddenly Posy was wide awake again. With a nod towards Caro, who smirked, damn her, she went to find out how his evening had gone.

'So, when you said you might be a little late . . .' She watched as he shoved his car keys in his pocket and hung his coat on the end of the nearly empty rail that had served as their cloakroom for the night.

'I know, I know.' He turned back towards Rebecca behind the bar. 'Any chance of a whisky?'

She rolled her eyes and reached for a glass. 'Since it's you.'

Caro emerged from the back room, Tristan close behind.

'You missed all the fun,' she called across to Kit. 'I might have done better at blackjack if you'd been here.'

'I doubt it. I'm rubbish at gambling.' Kit flashed her a grin, but Posy couldn't help but notice it didn't reach his eyes.

'Do you want to talk about how it went tonight?' she asked, softly.

Kit grimaced, and took another gulp of his whisky. 'Honestly? I just want to sit here and get drunk.'

The fumes from his glass were strong and, even though she'd managed all night without even wanting to touch a drink, Posy really didn't want to push her self-restraint any more. Because she never just wanted *a* drink. More was always better with her.

'Right. Okay.' She left him sitting by the fire, and was pleased to see that Anton, of all people, joined him a moment or two later, nursing his own tumbler of whisky. On set, Anton might forget that they were human, but he and Kit had worked together before. Maybe Kit needed male company tonight.

'Everything okay?' Caro asked, and Posy nodded. Caro didn't look entirely like she believed it, but she let it go. 'I couldn't get much from Gabriel, but I've had a few interesting conversations tonight. Debrief in the morning? I want to check on Rosalind.'

'Sounds good.' She waved Caro off to bed, and was about to join Tristan and Rebecca, who were chatting at the bar, when she heard a smack from the room they'd been using as a casino. Like a hand slapping down on a wood table.

Automatically, she veered off course to see what was happening, and almost barrelled into Dominic coming the other way. Gabriel was right behind him, his face tight and pale in contrast to Dominic's almost purple complexion.

'I said I don't want to talk about it,' Dominic whispered harshly. Then, raising his voice and his cheer for the rest of the room, he said, 'Excellent night, all! Well done. I'm for bed, but I hope to hear in the morning just how much we raised for . . . such a worthy cause.'

Whatever it was, Posy imagined him finishing in his head.

Gabriel trailed Dominic out into the courtyard behind the inn and, once she was sure no one was watching her, Posy followed, closing the door silently behind her and staying in the shadows. Gabriel hadn't looked like a man who was about to let whatever was bothering him drop, not yet.

She was right.

Even with the lights that lined the path, most of the courtyard was in total darkness. Posy followed the sound of muted voices to the far side of the courtyard, away from the car park, between two of the barns that had been converted into luxury suites. She tucked herself behind a large planter and wished she'd brought a coat.

'Are you *really* trying to blackmail me into this?' By peering around the brick planter, she could just make out Dominic in the shadows.

'Of course not!' Gabriel's denial wasn't entirely convincing. 'I'm just saying. Well. I'm not the only one who knows. Keira—'

'That bitch,' Dominic spat. Was it fear or frustration making him bullish? And was this what Caro had heard Keira and Gabriel arguing about earlier? 'Did she get to you too? Or Brigette? Is that what this is about? Is she behind this?'

'Behind what?' Gabriel sounded genuinely confused at the question.

'It doesn't even matter. Your word against mine only goes so far, you realise. And so does hers.'

'That's . . . the truth isn't even important, these days. Just the stories.' Gabriel sounded weary, just saying the words. 'And trust me, I know. The damage is already done. But if we just work together . . .' Gabriel broke off, and the sudden crunching on gravel told her one of them was moving in her direction. Not good.

She inched around the corner of the planter, keeping low and – hopefully – out of sight as Dominic crossed the courtyard, away from Gabriel and towards his own room.

'There are no secrets here, Gabriel,' he called back, across the darkness of the night. 'Only stories. And I get to choose which ones we tell. Remember that.'

Posy stayed crouched, listening to Dominic slam his door behind him so hard she thought the walls must shake.

Gabriel's sigh echoed around the courtyard. She saw a flicker of light – a cigarette, she assumed – fall from his hand to the ground and go out. Then he crunched off across the gravel to his own room, and Posy let out a long breath.

At least she had something interesting to share with the others in the morning.

Chapter Nine

'There's nothing like a murder to completely upset any person's plans.'
Dahlia Lively *in* Murder Looks Lively
By **Lettice Davenport, 1933**

Caro

Caro had been anticipating a debrief with the other Dahlias over coffee and pastries the following morning, but the day did not get off to the start she had been hoping for.

She awoke to the sound of voices outside – unfamiliar ones. Local accents. Serious tones. Not the courtyard side, she realised, which meant they had to be in the car park.

Keeping the duvet wrapped around her, she knelt up at the window, peering out through the gap between the plush curtains. From her daybed, she had a good view of the tarmacked parking area before the more stunning view of the hills beyond. She could see the skip by the trees, the few cars that cast members had brought (most, it seemed, had been driven or at least caught a cab from the nearest mainline station), her own red convertible – and a police car.

Not a good start to the day.

Rosalind remained fast asleep in the next room and, having listened to her toss and turn through the wall between them all night, Caro decided she probably needed the rest while she could get it. So, she washed and dressed as quickly and quietly as she could, sending an urgent message to Posy. *Look Lively*, it read, which she knew would make the youngest Dahlia groan, just as she intended.

It was early still, but when Caro stepped into the pub it was already busy. A police officer in uniform was at the bar, talking to Rebecca and Owain, while Anton stood a little away, beside the not-yet-lit fire, looking anxious. The decorations and screens from the night before remained in place, the tables still pushed against the walls, although she'd seen the temporary staff clear away the glasses and plates before they'd left for the night.

At the table on the other side of the fire, Kit, Nina, Scarlett and Tristan were sitting together, watching.

'What's happening?' Caro slipped into the last chair at their table.

'Not sure yet,' Kit said, but there was a tension in his voice that wasn't normal for him. 'We had an early call. We were waiting for Posy, Keira and the shuttle bus, but there's no sign of the bus. Just the police.'

'Oh.' A crash, then, maybe? An accident with the bus bringing the crew to Tŷ Gwyn from the town?

Posy appeared in the doorway, her hair pulled back into a knot on the top of her head, her face make-up free and fresh, and a cup of coffee from the expensive pod machine in her room still in her hand. With a cautious look in the direction of the police, she headed for Caro and the others, snagging a stool from the nearest table.

'*Look Lively*? Really?' she muttered to Caro, who shrugged.

'Got you here, didn't it?'

'Where's Rosalind?' Posy asked.

'Still sleeping.'

'Lucky her,' Kit grumbled. Caro wondered how many more whiskies he'd had with Anton after she went to bed.

The police officer nodded at Rebecca and Owain, then turned to face the rest of them.

'I'm sorry to have to tell you that there has been a serious incident on the road between here and Glan y Wern village, and the road will remain closed until we have finished our investigations,' he said. He looked, Caro determined, about twelve, but suitably sombre about the matter in hand.

'What's happened?' Anton asked. 'Is it *really* that serious? We need to get our crew up to Tŷ Gwyn to start shooting, and at the moment they're telling me they're not being allowed into the road.' He waved his top-of-the-range phone around for emphasis.

'Unfortunately it seems that a woman was hit by a car on the side of the road overnight. Her body was found by a local woman from the village walking her dog this morning, and reported to us directly.'

Caro felt the air being sucked from the room at the news. For a moment, there was total silence – until Anton began demanding more information.

The young police officer fended him off reasonably well, but even the best training was no match for an egocentric and determined director, it seemed.

'We believe the victim may have been staying here at Saith Seren,' the police officer finally admitted. 'We're awaiting a formal identification, but she was carrying ID and a key to a room here.' From the look on his face as he finished speaking, he really shouldn't have told them that last bit, Caro suspected.

'Here?' Rebecca repeated, the word echoing in the silent pub. 'Who?'

'As . . . as I said, we're awaiting formal identification . . .' the policeman started, stammering slightly as he tried to backtrack, but it was pointless. With just a glance around the room, the answer to the question of who was missing was obvious.

'Oh my God, it's Keira, isn't it?' Kit jumped to his feet, stalking across to the policeman. 'She's the only woman missing from the cast this morning. Keira Reynolds-Yang?'

The policeman looked as if he'd just swallowed something incredibly unpleasant. 'I cannot officially confirm that.'

But it was. Of course it was. And everyone in the room knew it.

There was a long, stretched, second of utter shock and silence.

And then chaos.

Anton swore and demanded more information, Scarlett sobbed loudly and was comforted by a distraught-looking Tristan, and Kit started to pace the length of the bar. Caro shared a look with Posy, and saw her own feelings reflected. Not shocked, or particularly distraught. Rather, horrified, but accepting.

'My colleagues may wish to talk to some of you shortly,' the policeman went on, as things started to calm down. 'Until then, I'll have to ask you to let us get on with our jobs undisturbed.'

He turned quickly to escape via the side door, back into the car park and towards the road that led to the village. The road where Keira had died.

'It's a dead end,' Caro whispered, realising.

'What?' Posy said, sounding startled out of her own thoughts.

'It's a dead end. This road, I mean. It leads up to Tŷ Gwyn, but nowhere else. Even the road at the bottom of the lane only goes between the village and a cul-de-sac of houses. Anyone who was on this road last night would have been coming to or from the Seven Stars or Tŷ Gwyn.'

'They could have taken a wrong turn,' Posy suggested, half-heartedly. 'Been turning around when they hit her?'

'Perhaps.' But Caro wasn't convinced. 'If they're checking CCTV maybe they'll find something. And I suspect they're checking the cars in the car park, too.' Why else would there have been more officers out there?

'There were a lot of people coming and going, after the fundraiser,' Posy pointed out. 'They'd need to check every car in the village to be sure.'

'It's a small village. They might.' Caro tapped a finger against her lips. 'But they might *not* need to. I'm trying to remember. When did Keira go to bed?'

'Before us,' Posy answered. 'In fact, I think she called it a night not long after Owain officially closed the bar.'

'Except she *didn't* go to bed,' Caro said. 'Because if she had, she wouldn't have been on the road to be hit. Would she?'

Posy nodded. 'So where was she going? And why?'

'I guess that's what we need to find out,' Caro said. 'Just in case.'

She didn't need to say in case of what; Posy would know. If there was any chance at all this was linked to the letters Rosalind had been receiving, they had to find out what was going on.

Time to take it back to basics. 'We need to figure out who knew she was going. And, if we think this was deliberate, who could have followed her. And why.'

'*Do* we think it was deliberate?' Posy asked.

'I think . . . we have to assume that it *could* have been,' Caro said. 'Given everything that's been going on here, it seems likely it could be connected.' Or, Caro thought to herself, an escalation of what had gone before. Threats, secrets, an accidental almost-stabbing . . . and now an actual death. It all had a horrible feeling of rising tension, like a horror movie in progress.

Or like one of Lettice Davenport's Dahlia Lively books, of course.

'So we talk to people, I guess.' Posy's expression was strained, and

Caro reached out to put an arm around her shoulder and rub the sleeve of her jacket sympathetically.

This movie was Posy's big break – well, big revival, actually – and, once again, it seemed under threat.

'Why don't you wake up Rosalind?' Caro suggested. 'We're going to need her for this.'

Posy turned towards the back door, then paused. 'All this . . . does it feel familiar to you? Like . . . the curse, last summer.'

Ah, the fabled movie curse. Of course. No wonder Posy was worried. Last time, they'd all been blackmailed, and she'd been set up for humiliation – by her own director. Across the room, Anton was already on his phone, his hair in disarray as he raked his fingers through it.

Whatever his many, many faults, Caro found it hard to believe he was sabotaging this movie again. Not like this.

'Anton never went as far as murder, last time he tried to put an end to the movie. And given how much has changed since then, I don't imagine he'd be trying again. He's in too deep now. Look how invested he was in that fundraiser last night, to make sure the locals were onside. He needs this movie to succeed as much as we do.'

Posy nodded, looking reassured, and went to find Rosalind.

Caro, meanwhile, began mentally compiling a list of everyone to whom they needed to speak.

Gabriel, definitely. And Dominic. It hadn't escaped her notice that they were the only two not already there this morning, beside Rosalind.

The rest of the cast, too, of course. And everyone else who'd been at the Seven Stars for the fundraiser, if they could. Keira had left the bar almost as soon as it ended, and Nina hadn't been far behind her. That was a lead – Nina could have seen something.

Unless they got any further information from the police to narrow their focus, they had to assume that anyone with access to a car who was at the inn the night before could have been responsible. By that time it would have been pitch black out there, and the policeman had said her body was found on the side of the road. There was no street lighting, that Caro had seen, away from the inn and the junction. Any drivers who went down that road afterwards, if they weren't right behind the car that hit her, probably wouldn't have seen anything.

'Might be useful to find out who that dog walker was who found her, too,' Caro mused aloud, wishing Posy was there with her notepad to write all this down. Beside her, Nina gave her an odd look.

The front door to the pub flew open again, and a man in a silver-grey suit walked in. Older – by far – than the twelve-year-old uniformed police officer who'd informed them of Keira's death, he had the look of an authority figure about him. Silver-haired, trim of build, strong-looking shoulders. Yes, Caro would cast him as the DCI in a TV version of this story, quite happily.

She wondered if he had a good name for a detective.

'Jack?' Rosalind's voice rang out through the pub. Caro glanced over to see that she and Posy had entered via the back door from the suites.

Rosalind smoothed a hand over her hair which – despite her having just been woken up – still looked immaculate. As did her cashmere sweater and tailored trousers, for that matter.

The newcomer – Jack – just stared at Rosalind like she was the second coming.

Caro smiled.

Well, now. And she'd thought the day couldn't get any more exciting.

Rosalind

Jack. Jack Hughes was standing in the middle of the Seven Stars Inn, and Rosalind simply didn't know how to process that information.

'Rosalind King, as I live and breathe. If they'd told me *you* were here I'd have got here faster.' His voice was just as she remembered, Rosalind realised.

She recalled describing it to Frank, after the first dinner where they'd met. Sleepily, after too many glasses of wine at that bistro on the river, when Frank had asked what she thought of their new friend. *He has a nice voice*, she'd said. *Slight accent, but not too valleys. Pitched mid to low. Good for voiceovers.*

Frank had laughed. *I'm not asking if you want to cast him in a show*, he'd said. *I'm asking if you think we can be friends.*

She'd considered the question, then nodded. *I think he might be good for you.*

She'd been right, too.

'What *are* you doing here?' Rosalind asked. 'I thought you and Milly retired to . . . oh, that place I could never say.' Back home, he'd called it. The whole time she'd known him – all the decades he'd worked for the Met and he and Milly had lived in London, he'd still called North Wales home.

'Llangollen,' Jack said, helpfully. 'We did. I'm still there. But since Milly . . . well. I needed something to do, and the local force were a bit short-handed.'

He'd never been one for sitting around doing nothing, either, Rosalind remembered.

That was how they'd met, originally. Jack had been the younger brother of a friend of Frank's from university – a rugby teammate, she thought. And when Jack had moved to London in his early twenties, his brother had asked Frank to keep an eye on him.

It had been an obligation, really. So they'd agreed to meet him for dinner at that bistro, hoping that would be enough. Maybe they could recommend the odd restaurant, or a neighbourhood, put him in contact with someone he might get on with better. After all, what did *they* have in common with a policeman?

But it had only taken that one dinner for them to realise that Jack was more than just a policeman. He was someone who could become a friend.

A best friend, for many years. Until Frank died, and Rosalind . . . let that friendship drift. Jack had come to the funeral, and the wake, she remembered. But she'd been out of the country, filming, when Milly died. Had she even seen him since?

Another reason for the guilt that always seemed to hang heavy around her neck these days.

Jack turned towards the bar, where Owain and Rebecca were watching with obvious curiosity. 'I'm Jonathan Hughes, a civilian investigator assisting with this case. You two must be the owners, Mr and Mrs Morgan?'

Owain and Rebecca nodded in tandem. Jack had always known how to command a room.

You should have been an actor, Rosalind remembered telling him, one night, so many years ago. After his promotion to inspector, she thought. *You have the stage presence.*

I'd rather be a policeman, thanks, he'd replied with a laugh. *It's all I've ever wanted to do.*

She shouldn't be surprised he was still doing it, even if he was meant to be retired.

You've got the name for it, too, she'd said, but he'd looked at her blankly. *Jack Hughes* – J'Accuse? *Like at the end of a murder mystery, when the detective gathers them all together to tell them whodunnit.*

He'd roared with laughter at that. But now he was here to potentially do it for real.

'Excellent. Well, if it's okay by you, I'm here to talk to you and your guests individually about the poor young woman who was killed last night. All right?' Jack smiled. His tone was friendly, reassuring even, but still gave the impression that he wasn't used to people saying no, and that he'd be talking to them all whether it was okay with the Morgans or not.

He turned back to Rosalind, and she felt the weight of his smile on her again.

What must he have thought when he read all those lurid newspaper reports last summer? Heard not just about her solving a murder, but about her decades-long affair with Hugh Davenport. When he'd realised she'd been lying almost the entire time he'd known her. To him, and to the man who'd been his best friend.

What did he think now, seeing her here?

She couldn't tell. His eyes gave nothing away.

But if he was going to be here figuring out what had happened to Keira . . . maybe she'd find out. There'd be time for them to talk, she hoped. Clear the air.

Although she had no idea at all what she was going to say.

Maybe I could tell him about the death threats. No. Not if he thought she was fishing for pity, or making excuses. And besides, someone *had* been killed, and it wasn't her. That had to be the focus now.

Which only left talking about their shared past.

Something no one ever mentioned about growing old. It wasn't just the accumulating aches and pains, the worn-out joints or the physical damage done that wore you down.

It was the memories.

Every mistake ever made, every word spoken without thinking, everything never said when it should have been. Every choice regretted later.

They all hung off the body, the added weight of years, however much she thought she'd put things behind her. She was only ever one reminder away from reliving it all again in her head.

The world had changed so much and so fast, over the years she'd lived. There were so many things she'd do differently, if she'd known then what she knew now.

She wished she'd called Jack after Milly died.

She wished she could talk to Frank one last time.

But time never stopped for wishes, did it?

'I'll talk to you later, Rosalind,' Jack said, now. She couldn't quite decide if he sounded like he was looking forward to it or not.

But then, she didn't know if she was, either.

He turned back to the Morgans with a question about where best to set up his interview room, and Rosalind moved away, back towards Caro and Posy, who would both be wanting answers.

A woman was dead here. Maybe it was connected to the threats to her life, maybe it wasn't. But either way, finding out what happened to Keira had to come before dealing with the ghosts of her past.

Rosalind needed to remember that.

Chapter Ten

'I knew we should have taken my car,' Johnnie said, as Dahlia's motorcycle and sidecar swerved around the bend in the road at what she supposed could be considered an unnerving speed.

Dahlia Lively *in* Death Comes to Hazelwood
***By* Lettice Davenport, 1944**

Posy

Jack Hughes set up in one of the private dining rooms, just off the room where the casino was still being disassembled. With a table for four, a recording device and his notebook and pen, he invited Owain Morgan in first, then shut the door. Caro, Rosalind and Posy took the opportunity to grab their coats and slip out into the courtyard to talk.

'So, Jack Hughes?' Posy hopped up to sit on the low wall surrounding the raised beds in the centre of the courtyard.

'He was an old friend of my husband's,' Rosalind said, wearily. 'He and his wife moved to Wales a few years ago, after he retired from the Met. I'd forgotten all about him, to be honest.'

Except she'd recognised him and remembered his name, rather quickly for someone she'd completely forgotten, in Posy's opinion. She knew, better than most, how a person from the past could suddenly appear and blindside a person.

'He clearly hadn't forgotten you.' Caro leaned a little closer and nudged Rosalind with her elbow, earning herself a scowl.

'Yes, well. I imagine he'd been reading all about how I cheated on my husband, his friend, for decades in the papers recently. That probably brought me to mind.' Posy looked down at her knees at that. Sometimes she forgot that her past wasn't the only controversial one for a Dahlia, these days. Even Caro had her own rumours and gossip.

Caro sighed. 'Ah. Yes. I was going to ask if you wanted to be the one to try and pump him for information, given that you already have a connection, but under the circumstances . . .'

Rosalind moved to lean against the wall beside where Posy was sitting. 'No, it's okay. I'll do it. I mean, if there's any chance that Keira's death was murder, and possibly linked to the death threats I've been receiving, then I have to do whatever it takes to find out the truth.' Her shoulders slumped a little, despite her determined speech. 'Besides, Jack was a friend, for years. I owe him at least a catch-up conversation, right?'

'Perhaps over dinner,' Caro suggested, far too innocently. 'There's a nice-looking bistro in the village . . .'

'If they ever let us leave the Seven Stars again,' Rosalind grumbled.

'They'll have to, before too long,' Posy said. 'Once the initial shock has worn off, I imagine Anton will be on at them. And besides, after they've combed the area for evidence and moved the . . .' She stumbled at the thought of calling Keira a body. 'Once they've moved her, I can't imagine there's much point in keeping it closed any longer.'

'And until then we'll talk with everyone here. See if anyone knew where Keira was going or why. If she'd been worried – or scared about anything.'

Rosalind looked at Caro in surprise. 'You think she might have been getting death threats too?'

Caro shrugged. 'Not really. She didn't act like someone who was scared for her life, did she?'

'People react to that kind of fear in different ways, though.' Posy thought back to the conversation between Gabriel and Dominic the night before. Dominic had sounded angry, sure. But had he also been afraid?

Looking across the courtyard, she could see that Dominic's curtains were still closed.

'I think it's time to wake some people up,' Posy said. 'I heard an interesting conversation between Dominic and Gabriel last night, for a start, and I'd like to follow up on that.'

Promising to fill them both in properly later, she headed across the courtyard and knocked on Dominic's door, peering around the edge of the heavy linen curtain hanging inside the front window while she waited for him to answer. The room seemed to still be in darkness, so apparently Dominic really had slept through all the goings-on. Posy supposed it was still early, and he wasn't on the call sheet for the morning at Tŷ Gwyn. Plus it had been pretty late when she'd seen him talking to Gabriel the night before. She knocked again and, after another long moment, the door creaked open to reveal a very bleary-eyed Dominic.

'Posy?' Her name came out as mostly a croak, and he cleared his throat before trying again. 'Whatever is it? What time is it?'

'I'm so sorry to wake you, Dominic.' Posy placed a hand against the door, easing it casually open until he had no choice but to step back and let her inside. His suite, like hers, only had one main room, but was large enough for a small seating area by the kitchenette. 'But I knew you'd want to hear the terrible news before it hits social media.'

She was watching carefully, so she saw clearly how Dominic's whole body froze, just for a second, before he forced it to relax again. However good an actor he was, he couldn't hide that he was worried about something getting out. Something Gabriel knew. 'Whatever are you talking about, my dear? I appreciate you coming to talk to me, but I can't imagine—'

'Oh, it's so awful! The police are here. They're saying . . . they're saying that Keira's dead.' Dominic liked his younger actresses lost and in need of guidance, she suspected. So, as much as she disliked that, she'd play into it to get his answers. 'I just don't know what to do!'

Dominic blinked, his bloodshot eyes confused. 'What? Keira?'

'Keira Reynolds-Yang,' she prompted, her voice eager. 'She's playing your wife in the movie . . .'

'I know who she is,' he snapped, before taking a breath and placing what he obviously thought was a soothing hand on Posy's arm. She resisted the urge to shake it off. 'But what do you mean . . . how can she be dead? She was at the fundraiser with us last night.'

'People are saying that she must have gone out for a walk, because she got hit by a car and left to bleed out on the side of the road until someone found her this morning.' Posy had no idea whether she had actually bled out or been killed instantly, but for her purposes the former sounded more dramatic. 'It's just so awful!'

Dominic turned away, staggered back a few paces, and dropped to sit on the edge of the bed, staring down at his hands. She gave him a moment to collect himself, then pressed on.

'I just know I won't sleep again until I can understand how this happened. I saw you head back to your room a little before me,' she said, moving closer. 'I wondered if you might have seen her? You see, I just can't figure out why she was out on the road at all. She said she was going to go to bed, where she should have been safe.' Posy shivered, and wrapped her arms around herself for good measure.

'I didn't see her,' Dominic said, almost too quickly. 'I don't know anything. Why would I? Barely knew the girl. Probably she went out for an early morning run or something. I don't know.'

Posy hesitated. *Could* Keira have gone out this morning, rather than last night, like they'd assumed? The police had said last night, and it must have been very early when the dog walker found her body. But Keira had an early call, and if she'd wanted to get a run in, she'd have needed to have gone long before first light. So it wasn't impossible.

Except who would have been driving up the road to Tŷ Gwyn at that time in the morning? And where were they now?

Dominic got to his feet, still looking a little shaky, but it was hard to tell if that was because of the news or last night's alcohol. It was hard to imagine him being in any fit state to drive a car, but he'd been angry enough with Keira, that was for sure. She'd watched him go into his room the night before, but after that he'd been alone, without an alibi.

If someone *had* wanted Keira dead, and this was something more than a tragic accident, Posy had to assume that Dominic, and maybe Gabriel, were her prime suspects right now.

'I need to get ready for my call.' Dominic staggered towards the bathroom.

'I don't think we're going to be filming today,' Posy replied, thinking of Anton's frustration at realising the road was closed. But Dominic didn't seem to hear her, shutting the bathroom door behind him.

Caro

Caro watched Posy inveigle her way into Dominic's room, and was about to follow Rosalind back inside the inn when she spotted Anton leaning heavily against one of the wooden posts that held up the pergola over the beer garden, phone clamped to his ear, and changed direction.

'So you're telling me there's nothing you can do,' he snapped into the phone. 'Then what's the point of you?' Caro watched as he stabbed the end-call icon and shoved the phone back in his pocket.

'No dice getting that bus through?'

Anton's head jerked up at her words, his expression settling into an even deeper scowl as he realised who it was.

'Obviously we wouldn't be filming today anyway. Out of respect.'

'Obviously.' Except he'd clearly just been on the phone trying to do exactly that. Who would he have been calling?

Then she remembered Posy mentioning Anton arguing with Rhian, the house manager at Tŷ Gwyn, and decided she could make an educated guess.

'Rhian couldn't find you a back route to Tŷ Gwyn, then?' She raised her eyebrow, Dahlia style, and watched Anton's face darken further.

'Apparently not.' His words were clipped. 'Now, if you'll excuse me . . .'

Caro moved to block his path. 'Actually, I just wanted to ask you a couple of questions.'

Anton's eyebrows jumped to incredulous heights hers could only dream of. 'Tell me you're not trying to start another bloody investigation on *my film set*.'

'What could I possibly be investigating? Keira's death was clearly just a tragic accident.' Caro used her most innocent voice but it was obvious that Anton, like most people she tried it on, wasn't buying it, so she gave up the attempt. 'Okay, fine. But has it occurred to you that the sooner the police get to the bottom of this the sooner your film can carry on smoothly?'

'Once I find someone to body double for Keira's final scenes and re-block them,' he muttered. 'Thank God she'd finished filming all her speaking parts. Anyway, what makes you think you can solve this faster than the police?'

Caro shrugged. 'I've always liked a challenge. And it's not like I'm particularly busy right now.'

'I *knew* you weren't really writing a book!'

'Oh, actually, I am.' Caro beamed at him. 'You see, Libby thinks it's a *marvellous* idea and personally asked to me write it. But luckily for everyone, I am excellent at multitasking.'

Anton's war with himself – whether to continue the fruitless argument or walk away and let her have the last word – showed clearly on his face, and Caro took advantage of his indecision to get in with her first real question.

'I just wanted to know if you saw Keira last night, after she went to bed. I know you stayed up in the bar with Kit for a while.'

'I didn't see her,' Anton said shortly. 'Now listen to me, and listen carefully. This is not a game. This is a tragedy, and one that is going to be all over the bloody news. The last thing this movie needs is you three sticking your noses in where they don't belong and causing trouble. We've had enough problems with this bloody cursed film as it is.'

'And remind me, who was responsible for that so-called curse?' Caro asked, innocently.

He ignored her. 'If you want your friend's big comeback to be a big success, stay out of this, okay? You were right – this *is* a tragic accident. And I don't want to hear a single word – or even a hint – anywhere about this being anything else.' Anton pushed past her, stalking off towards his own room, and Caro watched him go before turning to head inside, still turning his words over in her mind.

Back in the bar, it seemed that the rest of the cast had all congregated, to share either their grief or their gossip. Gabriel had obviously woken and joined the others while Caro was outside, and even Dominic had managed to stagger in just behind Caro. Now Posy was sitting in the middle of them all, soaking up everything they said – or didn't say. She caught Caro's gaze across the room, and gave her a tiny smile. They'd have a proper debrief later, and figure out what they'd all learned.

Behind the bar, Owain was handing out plates of what looked like a very artistic chef's take on a full Welsh breakfast that made Caro's stomach rumble, even with the inclusion of laverbread. She took a plate, and sat with the others at the long table by the window that they'd occupied. Rosalind joined her a moment later.

'It's already hit the socials.' Scarlett swiped a finger across the screen of her phone, then held it up to them all. 'Not officially, but there's talk on Twitter already.'

'And on the local Facebook page,' Caro added, checking her own phone. 'Lots of rumour and no confirmation yet, but in a place like this . . .'

'It won't take long,' Posy finished for her. From her stormy eyes, Caro imagined she was remembering how often the online gossip had been about her. 'As soon as her family have it confirmed, her management team will want to get out in front of the story. Before anyone starts asking too many questions.'

'What story could they need to be in front of?' Kit asked, sounding incredulous. 'I mean, she went out and was hit by a car. It's not exactly a scandal.'

'Depends who hit her,' Dominic murmured, lifting his pint glass to his lips. Apparently hair of the dog was the way to go this morning, although the rest of the cast seemed to have stuck with coffee.

'It could have been anybody,' Nina said, softly. But from the way her gaze darted around the table, Caro wondered if she really meant, *It could have been any of you.*

'Anton has cancelled filming for the day, he tells me?' Caro said, mostly to fill the awkward silence that followed.

Posy nodded. 'The police are hoping to have the road open again this afternoon but under the circumstances . . .'

'Right. Decency and all that. Especially since the news is already out there.'

'Should *we* be posting something, do you think?' Scarlett asked, looking around for approval. 'I mean, about Keira? We're the last people to see her alive, right? Her last cast mates. Friends, even. We should post something in memory of her, yeah?'

'I'd think the most respectful thing would be to *not* try and garner likes and follows from a tragedy, especially before the family have even confirmed her death,' Rosalind said, scathingly. 'But I'm barely on social media, so what do I know?'

Scarlett nodded, as if Rosalind had agreed with her. 'I think people would expect us to post.'

'As long as we say the right thing.' Tristan shuffled his chair closer to Scarlett's. 'Perhaps a group post? But wait until her family have posted first?'

'Yeah, definitely wait for that,' Kit agreed. 'I mean, Keira's family are . . .'

'Exactly,' Tristan finished for him, without Kit having to find words for exactly what Keira's family were. 'We want to get the tone right. And we don't want to get in trouble with our uniformed friends out there, either.'

'Sometimes I just think this whole movie is cursed.' Scarlett threw herself back in her chair, her phone on the table, memorial to Keira still unposted. 'I mean, first Brigette walking off, that mix-up with the knives, and now this?! I thought this was going to be my big break. Now I'm just hoping the film gets finished at all.'

From the wry smile on Posy's face, Caro imagined her sister-Dahlia knew exactly how Scarlett felt. 'We thought that last summer, remember?' Posy said. 'But here we are filming. We'll get through this too.'

Tristan leaned across the table towards Scarlett, a mischievous smile on his face. 'Besides, don't you know, Scarlett? Some of the most famous movies are the ones that never even got made at all.'

'Kubrick's *Napoleon*,' Dominic said.

'Ken Russell's *Dracula*,' was Gabriel's suggestion.

'Gilliam's *Don Quixote*,' Tristan said.

'*Gladiator 2*,' Kit added, which felt like a bit of a step down.

'*The Castle on the Hill*,' Posy said. Caro didn't recognise the name instantly, but it was clear from Dominic's suddenly stormy face that he did. One he'd been involved in personally, perhaps?

'I'm going to go check on Anton,' he said, placing his pint glass heavily on the table. 'See when he thinks we'll be able to get back to work.' He lumbered off towards the door.

'I don't get it.' Scarlett's forehead crumpled into a frown. 'How can they be famous if they never existed?'

Tristan shrugged. 'They're always the ones with big names attached – a huge star or a brilliant director; or incredible vision or innovation. Think about it. All the time and money, all the hype and excitement, a whiff of scandal or worse . . . and then nothing to show for it in the end. Always leave the audience wanting more, right?'

'Well, I'd rather just make a movie, get paid and get famous, thanks,' Scarlett replied, her arms folded across her chest. 'And we still haven't decided what to do about Keira's memorial post.'

One thing Scarlett had right, Caro realised, was that Keira's death was going to be huge. It wasn't just about how famous she was in her own right, or the tragedy of a young star cut off in her prime. Keira Reynolds-Yang was the product of two separate film and fashion dynasties, a famous name and face even before she forged her own career as an actress.

Everyone was going to be talking about this. The local police, if they'd realised who they had in their morgue, were going to be all over this too. They'd want to find any evidence that could lead them to a culprit as soon as possible – ideally before the town was flooded with Keira fans coming to pay their respects, and paparazzi wanting to capitalise on the moment.

Caro pushed aside her finished breakfast plate just as her phone rang.

Ashok.

She stepped outside to take the call.

'What have you got?' Across in the car park, the police were still going car to car, presumably checking each of them for any sign of a collision.

'The conspiracy theory seems to have popped up on a few different forums under different usernames, but at exactly the same time. That means—'

'It was probably the same person using different accounts,' Caro finished for him. 'I may be old enough to be your . . . young and cool aunt, but I did spend my later teenage years with internet access, you realise. I get how this works.'

'Right. Sorry. Anyway, my point was that it seems to have been started purposefully. Like someone had a vendetta out against Rosalind and wanted to spread it as far and as wide as possible.'

That was interesting, Caro had to concede. 'But who?'

In the car park, two police officers has stopped alongside one of the cars – a low-slung, silver sports car. She pushed away from the wall, creeping closer and hoping they didn't notice that they had an observer. But their bodies were blocking her view of the car, so she couldn't tell what it was that had gripped their attention.

'That I don't know yet,' Ashok admitted. 'But I'm still looking into it. The people caught up in believing the theory seem to talk a lot about "out-of-date and out-of-touch" stars, saying how their time has passed. So it could be linked to things like Me Too and cancel culture, except it doesn't quite seem to have that vibe. I don't know. Maybe it's someone who genuinely believes the wrong person was blamed for the deaths at Aldermere last year?'

'How could anybody genuinely believe that?' Caro asked, incredulously. 'They confessed!'

'Oh, people can choose to believe anything they like, in my experience,' Ashok replied. 'But yeah. I'll keep looking. Maybe it's just someone who has a grudge against Rosalind.'

As she watched, the police officers straightened, and one nodded to the other before they turned in unison and began striding towards the front of the pub.

They'd found something.

'Given the death threats and the incident with the dagger on set, I'm thinking that's looking likely,' Caro said, distractedly, as she tried to concentrate on both the conversation and the police antics at the same time.

'Except if the same person is behind that thing with the dagger, that means it's someone there with you,' Ashok pointed out. 'So you're probably in a better position to find them than I am.'

'True.' Caro thought about the cast, sitting around that long table with their coffee and their cooked breakfasts, talking about a social media post to commemorate their late colleague. Was one of them really threatening Rosalind? And if so, were they also behind what had happened to Keira? 'There's something else that's happened, too. Might not be connected, but . . .'

'We have to assume *everything* is connected until we can prove otherwise.'

'Exactly that,' Caro said, approvingly. 'Keira Reynolds-Yang was killed in a hit-and-run last night or early this morning.'

She heard Ashok's sharp intake of breath, then the sound of his keyboard clicking as he obviously looked up the information. 'I hadn't seen that. I should have seen that – I've got alerts set up for everyone on the cast. It must not have hit the news websites yet.'

'It's on the local socials, but not confirmed yet.' One of the police officers was standing guard by the silver car, now. Whose was it, anyway? 'Keep looking into the cast, will you? Any reason any of them might have it in for Rosalind. Maybe that will throw up something.'

'Will do, boss.' *Boss.* She liked that.

Ashok hung up, and Caro slipped her phone back into her pocket as she stared out at the car park, waiting to see what happened next.

Suddenly, Rosalind and Posy rushed through the back door to join her – just as the first police officer returned to the car park, talking to someone beside him as they approached his colleague. 'And you are the owner of this silver Audi TT?' His words carried the short distance in the still morning air.

'I . . . yes? Why?' The police officer was blocking Caro's view, but she recognised the voice all the same – and her heart sank.

'They asked Kit to join them outside,' Posy said, her voice hushed. 'What's happening?'

'I'm afraid you're going to have to come with us, sir. Your car has damage consistent with hitting a person at speed, and by your own account you arrived back here after the victim left last night.'

'I . . . what?' The confusion in his voice *sounded* real, Caro had to give him that. But then, he was an actor, wasn't he? 'No. I didn't do it.' He turned around, and spotted them watching from over the wall. 'You have to believe me. It wasn't me.'

Posy clutched Caro's hand so tight her bones ground together. 'No.'

'Kit Lewis, I am arresting you on suspicion of causing death by dangerous driving.'

Chapter Eleven

Wendell stopped dead in his tracks. 'Cousin Dahlia. I didn't expect to see you here.'

From his tone, she couldn't entirely tell if he was pleased about this turn of events or not. 'Trust me, kiddo. I didn't expect to see me here either.'

Dahlia Lively *in* Murder Looks Lively
***By* Lettice Davenport, 1933**

Rosalind

Rosalind watched Kit being led away towards the police car parked outside. His head was bowed, his shoulders slumped, and she hoped to God that none of the local press was out there yet with cameras. For his sake.

Kit. Could he really have been behind the wheel when Keira was killed? The idea was hard to reconcile with the young man she'd got to know since they met last summer. He always seemed so light-hearted, so jovial. The person in the room that lifted the mood, or made a joke to distract from the disappointments.

He'd reminded her of her late husband, that way. He'd always smoothed over *her* sharp edges, too.

'You have to talk to Jack and get this fixed, Rosalind. Rosalind?' Posy's voice was insistent.

'Posy . . .' Rosalind broke off. What was she supposed to say?

'I was watching the police outside,' Caro said. 'They saw something in the car park that made them pretty damn certain that it was Kit's car that hit her.'

'Come on.' Rosalind took Posy's arm. 'Let's get back inside.'

Back in the bar, it seemed the Dahlias hadn't been the only ones watching Kit's arrest. The rest of the cast milled round, their voices low as they absorbed the latest shock to rock their production. To not only lose a cast member so tragically, but have another accused of causing her death . . . Rosalind wasn't sure how any of them were going to be able to continue filming after this.

'He didn't do it,' Posy said, stubbornly. 'He couldn't have.'

'*We* know that,' Caro replied, even though they didn't. Not really. 'But he wasn't here last night, was he? Not until late – after Keira had gone. Do you know where he was?'

'Sort of.' Posy dropped down to sit in the nearest chair, her face greyer than Rosalind liked. 'He was meeting someone – I can't tell you who. And when he got back, he wouldn't talk about it. But I asked him this morning if he'd seen anything. He said he didn't see her.'

He didn't see her. Didn't see her body on the side of the road? Or didn't see her before he hit her?

Rosalind didn't want to think Kit was responsible any more than Posy did. But the police wouldn't have arrested him without a bloody good reason. Would they?

When Posy had burst into her room that morning, telling her that Keira was dead, Rosalind's first thought had been that it *had* to be linked to everything else – the threats to her, the swapped dagger, all of it.

But if Kit *was* behind Keira's death, that would mean he had to be behind the threats to her, too. And that Rosalind couldn't bring herself to believe. So either the events weren't linked, or—

'He didn't do it,' Posy said again, mulishly.

'And we're going to prove it,' Caro agreed. 'But . . . he wasn't in a great mood when he came back last night. Was he?'

Posy glared at her, but Rosalind could see the fear behind the look. 'He'd had a bad night, that's all. He wanted a drink. That doesn't mean he'd killed someone on his way back.'

'No, of course it doesn't,' Caro soothed. 'It's just . . . it might not look good. That's all.'

'I don't care how it looks,' Posy replied. 'I know.'

But did she?

Maybe it really was just a tragic accident. A coincidence.

Maybe it wasn't all about her, after all.

From her seat at the next table, Scarlett gave a small, shocked sob, and Rosalind's heart sank as she wondered what else could possibly go wrong now.

'It's up on social media now. Official. Look.' Scarlett angled her phone towards them, and the rest of the cast gathered closer to see.

A black-edged photo of Keira, smiling out angelically, filled the screen. Rosalind couldn't quite make out the caption below – really, she should find those reading glasses – but she could imagine how it read.

'Is that Keira's page?' Posy asked, frowning slightly.

Scarlett shook her head. 'Her brother's – the one who's a director, not the musician. But it's the same post on her mum's page and her dad's, too.'

'And it's up on her other brother's page now, too,' Tristan added, showing them his own screen.

'It just makes it feel really real, doesn't it?' Scarlett said, eyes wet with tears.

Rosalind rather thought the police, the arrest and the crime scene had done that better than social media could, but everyone else seemed to nod, all the same.

Caro gave her a meaningful look.

'I'll talk to Jack,' Rosalind said. 'See what I can find out.'

Jack had left his interrogation table in the dining room and come into the main bar when the police officers had arrived, and stood chatting with one of the other officers by the counter. Presumably his job at the Seven Stars was done for now, if they'd made an arrest, unless they needed more evidence. She wondered if other officers were searching Kit's belongings right now. Probably, she decided. Even if they were sure the car was the one that had hit Keira, surely they'd need to prove that Kit had been the one driving it? A witness would probably be nice. Perhaps he'd learned something interesting while he was questioning Owain or Rebecca or one of the others.

She waited until Jack clapped the other officer on the arm and stepped away, before moving in.

'Jack?'

The smile that stretched across his face was gratifying, in a way. 'Rosalind! I didn't even get around to talking to you yet. That was the part I was looking forward to most!'

'I suppose it's rather surplus to requirements, now you've caught your man.'

Jack shook his head. 'Not at all. Got to be thorough about these things, after all. And it won't take a moment.'

He gestured towards the dining room, waiting for her to walk in first. With a glance back at a watching Posy and Caro, Rosalind complied, as Jack went through the standard police spiel she imagined he'd given to everyone he'd spoken with this morning.

'So, just for the record, your name and reason for being here at the Seven Stars?' Jack asked, turning to a fresh page in his notebook and eyeing her expectantly.

Rosalind raised her eyebrows at the ridiculousness of the question. 'Rosalind King. Actress. I'm here filming the new *The Lady Detective* movie.'

'But not as Dahlia Lively, eh?' Jack shook his head sadly. 'Time just keeps moving on, whether we like it or not, doesn't it? New bucks coming through to take over, convinced that only *they* know the right way to do the job.'

She suspected he was talking more about himself than her. 'I haven't been Dahlia in over thirty years, Jack.'

'Ah, but you'll always be *my* Dahlia.' There was a twinkle in his eye, a hint of something Rosalind wasn't sure she wanted to explore. But she wasn't completely convinced she *didn't* want to, either, which was something of a surprise.

After Hugh, she hadn't been sure she'd been capable of contemplating that sort of twinkle, any longer.

'So, these "new bucks" doing the job. Do you really believe they're right about Kit?' That was what she was here for, after all. Answers. Not flirting.

'Could be,' Jack admitted, with a shrug. 'Probably, really. They'll be keeping an open mind, looking at all the angles. But from my happily retired civilian position, I have to say it looks fairly open and shut.'

Rosalind leaned forward, her elbows resting on the scuffed wood of the table between them. 'How so?'

Jack ticked the points off on his fingers. 'Damage to his car, consistent with hitting something – potentially a person – at speed. And he already admitted he drove back here after the victim left the rest of you in the pub, so the times line up too.'

'Is that enough to convict him?'

'Not on its own, no. Like I said – they'll be keeping an open mind. Waiting for the forensics lot to do their job, mostly. Checking for fibres and blood and DNA. That's what'll solve the case – that and anything the post-mortem throws up.' She must have looked surprised, because he added, 'They're not amateurs, you know. They'll get this right. But right now it's not looking good for your friend.' Jack leaned back in his chair, his arms folded across his barrel chest. 'Unless you're about to tell me you saw something last night that changes everything.'

'No, no, I don't imagine I am.' She forced a small smile. 'I was here for the fundraiser, then went to bed shortly after it finished. Keira left for her room just before me, actually.'

'And did you see her at all after that?' Jack lifted his black pen to make a note on his pad.

'No.' But she was really hoping somebody had. 'Do you know what she was wearing when she was hit?'

Jack gave her a quizzical look. 'Why?'

'Oh, someone suggested that maybe she'd been for an early morning run, rather than going out last night, that was all.' Rosalind shrugged. 'If she was in her running gear, that might change the assumption about time of death.'

'I'm fairly sure we'll get time of death from the body – temperature, rigor mortis, that sort of thing.' He looked amused at her old-fashioned question. Dahlia wouldn't have had access to forensic evidence, though, and even the post-mortem evidence in the books was never very accurate. 'However, if it helps, I believe she was wearing jeans, a black sweater, boots and a raincoat.'

Rosalind's heart sank. 'Probably not running then.' But she had changed out of her dress for the Classic Hollywood Night.

He gave her a long, contemplative look. 'So, assuming she left the pub shortly after the fundraiser finished . . . Kit wasn't back from wherever he'd been before then? A number of witnesses have confirmed he returned late to the Seven Stars.'

'No, he wasn't back. I don't suppose I've been any help at all, really.' To Kit, or to the police.

She couldn't even figure out who on set wanted her dead. How was she supposed to prove Kit's innocence?

'It all helps,' Jack said, reassuringly. 'We're building up a picture of what happened, see. Until the victim's movements can run as smoothly as a film clip, up until the end, when we see exactly who was responsible for her death – and what they did next.'

'Of course,' Rosalind murmured. In some ways, it really was just like filming a movie. All the pieces – or scenes – were already there. They just weren't ever filmed in the correct order, so they had to be edited together to make sense afterwards.

The question was, who was directing this thing? The police? The killer? Or them – the three Dahlias?

She didn't have all the pieces yet. That was the problem. There had to be a way that all of this made sense. Brigette leaving, her death threats, the dagger, Keira's death, Kit's arrest. There was a story there somewhere.

And it was up to her, Caro and Posy to find it.

She considered telling Jack everything – about the dagger and the letters, at least. But what if that only made things worse for Kit? He'd been on set that day. He'd been at Aldermere, too. What if they decided he was behind everything from the conspiracy theory onwards?

Besides, she'd already told one police force about previous letters and nothing had happened. What good would it do to tell another?

And if they knew about the knife, they might stop filming completely. Unless they were convinced it really was just another accident – a careless oversight by the prop master. She could get him fired, when it might not have even been his fault.

She remembered Jack once telling her, years ago, how investigators really didn't like coincidences. And she knew, deep down, that he – and the local police – would take the letters more seriously now, in the light of Keira's death.

But she still couldn't bring herself to tell him.

Not yet. She needed more pieces of this puzzle, more clips of this film, before she talked to Jack. Once she had that, she'd tell him everything.

'If that's all . . .' Rosalind moved gracefully from the chair, and had already taken a couple of gliding steps towards the door when Jack's voice stopped her.

'Actually . . . I have to admit something. I told a lie, earlier, when I arrived.'

Rosalind paused, and turned to face him. 'Oh? What was it?' They'd barely exchanged a few sentences.

'I said that if I'd known you were here I'd have arrived faster.' Jack gave a shame-faced smile. 'But, of course, I already knew you were here. That's why I volunteered to come.'

Rosalind let his words settle in her mind, in among the memories of their friendship before Frank died, and Milly, and between the revelations that had come out since, and the guilt and the shame she'd carried and shaken off.

After a moment, she returned his smile. 'I'm glad that you did.'

Caro

Caro and Posy were waiting for Rosalind the moment she emerged from her conversation with Jack.

'Well?' Posy asked, impatience clear in her voice.

Caro glanced around the crowded bar. It seemed all the cast and crew in residence had congregated there to gossip, and the last thing they wanted was any evidence against Kit Rosalind had uncovered hitting social media before they'd had a chance to debunk it. If they could.

'Not here,' she muttered, and jerked her head towards the courtyard.

From outside the inn, they had a perfect view of the car park, and the scene-of-crime officers meticulously recording every detail of Kit's car. Even from a distance, now she knew what she was looking for, Caro could see the damage to the front bumper that the police had noted, and had led to Kit's arrest.

As they watched, Rosalind filled them in on the little she'd learned from her conversation with Jack.

'I just don't believe that Kit could have done it, whatever the police say,' Posy said, stubbornly, as she wrapped her coat more tightly around herself. 'I mean, maybe they just saw a black guy driving an expensive car and leaped to conclusions.'

'Perhaps,' Rosalind said, gently, but Caro could tell she didn't believe it.

'Or . . .' Posy stumbled to a stop, then started again, her eyes big. 'They might think that because of his history with Keira, he did it on purpose. That it really was murder.'

'What history?' Rosalind shot a quick look at Caro. Clearly she didn't read enough gossip mags.

'They dated, didn't they?' Caro asked.

'On and off, for a couple of years,' Posy said, with a nod. 'Kit doesn't like to talk about it much, but when Scarlett made some comment about it on our first day on set, I did a little digging just to see what she was going on about.'

Caro tried to think back over the years' worth of celebrity gossip that was filed away in her brain. 'I remember seeing some photos of them together in the mags, and then some of those ones where they put a jagged line between them, but I can't remember what it was all about.'

'Best I can tell, they met on the set for *Chasing Francis* – you know, the romcom they did together about four years ago? It was Keira's first big movie, and one of Kit's first films too – he was the best friend rather than the love interest, I think, but in the end it was the two of them that had the most chemistry.'

'On and off screen, clearly,' Rosalind murmured. 'Go on.'

'So, they dated for a bit, and it was kind of a big deal online because of Keira's fanbase, of course. Then there were rumours about a secret engagement—'

'Aren't there always?' Caro said. Even she'd been secretly engaged to a few co-stars – once after she'd *actually* married Annie.

'—but then a few weeks later they split. There were the usual "are they back together?" features, but really, that might have been it if it wasn't for an interview Keira gave on some American show a few months later where she accused Kit of cheating on her.'

'Was he?' Caro would like to give him the benefit of the doubt but, under the circumstances, the truth would be far more useful.

'No idea,' Posy admitted. 'But he hadn't been seen or photographed with anyone else, so it seems unlikely. And in the interview Keira seemed a little . . . unhinged, to be honest.'

'Didn't she take some time off in a "de-stress and detox retreat" afterwards?' Caro asked. 'I remember reading that.'

'Code for rehab, I assume?' Rosalind added.

'Possibly,' Posy replied. 'But whether she was burned out or whatever, she had a few weeks in the foothills of the Himalayas at this retreat and came back a new person. Well, mostly.'

'Mostly?' Caro raised an eyebrow. 'You know, I'm getting the impression you didn't really like Keira.'

Posy sighed. 'I didn't really know her well enough to judge, but . . . no. I didn't like her. She was snide and cruel and superior to everyone. She was forever making digs at Kit, even though she made a point of publicly forgiving him on her first day on set. And she ran cold and hot, you know what I mean? Especially with Scarlett. One moment they were best friends, the next Keira was complaining about her acting to anyone who would listen. I think the only person she actually liked in the cast was Tristan, because they've been friends forever. God knows how he puts up with her.'

'It seems to be there's a whole list of people on this film who might not be too distraught that Keira's no longer here,' Rosalind said. 'But that's not the same as wanting her dead.'

They were all silent for a moment as they watched the police team work.

'It could have been a genuine accident, you realise,' Caro said, eventually, because she felt one of them should. 'And we're reading too much into it because of everything else that's going on.'

'Even if it *was* an accident, Kit didn't do it,' Posy said.

'Then we need to prove that.' Caro pulled out her phone. 'I've been checking the local Facebook groups – the story is *definitely* getting around, by the way – and I haven't seen anything about Kit.'

'What have you seen?' Rosalind pressed.

'Well, there's this one comment on someone's post about Keira being the hit-and-run victim . . .' She held the phone up so they could both read it.

Can't believe it, it read. *Just saw her last night on the green, on my way home from the pub. Was going to ask for her autograph, but the missus said it wasn't her.*

'The green – the village green?' Posy reached into the small bag that hung across her body, and pulled out a small red notebook and a biro. 'So she left the pub and went into the village?'

'That's hardly conclusive,' Rosalind said. 'The drunken ramblings of an attention-seeking local on social media? He's not even sure it was actually her.'

'But if it was . . .' Caro drummed her fingers against the edge of one of the wooden posts that held up the small porch shelter outside the back door. 'If she walked all the way into the village for some reason, then came back again – and was knocked over on her return trip . . . Surely that's got to put Kit out of the frame? He was back before she could have done that, wasn't he?'

'I think so,' Posy agreed with a nod. 'It might be close, though . . .'

'Won't the police just say he could have gone back out again?' Rosalind asked.

Caro considered. 'Depends on the timing. He was talking to Anton before we went to bed. That buys him an alibi for a while, I should think.'

'Let's see if we can find out how long for,' Posy suggested, as she opened the door back inside.

In the bar, the others were already discussing the case against Kit as if it were a foregone conclusion.

'I wouldn't have thought it of him,' Dominic said, holding court at the top of the long table by the fire. 'But I have to admit, he was a bloody menace in that car of his.'

'Oh, I wouldn't say that.' Tristan topped up his coffee from the cafetière on the table. Apparently the fancy coffee machine behind the bar simply couldn't cope with the caffeine needs the day seemed to be requiring. 'But that car is a thing of beauty.'

'Beauty?! He almost winged me the other day, turning into the car park,' Scarlett said.

'Oh, he did not.' Tristan laughed, then stopped abruptly, obviously remembering the circumstances again. 'And anyway, if you hadn't been trying to take the perfect selfie, you wouldn't have been standing in the middle of the road.'

'I just can't believe it, to be honest,' Gabriel said, staring morosely into his coffee cup. 'Some people in this business, you know they'd leave you bleeding at the side of the road to save their own skin. But not Kit.'

There were a few sombre nods around the table at that, although no one else actually came out and said that they thought that the police had got it wrong. Caro supposed that, in face of a tragedy like Keira's death, having a simple, fast answer to what happened – especially one that lifted suspicion from the rest of them – was probably a bit of a relief.

Well, for everyone except Kit, anyway.

'I'm just saying that the speed he took some of those corners at yesterday, I had to hold on to the seat to stop flying out the window.' Dominic reached for a muffin from the basket on the table.

'At least you were in the front seat,' Tristan said. 'It was even more lively in the back. Right, Nina?' He nudged Nina Novak, sitting next to him, but her answering smile was faint.

'That's right. You all got a lift into Glan y Wern with Kit yesterday, didn't you?' Posy shimmied between the chairs to take a seat between Tristan and Gabriel. 'Keira didn't go with you, though?'

141

The others shook their heads.

'What about later, after the fundraiser?' Posy's wide eyes suggested an innocent curiosity, but Caro knew better. 'Did any of you see her after she left the bar? I mean, if they think Kit hit her coming back from town, she would have to have gone out pretty soon after she left us. He didn't get back *that* late, did he?' Caro hid a smile. Posy knew *exactly* what time Kit had returned, she was sure.

'And if any of us saw her later, we could put Kit in the clear,' Gabriel surmised. He was quicker off the mark than Caro had given him credit for – quicker than any of the others around the table, judging by their startled looks.

They began a jumbled debate about who had been where and when, one that Caro saw Posy taking some discreet notes from, but the conclusion was the same. No one knew when or why Keira had left the Seven Stars the night before.

And Kit was still the best suspect anyone had.

Chapter Twelve

Dahlia tossed the newspaper aside in disgust. 'Some people will believe anything, no matter how ridiculous, if it makes them feel better about themselves.'

Dahlia Lively *in* Fame and Misfortune
***By* Lettice Davenport, 1967**

Posy

The day dragged on unbearably as they waited for the police to reopen the road into the village. They wouldn't even need to reopen the *whole* road, Posy reasoned. Just enough that they could pass by. Then they could get a look at the crime scene, too. *That* could be useful. But mostly, Posy wanted to find someone in the village who had seen Keira last night, preferably *after* Kit returned to the Inn.

The rest of the cast had drifted back to their rooms, once they ran out of things to say about Keira, or Kit. In the immediate aftermath of the news, they'd seemed to want to cling together, to share the horrors. But the longer they remained trapped at Saith Seren, the more the horror seemed to fade into mundanity.

Caro and Rosalind had stayed in the bar, but were giving Posy a wide berth after her patience had started fraying and she'd snapped at them both. She'd have to apologise for that, later. Once they were out of there.

Posy cast a hopeful glance at the police officer standing by the door. She'd asked if and when she could leave so often now she didn't even need to use the words. He just shook his head when she met his gaze.

Not yet.

And every moment she sat there, Kit was stuck in some police cell somewhere, waiting for her to find a way to prove his innocence. Because he couldn't have done it. She *knew* Kit. Even if it was a terrible accident . . .

The sick feeling that had been swirling inside her all morning started to rise again as she remembered his face when he'd come in the night before. The way he'd pushed her aside, had started drinking knowing she wouldn't stay.

No. She wasn't going to let herself start thinking that way.

With a sigh, she flipped to a new page in her notebook and started writing out everything she knew, again, in the hope it would spark some new insight. Mostly it just left her with more questions, though.

Questions like, if Kit's car had been used, but he wasn't driving, where were the keys? He'd hung his coat in the cloakroom area when he'd come in, and she was sure she'd seen him put the keys in his pocket. Could someone have taken them from the cloakroom? Or later, from his room? And where were they now?

All questions she could ask Kit if he was there with her, and not in police custody.

Questions the police were probably asking him right now.

She looked down at her notepad again. No answers had miraculously appeared.

This was hopeless. Posy tossed her pen onto the table and looked up at the police officer again. Except this time, he didn't look back, because he wasn't alone. He was talking to another uniformed colleague.

Posy gathered up her stuff quickly, shoving it into her bag, and got to her feet. Just in case. Caro and Rosalind followed suit.

The officer at the door sighed with long-held frustration at the sight of the three of them approaching. 'Yes, fine. The road is still closed, but if you want to go down there I won't stop you. But . . .'

There were no buts that were going to stop Posy.

'You realise we're trained to look out for people showing too much interest in crime scenes,' he called after her.

'Why is that, do you suppose?' Rosalind asked, as she and Caro followed Posy out the front door of the inn.

'Perpetrators of violent crime often return to the scene,' Caro replied promptly. 'They even talk to the police.'

'Why?' Posy wondered if the real murderer was down there already, watching the police work.

'Curiosity. Or to figure out how much the police know. Or just for the power kick.' Caro shrugged. 'One of the police consultants on set told me once.'

'Maybe we'll get lucky down there, then,' Rosalind said, echoing Posy's own thoughts.

But as they got closer to the scene of the accident, cordoned off and guarded, Posy realised the only people waiting there had more questions than answers.

On the far side of the police cordon, a gaggle of reporters had already gathered – along with some curious locals, she assumed. Not that there was much to see. She'd been anxious, she realised now, about seeing another dead body – not her first, not even before Aldermere – but the police had erected a tent over where the body must be, hiding it from view.

Was that standard procedure, or an extra measure to keep things out of sight of the eager paparazzi? Or maybe just to prevent any of

Keira's local social media followers congregating for a vigil. Posy could already see flowers, and sobbing teenagers being kept back by police. Maybe the officer at the inn had been right. They really shouldn't be here.

Posy fell back a step or two, but it was too late. They'd been spotted. She heard the buzz of chatter on the far side of the cordon rise, and then suddenly . . .

Flashes. Lights. Voices. Cameras.

'Posy! Posy! How do you feel about Keira's death?'

'Posy, is this the end of your big comeback? Is the film dead?'

She froze midstep, knowing that they were taking photos of her stunned, unprepared face.

'I . . . I . . .' She didn't have any words. She didn't have the voice to make them heard, anyway. She didn't have any fight left for these people.

They'd almost broken her apart last time she became the centre of their attention – after it was discovered that her parents had embezzled her earnings from her childhood of filmmaking, and it was all gone.

Posy didn't know if she had the strength to face that kind of attention again.

Hands grabbed her arms and pulled her back. Rosalind and Caro then stood in front of her, with their backs to the crowd.

'Well, at least we can confirm that the media have the story now,' Rosalind said. 'I wonder who tipped them off?'

'Does it matter?' Posy asked, tiredly.

She knew the procedure here. They'd stick to a studious silence in the face of the reporters' questions, but from the rapid-fire flashes of the cameras, Posy knew they'd all be on the news sites soon enough. Probably people would interpret their lack of tears or grief-stricken statement, as an insult to Keira or even a sign of guilt. If the news had broken that Kit had been arrested, someone would probably have her down as an accomplice soon enough.

Maybe Rosalind wouldn't be the only one getting death threats, when that happened.

Posy bit the inside of her cheek to force her expression to stay blank. She wasn't giving these vultures anything at all to work with.

A rustle of leaves sounded to her left, and suddenly a man with a camera appeared through the hedge at the side of the road. *He must have gone through the field*, she realised. How long before the rest of them thought of that?

His camera flash blinded her, even as he called out, 'Posy! Is it true they've arrested Kit Lewis?'

Another figure appeared through the new hole in the hedge. 'Are you standing by Kit? Can you confirm you two are a couple?'

'How does it feel to be involved with a murderer?' the first reporter yelled.

Posy froze again, as she realised that Keira may have been the one who had died, but the press had already decided to make this all about Posy. She was the face of the movie. She was rumoured to be in a relationship with the man accused of causing the accident. She was the one with the history they could mine for horrendous stories.

Keira was news enough on her own, and Posy was sure there'd be plenty of pieces about her. But there was only so much you could say about a tragic death before it just got depressing – and none of the papers would want to tear down and denigrate a dead girl with a powerful family.

But Posy was still here, ripe for the taking, and without any family at all these days.

Her and Kit. That's who the press were going to hang this on.

And it was going to be horrific.

If they found out she was sniffing around, investigating, trying to get Kit off the hook, it could be even worse.

'Caro! Are the three Dahlias investigating again? Is that why you're here?'

Posy stumbled back a few steps, then turned, even as Caro tried to take her arm and help her keep her balance. She shook her off, ignored her concerned expression, and started back up the hill towards Saith Seren.

There was a small pause before she heard Caro and Rosalind's footsteps behind her.

'You're probably right, Posy,' Rosalind said, carefully, when they were clear of the police, the reporters and the sobbing teens. 'We should wait until the furore dies down before we try to ask any questions.'

'Anybody notice anything at the crime scene?' Caro asked.

My future, my reputation, everything I worked so hard for, circling the drain.

Beside Posy, Rosalind shook her head. 'Couldn't *see* anything, the way they had it all blocked off. Certainly not enough to read anything into it.'

'She must have been either coming out of or going into the woods, I think,' Caro said. 'The shortcut was blocked off by that cordon, did you see? If she was coming out, on her way back from the village, she might not have noticed a car coming the other way – and they might not have noticed her, if she moved suddenly and quickly.'

'A car with its lights on?' Rosalind sounded unconvinced. 'Hard to miss, I'd have thought.'

'Still, a possibility,' Caro said. 'It *could* have been an accident.'

An accident Kit was involved in. That was what she was really saying, Posy knew. That Keira's death, horrible as it was, might not be connected to anything else they'd been investigating.

That Kit could be responsible.

That was something Posy been refusing to admit thinking, even to herself. The possibility that Kit could have hit Keira by accident on his way back, then pretended not to know it had happened. Or maybe not even realised — there were deer in the woods, weren't there? Or sheep, or something? Maybe he thought he'd hit an animal . . .

He'd been so shaken up when he got back to the pub. Hadn't wanted to talk to her at all.

No. He'd said he didn't do it. She had to believe him.

Kit had been on her side at Aldermere. And since then, he'd been the one in every cast interview or event, talking up how great she was going to be as Dahlia. He'd been a good friend, and he needed her help.

And if she'd thought that maybe he was on the verge of becoming something more than a friend, before they came here . . . well. She couldn't think about that right now. She had to focus.

But on what?

Filming was on hold. She couldn't try to find evidence to prove Kit was innocent without half of the UK's media following and shouting questions at her. And even if she did nothing at all, half the stories in tomorrow's papers were going to mention her involvement, and her past screw-ups.

Not for the first time since she accepted the role of Dahlia, Posy started to wonder if it might have been a mistake. And if the best thing she could do was get the hell out of Wales before things got any worse.

Rosalind

Anton was waiting for them when they reached the back door of the Seven Stars, his arms folded across his chest, his face settled into a scowl.

'I don't want to know where the three of you have been,' he said, in a tone that suggested he already knew. 'Rosalind, Posy, I've got a job for you.'

Rosalind arched her eyebrows and met his gaze, aware that, at her side, Caro had shifted to shield Posy from the director's sight. The youngest Dahlia had been silent all the way home, but Rosalind had no doubt her mind was moving fast.

She hadn't considered what the press furore around Keira's death would mean to Posy. Rosalind had been at the centre of such things before, of course, in her personal life and related to movies she'd been involved in that had found themselves with scandals attached. But it was different for Posy. The press had picked apart her whole life before she was even really an adult.

And with Kit on the hook for Keira's death . . . Rosalind had to admit, this had the potential to get very ugly.

She just hoped that Anton had a plan to get the movie, at least, back on track. 'What do you need us to do?'

'Go to London,' Anton replied. 'I've got you both on one of the morning shows tomorrow to talk about the movie. And Keira, of course. Nothing controversial, no comment on Kit, just there showing that we're all devastated, but committed to finishing the movie in her memory. Okay?'

'Are you sure that's a good idea?' Caro asked. 'You know they're going to want to ask Posy about her relationship with Kit.'

'I don't have one,' Posy said, softly, and Rosalind turned to her in surprise. 'And I think we should go.'

'You do?' Even Anton sounded surprised she wasn't fighting him on this one. 'I don't want any investigative nonsense from any of you. Just normal celeb platitudes, okay? Ideally, by the end of the interview no one will remember anything you said, just feel like you're suitably grieving but the movie will be a must-see. Think you can manage that?'

Posy nodded and, after a moment, Rosalind followed suit. 'I suppose so. It's not like we'll be filming for a few days anyway.'

'Exactly.' Anton looked suspiciously between the three of them. 'Right. In that case, go pack a bag, you two. My assistant has booked you on the evening train from Crewe. We'll get a car to meet you at the end of Dark Lane to take you there. I've spoken to Owain, and he says there's a path from the car park, past the police cordon, through the field on the other side of the hedge.'

'So we noticed,' Caro muttered.

'You realise we'll have to walk past a dozen or more reporters to get there,' Rosalind said.

Anton shrugged. 'Sunglasses and no comment.'

He headed into the bar, leaving the three of them alone in the weak, February sunshine.

'My suite,' Rosalind said, after a moment. 'We need to talk about this.'

'So, do we think Anton is sending you away to stop us investigating, or because he genuinely needs you to save face for the movie?' Caro threw herself onto her daybed as Rosalind shut the door behind them. Posy, meanwhile, lingered near the kitchenette, not even taking a seat.

'Does it matter?' Posy said. 'We have to go.'

'Do we?' Rosalind studied her young friend carefully, but Posy's face was locked up tight. 'Are you sure you even want to?'

Posy shrugged. 'There's not much we can do around here. And if it's good for the movie . . .'

'Posy, you saw what the press mob was like out there.' Caro sat forward, her arms resting on her knees, looking more serious than Rosalind was used to seeing her. 'Do you really think it's going to be any better in London?'

Posy shrugged again, but didn't answer.

'What about finding Kit an alibi?' Rosalind crossed to the wardrobe in her room and pulled out her small rolling case from the bottom, calling back into the main living space. 'I thought *that* was your focus.' Not to mention finding who was behind her own death threats.

'Caro is still here,' Posy pointed out. 'Besides, it's not like I can do much investigating if I'm being followed by the paparazzi everywhere I go.' Rosalind had to admit she had a point there.

'And maybe I just think . . .' Posy trailed off.

Rosalind could guess what she was thinking. Her lips tightened as she set the suitcase on the bed and waited to see if Posy would say more.

When she didn't, Rosalind turned to face her through the doorway and said, 'You think we should do what Anton says and stay out of things. Even if Keira's death could be linked to the threats on my life.'

'I just think we have to work with Anton here and keep things on track.' Posy stared down at her hands. 'Besides, even if it *is* linked – and I can't really see how – then we know whoever is after you is here in Wales. Wouldn't you be safer in London?'

'She'd be safer if we found out who was behind it and stopped them,' Caro shot back from her seat on the daybed.

Rosalind appreciated her support. But she had a feeling that wasn't all that was behind this. She reached back into the wardrobe and pulled out a favourite trouser suit to wear on camera tomorrow. 'Posy. Whatever you think you're running from—'

'I'm not running.' Posy's head snapped up to look her directly in the eye. 'I'm just trying to be a professional. I'm an actress, not a detective – and so are you. So maybe we should be leaving all this to the professionals and getting on with our actual jobs.'

She was scared. Rosalind could see it in her eyes, the way her gaze skittered away the moment her words were done. But knowing Posy was afraid didn't make her any less angry.

'So I should just ignore the fact that someone is trying to kill me, and run off to London and smile for the cameras instead?' Rosalind yanked open the drawers beside her bed rather more forcefully than she'd intended.

'Jack's here,' Posy said, desperation leaking into her voice. 'Can't you turn the letters and everything over to him?'

'He's not on set every day,' Caro pointed out. 'You'll be in London for, what? Twenty-four hours? Less? What about after that? Do you want to just leave her to whoever is out to get her?'

'No! Of course I don't. I just . . .' Posy shook her head.

'You just think we should back off, like Anton wants.' Rosalind's voice sounded sharp, harsh, even to her own ears. 'Because the movie – your career – is more important than my life. I get it.'

'That's not what I said!'

'Isn't it?' Rosalind crossed back to the main door to the suite and pulled it open. 'You need to pack. Go on. You're off the hook. You can leave the investigation to us.'

Posy looked between them for a long, silent moment, then walked out.

The empty space in the room seemed louder than any argument, as Rosalind shut the door again, far more softly.

'Well.' Caro sucked in a deep breath and sighed. 'That's all very well, but while you two are off having fun in London, I'm the only Dahlia here doing any actual work, you realise?'

Rosalind twitched the curtain to one side, hiding her face but increasing her view, so she could see Posy crossing the courtyard to her own suite, her shoulders rounded.

She let the curtain fall, and went back to her packing. 'I don't think we're going to be having any fun in London.'

Chapter Thirteen

Bess eyed the filthy windows and the battered door with dismay. 'Are you sure we really need to speak to Mr Yarrow? Couldn't we just leave this one for the detective inspector?'

Dahlia shook her head. 'Bess, when a promising lead presents itself, you have to follow it wherever it goes. Even if it leads you to a less than salubrious character like Mr Yarrow.'

Dahlia Lively *in* Disaster, Death and Dahlia
***By* Lettice Davenport, 1935**

Caro

Caro waited for Posy and Rosalind to leave before sneaking past the paparazzi at the crash site. In fact, she changed her clothes, and even put on a grey felt cloche hat that Rosalind had packed for reasons past understanding – apparently, while she'd travelled up with only one small suitcase, another two had been shipped up to meet her on arrival – before following behind them.

As she'd guessed, the photographers were far more interested in Posy and Rosalind leaving town than anyone creeping along in their shadow. One of the paparazzi had recognised her earlier, which was moderately gratifying, but the other two Dahlias were the stars here on the movie.

It helped, too, that Anton had escorted them down, looking sombre but relaxed as he spoke to reporters while Rosalind and Posy climbed into the car waiting on the other side. The reporters hurried out if its path as it drove away.

She didn't hang around to hear what Anton was saying – something about waiting a respectful few days before resuming filming, from what she caught on the breeze. Instead, she kept close to the hedge on the far side and hurried past while all attention was on him. She only paused for a second to watch the retreating car take the last bend in the road.

And then she was alone. One Dahlia instead of three.

The path through the woods was blocked by the crime scene, so Caro took the longer route along Dark Lane, all the way to the T-junction and the turning she'd missed on arrival. At the end of the road, she saw the row of neat, new brick houses, continuing along into the cul-de-sac.

Obviously built within the last handful of years, they were a sign of the increased prosperity of Glan y Wern – or perhaps just that the locals weren't the ones buying up property around here. Each house was detached, with a large driveway and lawn out front and, from what Caro could tell, plenty of land out the back, too.

She paused to study them a little longer, something niggling at the back of her mind. What was different about these houses, compared to the ones in the cul-de-sac she'd turned around in the day she arrived?

She blinked, and got it.

Gates.

These houses, there on the main road, not tucked away in the dead end, were gated properties, with keypads and spikes and other things that screamed 'keep out'. Caro recalled, in a flash, another post she'd seen on the local Facebook group she'd joined looking for information on Keira's movements. A post about locals breaking into second homes, or vandalising the walls with spray paint and messages

– hence the gates. But that wasn't the only post about local problems. Another had talked about boy racers, and cars speeding along this road and up into Dark Lane.

Couldn't one of them have been responsible? Even if it turned out the police were right about Kit's car, couldn't one of the local staff Owain and Rebecca had brought in for the fundraiser have stolen Kit's keys from his pocket and taken out the car?

Caro placed her hands on her hips and surveyed the houses again. Now she knew what she was looking for, it took only a moment to find it.

One house, directly opposite Dark Lane, had a video doorbell on the gate.

With a smile, she stepped forward and pressed it.

Mr Grey, who owned the house, was more than happy to help – especially when Caro explained that she was writing about events in Glan y Wern. She might have led him to believe that she was a journalist covering the local 'unrest', as he referred to it.

'You look familiar,' he'd said, eyes narrowing. But Caro knew that, without Dahlia's trademark red lipstick and pin-curled hair, she wasn't all that recognisable.

'Just one of those faces,' she'd assured him, and he'd invited her in for tea and biscuits.

'Three times they spray-painted my car!' His hands shook with rage as he placed the tea and biscuits on the coffee table. 'And I grew up just two villages over. Went to London to seek my fortune and moved back when they built these houses five years ago. It was supposed to be a peaceful retirement, but they couldn't let me have that, could they?'

'That must be incredibly frustrating.' Caro chose a chocolate digestive. 'I noticed that you had a video doorbell on the gate. Is that why? To capture everyone who comes near the house?'

Mr Grey nodded as he took the armchair opposite her. 'That's right. That stumped them! Sent the footage to the police last time and they haven't been back since. Some of those doorbells only activate when someone presses it – but that wasn't good enough for me. I got one with a motion detector, see. It films every time someone walks by, drives past or tries to scale the gate!'

Clearly the local vandals weren't smart enough to figure out how to wear a balaclava, let alone disable the doorbell. 'I wonder if it might be possible for me to see some of the footage from it? Say, from last night?'

She'd already established that the Seven Stars didn't have any security cameras covering the car park, which meant that a camera like this might be the only evidence of which cars had come and gone up Dark Lane around the time Keira was killed.

Mr Grey reached for the tablet on the table beside him. 'As it happens, I have last night's right here – but it's not very interesting. Already sent it to the police after they came knocking this morning – assume you heard about the hit-and-run on Dark Lane?' She nodded, and he kept talking, as he scrolled through the footage. 'But I can show you my greatest hits. My grandson put it together for me. See!'

He handed her the tablet with a video already playing. Caro watched as various teenagers and young men walked past shouting, drinking, occasionally throwing cans, scaring a cat and, once, tried to climb Mr Grey's gate. 'You see?' he cried. 'Total chaos.'

Caro nodded sympathetically. 'I can see why you're keen to get more exposure for this story – and I'd love to help you. But about the footage for last night . . .'

Mr Grey's eyes turned shrewd, as he took the tablet back and scrolled through. 'You're thinking those yobs might have had something to do with the accident, aren't you? Well, I wouldn't put it past them. But there's nothing definitive in the footage, I'm afraid.'

'Still, it could be helpful to see it,' Caro said. 'For, uh, background.'

This time, the video ran at a speeded-up rate. It started from early evening, with cars taking the turn up Dark Lane, presumably for the fundraiser at the Seven Stars. Then there was a skip in time; the next few times it activated must have been people leaving again. Then a final break, until the video activated at 11.10 p.m. to show a familiar silver car as it came into view. Caro couldn't quite make out the person driving, but she assumed it had to be Kit, given the timestamp. It showed that he'd made the turn into Dark Lane just five minutes or so before he'd entered the Seven Stars. Surely not enough time for an accident to have taken place?

'Is there any more?' she asked Mr Grey. 'Any other cars coming in or out of Dark Lane, for instance?'

He shook his head. 'Nothing. After all the noise and fuss from people coming and going to that event they had up there at Saith Seren, that was the last time the camera came online.'

So nobody had passed this way at all after Kit returned. Which meant, if Kit wasn't responsible, then whoever had hit Keira had to have driven out from the Seven Stars, then turned around and headed back before they reached the T-Junction and Mr Grey's camera. Then they'd left the car in the car park and either escaped on foot – or headed into their room at the inn.

So much for finding a smoking gun – or at least some evidence Kit couldn't have done it. He was still by far the most likely suspect, and nothing she'd learned here was going to convince the police otherwise.

Caro thanked Mr Grey for his time, and promised to keep him updated on her work, before leaving to trudge back up to the Seven Stars, wishing that Rosalind and Posy were there to talk things through.

Posy

Their train ride to London was silent. At least the first-class compartment was empty, so she and Rosalind could spread out from their assigned seats and ignore each other in peace. Or, in Posy's case, try to figure out where things had gone so wrong. *Of course* she cared about Rosalind's safety, and finding the person threatening it.

But was it so unreasonable to suggest that the professionals might have better luck finding out who that was? Or that they'd be better off sticking to what they were actually good at?

Things didn't improve when they reached the hotel they'd been booked into for the night. Rosalind took her key and muttered something about room service before disappearing towards the lifts. Posy sighed and waited for her own room key, resigning herself to a long night spent overthinking things.

The following morning started with an early wake-up call from the publicist looking after them for the trip, and another silent journey by car to the TV studio where they'd be filming. At least Posy could almost pretend that the awkward silence between them was due to the early hour, rather than lingering tensions from yesterday's disagreement.

She wanted to say something, to smooth over the argument. She just had no idea what.

Before she could come up with anything, they were both sitting in hair and make-up, side by side in front of a long mirror, while the professionals did their good work to make them both look alert and beautiful, despite the ridiculous hour and – in Posy's case, at least – a sleepless night.

She watched Rosalind in the mirror, barely registering the chatter from the make-up artist behind her. Rosalind's eyes were closed, and Posy could almost believe she was asleep, except there was a tension in her hands as they lay on the arms of the chair, and in her shoulders as she sat.

She's still half expecting an attack, Posy realised. *Even here.*

How terrified must Rosalind be, all the time? She'd been shrugging it off, talking about similar letters she'd received in the past or the natural risks of being in the public eye. But this . . . this was different, and they all knew it. Behind her determination to solve this themselves and protect her reputation, and her insistence that they do it without involving the police, just how scared was Rosalind really?

Posy suspected it was more than she'd realised before now.

The make-up artist – Lucy – was still talking, high and a little too fast. 'And you're working on the new Dahlia Lively movie. So exciting! Actually . . . a friend of mine was working on that too. As the casting director.'

Rosalind's eyes snapped open and met Posy's gaze in the mirror.

'You're a friend of Brigette's?' Posy said, smiling at the reflection of the make-up artist. 'How brilliant! Have you spoken to her lately, by any chance?'

Maybe it was nothing, but Brigette's disappearance still niggled at her. If a friend had spoken to her and could tell Posy that all was fine, maybe she'd be able to let it go.

But Lucy bit down on her lower lip, her eyes worried, and Posy knew that she wasn't going to be able to let it go at all.

'Actually . . . I was hoping *you* might have,' Lucy said. 'I swapped with a friend to work on this show this morning because I knew you'd be here. You see, I haven't been able to get hold of Brigette at all – ever since it was announced that she had left the production. She's not answering texts, emails – even social media messages.'

'But she has been posting on social media,' Posy said, slowly. 'Hasn't she? From a retreat in California somewhere.'

Lucy nodded. 'She has. Except . . . after that photo of the departures board at Heathrow, every picture she's posted since is, well, fake.'

'Fake?' Rosalind asked, obviously giving up on pretending she wasn't listening in. 'Fake how?'

'They're from last year,' Lucy said, in a rush. 'We took a retreat out there together last year, and the photos she's posting now, they're from then. I'm sure of it. Look!' She pulled out her phone and scrolled through a year's worth of photos before showing Posy a selection that certainly looked similar to the ones she'd seen on Brigette's Instagram page.

'Couldn't she have just gone back to the same place?' she asked, doubtfully.

Lucy shook her head. 'She might. But the photos are *exactly* the same. Like, I think you can even see my foot in one of them, and I'm definitely not there, right?'

'We haven't heard from Brigette since she left Wales last month,' Rosalind said. 'But I think we – well, I – would like to talk to her, too.' She gave Posy a pointed look at that, and Posy knew exactly what she was saying.

This is our best lead so far. Are you in, or are you out?

She should be out.

Being in meant throwing herself in the view of the cameras – not for her work, but for her personal life. It meant having her whole history rehashed in a way she might have avoided if she'd just stuck to being a good Dahlia. Articles about the film might have one line on her troubled past. Pieces about her investigating a murder, trying to prove the innocence of her rumoured boyfriend, alongside two other famous actresses . . . that was going to cause more of a splash, and people were going to dig deeper.

The focus should be on the work, the film, and nothing else.

But . . . this was Rosalind. And Kit. And even Keira and Brigette.

How could she look her reflection in the eyes every time she sat down in the make-up trailer if she didn't help them? If she didn't fight to find out the truth?

If she let someone hurt Rosalind?

She couldn't.

So she nodded, and said, 'Yes. We *both* want to talk to her,' and watched Rosalind smile for the first time in what felt like days.

An assistant stuck their head around the door to say they were ready for them, and Posy and Rosalind were hurriedly given a last check over before being declared camera-ready.

'DM me your photos,' Posy told Lucy, as they left for filming. 'I'll check them out and see what I can do.'

Finding Brigette had suddenly leaped up her to-do list.

Because if Brigette wasn't where she said she was . . . where was she? And why was she lying about it?

Caro

Caro watched Rosalind and Posy live on the morning show from a prone position on Rosalind's king-size bed, since it was far comfier than her daybed, and the TV in the bedroom got better reception, anyway. They both looked tired, she thought, despite the make-up, but they did a good job of following Anton's orders to the letter. Sorrow displayed appropriately at Keira's untimely death, echoed by the plain black outfits they both wore. And a dedication to completing the film in her memory, although they didn't go into details on timescales.

What she couldn't tell was whether they were actually speaking to each other again yet.

With a sigh, she clicked off the television with the remote and went to get dressed. She had more investigating to do before they got back.

It was market day in Glan y Wern, life continuing despite the tragedy. She easily dodged both the cameras and the police officers conducting their own investigations around the village, and spent her time asking questions of market traders and local shop owners, hoping to find somebody – anybody – who had seen Keira in the village that night. Within the first hour she'd bought a jar of local honey, a hand-knitted beret and a pastry in lieu of the breakfast she'd skipped. But no sign of Keira.

The most obvious place she might have gone at that time of night, Caro decided, was the Drunken Dragon pub – so she was waiting outside the front door the moment they opened at 11 a.m. There was only one staff member behind the bar when she entered, so Caro headed directly for him, hopping up onto the stool nearest to him and hoping it looked effortless – even if a slight twinge in her back told her it wasn't.

'What can I get you?' The young bartender gave her a friendly smile as he turned to face her. A tag on his shirt said his name was Ben.

'Oh, a . . .' Too early, really, for wine. And probably not appropriate for an investigation, either. But it was rude to ask for information without ordering anything, and she didn't want to stay long enough to drink a coffee . . . 'A lime and soda, please,' she said, finally, and was pleased with her choice when she realised that the soda dispenser was right by her stool.

'Actually, I was hoping I could ask you a couple of questions,' she said, as he fetched a glass down from the shelf for her.

'Questions?' Ben raised an eyebrow in a way that would have made Dahlia proud. Maybe she could get him to give Posy lessons. God knew she and Rosalind weren't having any impact on her.

'I'm sure you heard about the terrible accident on Dark Lane the other night.'

Now, she had his interest. 'I just can't believe it. Keira Reynolds-Yang. I mean, she is . . . was . . . a real star. Right?' He leaned over the bar, his arms folded on its polished surface, eager curiosity in his eyes.

'I know. It's just terrible. In fact . . . I'm trying to figure out what she was doing out that late in the first place – we all thought she'd gone to bed, you see.'

'Aren't the police doing that?' He handed her the drink she'd ordered, and she passed over her bank card in return.

'Well, yes. But . . .' What *was* a valid excuse for asking these questions? Would he buy the same reporter spiel that Mr Grey had? The suspicious look in his eye suggested not, and Caro really didn't want to get thrown out on her ear. 'I'm working on the film too, you see. Behind the scenes. And the cast are all very distraught, as you can imagine. We're all just looking for some peace of mind, I suppose, by answering some of the lingering questions, like what possessed her to go out into the night.'

The barman shook his head, pulling another pint glass from the shelf and polishing it with a towel. 'Those famous types. Who knows what goes on in their heads. Different world, right?'

'Right,' Caro said, trying not to feel needled that he obviously didn't recognise her own participation in that world. 'Were *you* working that night? Can I ask . . . did you happen to see her? Or anyone from the movie, for that matter?'

He gave her a long, assessing look. 'You're working on the film?'

Caro nodded. Well, she *practically* was.

'And you're not a reporter? Because I don't want to read all about it in the papers tomorrow. I don't hold with all that using tragedy just to sell papers.'

'I promise you I am not a reporter.' Oh, she hoped Mr Grey didn't come in here for a lunchtime pint every day or anything.

Ben was silent as he finished polishing the glass he was working on. 'Well, that Dominic Laugharne was here for dinner. And then Keira Reynolds-Yang came in later and stayed until closing.'

Caro sat up a little straighter. 'You're sure it was her?'

Ben nodded. 'I wasn't, to start with. I mean, she *obviously* wasn't a local, but we get a lot of tourists in here these days. But it wasn't all that busy the night before last – lots of people were up at the fundraiser at Saith Seren, I guess. And Julia and Lucia – they were working that night too – they started whispering about it. They'd found her Instagram and compared photos. It was definitely her.'

'Did she look . . . how did she look? I mean, was she upset? Or angry? Or . . . anything?'

Ben looked surprised at the question. Like he didn't imagine celebrities had feelings. 'Honestly? She looked a little bored. She sat on her own at that table over there.' He pointed towards an isolated table, tucked away in one corner of the bar. 'Had one drink, and spent the whole time staring at her phone or checking the door.'

Caro considered the table Keira had chosen from her own seat. If she'd sat with her back to the wall, she'd have had a perfect view of anybody entering the pub, and everything else that was going on. So either she'd been wary or nervous about being seen there, or . . . 'Did you get the impression that she was waiting for somebody to join her?'

Ben gave a small shrug. 'If she was, they never came. She sat there alone the whole time, then left shortly after I called last orders.'

'What time was that?'

'Eleven? Around then, anyway. We like to try and get the place clear by eleven-thirty, on weeknights.'

Caro thanked Ben for his time, paid for her half-finished drink, and headed back out.

If Keira had left at eleven or before, she could have made it to Dark Lane just as Kit was driving up. Which meant she still had nothing.

Chapter Fourteen

'Untruths and lies can sometimes help us get to the real facts of the matter almost as quickly as the honest truth, if they're challenged right.'

Dahlia Lively *in* **Lies and Lilacs**
By **Lettice Davenport, 1966**

Rosalind

First class was empty again on the way back to Wales, but this time Posy and Rosalind sat together, huddled over their phones as they scrolled through the photos on Brigette's Instagram feed and compared them to the ones that Lucy the make-up artist had sent over.

Each of Brigette's photos was a bland image of her surroundings – the view from her balcony, a shot of a fountain in a courtyard – with only the occasional shot of her feet or her face in shadow. The captions were non-descriptive, too – mostly quotes from Buddhist icons or motivational speakers.

'I think this one is the clincher.' Posy took both phones and held them side by side. Rosalind peered at the images. One showed a sunset view from a balcony with a single pair of feet in it – Brigette's, she assumed, since it was from her feed. The other showed the same view from a minutely different angle, with an additional pair of sandalled feet – Lucy's. Rosalind's gaze flicked back to the first image again. There, just at the edge of the shot, she could make out the glint of a buckle from Lucy's sandals, and the edge of a shadowed foot.

Rosalind sat back in her seat. 'So the only question is, why is Brigette pretending to be in California?'

'And where is she really?' Posy finished. 'We could ask Caro to get Ashok on it?'

'We will,' Rosalind agreed. 'When we're back in Wales.'

Posy went quiet and when Rosalind looked over, she was biting her lip.

'Are we . . . you know . . . okay?' Posy said, when she caught her looking.

Rosalind sighed. If she'd learned anything in sixty-odd years of life, surely it had to be that wasting time holding grudges or dragging out arguments never helped anybody.

'We're fine.' Or they would be, once they figured out what the hell was going on around the set and cast of *The Lady Detective*.

She dozed for most of the rest of the train journey, leaving Posy making notes in her ever-present notebook. Thoughts that were almost dreams floated through her mind – a dagger above her chest, the sound of a car engine in the night, and a hundred movies rolling at once – until she opened her eyes to find they were nearly at Crewe.

They called Caro from the car back to the Seven Stars.

'We might have something,' Posy said, with a cautious glance towards the driver at the front of the car. 'Not on Kit, though. Brigette. How about you?'

From the way Posy's face fell, Rosalind assumed Caro didn't have much at all.

Posy hung up. 'She says to meet her in the village. She's still talking to people.'

If she hadn't found anybody to help clear Kit's name by now, Rosalind doubted they were going to jump out of the woodwork before they arrived. Still, after they'd dropped their things back at the Seven Stars – the road now fully open again – Rosalind forewent the shower and nap she was craving, and they headed straight into Glan y Wern to meet Caro at WelshCakes, the cafe-cum-bakery opposite the village green.

There were reporters doing the rounds in the village still, too, but Rosalind noticed that Posy didn't shy away from them today.

Inside, WelshCakes was decked out with red fabric heart bunting and pink honeycomb paper balls.

'I put them up for St Dwynwen's Day on January the twenty-fifth, then leave them up until after Valentine's,' the owner Bethan explained, when Caro asked. Rosalind had a feeling that she'd seen her at the fundraiser. 'The place needs a bit of brightening up at this time of year, anyway. Now, what can I get you all?'

By the time they'd finished ordering teas and cakes, they'd also established that Bethan hadn't seen anything out of the ordinary after she'd left the Seven Stars following the fundraiser. As reporters gathered at the window, Bethan pointedly locked the door and flipped the sign over to closed. When Caro thanked her, she gave them all a grim smile.

'Everyone deserves some privacy, especially at a time like this. And, well, I was the one, you see,' she said, in a low whisper, 'who called in the body. I had to wait there in the freezing cold with the dog until the police and ambulance arrived. And even then, they had so many questions . . .' Bethan shook her head. 'My husband told me to close up for the week, until this all passes, but I'm always better with a distraction. Keeps your mind off things, you know?'

'We know,' Rosalind agreed. 'I'm sorry to dredge it all back up again for you. But I have to ask . . . was there anything unusual that you noticed?'

'Unusual? No. Well, I mean, none of it was bloody usual, was it?' She shuddered. 'Now, if you don't mind, I'll go get your orders. I need to keep busy.'

'No help there, then,' Caro said, after Bethan was out of earshot, fetching their drinks. 'You'd think the person who discovered the body would have *something* to tell us. Now, what did you guys find out in London?'

'Only that Brigette isn't on some retreat in California like she wants everyone to believe.' Posy explained about Lucy the make-up artist, and showed Caro the photos to prove her point.

'Think we can get Ashok looking into where she might really be?' Rosalind asked.

'I'm sure we can,' Caro agreed. 'Now, let me tell you what I've found out here.'

What Caro had found out, it seemed to Rosalind, was that Kit was still the prime suspect.

'The timings line up,' she said, ignoring Caro's wince and Posy's glare. 'If Keira left the Drunken Dragon at eleven, she'd have been coming out of the woods path onto the main road just when that camera has Kit driving up it. He couldn't have just hit her and come into the bar like nothing happened though, could he?'

Posy and Caro exchanged a look. 'He wasn't . . . exactly himself when he arrived,' Caro said.

'And do we know where he'd been?' Rosalind looked to Posy for an answer on that one.

'I do.' Posy toyed with a paper-covered sugar cube, the sort Rosalind remembered getting in France. Frank had used to build vast structures out of them, delighting the children at nearby tables. Posy seemed satisfied with a small tower. 'But it's not my secret to share. I can tell you it doesn't have anything to do with *this* though.' She waved her hand to illustrate *this*, and knocked over the sugar-cube tower.

Rosalind watched Posy a moment longer, wondering how much they could trust her judgement on what was or wasn't connected, when they didn't really have a clue whether there were any links at all between Keira's death, Brigette's disappearance and the threats on her own life.

Bethan brought their tea and cakes, and they ate in contemplative silence. Rosalind assumed the others were just as aware as she was that they were nowhere with this investigation.

It wasn't until their cakes were reduced to crumbs on their plates, and the teapot was empty, that hope arrived – in the form of a teenage girl.

Seren slid into the last empty seat at their window table casting furtive looks over her shoulder to make sure she wasn't being watched by her aunt, who was taking a phone call at the counter.

'Where did you come from?' Caro asked. 'I thought the door was locked.'

'I'm good at getting into places,' Seren said, loftily. Then she gave a cheeky grin. 'Nah. There's a key hanging on a nail just behind a tin plaque on the back door. Worst-kept secret in Glan y Wern.'

'Might want to get your aunt to move that.' Rosalind glanced out of the window. No sign of reporters right now – probably they were investigating inside in the warm somewhere, if they had any sense. But they'd be back.

'I heard you talking.' She addressed Caro, but Rosalind knew she and Posy were hanging on her words all the same. 'About the accident the other night. Are you investigating it? Like you did at Aldermere last summer?'

The three Dahlias exchanged a look. 'You know about that?'

Seren scoffed, in the way only a teenager could manage – with true disbelief of the idiocy of adults. '*Everyone* knows about that. I mean, it was all over the internet.'

'Apparently so,' Rosalind said, remembering that website full of conspiracy theories about her. Although she'd bet that Seren *hadn't* heard all about it until she went looking into the film crew and cast, once they'd arrived at Tŷ Gwyn. Maybe not even until Caro had shown up, since she hadn't seemed to know who she was when she met her.

'Besides, I *love* murder mysteries – especially the Dahlia Lively ones.' Seren shrugged. 'So I looked you all up. And I reckon you're investigating again. Aren't you?'

The three Dahlias shared a quick look, and a brief, unspoken conversation, before Caro answered.

'Yes. We're trying to find out where she was, and when, to help clear our friend's name,' she said. 'Did *you* see something?'

The girl looked to be in her very early teens and should surely have also been safe in bed by nearing eleven at night. Rosalind didn't remember seeing her at the Seven Stars the night of the fundraiser, but if she'd thought about it at all, she'd assumed she must have been in the family accommodation above the inn.

But apparently she was wrong, as Seren nodded enthusiastically.

'I did! I saw her, outside the Drunken Dragon. Must have been after eleven, because it was after the fundraiser was over that I snuck out—' she broke off suddenly, glancing back over her shoulder again. Luckily, Bethan was still engrossed in a long conversation about an order for a birthday cake.

'You waited until everyone was asleep before you climbed out your window?' Posy suggested, looking more amused than horrified at the idea. Seren nodded.

'I was babysitting for Auntie Bethan that night, at her house,' Seren explained. 'I always stay over at her house when I do, see. So I had to wait until she and Uncle Rhys got home and had gone to bed before I could sneak out. Much easier than at home. The stairs at Saith Seren creak too much, and Mum's a light sleeper.'

'Where were you going?' Rosalind asked, not entirely sure she wanted to know the answer. At fourteen, her idea of excitement had been a trip to the milk bar in town. She suspected Posy's – and perhaps even Caro's – experiences at that age were rather different.

'There was a full blood moon last night,' Seren explained in a low whisper. 'And I wanted to get some footage of it over the old castle ruins.' She gestured through the window towards the bridge by the pub that led out of the village and towards some sort of heritage site, according to the brown signpost Rosalind had seen earlier. She assumed that the assortment of broken rocks and walls barely visible on the hill in the distance were the castle ruins Seren was referring to.

'You climbed up there in the dark?' Caro sounded impressed. 'Alone?'

Seren shrugged nonchalantly. Rosalind suspected that meant this wasn't the only time she'd done it. Not for the first time, Rosalind was grateful she and Frank had been of the same mind when it came to children. At the time, she'd just thought that becoming a mother would derail her career. Now, she thought that the stress of being responsible for another human might have been the death of her. Keeping an eye on Posy and Caro was tough enough.

'It'll look great in my final piece about the film being made here,' she explained. 'And that night was actually clear for once. I couldn't miss it.'

'Makes sense,' Caro said, even though it didn't – at least, not to Rosalind. 'So, you saw Keira outside the Drunken Dragon. Can you tell us what she was doing?'

Seren gave them a very self-satisfied smile. 'Better. I can show you.'

'You were already filming when you saw her,' Rosalind realised. 'Clever.' She bet Jack hadn't thought to talk to Seren. His loss.

'Can we see it?' Posy asked, eagerly.

With a last check that her aunt was still occupied, Seren nodded.

'Did you film it on your phone?' Caro asked.

'Yeah. I'm saving up for a proper camera, but for now—'

'Even the greats have to start somewhere,' Posy said. 'Maybe we can get you on set to meet with some of our camera guys, if you'd like?'

Seren's face lit up with such joy that, suddenly, she looked much younger than her fourteen years again. 'That would be awesome. I mean, now this has happened, I'm even more desperate to film you all!'

'Posy will get you on the list,' Rosalind promised. 'As long as you won't get in trouble with school?'

Seren shook her head, still grinning. 'It's fine. It's half term this week anyway!'

She fiddled with her phone case, setting it up on the table so it stood up on its own for them all to watch. Rosalind shifted her chair a little closer to Caro's for a better view, and saw Posy doing the same on the other side.

She'd turned the sound right down, but they didn't need it anyway. She pressed play, and the high street of Glan y Wern came into focus, the shops and the green dulled by the darkness of night. The few lampposts that lined the street gave an eerie, orange glow to the scene, but also illuminated the clock that hung above the pharmacy next to WelshCakes.

Eleven-ten. The same time that the video doorbell had Kit taking the turning into Dark Lane.

A surge of relief raced through her, and she saw Caro squeeze Posy's hand tight in anticipation. If it really was Keira on Seren's video, then they'd been right. Kit couldn't have been responsible.

Above it all, that full moon shone down on the village, just as Seren had said it would. The camera started to move, relatively smoothly considering Seren had to have been holding it as she walked.

They watched as the video moved through the village, past the war memorial, over the grass towards the pub and the bridge beyond and then—

'There!' Caro jabbed at the screen to pause the film. 'There she is.'

Rosalind peered closer, refusing once again to admit that it might be time to start *wearing* her reading glasses. 'Where?'

Caro pointed again to the phone screen, and things clicked into focus. There, standing outside the Drunken Dragon, was Keira Reynolds-Yang. 'What's she doing?'

Seren pressed play again. 'I think she was talking on her phone. I wasn't really paying all that much attention to her, though.'

'Don't suppose you heard what she said?'

Seren shook her head. 'But I walked right past her. Hang on.'

Bethan had disappeared into the back of the shop now, thankfully. Maybe she was even hiding that damn spare key. Seren pressed the button on the side of the phone to increase the volume, and the sound of the wind whistling past the microphone suddenly became audible, making Rosalind wince. But then, as the camera passed where Keira stood, the recording caught a snatch of one-sided conversation.

'—know what game you're playing now, but I'm not waiting any more, okay? We're gonna talk when I get back, though. You can't—'

'Play that back?' Caro asked, and Seren obliged. They all listened in silence again to Keira's voice, talking from beyond the grave, presumably into someone's answerphone.

Rosalind shuddered.

We're gonna talk when I get back. Whoever Keira had planned to meet in the village that night, they were waiting back at the Seven Stars. Which narrowed down the list of possibilities considerably.

This time, they let the film keep playing – over the bridge and up the hill towards the ruins, the footage getting rather more jerky as the terrain worsened – before Seren stopped it, skipping forward to the end. 'I kept filming on the way back, too.' She pressed play again, and this time they were approaching the Drunken Dragon from the bridge direction. 'She was gone by the time I got back.'

'What time was that?' Posy asked.

Seren skipped forward a few more frames. 'Pharmacy clock says eleven forty-five. I didn't go all the way up to the castle. Just got the shots I wanted of the moon over the ruins and headed back to Auntie Bethan's house. I was back in bed long before she got up to walk the dog. They never knew I was gone.'

It was almost a shame she hadn't been heading back to the Seven Stars, Rosalind thought, because then she might have discovered Keira's body hours earlier. Maybe even soon enough to help her. Except she wouldn't wish the trauma of that discovery on a fourteen-year-old.

'Okay. So, somewhere between ten past eleven and eleven forty, Keira left the Drunken Dragon to head back to the Seven Stars to talk to whoever stood her up that night,' Rosalind said.

'And we have to assume she never made it back there,' Posy added. 'Because she was hit by a car on Dark Lane. But not by Kit – he was already back by then.'

But someone could have taken his car back out again and hit her. Someone who knew she'd be heading back to the Seven Stars just then. The same someone she'd left that voicemail for.

Caro raised her eyebrows. 'Maybe the person she was calling *really* didn't want to have that conversation.'

Seren's eyes were huge. 'You really think somebody killed her on purpose? That this was murder?'

Rosalind shared another quick glance with her fellow Dahlias. Of course they did. They all did. The death of a cast member was too much of a coincidence after everything that was going on. But there was always the possibility that it *was* a coincidence.

'It was probably just an accident,' she said, deciding that it might *not* be a lie, so that was okay.

'But you're investigating,' Seren pointed out. 'If you really thought it was an accident, you wouldn't bother.'

'The police think a friend of ours was responsible,' Posy explained. 'And your video shows that he couldn't have been.'

'I'm someone's alibi?' Seren asked, brightly.

'Well, not exactly, but . . .' Caro obviously caught Seren's drooping expression. 'Yes, for all intents and purposes, you are his alibi. You are the evidence we need to set him free.'

'So what do we do now?' Seren asked, bouncing on her toes with excitement.

Rosalind felt Caro and Posy's gazes swing towards her, and sighed. 'I'll call Jack,' she said.

Chapter Fifteen

Rosalind

Jack agreed to meet them at the Seven Stars, so they ran the gauntlet of paparazzi back to the pub, still refusing to offer anything in the way of a comment. Posy held her head high through the experience this time, which Rosalind thought was just as well. The photographers and reporters seemed pretty entrenched. It was hard to imagine they were going to leave in a hurry.

The time it took for Jack to drive in was conveniently sufficient for Rosalind to finally shower and fix her make-up.

But now Jack sat opposite her, leaning back in his chair with his arms folded across his chest, a black coffee on his side of the table.

'So, I understand you have something to show me?' he said, as Rosalind took a seat with the others. 'This young lady here tells me it's vitally important to the case, but that she can't show me until you're all here.'

Seren sent a panicked look towards the bar, but fortunately for her, both her parents were currently absent. She noticeably relaxed.

'Shall I show him now?' Seren asked, obviously keen to get it over with before her parents returned. All three Dahlias nodded.

Jack watched Seren's video in silence, despite Caro's helpful running commentary of what he was watching. Then, when it had finished, he watched it again. And this time, he asked for the sound on.

'So, what do you think?' Posy asked, when he'd finished. 'It proves Kit *couldn't* have been the one to hit Keira on his way back to the pub. He was already here and at the bar with me before she could have got back to Dark Lane.'

Jack raised an eyebrow. 'That sure of your timings, are you? I thought Kit got back here "shortly after eleven" according to all of you. Could have crossed over.'

The Dahlias exchanged a look. 'We understand that there might be some video-doorbell footage that shows Kit turning into Dark Lane at eleven-ten,' Rosalind said, carefully.

'CCTV is notorious for having inaccurate timings. Besides, how, exactly, did you become aware of that information?' Jack's voice was tight, restrained, and Rosalind had to force herself not to wince.

'Oh, because I spoke to the owner of Gable Cottage, of course,' Caro said. 'Our friend is being falsely accused, so I will speak to anyone I need to in order to get him freed.'

'I see,' Jack said, not sounding as if he did anything of the sort. 'As if happens, I am *also* aware of that footage – since I am actually involved in this investigation.'

'So, you know that Kit was back here by, say, eleven-fifteen, like everyone here that night said – and when we know Keira was still outside the Drunken Dragon. And *I* know that, after that, Kit was sitting in the bar with Anton until late,' Caro said, triumphantly.

'Perhaps,' Jack said. 'But it's still not conclusive.'

'What do you mean?' Posy sounded outraged. 'We found you honest to God *evidence* that Kit couldn't have done it—'

'Except it was still his car involved in the accident,' Jack pointed out. 'There's no other car in the car park here at the Seven Stars that has the same sort of damage to it. And it has to have been a car from here, because—'

'Because no other car showed on the CCTV, we know.' Rosalind sighed. She'd known that find would prove too good to be true. 'So, what? You think he arranged to meet Keira in town, didn't show up, drove his car back here and was seen with us all, then took it back out again to hit her when he knew she was on her way back – some significant time *after* she called and said she was leaving? Where do you think she went in the meantime? And when was Kit supposed to have gone out and done that with no one noticing?'

'Well, *someone* must have,' Caro said, thoughtfully.

Posy swung her head around to glare at her. 'What do you mean?'

Rosalind was amused to note that Seren's eyes were wide and bright as she looked from one face to another as the conversation ping-ponged around the table. From the careful way she angled her phone towards Caro as she spoke, Rosalind suspected she was filming them even now.

'I mean if Kit didn't do it – oh, stop glaring, Posy, you know I am firmly on Team Kit – then someone else must have stolen his keys and taken the car out to hit Keira. I mean, it *could* still have been an accident – someone borrowing the car for a joyride. But the fact she was waiting for someone who didn't show—'

'Someone staying here at the Seven Stars,' Rosalind put in. The others stared at her. 'We heard her. She said that they'd talk about it when she got back. That means the person she was expecting to meet was here, too. Doesn't it?'

'It does seem likely,' Jack allowed. 'But still—'

'But nothing,' Caro interrupted. 'Someone didn't want to have that conversation. They knew when she'd be leaving the Drunken Dragon, because she called them. Have you even checked her phone?'

'I'm not at liberty to discuss an ongoing investigation,' Jack said, stiffly.

Rosalind rolled her eyes. 'Oh, come on, Jack. What do you think we're all doing here? Besides, we've just given you your best bit of evidence for Keira's movements last night.'

'The officers on the case had already spoken to the staff at the pub—'

'And learned, like I did when I spoke to Ben, that Keira left there at around eleven,' Caro said. 'Now we know she didn't come straight back here, *and* that she was waiting for someone who didn't show up.'

'We've cracked this case *wide* open,' Seren said, cheerfully. They all gave her a look. 'Okay, maybe not *wide* open. Like, a small crack or something. I mean, it's a start. Isn't it?'

It was a start, Rosalind had to admit that. From the uncomfortable expression on Jack's face, so did he.

He looked around the table – from Seren to Posy to Caro – before his gaze landed firmly on Rosalind. 'Can I have a word in private?'

Rosalind held back a sigh. She knew what was coming and, as much as she'd like to give the 'anything you have to say to me you can say in front of my friends' spiel, there was no real reason to subject the others to it. 'Of course.'

'What is it, Jack?' she asked, once they were seated at a small table in the private dining room.

He took a moment to find the right words. She'd always liked that about him. So many of her and Frank's friends as a couple had been the impulsive types – the sort to say whatever flippant remark came into their heads, just for the laugh it would earn. The sort to keep everything close to the surface, so they never had to think about what was buried underneath.

But Jack and Milly had been a different breed. When he first moved to London with his young bride he'd been an obligation, a responsibility. A favour to an old university mate. *Just keep an eye on Jack, will you, Frank?'*

Over time, though, they'd become real friends. The genuine sort capable of meaningful conversations that lasted into the night. Oh, they'd laughed plenty, too. But they were interested in more than just the surface.

Rosalind hadn't realised how much she'd missed that, until she met Caro and Posy last summer. Until Jack walked back into her life, now.

Which made the fact that she knew he was about to reprimand her – and she was about to disappoint him – all the harder to bear.

'Rosalind, I know it can be hard to stand back and watch from the sidelines when something terrible happens to someone you know and like. Or when you think something unfair has happened to a friend of yours.'

'Very hard,' Rosalind murmured in agreement.

'But I have to ask you to stay away from the police investigation into Keira's death. I know—' He spoke over her objections. 'I know you want to help Kit. That you genuinely believe in his innocence. But you have to accept that, at present, he is still the best suspect we have.'

'And you'd rather nobody found a better one, to mess up your open-and-shut case.'

Jack sighed. 'Firstly, it's not *my* case. I retired, remember? I am nothing more than an investigating officer here – I leave all the hard work to the younger ones.'

She scoffed at that. 'Like you could ever walk away from a really good investigation. I know you, remember, Jack?'

'And I know you.' There was a heaviness in his voice she didn't like. Were they finally going to talk about all the revelations that had come out over the last six months about her personal life? All the things he *hadn't* known, despite being one of her oldest friends? Apparently not. 'I know you hate to be sidelined, but—'

'This isn't about not being centre stage anymore, Jack,' she interrupted. 'In case you missed the news out of Aldermere last summer, this isn't the first murder that Caro, Posy and I have investigated.'

If he knew about the death threats. About the accidents on set, and Brigette's disappearance. About her fear that they were all connected – that they were all connected to *her*. Maybe then he'd understand that this was about more than just meddling.

She *should* tell him. She knew that. But she didn't, all the same. It was bad enough him looking at her like a meddling old woman. The last thing she wanted was him thinking she was an hysterical, interfering old woman, who had let the drama of her career bleed over into her character.

Besides, if he wouldn't listen to her about Kit, why should he listen about anything else?

'There's no clear evidence that this *was* a murder,' Jack shot back, and the moment had passed. 'That's just one of the many reasons that amateurs should never get involved in police work. Quite apart from your lack of knowledge about how evidence needs to be obtained to be admissible in court, the worst thing is that you start with an idea of what you think happened and you'll go to any lengths to prove it. That's not how investigations should work.'

The amateur tag rankled, even though Rosalind knew it was true. But what offended her more was the idea that they would be blinded by their own assumptions.

'The only thing we're trying to prove is that the truth matters,' she said, tightly. 'My apologies if that isn't true for you any longer.'

It was the kind of incendiary comment that would end a conversation flat with most people. The sort of bomb she'd throw into an argument to win, even if it was unfair and he didn't deserve it. With anyone else, she'd have been able to walk out and leave him fuming.

But Jack wasn't just anyone.

Before she'd even got to her feet to start her flouncing exit, he'd sighed, his previous brief display of temper over, and said, very calmly, 'Rosalind, you have to know that I care about you – at least as much as you seem to care about Kit. You're possibly my oldest surviving friend.'

'You haven't seen me in years.' Did friendships still count when one person had been lying to the other for decades, anyway?

'It doesn't matter,' he said, heavily, almost as if he wished it did. 'Much as you are trying to protect Kit, *I* am trying to protect *you*. Like I said, there's no evidence it was murder, yet. But there are a number of concerning features to the case. Kit claims his car keys were in his coat pocket after he got back that night, and that his coat was hanging in the cloakroom. He says someone else must have taken them, driven the car, put them back again while he was drinking with Anton, because they weren't missing the next morning. So if your Kit *is* innocent, then that means someone else is framing him – or at the very least not coming forward to clear his name. And we don't know how far that person would go to stop the truth coming out, do we?'

There was no fireplace in the dining room. That was probably the only reason for the chill that went through Rosalind at his words.

Jack stood. 'Leave finding the truth to us, please, Rosalind. I promise we won't stop looking for it.'

He left the room, without a flounce or a last barb or even a huff. Leaving Rosalind sitting alone with her thoughts.

Caro

Filming resumed the next day, and Posy and Rosalind were on the first revised call sheet up at Tŷ Gwyn. Anton and his ADs had been frantically reworking the schedule to figure out which scenes they could film without Kit, and without a body double for Keira's last few appearances, which thankfully were minor and didn't involve lines.

Kit's absence was more of a problem, and Anton had seemed genuinely pleased about Caro's presence for the first time when she'd told him, the night before, that she might have found the evidence they needed to prove his innocence – as long as Anton was happy to stand as his alibi after he returned to the Seven Stars. Anton had agreed enthusiastically.

On another movie, Caro might have expected production to shut down for a couple of weeks after such a tragedy. But with everything that had delayed the making of this film so far, she wasn't all that surprised that Anton was ploughing on regardless.

Before they headed up to Tŷ Gwyn, the Dahlias snagged Seren and took her with them, handing her over to one of Anton's ADs, Harriet, as an unpaid intern. Caro didn't think she'd ever seen anyone so excited not to get paid.

They'd talked over what Jack had said the night before, but everyone had been too tired to make much progress. Now, Caro intended to get them back on subject.

'Okay, so we're not *actually* giving up on this investigation, right?' Caro swung her legs as she sat on the counter in the hair and makeup trailer, while Rosalind was aged up into an older version of herself as Hermione, and Posy was given pin curls and red lipstick to transform her into Dahlia.

'No. Of course not.' Rosalind's smile in the mirror didn't quite reach her eyes, though.

'I just can't believe it wasn't enough.' Posy stared down at the coffee cup in her hands as the hairdresser fussed with her curls. 'We proved he couldn't have done it, and it still wasn't enough.'

'It might be yet. Kit could be back here with us before you know it.' Caro nudged Rosalind and waggled her eyebrows to suggest she should also say something encouraging.

Instead, Rosalind said, 'Jack had a point.'

'Rosalind!' Caro groaned, as Posy looked up, furious.

'Oh, not about Kit.' Rosalind waved a hand to clear their objections. 'That someone might be trying to frame him. It seems clear that it was Kit's car that was used to kill Keira, which means that if Kit didn't do it, someone else must have.' She didn't add 'someone on the cast', but Caro knew they were all thinking it.

'And if we can find out who, that would *definitely* clear him,' Caro noted.

Posy had abandoned her coffee cup and was already scribbling down a list of names, much to the annoyance of the hairdresser trying to pin the waves of her hair.

Dominic

Gabriel

Nina
Tristan
Scarlett
Anton

'Better add Kit on there too – just for completeness,' Caro said.

Scowling, Posy wrote, *Kit*, then put down her pen. 'That's everybody.'

Except it wasn't, quite. Was it? She was missing something . . .

As the hair and make-up people worked, Caro mentally ran back over everyone she'd spoken to while the others were in London.

Mr Grey, of course. And Ben at the Drunken Dragon . . .

And Owain, back at the Seven Stars, the night Rosalind and Posy were away.

'Not quite,' she said. 'Add Owain and Rebecca on there.'

'Why?' Rosalind asked, as Posy wrote down the names.

Owain
Rebecca

Caro shrugged. 'Just a hunch. Probably they had nothing to do with it, but . . . they were both there, right? And when I asked Owain about the CCTV in the car park, he said it had been broken for ages but they hadn't got around to fixing it.'

'That's it?' Posy asked. 'Nothing else? He didn't see or hear anything that night?'

'Well . . . He said Rebecca sent him to bed early because he had a headache.' Caro gave them a meaningful look.

'So he could have sneaked out?' Rosalind said. 'Is that what we're thinking?'

'Opportunity,' Caro replied. 'And means, since it's his inn and no one would have questioned him being in the cloakroom or the car park. Motive is a mystery, though.'

'Still, someone else to consider,' Posy said, thoughtfully. 'The family flat is above the bar, right? He didn't see anything out the window on the road?'

'He said something about seeing a light on in one of the unfinished suites when he closed the curtains,' Caro remembered suddenly. 'But God knows if that means anything. I was going to ask him more, but then Rebecca dropped a whole tray of glasses and he hurried off to help her clear up.'

'What about Seren?' Posy asked. 'If we're being completists.'

'She's too young to drive,' Caro mused. 'Legally anyway.'

'She's also the only one with a real alibi,' Rosalind observed. 'She was up at the castle filming when Keira must have been killed, then staying at her aunt and uncle's. She never came back here that night.'

'As far as we know,' Caro said, remembering Aldermere. 'Put her on anyway. Just in case.'

Posy wrote, *Seren*, then put down her pen. 'That's it. That's everyone who could have been in the pub after Kit got back, to take his keys from his coat, drive the car, kill Keira, then put the car and the keys back where they belonged. Isn't it?'

Rosalind nodded, but Caro was staring into the distance, out the window of the trailer, thinking again.

'*Isn't* it?' Posy repeated.

Caro held up a finger. 'Hang on. I'm thinking. There's something . . .' It was just out of reach. A memory of something else someone had said, somewhere, in the last few days. Something to do with who could have been there . . .

She snapped her fingers. 'At the fundraiser, Bethan told me a story about some star-crossed lover types – a girl from the inn who fell for the son of the lord of the manor up at Tŷ Gwyn.'

'Unless you think her ghost can drive a car, I'm not entirely sure how that's relevant,' Rosalind commented drily.

'*Because* Bethan also said that they used to meet in some secret place that linked the inn with Tŷ Gwyn.'

'You think there's a secret passage between the house and Saith Seren?' Posy said, dubiously. 'I mean, I know Lettice Davenport loved a secret passageway in her mysteries, but how often do they really show up in real life?'

'It would explain how Brigette disappeared from the study,' Caro pointed out, not ready to give up on her new theory yet.

'Okay, but say it's there,' Posy said. 'What does that add to our list?'

'I'm not sure,' Caro admitted. 'But it's worth keeping in mind.' Maybe they'd even have to add Brigette to Posy's list. If this really was a Dahlia Lively mystery, it would probably turn out she'd been living in the secret passage ever since she disappeared, and was secretly behind it all.

'Rhian,' Rosalind said, suddenly. 'She wasn't at the fundraiser, but she could have been up at Tŷ Gwyn. Even without a secret passage, she could have crept in, couldn't she?'

Posy wrote *Rhian* at the end of her list, just as she and Rosalind were declared done by the hair and make-up team.

Outside the trailer, they strolled through the chaos of the film set, ignored for the most part by the crew. Caro spotted Seren helping Harriet, the third AD, with something and waved.

'Okay. So we've got our list of suspects. What do we do now?' Posy asked.

'We talk to them all,' Caro said, confidently. It was, after all, what Dahlia would do. 'Try to find out who Keira was meeting in the village that night.'

'And how are you intending to convince them to talk to us?' Rosalind asked.

That was a good point, not that Caro intended to admit it. Posing as a reporter or staff on the film had been fine for people who didn't know them. But it wouldn't work with the cast.

She tapped her fingers along her thigh as they followed the path around the side of the house. 'Well, if we succeed in convincing the police that Kit couldn't have done it, they'll be looking for someone else, right?'

'I guess,' Posy said, dubiously.

'So maybe we spread that fear a little bit,' Caro suggested. 'Get them worrying who'll be next. They'll be falling over each other to give us their alibis.'

Chapter Sixteen

Johnnie threw his pen across the desk in disgust. 'We simply have to narrow down the number of suspects in this case. Right now, it seems like any resident of London could be responsible.'

Dahlia retrieved his pen and threaded it through her fingers. 'That's because you're not looking closely enough, darling. If you pay proper attention, you'll see that there are actually only eight possible culprits.'

Dahlia Lively *in* Violet Murder
***By* Lettice Davenport, 1964**

Posy

They started with Nina, since Posy was due to film a scene with her that morning anyway. They found her in the wardrobe trailer, being stuck with pins by the wardrobe assistant as she adjusted Bess's maid outfit.

'While you're just standing there, do you mind if we ask you a few things?' Caro asked, then ploughed on without waiting for her to answer. 'Great. You see, we've found some evidence that suggests Kit couldn't possibly have been driving the car at the time Keira was killed.'

'At least, it's highly unlikely,' Rosalind put in, and Posy shot her a quick glare, which she ignored.

'I don't see . . .' Nina trailed off, her eyebrows knotted together in confusion.

Posy perched on the edge of the counter holding pins and threads and other sewing bobbins. 'We think the police are going to start to look more widely at who was where that night, and who might have taken out Kit's car without him knowing.'

'And you think they might suspect *me*?' Nina's incredulity shone through even though her voice stayed soft.

'Oh, no,' Caro said, unconvincingly. 'Not necessarily, anyway.'

It was enough. Nina's gaze darted between them nervously, and Posy knew she'd want a chance to prove her innocence – or at least stop any rumours before they started.

Rumours might not be evidence, but they were more than enough to bring a celebrity down. Everyone knew that.

'You left just after Keira that night, didn't you?' Posy didn't need to check her notes to know that. She'd been over the events of that night so many times in her head it was all stuck there, rolling like a movie. 'Did you see her leave Saith Seren?'

Nina shook her head, and the movement was obviously enough to shift the rest of her too, since she winced as the wardrobe assistant placed another pin. 'I just saw her go to her room.'

Because obviously she had to get changed out of her gown for the fundraiser.

'We think Keira might have gone out to meet somebody in the village, that night,' Caro said. 'And we're trying to figure out who.'

'Why would I know?' Nina looked away as she spoke.

The wardrobe assistant stood back. 'There we go. That should be more comfortable for you now. If you want to change out of it, I'll get the adjustments made.'

'Thanks.' Nina flashed her a grateful smile, before stepping behind a curtain to change.

'So. What did you *really* think of Keira?' Caro asked, in a conspiratorial tone that made Posy smile. Caro was such a gossip – which was incredibly useful for investigating.

Nina laughed over the rustle of her costume. 'I thought she was an entitled bitch. But that doesn't mean I didn't respect her, just a little bit.'

'Oh? And why was that?' Caro inched closer to the curtain.

'The entitled bitch bit? Or the respect?'

'Both,' Posy replied, promptly. Her notepad was out again, pen tapping against the page. If Nina was going to give them anything useful, she wanted it down in writing before they forgot any of it.

'The first is easy. She had her family name, her family money, and she knew how to use both to get anything she wanted – from men to friends to endorsements to acting roles.'

'Which one of those did she take from you?' Rosalind asked, getting straight to the heart of the matter. Posy supposed she knew exactly how their industry worked, after so many decades in it.

'None, really. I've mostly been doing theatre here in the UK before now, so it's not like we were competing for roles or anything. She just walked into her first job the moment she declared she wanted to try acting, as well as modelling. Same with this movie – the part was just given to her. I had three rounds of auditions before they offered me the role of Bess.'

'What about the respect part, then?' Posy considered Nina as she stepped back out from behind the curtain. 'What made you respect her?'

Nina paused before replying. 'Working with her on this movie . . . I mean, yes, she was as catty as anything, and always knew just where to stick the knife.' An interesting turn of phrase, under the circumstances. One that made Rosalind shudder, Posy noticed with a frown. 'But she was dedicated, all the same. Showed up, did the work. Bitched about it – and everyone else on the cast – but she took it seriously. And the other night . . . I saw her and Scarlett at the Drunken Dragon in the village, having some sort of girls' night I hadn't been invited to.'

Caro raised an eyebrow at that, but since Posy doubted that Nina had committed murder because she'd been left off an invite list for a night at the local pub, she just kept listening.

'Dominic was there, as always, and he'd had a few too many drinks.'

'As always,' Rosalind muttered.

'I was getting ready to leave, and was just coming back from the loos when I saw him cornering Scarlett against the wall at the bottom of the stairs.' Posy tried to remember the layout of the Drunken Dragon. The bathrooms were set back on the other side of the building from the bar, up a staircase, with at least two doors between the main bar area and them. Yes, it would be easy to get someone alone there, without being noticed. 'He was just talking, as far as I could see, but she was obviously uncomfortable. He was crowding her body, imposing on her. You know what I mean?'

They all nodded at that – even the wardrobe assistant. Posy figured they'd all been there. She knew she had.

'I was about to head down and interrupt,' Nina went on. 'You know, make a lot of noise, get him to back off naturally so Scarlett could get out of there. I mean, Dominic's a big name, you don't take him on without consequences, but he's been there before with the accusations, right?'

'He was lucky to come back from the last lot,' Caro agreed. 'But then, that's always easier for men, isn't it?'

Nina nodded. 'I knew he'd claim he wasn't doing anything anyway, just talking. But he'd leave, at least, I hoped.' Posy wished she didn't know exactly what Nina meant. 'But then Keira came storming through the doors from the pub. I don't know if someone else had told her what was happening, or Scarlett phoned her without Dominic noticing, or if she just got suspicious when Scarlett was gone so long. But she walked in ready for a fight, so I stayed where I was and watched.'

'What did she do?' Posy's eyes were wide with anticipation.

Nina gave a small, sad smile. 'What I wished I'd had the courage to do. She shoved him aside and said, "Just because you can't go after me because of my family and my connections, doesn't mean I'm going to let you go after anyone else either." Then she grabbed Scarlett's arm and dragged her out of there.'

'What did Dominic do?' Caro asked.

'Nothing. I mean, what *could* he do? Keira was right. He'd never try anything on with her because of who her parents are, and because the world would listen and believe her. They might even choose her over him. He'd never risk that.' Nina sighed. 'So, he dusted himself off, and walked back out there as if nothing had happened. I mean, I guess for him nothing really had. Nothing changed, I mean, did it?'

'No. Nothing changed,' Posy agreed, softly.

Sometimes, it felt like nothing ever would.

Rosalind

'We need to talk to Dominic,' Caro said, as they made their way down the metal steps of the wardrobe trailer.

'He's not on set today.' Rosalind clung onto the hand rail as she descended. 'He'll have to wait until we get back to the Seven Stars.'

'And I need to get on set before Anton sends someone to fetch me,' Posy added, hopping down the last of the steps behind them both. 'What are you two going to do while I'm filming?'

'Since Dominic's not here, maybe I'll try and find Scarlett,' Caro said. 'See if she backs up what Nina told us about Keira and Dominic. And if I get a chance, I'd like to talk to Gabriel too, since he was the one we know was arguing with Dominic the night of Keira's death.' She turned to Rosalind. 'What about you? Want to come with me?'

Rosalind was needed later in the day for a scene with Posy and Nina, as well as Gabriel and Scarlett. But until then, her time was her own.

And she had a secret passageway to prove – or disprove – the existence of.

'I want to search the study again,' she said. 'See if I can find any evidence of this secret passage of yours.' Maybe it wasn't the most important part of the puzzle, but it was a loose end, and Rosalind hated those.

The day of Brigette's disappearance felt like the day it all started. She'd found that first note tucked into her script when she returned to her seat after they all went to watch Rhian unlock the door. And since then . . .

Well. Maybe solving one small mystery could lead to them solving all the others.

The three Dahlias split up, and Rosalind ducked past cameras and crew to reach the study off the main hallway from where Brigette had disappeared – fortunately not the setting for any filming that day.

She shut the door quietly behind her – checking that the small key was on her side of the door, just in case Rhian had been right about them locking themselves, somehow. Then she stood in the centre of the room and tried to put herself in Brigette's shoes – or mind. What had happened that day? What did they actually *know*?

Rosalind had seen Brigette going into the study, same as everyone else. They'd assumed she must have slipped out again when no one was looking, but it was hard to imagine when. Anton and the others had been passing through the entrance hall on their way to the table read, and would have called out to her to join them if they'd seen her. And when Rhian had unlocked it, there had been too many of them cramming in for her to slip out once the door was open.

So maybe Caro was right. There was another way out of this room.

Slowly, Rosalind turned in a circle, her gaze taking in all the details of the study. Bookcases – they often held a secret door in movies. Or the painting over the fire, although they more often hid safes, in her experience as Dahlia. What else? The window seat? Could that conceal a passageway?

She was half-heartedly pulling books off the shelf, looking for the one that might work a lever to reveal a whole different room behind the fireplace, aware that Caro had probably already done the same thing, when another thought occurred to her.

How would *Brigette* have known about any secret passage in the first place? How would anybody? According to Caro even Bethan only knew of a rumour that there was some hidden meeting place linked to the Seven Stars. It seemed unlikely that Brigette would have just stumbled across it.

But who *would* know?

She paused, hands on the desk, and considered.

Their location scouts might, but they hadn't been on site that day. Perhaps they had told her? But if they were telling people, surely the story would have got around more? And it obviously hadn't.

But the one person who *would* know, if anyone did, was the house manager – Rhian Hassan. When they'd been introduced on their first day, Rosalind remembered suddenly, Rhian had told them that if they had any questions about Tŷ Gwyn at all, her office was back by the kitchens . . .

'A secret passageway?' Rhian's eyebrows rose politely. 'Whatever gave you that idea?'

Rosalind began to regret accosting the house manager at her desk. No, mostly she was regretting listening to Caro's crazy hidden-tunnel idea. She should have left Caro to do this, and *she* could have gone to question Gabriel and Scarlett instead. 'I appreciate it sounds a little . . . outlandish.'

Rhian gave a light laugh. 'No, I was just . . .' Her smile faded, her eyes suddenly serious. 'Is this about the day Brigette Laugharne left? Are you thinking she used a secret passageway to escape?' Something in her voice caught at Rosalind's investigative mind.

She eased herself into the chair opposite Rhian's desk. 'I'm wondering . . . if there was something she was *trying* to escape. And if you might have some idea what that was.'

The way that Rhian shifted in her seat told Rosalind she did. 'Not really. It was just . . .' Rosalind waited. The easiest way to get people to talk, she'd always found, was not to fill the silence for them. 'I saw her talking with someone, the day of the table read, just before she, well, disappeared. Then she answered her phone, and I watched her walk into the study to take the call.'

'But you didn't see her walk out again.'

'I wasn't looking for it.' Rhian's cheeks were pink with indignation. 'It's still more likely that she slipped out unnoticed than escaped down some legendary secret passage, isn't it?'

'Legendary? Does that mean you *have* heard the story of the secret passage?'

'Well, yes. Obviously.' Irritation crossed Rhian's face. 'There's a whole section about it in the new guidebook we're developing, about the links with Saith Seren. But if any tunnel ever really existed, it must have been sealed up or bricked over years ago. I've worked here for three years, been in that study hundreds of times and never seen a single sign of it.'

She pulled a file over from the side of her desk, opening it and focusing on the paper inside with the single-mindedness that told Rosalind she was dismissed.

She wasn't going to get anything more here. Rosalind creaked to her feet and moved towards the door, only pausing as she stood on the threshold to the hallway outside.

'Can I ask you just one more thing, Rhian?'

The house manager looked up, and gave her a reluctant nod. 'What?'

'How would you say Brigette looked, when she took that call?'

A small, snide smile. 'Honestly? Relieved to get away from Keira Reynolds-Yang.'

Rosalind walked away, thinking how everything seemed to come back to Keira again.

Then she stopped, stock still, in the centre of the hallway, barely aware of the crew member who had to swerve suddenly to avoid her, as another thought struck.

She hadn't received a death threat since Keira had died.

Caro

Caro didn't remember there being any swordplay in the original novel of *The Lady Detective*, which might have been why it took her a while to find Gabriel and Scarlett. But when she finally ventured into the gardens at the back of Tŷ Gwyn, there was Gabriel, a thin cage mask over his face, a fencing rapier in his left hand, trading parries and blows with another man.

They both wore the thick, padded white jackets and masks she associated with fencing, but not the full body whites – which was probably just as well for the costume department. Their shoes and jeans were already soaked with dew.

She wouldn't have recognised Gabriel if it hadn't been for his voice; he was shouting mock insults at his opponent that had Scarlett, sitting on the sidelines watching, in stitches.

'You scurvy knave!' Gabriel called. 'You black-hearted brigand!'

'Who are you calling a *brigand*?' his opponent called back, and Caro instantly recognised the laughter in his voice, too. Tristan.

'Did I forget a sword fight in this story?' Caro asked, hopping up to sit on the low garden wall beside Scarlett. She had to wonder at the sense of having *more* weapons on a set where someone had already almost been stabbed.

'Isn't there one in the book?' Scarlett blinked at her, with a blank expression. 'There's definitely one in the script.'

They'd chosen one of the lawns of a large, walled garden for their fencing bout, hidden away from the main house. The sun hadn't quite reached all of the lawn yet and, even where it had, sprinkles of frost still remained, and it crunched underfoot as they fought.

Finally, Gabriel disarmed his opponent with a flashy move that made them both laugh. Tristan put up his hands in the universal gesture of surrender, and they both pulled off their masks before heading over to where Scarlett and Caro were sitting.

'So, does Dahlia's cousin challenge her ex-fiancé over her besmirched honour in Anton's version of *The Lady Detective*, or what?' Caro asked, while Gabriel and Tristan gulped down icy water from the bottles sitting on the wall.

Gabriel shook his head, sending droplets of sweat flying from his hair, despite the icy chill. She was surprised they hadn't frozen to his mask. 'Not exactly. He just thought that there was an awful lot of sitting around drinking tea and asking questions in the story.'

'It is a hallmark of a Dahlia Lively mystery,' Caro admitted. 'The cakes are usually good, too.'

'Yes, well, Anton thought it would be good to imbue it with a bit more . . . action. So he asked Libby to turn one of the investigative scenes into a fencing bout. So Dahlia and Johnnie are asking Charles and Bertie questions while they practise fencing, you see.'

'It's a visual representation of the way they're both fighting over me – I mean, my character, Rose – in the story,' Scarlett said. Caro suspected she was quoting Anton directly.

'Gabriel and I have both done loads of fight training for other projects,' Tristan added. 'So we figured we'd see if we could figure out some choreography for the fight between ourselves.'

'Oh, so *that's* why you lost.' Caro smiled, knowingly. 'Because that was the choreography.'

'That's my story.' Tristan smirked back at her. 'And I'm sticking to it.'

'Want to go again?' Gabriel asked. 'See if you can beat me this time?'

Tristan slammed his mask back into place. 'You're on!'

Caro jumped down from the wall and followed them towards the grass, aware of Scarlett trailing behind her. 'Actually, I was hoping I could ask you all some questions, while I have you?'

Tristan shrugged. 'Sure. It'll be good practice for the actual scene.'

'Questions about what?' Gabriel asked. 'And why?'

'About Keira, mostly,' Caro admitted. 'It seems the police now have evidence that Kit couldn't have been the one driving the car when she was killed, so they're going to be looking for other suspects.'

'Meaning all of us,' Gabriel guessed, and Caro nodded.

'I know Anton's really worried about more disruption to the film,' she went on, thinking on her feet. 'So I thought we might be able to help by figuring out some stuff between ourselves, to save time. Don't you think?' She didn't give them time to disagree. 'For instance, it looks like Keira was supposed to be meeting someone at the Drunken Dragon in the village that night, so we're trying to find out who, in case it's connected.'

'Meeting someone?' Tristan moved smoothly into the *en garde* position. 'She said she was going to bed.'

'Because Keira never lied,' Gabriel murmured, before pulling down his own mask.

She wanted to ask him more about that comment, but he quickly moved away to take up his own position. Caro got the impression he hadn't meant her to overhear, and she didn't want to spook him by pushing too hard, too fast.

'You and Keira were friends, weren't you, Tristan?' Caro asked.

Gabriel thrust towards Tristan, and he parried before replying. 'Yeah. I'd known Keira for years. We worked together on a few episodes of this edgy teen show a few years back – you won't remember it. *Cases*?' He was right. Caro didn't remember it.

Tristan launched his own attack now, forcing Gabriel back a few steps. 'Anyway, we stayed in touch. It was when Keira was going through her "I can make it on my own without my family name" phase, and trying acting for the first time, as Keira Buckley, I think. Before she went back to modelling and using her real name again. We even ended up sharing a flat for a while, before her family convinced her that a life of comfort and automatically opening doors was more fun.'

Now *that* was interesting. 'So you knew her when she was dating Kit?'

Gabriel came back on the attack, and it took a few fast flurries of the foils before Tristan gained enough breathing room to answer. 'I did. I mean, that was later, and they were both in kind of a different circle of fame by then, as you can imagine. But we kept in touch. I went to a few parties with them both, that sort of thing.'

'And how were they as a couple?' Caro couldn't quite imagine them together, even though she'd seen the photos.

'Honestly? They didn't bring out the best in each other. You know? Individually, they were both lovely people—'

Gabriel gave a small snort at that, even as he lunged forward again with his foil. 'You have to be one of the only people in the world who'd call Keira Reynolds-Yang "lovely". I mean, I admired the hell out of her for a lot of things, but she wasn't exactly a . . . you know.'

'Kind to animals and children type?' Caro suggested, and Gabriel nodded.

Tristan laughed, as he sidestepped another thrust from his opponent. 'Okay, maybe that's the wrong word. You're right – she wasn't Snow White. But she wouldn't have got where she did if she was. I mean, lots of people say she only got opportunities because of her family and her face, but that's not true. She worked damn hard for all of it. And in this business . . .'

'Being kind doesn't get you very far,' Caro finished for him.

'Exactly. But she was a good friend to me. A few years back . . . I lost someone close to me. My roommate, actually. And Keira was there for me.' He shrugged. 'Maybe I just saw a side of her others didn't.'

Interesting. Caro had pegged Tristan as being close to Nina, but hadn't really banked on him being a friend of Keira's too. But then,

Tristan was a friendly, extroverted sort. He seemed to have no problems making friends wherever he went.

'Well, I guess we can assume that Kit did too, since he dated her for so long. What about you, Gabriel?' Caro asked. 'Did you know Keira well?'

Tristan lunged forward and Gabriel had to jump back out of the way, narrowly avoiding the tip of Tristan's foil touching his jacket. 'Never met her before this movie,' he said, his breath starting to come fast.

'Really? That surprises me.' She watched him carefully as he launched into an overeager attack. 'I was sure I heard you talking with her, my first day on set, and you sounded . . . well acquainted.'

'You get to know people fast on a movie set,' Gabriel replied, his eyes never leaving his opponent's foil.

'Yes, but Posy also heard you talking to Dominic *about* her, the night she was killed.'

Gabriel didn't fumble this time, or show any sign of hearing her at all as he parried and riposted, until Tristan was forced back with the tip of Gabriel's foil pressed to his chest.

He stepped back, and pulled up his mask.

'She must have been mistaken,' he said, through panting breaths. 'I talked to Dominic that night, yes – I heard him staggering around out in the courtyard and went to check he was all right.'

'And was he?'

'Drunk, mostly. And Dom's a horrible drunk, everyone knows that. Started bringing up past grievances – you know, the sort of thing everyone else forgot years ago.'

'Posy told me Dom said something about Brigette, too.' Time to give up on subtle. 'Something to do with her disappearance?'

Gabriel scoffed as he stalked past her, towards the water bottles on the wall. 'I think calling it a disappearance is a bit much, don't you?

Brigette always did know when her horse was losing, and she's a pro at getting out before anything hits any air-conditioning devices, if you know what I mean. And she always used to like a bit of drama, too – I'd bet she still does.' Gabriel sounded fond of Dominic's ex-wife – certainly fonder than he was of Dominic, by all accounts. 'She'd have been a wonderful actress, but there was only room for one diva in that marriage. No, you mark my words. She'll be lying low somewhere, waiting for the storm to pass.'

'What storm, exactly?' Gabriel knew something – a lot more than he was saying, if Caro had to guess. But how to get it out of him? That was the question.

Gabriel gave her a long, assessing look, then glanced at Tristan and Scarlett before answering. 'That's what we'll have to wait and find out, isn't it? Brigette always was a much better forecaster than the rest of us. It's what makes her such a great casting director. She knows who the next star the world will love is before they do.'

He picked up his water bottle and his foil, and headed for the house, leaving Caro staring after him, wondering. Was Brigette the key to all of this after all?

Chapter Seventeen

'There's always a link, Bess.' Dahlia tapped the three faded photographs on the desk in front of her. 'Even when you can't quite see it yet, there's always *a link somewhere, waiting to be discovered.*'

Dahlia Lively *in* **A Very Lively Christmas**
***By* Lettice Davenport, 1943**

Rosalind

By the time Anton called it a day for filming, the bright skies of that morning were a dull grey and rain was threatening. The mood on set had declined, too, after some difficult scenes that took too long to shoot. By the end, their eccentric director's famous temper had definitely started to fray.

Rosalind, Caro and Posy huddled together under the stone porch at the front of Tŷ Gwyn, waiting for the transport to take them back down the road to the Seven Stars, rather than risking getting soaked on the walk. Besides, at the gates, they could see a gaggle of reporters and TV cameras, filming despite the weather, and Rosalind knew they'd all rather not walk that gauntlet again. The number of security guards seemed to have increased too, she noted.

'So, what have we learned today?' Caro asked, cheerfully.

'That Tristan is *never* going to get that line right in the parlour scene,' Posy grumbled.

'And that it really does always rain in Wales,' Rosalind added.

'I meant about the *murder*.' Caro dropped her voice on the last word, as some of the crew hurried past, trying to get equipment between the house and the trucks without it getting too wet.

Rosalind sighed. 'We know. It's just hard to think in this weather.'

'And with Kit still accused of something he didn't do,' Posy said.

What, exactly, *was* going on between Posy and Kit, Rosalind wondered? They'd seemed to have become friends since last summer, but she hadn't got the feeling that things had progressed any further, despite the gossip online. But now she wasn't so sure.

Something to ask Posy about, once they'd got Kit out of jail, perhaps.

'Well, I can confirm that Scarlett corroborated everything Nina told us,' Caro said. 'And this is what I got from Gabriel and Tristan . . .'

She filled them in as they drove back to the inn, while Rosalind and Posy listened in grumpy silence, even the transport splashing the reporters not cheering them up. But the sight of Jack's car parked outside lightened the mood considerably. Or rather, not the car itself, but the man getting out of it . . .

'Kit!' Posy was off the bus and at his side in seconds, Caro not far behind. Rosalind followed at a rather more sedate pace.

'They let you go, then?' Caro asked, as Posy embraced him.

'Late last night. But obviously I didn't have my car and I . . . I just needed a few hours to process everything. So I checked into a hotel in the town and then Jack offered to drive me back today.' Kit pressed a kiss to the top of Posy's head and let her step away. 'And I understand my freedom is all thanks to you three!'

Leaning against the driver's side, Jack cleared his throat. 'That's not *entirely* true.'

'Isn't it?' Rosalind asked, eyebrows raised. 'Then why *are* you letting him go?'

'I'm just playing chauffeur,' Jack said. 'But I understand that Mr Lewis's lawyer pointed out that, since there was now video evidence of the victim alive *after* he returned to the pub that night—'

'Thanks to us,' Caro put in. 'And Seren.'

'And since Kit has an alibi for the hours after that—'

'Also me,' Caro said. 'And Anton.'

'And since the time of death is most likely to have been soon after Keira was seen at the Drunken Dragon, and Kit's car keys were easily accessible to everyone in Saith Seren after his return that night,' Jack continued regardless, 'there was not enough evidence to apply to continue to hold him without charge any longer. As such, he has been released under investigation, but asked not to leave the vicinity.'

Something that had been niggling at the back of Rosalind's brain jumped to the front.

'I'd have thought that, if you had Keira's phone, you might have been able to find out who she was meeting by now, and who she called to say she was leaving.' Rosalind carefully didn't look directly at Jack. 'If you had it.'

Jack stepped forward, taking a light hold of her elbow as he turned her away from the rest of the group and spoke in a low whisper. 'Swear to God, Rosalind, if you know where the victim's phone is you need to tell us now, or—'

'I don't,' Rosalind replied. 'And, from your reaction, I assume that neither do the police.'

He let her go, stumbling back a step and staring at her. Then his jaw tightened, and he spoke in a clipped voice. 'I would appreciate it if you did not use our friendship, and my concern about your well-being, to further your ill-advised investigation from now on.'

With that, he turned on his heel, got back into his car and drove away.

Rosalind watched him go, thinking hard.

'Rosalind? Are you coming?' Posy asked. 'We're going to get in out of the weather and have a celebratory drink with Kit.'

'And find out what he picked up at the police station,' Caro added, from her other side.

'Yes. I'm coming.' She took one last look down Dark Lane, then followed them into the pub. They'd get their information from Kit, not Jack, for now.

And then . . . then they still needed to have a word with Dominic Laugharne.

But Dominic didn't appear in the bar at the Seven Stars to celebrate Kit's return, or for dinner. Rosalind might have thought he'd gone down to the Drunken Dragon instead, except the rain hadn't let up and Dominic didn't have a car with him, and she didn't think the scampi and chips at the village pub were worth getting that drenched for, even for Dominic.

Still, she kept an eye on the road outside, through the front window, while Kit filled them in on everything that had happened since he was arrested.

'They told me they've got forensics going over the car.' He took another swig of his pint, like he'd been locked up for years instead of hours. 'I don't know how much it'll tell them, though. I mean, if it was my car that hit her, anyone could have taken my keys from my coat that night then slipped them back again while I was drinking with Anton. And half the cast has been in and out of my car getting lifts into the village and back since we got here. But if it was someone else – a local or something – maybe they can find some evidence that helps.'

'It sounds like they're pretty sure you didn't do it.' The eagerness in Posy's voice didn't quite match the wry expression on Kit's face.

'Or that it was too much bother to ask a magistrate to let them keep me longer right now,' he said. 'I'm certain they'll still be looking for evidence against me. And if they think it was deliberate, well . . . they won't have to look very far.'

'Keira was your ex,' Rosalind said, mostly so Posy didn't have to. 'We heard things were . . . volatile between the two of you?'

'Not when we were together.' Kit sighed. 'Have you ever had one of those relationships that you sort of fell into because everybody thought you *should* be together?' They all nodded. Thankfully he didn't ask for details. Rosalind didn't fancy revisiting her marriage right now. 'It was like that. One day we were just co-stars, the next . . .'

'You were the new it-couple,' Caro finished for him.

'But you were together for almost two years, on and off,' Posy said. 'It must have been more than that.'

Kit shrugged. 'It was. I mean, it *became* more. I liked her. Underneath all that armour, and her name, she was . . . someone else, I guess. Someone I . . . I don't know if I loved her, exactly. But I cared about her. I loved being with her, at least most of the time. But then other times – usually when she'd been back to spend time with her family, or I'd been away filming – she'd get . . . different.'

'Jealous?' Rosalind asked. Frank had never been jealous. She'd wondered about that. Whether he'd known the truth about her and Hugh and just never let on, for fear of losing what they'd had together.

Kit shook his head. 'That was part of it, maybe – I mean, we all know that long-distance relationships aren't easy, and when your partner is off filming with beautiful men or women and kissing them for work every day . . . that's hard. And the closeness, the bonds that form on set . . . I mean, that was how Keira and *I* got together. It happens, and yeah, maybe she was worried about that. But that wasn't all of it.'

'What else?' Posy had shifted her chair a little, Rosalind noticed. Nothing big, but whereas she'd been sitting right up close to Kit before, now she was angled slightly away, a few more inches between them.

'It was like she was a different person. A harder one. Like any of the walls I'd broken through had been rebuilt when I was away. She'd pick fights, talk down to me, accuse me of stuff I hadn't done . . . in the end, I was just done with it all. So I walked away.'

'But that wasn't the end of it. Was it?' Caro said. Rosalind wondered what gossip rags she'd been reading now.

'It should have been. And honestly, at the time, she seemed fine. Like, it was a perfectly amicable break-up.' He looked helplessly up at them all. 'Then she went on that talk show and started accusing me of cheating, of lying, saying I was emotionally unavailable . . . and I don't know where any of it came from. Like, at all.'

'What did you do?' Posy asked, softly. Rosalind could hear the pain in her voice – for him, or for the younger version of herself, who'd suffered the same sort of public humiliation.

'Kept my head down and hoped it would go away. That people would get bored of the story.'

'And they did,' Caro said. 'They always do, eventually, if you don't engage. There's too much other gossip in the world to get on with.'

Rosalind hid a smile when she thought of Caro gleefully stoking the gossip a little longer when her own husband had left her for another woman. Everyone had their own way of dealing with these things, of course – and Caro's style was definitely more 'do as I tell you, not as I do'.

But she couldn't help but think of the reporters outside Tŷ Gwyn, and the security guard Anton had added at the Seven Stars to keep the paparazzi out. It was hard to imagine this just blowing over anytime soon.

'Keira went off to some retreat or another, and came back totally over it and ready to flaunt her newest romance,' Kit said, with a shrug. 'And I just got back to work.'

Rosalind tried to picture the Keira Kit had described – a woman capable of intense emotion, of anger and rage, but also of love and kindness. Wait. Wasn't that *all* women?

Was a turbulent relationship and unhappy break-up a reason to commit murder? Well, yes – such had been proven over and again in the courts. But she didn't believe it was enough for *Kit* to kill – especially for a relationship that had been over for years.

She left Posy and Kit sitting together by the fire, and made her way back to her suite, Caro following.

'I had a thought today,' Caro said, as she dropped onto her daybed and kicked her shoes off into the middle of the floor.

Rosalind picked up the shoes and stacked them neatly by the door. 'Just the one?'

'Have you received any notes in the last few days?' Caro asked. 'Say, since Keira died?'

'No.' Rosalind straightened and turned to look at her friend. 'I had the same realisation earlier, actually.'

'Hmm.' Caro drummed her fingers along the metal bed frame. 'Was Keira on set the day the knife was swapped? I can't remember seeing her.'

'She was on set, somewhere. In fact, she was supposed to be the one stabbing me first, but they got swapped at the last minute because . . . I think it was because she was late, so was still in hair and make-up.' She met Caro's gaze. 'Do you think that's significant?'

She didn't want to admit to the small bubble of hope forming in her chest. That if Keira was behind the threats on her life, it was over now.

'I don't know. But I don't think we can rule out the possibility,' Caro said, more serious than Rosalind was used to seeing her. 'Do you?'

Posy

The sun – such as it was – hadn't fully risen over the sea the next morning when Posy, Tristan, Kit and Nina stumbled onto the sand of the nearest photogenic beach to Glan y Wern to film a scene together. Their call time had been insanely early, and hair, make-up and costumes had been done in a blur of coffee. Unsurprisingly, Caro and Rosalind had not been up in time to say goodbye before she left, but she had woken up to a strange text message from Caro, sent the night before.

Try and find out if Kit received any threatening notes before Keira's death.

She had no idea what that meant, and she didn't expect her brain to be functioning at a high enough level to figure it out for another few hours.

'Bet you wish you'd stayed in custody a few more days, huh, mate?' Tristan muttered to Kit as they all sipped yet more coffee.

Posy pulled her padded coat closer over her Dahlia costume. She hated early shoots.

'Right!' Anton approached them, rubbing his hands together with purpose – or to ward off frostbite, Posy wasn't sure. 'This is going to be amazing! The light is just . . . aren't you blown away by it? Only thing is, we've not got long before the sun will be too high and we'll lose that gorgeous dawn feeling, so we need to nail it first time.'

'Yes, boss,' Tristan said, with a nod, as if he were their dedicated spokesman. Which maybe he was. No one else seemed awake enough to deal with Anton's early morning enthusiasm. Posy thought she might have actually fallen asleep again, just standing up. Still, if she got through today, they had a whole weekend off. The cast had worried that Anton would add extra days to the schedule over the weekend to make up time, but it seemed like there were enough crew members with pre-existing commitments for the time that it wouldn't work, so the weekend off had stayed.

Posy had big plans to sleep. And maybe investigate. But mostly sleep.

Once she'd got through this scene . . .

Posy was pretty sure there weren't any beach scenes in the book of *The Lady Detective*, the same as there wasn't any fencing. But Anton had decided that the deserted sands less than an hour's drive from the village of Glan y Wern were the perfect place for Dahlia and Charles to be taking a walk at sunrise – with Bess as chaperone, of course – only for DI Johnnie to show up and interrupt.

The original script had the walk at lunchtime, Posy was certain. But Anton really, really liked that early morning light. Apparently it fitted his vision.

'Now, remember. Tristan, Charles is trying to win Dahlia back – even though the audience know it's for nefarious means. Nina, Bess is trying to tell Dahlia – subtly – that they're about to have company. And Kit—'

'I'm just here for the investigation,' Kit interrupted. 'Nothing to do with distracting the lovely Dahlia from her worthless ex-fiancé.' The smile he flashed her way left Posy – and the others – in no doubt that Johnnie was *absolutely* there to steal Dahlia away. Even if he didn't fully admit to it for another seven books.

'Perfect!' Anton ran a hand through his already rumpled hair. 'Right, let's try and run a rehearsal. Tristan, you and Posy are going to walk along the edge of the water here . . .' He jumped across the sand, dodging seaweed, to show where he meant. 'Nina, you'll follow them at a discreet distance.' He skipped back, then walked the line again, as if he were Nina that time. Then he continued along the shoreline, the waves already washing away his footprints behind him. 'Then you two will walk down this way – try to hit the "not in this lifetime or the next" line as you're standing here, Posy, with the cliffs behind framing you and – hopefully – the sun rising. Then Kit, you'll come up from this side of the beach just in time to hear her say that, okay? Right. Let's try it.'

The cameras were already set up – Posy dreaded to think what time the crew had needed to get up to be there on time, and deal with the sinking sand, especially since they were staying so much further away. They ran through the scene once then, with the sun inching ever higher, Anton called for them to do it for real.

'And . . . action!' he called, probably waking up some of the sleepier inhabitants of the nearest village with his cry.

Dahlia. I am Dahlia.

She stepped forward, chin up, keeping a space between her and Tristan – no, Charles – as she walked. The seawater lapped at her boots, and she wondered how the sound crew were coping with the seagulls overhead and the crash of the waves further out.

'All I'm saying, Dahlia, is that it makes sense,' Tristan said, a condescending smile on his face. Charles probably thought that was friendly. Endearing. Seductive, even. 'You've always been the sensible sort, and I admire that about you. So you have to admit, you and me, together again . . . it makes sense.'

She didn't look at him as she replied, staring instead past the cameras to the hills beyond, and a ruined castle perched on the edge of a far-off cliff. 'Do you remember the reasons I gave when I broke off our engagement, Charles?'

'Well, yes. Of course I do,' Tristan said, making it very clear that Charles had no recollection of such things at all. 'But things have changed, haven't they?'

'Have they?' They were almost at the point Anton had specified. There was a conveniently placed rock to mark it. 'Seems to me the only thing that's changed is that you're suddenly even more frantic to get your hands on my uncle's money, and you seem to believe I'm your best chance of doing that.'

'Dahlia!' Tristan gave a notably desperate laugh. 'You always were such a joker, too. You know I've always loved you.'

Out of the corner of her eye, Posy could see Kit coming down the beach, as cued, but pretended not to notice. Behind Tristan, Nina was trying to catch her eye and pointing, but she ignored that too.

She hit her mark, felt the sun rising over the cliffs behind her, and looked Tristan dead in the eye. With one foot pointed out, a hand on her hip, and one eyebrow ever so slightly higher than the other, she said, 'Charles, if you only understand one thing about me, let it be this. I will not marry you. Not in this lifetime, or the next. Are we clear?'

Tristan stared at her, mouth slightly open, eyes buggy, the perfect image of upper-class expectation and entitlement gone awry. And behind her, Kit cleared his throat.

'Ah . . . Mr Baizey? Miss Lively? I wondered if I could just ask you both a few questions.'

The scene flowed into the investigative part, with Kit asking questions of Tristan, but looking to Posy for more informative answers when Tristan failed to give them. Already, even quite early on in the script, there was a fun, flirty undercurrent between Dahlia and Johnnie that she liked.

Finally, Anton called cut on the scene, and declared it good – either because it was or because there was no time left to do anything about it, anyway. If he hated it when he watched it back they'd either be called back out here some other freezing morning, or the scene would be trimmed or cut in edits.

But Posy felt in her chilled bones that it was good. She wrapped her padded coat back over her costume, and returned the smile of a passing crew member.

She'd been Dahlia, in that scene. For real.

Now she just needed to be her in real life, too.

Starting by asking Caro's question for her.

Posy caught up to Kit again as they all headed for the cars to take them back to Tŷ Gwyn.

'Hey!' He gave her a warm smile. 'That was good. Really good. Don't you think?'

'Yeah. I think it was.' She returned the smile, before letting it fall. 'Listen, Caro wanted me to ask you something. I guess she's still working on finding extra evidence to clear your name – or perhaps who might want to frame you.'

'I hadn't thought of it like that,' Kit admitted. 'I just figured my car was the most convenient. And, well, it is kind of awesome. I could see someone borrowing it and taking it out for a joyride, then panicking after the accident and just putting the keys back where they found them.'

Posy had to admit, it seemed the most likely explanation. At least, it would, if she didn't know everything else that was going on. 'You're probably right. But you know Caro . . . She wanted to know if, well, if you'd received any strange notes or threats or anything, before Keira died.'

'Notes?' Kit sounded puzzled. 'You mean, like . . .'

So much for subtle. 'Death threats. So, did you?'

Kit recoiled at the suggestion. 'Hell, no. Why? Has someone been sending them to you? Posy—'

'No, no, nothing like that.' She forced a weak smile. 'Like I said. Just Caro pursuing all investigative avenues. Oh, look. I think the cars are ready.'

She hurried off in their direction, ignoring the confused look on Kit's face as she went. She wanted to get back to Tŷ Gwyn and get this day over with – and find out what new theory Caro and Rosalind had come up with now.

Rosalind

With Posy and the others filming off-site that morning, Rosalind took the opportunity for a lie-in before heading up to Tŷ Gwyn in good time for her hair and make-up call. By the time she was done, Posy and the others had returned, ready for the rest of the day's shooting. There was still no sign of Dominic, though.

Filming seemed to go fast – whether because Rosalind was distracted with thoughts of murder, or because Anton was hurrying them along to make up time, she wasn't sure. Once she was done, she headed to craft services for a coffee, and found Posy and Caro there waiting for her – along with Seren.

'What is that?' Rosalind asked, gesturing to the badge pinned to Posy's coat, which was draped over the shoulders of her Dahlia costume. Tent-like structures had been put up around the grounds, with temporary flooring, to keep the actors – and more importantly, their costumes, hair and make-up – protected from the weather. Rosalind imagined Anton was grateful not many of the scenes took place outside – the ones that did already involved an awful lot of luck and checking of the forecast. Which was why poor Posy had been dragged from her bed at some ungodly hour that morning.

'Seren made it,' Posy said with a grin. 'Caro's got one too.'

Caro showed off her own badge where it shone brightly on her own jacket.

The badges were about the size of a ten-pence piece, shiny, and had the letters WWDD printed in a cream font on a bright background – red in Caro's case, blue for Posy.

'I made one for you too, of course.' Seren handed Rosalind her own gold-coloured badge. 'Auntie Bethan has this machine in the shop that the kids can use for a pound a turn, to make their own badges. I thought this one might help you all with your investigation. You can just ask WWDD?'

Posy, obviously recognising Rosalind's bafflement, took pity on her. 'What Would Dahlia Do? You see?'

'Of course.' Rosalind did not see how a badge with a meaningless acronym on it would help solve a murder, but she smiled all the same. 'Thank you, Seren.'

'It's nothing.' Seren shrugged, ducking her chin as if suddenly embarrassed by the childishness of her offering. But Rosalind did notice that she was wearing her own green version, pinned to her dungarees.

What would Dahlia do? Maybe that *was* the question they needed to be asking more.

Dahlia wouldn't be sitting around waiting for Dominic to come to her for questioning, that much was for sure.

'We need to find Dominic,' she said, and Posy and Caro both nodded.

'Leave Dominic to me,' a voice said behind them, and Rosalind turned to find Anton there. 'Trust me, I want to speak to him just as much as you do. But first, we've got the photographer from that magazine on set to take some photos so, ladies, it's time to go and smile nicely for the cameras please. Not you, Caro,' he added, before she could ask. His eyebrows dropped into a frown as he spotted Seren. 'Wait. Who are you?'

'Local intern,' Seren said brightly. 'Ask Harriet.'

'Right.' He didn't look convinced, but Rosalind suspected Seren was right to guess that he'd forget about her before he next spoke to his AD about anything other than filming logistics. 'Okay. Inside, please. Now.'

'Is that really appropriate?' Caro asked, as they headed back into the main hallway. 'A photo shoot right now, I mean? When somebody in it could be a murderer?'

'It's a Welsh crime-fiction magazine and, I think, festival,' Posy explained. 'They were out here interviewing the cast last week for a special edition feature, and the photos have been scheduled for today for weeks. I guess they're on a deadline.'

'They're going to have plenty to write about.' Caro peeled off with Seren as the main cast were shepherded onto the stairs to get into position. Rosalind suspected that, if it hadn't been for their teenage interloper, she'd probably have tried to get in on the photo, just to annoy Anton.

The cast gathered on the stairs, either side of the main hall, as the photographer directed them around in groups of three or four, snapping away the whole time. Rosalind tried not to look at Seren and Caro, who were pulling faces to make her laugh – although they seemed to be succeeding with Posy, who was giggling away on the other side with Tristan and Scarlett.

Rosalind's mind was too preoccupied for laughter. Besides, standing next to all these bright young things, and without Dominic for age-appropriate company, she could only look more ancient with her laughter lines on display.

She remembered a shoot she'd done for one of the glossy mags, a few years ago – after Frank died, but before Aldermere. It had been for an interview with her, after she'd been presented with a lifetime achievement award. The questions the interviewer posed seemed to assume she'd already achieved everything she wanted to in this lifetime, which was categorically not the case. So she was already in a bad mood when she headed to get changed for the photo shoot.

But then she'd been put in this magnificent, luxurious bronze shot-silk dress, that bared her décolletage even if it was a little crêpe-y these days, and she'd been posed perched on a cocktail stool showing off her calves and her sky-high heels.

And she'd felt like herself again.

Those photos had been some of her favourites ever taken of her. She suspected that today's images, with her dressed in her Great Aunt Hermione costume, would not match up.

Still, it was all part of the job, so Rosalind posed and angled her body and face the way she knew worked best, and let her mind wander to consider where the hell Dominic was.

He hadn't been required for shooting today, but he should have been here for this, if Anton's silent fuming on the sidelines was anything to judge by. So where was he? And why? Dominic might not be her favourite cast mate, and heaven knew he had plenty of faults, but he usually at least managed to be professional when it came to work projects.

'Okay, last one. Let's have you all spaced out on this side of the stairs,' the photographer called.

There was a hustle and bustle of movement as all the actors tried to find their best positions, and were then moved again by the photographer, or a cast mate who couldn't be seen. Rosalind hung back, only moving forward into the middle of the stairs at the urging of the photographer.

'Perfect!' The camera was snapping again. 'Try moving around, like you're catching up, chatting about your week!' The photographer seemed unaware that this week was the last thing any of them wanted to be talking about. Still, Rosalind posed and smiled and wished that it was over.

Until the front doors of Tŷ Gwyn burst open and Dominic appeared, red-faced but smiling broadly.

'Ah, here you all are!' he declared, as if he hadn't been supposed to be there too. 'Anton, our esteemed director, are we all done for the weekend? Only I have *just* the thing to brighten everyone's mood and get us all in a perfectly Dahlia Lively frame of mind before filming recommences on Monday.'

Scarlett squealed with excitement before Anton could comment. Nina, Rosalind noticed, rolled her eyes at the other woman.

'What's the plan, Dom?' Scarlett asked.

Dominic sauntered across the hallway to where Scarlett stood at the bottom of the stairs, and slung an arm around her shoulder. 'Well, my darling, we're all going to my place in France for a proper party. Come on, I've got a private plane on standby. Let's get gone!'

Chapter Eighteen

'Just because someone is a despicable speck of a human being, doesn't automatically *mean that they're a murderer, Bess.'*

Dahlia Lively *in* **Look Lively, Dahlia!**
By **Lettice Davenport, 1936**

Posy

As it turned out, they weren't *all* going.

'Sorry, old man, but I understand the police would rather you hung around here this weekend,' Dominic told Kit, not sounding sorry at all. 'Next time.' He slapped him on the shoulder, then moved on to tell Scarlett all about the local delicacies he'd arranged to be ready for their arrival in France.

'Do you want me to stay here with you?' Posy asked Kit.

He shook his head and gave her a small smile. 'At least one of us should have some fun. Dominic's a pain in the arse a lot of the time, but he's right about that. Everyone needs to let off some steam after this week. It's getting too tense to breathe on set.'

'Is it really appropriate, do we think?' Rosalind asked, standing with Dominic and Anton. 'To be partying, now? After everything that's happened?'

Dominic threw an arm around her shoulders and squeezed, something Posy could see Rosalind did *not* appreciate, from the sour look on her face.

'But that's *why*, Rosa. We need to celebrate Keira's life, to toast the time we spent with her and remember her with joy – not mourn her passing. We should be happy that she lived, and walked among us, rather than depressed because she is gone.'

'It's what she would have wanted,' Scarlett said, seriously.

Posy wasn't entirely sure about that, but it seemed the decision had been made.

Anton prevaricated about whether to join them or not, but in the end concluded that the movie would be best served if he was there to keep an eye on them all. Dominic's promises about the local seafood may have played into that decision, Posy suspected.

As promised, Dominic had his own private plane on standby at a nearby airstrip – a tiny, windswept place a short drive away. After a brief stop at Saith Seren for them all to pack their overnight bags and pick up their passports, they were whisked away in a stretch limo that struggled with the tight corners and narrow bridge of Glan y Wern, and taken to the plane.

'Wow, just look at this thing!' Scarlett already had her phone out taking selfies before they were all on board.

Posy had travelled by private plane often in her younger, more famous years, but it was still something of a jolt to see the fresh flowers laid out, and the afternoon tea prepared for them all to enjoy over the short flight. Having their passports checked on the plane, and landing at another tiny private airport a few miles from Dominic's house, with a limousine waiting to transport them, away from the prying cameras of the paparazzi, was another bonus.

Dominic's house squatted atop a cliff overlooking the ocean, square and white, with balconies and balustrades, and lush green foliage surrounding it. As they were led towards the heavy front door, Posy spotted an infinity pool outside, the water seeming to pour off the edge of the cliff into the sea, as the sun started to set over the water.

'There's spare swim gear in the pool house, if you fancy a dip later,' Dominic said, pausing in his conversation with a slightly harried-looking woman with a clipboard that Posy assumed was his party planner. 'The pool was always Brigette's favourite part of this place.'

'I can see why,' Posy murmured. 'It's stunning.' She hoped it was heated, though. Even in the south of France, February wasn't particularly warm.

Inside, she could tell the house would be cool and shady in the summer, with marble floors and white stone walls. The artwork hanging from them ranged from abstract modern pieces to more classic landscapes of the local area, and the whole place was furnished in neutrals and metallics. Posy wondered if Brigette had been responsible for the interior design, too.

Already, catering staff in black waistcoats and ties were setting up drinks tables and preparing for the party – including adding heaters to the terrace, she noticed. Musicians were setting up in the hallway, and Posy thought she saw circus performers practising in the garden.

'Looks like there's as many staff as guests, right now,' Caro murmured, as they passed through a large, open-plan living space, with a number of seating areas already laid out. 'Who else do you think he's invited?'

They were all shown up to their rooms, and Posy sank onto her bed with a sense of relief she hadn't expected to feel. Placed to make the most of the fabulous view out over the ocean, her bed boasted four wooden poles holding up a gauzy canopy, and a mountain of plush cushions over the silky bedspread. The room itself maintained the same, soothing colour scheme as downstairs, and the en suite wet room looked divine.

But Posy knew it wasn't just the luxurious surroundings that were making her feel so much more relaxed. It was being away from Wales, from the site of Keira's death and so many other unsettling moments. She'd sensed that feeling in the others too – the way they'd laughed more on the plane, smiled so much more as they'd arrived at the house. She suspected the party tonight would give them all a real chance to kick off their shoes and dance. To step out of the fear and uncertainty they'd all lived with for the last week – even longer.

Maybe Dominic had been right about them all needing this.

Except we probably brought the killer with us.

That was something she couldn't afford to forget.

She felt the tension return to her jaw and shoulders as she got to her feet and crossed to the stone balcony outside her floor-to-ceiling windows. White, almost transparent curtains fluttered in the breeze as she stepped outside, and she shivered. Her room was on the corner and, to the left, she could see the ocean stretching out for miles while, to her right, she looked back inland. Resting her hands on the stone railing, she surveyed the twisting road that wound up the hillside to the house, and spotted more long, black cars making their way up it. Caro had been right; the cast of *The Lady Detective* weren't the only people who'd been invited for a party here tonight.

She took a quick shower before changing into a silky, red, spaghetti-strapped dress she'd brought to Wales just in case. Brushing out the Dahlia curls her hair had been set in for filming left her with soft waves, which she fluffed and decided would do for the occasion. She'd removed the heavy film make-up before the flight, and now she replaced it with a much lighter dusting of cosmetics. She slipped into her heels, shoved her phone in a silver clutch bag, grabbed a wrap in case the heaters weren't enough, and headed downstairs to see if she could find Rosalind and Caro.

On the stairs, she saw a photo she hadn't noticed on the way up, tucked among a cluster of black-and-white shots in black frames. She paused to study it – a snap of Brigette and Dominic out on the terrace of the house she was standing in, both with their arms around each other, laughing. Judging by their ages, she suspected it must have been taken some years after their divorce. Interesting.

Downstairs, the house was already filling up with guests. A cocktail bar had been set up on the terrace, out the back of the house overlooking the sea, and the crowd was several people deep around it already. Posy found a waiter circling with a tray of drinks, and managed to snag an orange juice instead.

As she scanned the gathering, she spotted more than a few people she recognised – actors she'd worked with, directors she'd met, other industry people she'd been introduced to at parties like this over the years – but nobody she really wanted to talk to. They all belonged to that other, older part of her life. The Posy who went to parties like this every night of the week, and could never remember anything that happened past midnight.

She wasn't that Posy anymore, and she didn't want to be reminded of her this weekend. Eventually, she knew, she'd have to re-enter that world, but she wanted to prove her place in it by making this movie first.

It was easy enough to skirt the crowd, exchanging brief smiles and nods as she passed, but never slowing down long enough to chat. Snippets of conversation floated on the air and caught in her mind.

'Have you tried the crab puffs? They're divine.'

'Doesn't this place remind you of the Santa Monica house?'

'Who's the girl in the silver dress – do you know? Oh, really.'

'It's just like the parties we used to have at Dom's other place, isn't it? The ones he and Brigette used to throw in the old days.'

'Dom's on form tonight, isn't he?'

The last she had to agree with; Dominic was clearly in his element, holding court out on the terrace, speaking in his booming voice to the crowd of guests who had clustered around him rather than the cocktail bar.

'Looks like he's having fun, doesn't he?' Posy looked up to find Gabriel standing beside her, drink in hand, an unreadable expression on his face.

'He does,' she agreed. 'But you're not?'

Gabriel shrugged. 'One party is much like another, isn't it?'

'It's been so long since I went to one like this, I think I'd forgotten,' Posy admitted.

He drained his glass, and placed it on the empty tray of a passing waiter. 'Don't worry. It all comes back to you easily enough.'

Posy watched him weave through the crowd as he walked away in search of another drink, and wondered what he meant by that.

She didn't want it to come back to her. She wasn't the girl she'd been then, drifting through life uncertain of what or who she needed to be. Now, she had a purpose.

She wasn't here in France to party, not really.

She was here to investigate.

A burst of laughter from Dominic's group surprised her out of her reverie, and she turned in time to see Dominic moving away, inside the house, as the crowd around him dispersed, most of them heading down onto the lawn where three men were juggling fiery batons while above them a woman walked a high wire between two poles.

Searching the terrace for other cast members, she saw Tristan and Nina deep in conversation by the railings over by the cliff edge, and Scarlett sweeping past in her silver dress talking about a trip to the pool house. Anton she found sitting in a set of comfortable chairs around a fire pit, talking with men in suits she didn't recognise.

But she didn't spot Rosalind and Caro, until they appeared suddenly at her sides.

Caro took her arm. 'Are we ready to talk to Dominic, at last?'

Posy nodded.

It was time.

Rosalind

Dominic had obviously been making the most of the cocktail bar by the time they caught up with him. They'd trailed him through the house, lingering far enough behind to see where he was going but not draw his attention. Not yet, anyway. They wanted to speak with him alone, and if that meant cornering him as he came out of the bathroom, so be it. The house was packed from terrace to top floor with guests, so they'd take what they could get.

As it turned out, though, he wasn't heading for the bathroom. Instead, he staggered along a small side corridor off the terrace, one hand on the wall to support himself as he went, and unlocked a door tucked away around a corner at the end of it.

Rosalind exchanged a glance with Posy and Caro, before following him inside.

This room hadn't been decorated by Brigette, Rosalind was certain. She'd seen the casting director's style in every other space in the house – refined but relaxed, pared back but still luxurious. This room, by contrast, was crammed with heavy dark wood furniture and richly coloured, deep-pile rugs. A leather armchair sat in the corner, away from the desk, and it was this seat Dominic had sunk into, looking suddenly far wearier than he'd appeared out on the terrace.

Rosalind shut the door behind them.

'All three of you, is it?' After blinking a few times Dominic focused, more or less, on Rosalind. 'You've figured it out then, I suppose.'

Figured it out? It seemed unlikely that Dominic was preparing to confess to Keira's murder, but then, a lot of strange things had been happening lately. Rosalind wasn't ruling it out just yet.

He'd drawn the curtains against the moonlight and the noise of the party, but failed to switch on all but one of the lamps around the room, leaving everything gloomy. Dominic motioned for them to sit – although where, Rosalind wasn't entirely sure, as there was only one other seat, behind the desk. She leaned against the left side of the desk, leaving Posy to hop onto the right corner, and Caro to shrug and take the chair.

Dominic reached under his armchair and pulled out a bottle of brandy, offering it to Rosalind. She declined with a shake of the head.

'Would think you could do with a drink,' he said, before lifting the bottle to his mouth and taking a long gulp. 'You've been getting them too, I imagine?'

'Getting what?' Caro asked.

But Rosalind already knew. 'The death threats. You too?'

Dominic nodded. 'Started last month. All *I know what you did* and *you deserve to die for it.*'

Posy glanced over at Rosalind before asking, 'And do you know what they're talking about?'

Rosalind hadn't. When the notes first came, she hadn't understood them at all, had just stared at them blankly.

But there had been so many stories in the papers about her – and her role in what had passed at Aldermere. Exposing her personal life, her transgressions, her betrayals. Then, of course, there was that new conspiracy theory Libby had found. She wasn't a murderer, but she wasn't without guilt, either.

She'd understood that some people would hate her, when the truth came out. She hadn't anticipated death threats from it, but what other reason could there be?

But Dominic hadn't been at Aldermere last summer.

His gaze skittered away from hers as he answered. 'Not a clue. Load of nonsense, of course.'

A lie, and an obvious one at that.

'I got one yesterday morning, waiting on my bedroom floor when I woke up.' He fished into the inside pocket of his tux, and pulled it out. Rosalind didn't reach out to take it. She could tell from the black edges and the jagged writing that it was the same as hers. 'That's when I decided to escape here.'

Yesterday morning. Dominic had received a note after Keira's death.

Rosalind felt the same fear she thought she'd shaken start to rise up from her stomach again. This wasn't over at all.

Posy took the note from him and studied it. 'You weren't worried about bringing the murderer with you?'

'Safety in numbers, isn't it?' Dominic replied. 'Too many people here, too many witnesses to risk it.'

Rosalind didn't point out that he'd been alone when they'd all followed him to this room. A murderer could have done so just as easily.

'Besides, there's something about that place. Brigette would call it a vibe – a dark and threatening one . . .' Dominic shuddered. 'No. I don't believe it could be one of us. I think it's someone back there, in Wales. I just don't know who.'

Perhaps Dominic hadn't thought through the logistics of Keira's death as thoroughly as they had, or perhaps he thought they weren't connected. Because if Rosalind crossed the people who'd made the trip off their suspect list, it didn't leave many names at all.

'Do you think the threats might be connected to your ex-wife's disappearance?' Caro leaned forward in her chair as she asked the question. Obviously she wasn't buying his attempts at deception, either.

Dominic scoffed at that. 'Brigette? She's always known when to leave a sinking ship, hasn't she? She left me . . .' He trailed off, then shook his head before continuing. 'I got a message from her – an email – the day after she left. Didn't say much more than that damn Instagram post – that she was taking a break, going on retreat – except it had an extra warning, just for me. But nothing since. I've tried to call her, email, but nothing. Nobody's seen her, not even our son.'

'You called Grayson?' Rosalind asked, surprised. The falling out between father and son had been both epic and well publicised, a few years ago.

Dominic shrugged. 'She might be my ex-wife, but she's still the love of my life. I wanted to know that she was okay.'

Caro shot her a look, as if to say *Focus, Rosalind*. 'She sent a warning?' Ah, yes. That was probably more important, wasn't it?

Dominic took another swig of brandy, then nodded. 'A warning. Yes.'

'Had she received death threats too?' Posy had her notebook out again, jotting down his answers.

'She didn't tell me if she had,' Dominic admitted. 'But *something* drove her away, didn't it? I mean, one minute she was there, then next – poof! Gone. I know she had that argument with Anton, but really, who hasn't? It wouldn't be enough for Brigette to abandon a project. No, I knew it had to be something else.'

'What did her warning say, exactly?' Caro asked. 'I mean, did it tell you *why* she left? Or even *how*?' Caro was still hankering after her secret passageway, clearly.

'It said . . . hang on.' He dropped the brandy bottle onto the floor, where it wobbled ominously before settling, and reached for his phone. It took several attempts for him to open it – apparently his facial recognition system didn't believe he *always* looked like a drunken fool, which Rosalind felt was optimistic of it. Finally, he swiped through a few apps and handed Caro the phone with the email showing on the screen.

'"Get out of there, before it's too late,"' Posy read over her shoulder. 'Well, that's not ominous at all.'

'Gabriel said she was always a bit of a drama queen,' Caro said, doubtfully, but Dominic shook his head.

'Not like this,' he told them. 'Not when no one was there to watch, or to be entertained. Not to *scare* people.'

'She hated horror movies,' Rosalind remembered, absently. They'd been friends, once. It felt like so long ago. 'Or anything where people were hurt, or even embarrassed.'

'Which was most of my films at one point.' Dominic sighed. 'Maybe that's why she divorced me.'

'I'm sure she had plenty of other reasons,' Caro muttered, but he didn't seem to hear. 'Tell us more about these death threats,' she went on, a little louder.

'I didn't take them seriously at first.' Dominic reached for the brandy again, taking another long pull from the bottle. 'I mean, at our level you get used to the whackos and the obsessives, right?' He looked to Rosalind for agreement. She didn't give it, not least because she wasn't sure she wanted to be on whatever level Dominic thought they were both on. 'But then Brigette left, and I got that email. And still I didn't think . . . Until you burst in the other morning . . .' He waved the bottle in Posy's direction. 'And told me that Keira was dead. Until then, I'd thought it might be her. But after that, I knew it was something else. Even then, though, it was okay when I thought it was Kit. Just an accident, after all. But once the police let him go . . . That's when I started putting it all together. And I realised that I'm next. Well, me or you,' he added, swinging the bottle around towards Rosalind again.

'Putting it together how?' Caro asked.

'And why Keira?' Posy put in. 'Had she been getting letters?'

Dominic stared at her blankly. 'No idea. She wouldn't tell me if she had, would she?'

If only they'd managed to have this conversation a few drinks ago. Maybe then he'd be making more sense.

'We understand that she interrupted a . . . moment between you and Scarlett,' Rosalind said, carefully. Dominic had always been volatile, especially when drunk, and she knew he wouldn't like this insinuation. 'Does that have anything to do with this?'

'You think *I* killed her!' He exploded forward from the armchair, the brandy bottle crashing to the floor uncapped. 'She was an interfering uppity little bitch, but so are half the girls I have to work with these days. Can barely tell them apart. But I've never killed any of them!'

'We're not accusing you of anything.' Caro didn't sound totally convinced that there wasn't something she *should* be accusing him of, though, and Rosalind couldn't help but agree. 'We're just trying to figure out the truth here.'

'Like why the two of *you* . . .' Posy motioned between Rosalind and Dominic, '. . . are getting death threats, but Keira's the one who's dead. What's the link?'

The link. There had to be one, Rosalind supposed, but she was damned if she could figure out what it was – unless Keira was the one sending the notes. If Dominic thought she was behind it, he'd have had a motive to kill her. But if Dominic had received one since her death, that was that theory blown out of the water.

What connected her perceived crimes at Aldermere to Dominic? And what connected Dominic, and his dubious history, to Keira? She couldn't see the link.

Dominic had found it, though. He may have been a drunk, but he wasn't an idiot, Rosalind should have remembered that. And he knew better than anyone how stories could damage a person. Which secrets needed to be kept.

'You're looking for a link. Haven't you guessed? Doesn't this party remind you of anything?' His eyes cleared as he kept his gaze trained on Rosalind's face. 'It's because of *The Castle on the Hill*, of course.'

Her stomach lurched, sinking down towards the ground, as his words echoed inside her head.

This wasn't about Aldermere at all.

Suddenly, all too many things made sense.

Chapter Nineteen

'He's hiding something.' Johnnie slapped his hand against the steering wheel. 'I can feel it.'

'Feeling it's no good, darling,' Dahlia pointed out. 'What we've got to do is get him to admit it.'

Dahlia Lively *in* Dining with Death
By Lettice Davenport, 1954

Caro

'What was *The Castle on the Hill*?' Caro barely let Rosalind usher them all out of Dominic's study and shut the door behind them before she asked the inevitable question. She was missing something here – something the others knew – and she *hated* that.

'A movie.' Rosalind kept moving, down the corridor and back out onto the terrace, towards where the main bar was set up. 'Well, almost.'

'Almost a movie?' Caro frowned as she pushed past other party-goers to keep up. 'Wait! Posy, you mentioned it the other day, didn't you? One of those movies that never got made.'

Rosalind snagged two gin and tonics from the bar, plus something non-alcoholic for Posy, and they all made their way to the edge of the terrace. Down below, in the infinity pool, Caro could see Scarlett, Gabriel, Nina and Tristan all splashing around happily.

Clearly cast morale had been significantly improved by cocktails, bikinis and a heated swimming pool. Even if the same didn't seem to be entirely true for their host.

'Yeah, I mentioned it,' Posy told Caro, leaning beside her to watch the others. 'It was this hugely hyped-up movie, about eight, nine years ago, with all these big names attached . . . and then somehow it all fell apart.'

Rosalind took a sip of her gin and tonic. 'I'm surprised you remember.' So was Caro. Posy could only have been a teenager still. Twenty at most. But she had been a part of the movie industry since she was a child, so perhaps it wasn't so surprising.

Posy just gave them a tight smile.

'So, what happened?' Caro asked. 'And why don't I remember this? I suppose I was divorcing Thomas at the time. You were going to be in it, I assume, Rosalind?'

'Yes.' Rosalind frowned, as if she were trying to remember the details. 'It was not long after Frank died. My agent thought it would be a good move, and I liked the idea of being over in LA for a few months, at the time. There were . . . too many memories at the house in London. So I flew over, rented a flat on the production team's dime, and read my script and waited.'

'Did it even start filming?' Posy scrunched up her nose. 'I can't remember.'

Rosalind nodded. 'They started. I know I filmed a few scenes too, although my part wasn't huge. In fact, I think they were most of the way through when—' She broke off, just when things were getting interesting.

Sometimes Caro thought she just did it for the sense of drama.

'What happened?' she asked. 'Obviously it was something pretty awful, if Dominic thinks it was worth killing for. I can't *believe* I don't remember this. Something else to blame my stupid ex-husband for.' Like she really needed to add to the list.

'Do you remember the name Evie Groves?' Posy asked.

Caro's forehead scrunched up for a second, then cleared as she remembered. 'The starlet who walked into the sea and drowned herself one night in LA? Of course. Wait—'

Rosalind nodded, confirming Caro's suspicions. 'She was supposed to be the star of *The Castle on the Hill* when she died. Everyone was talking about her that year.'

'I remembered her, just not the movie she was working on,' Caro said, only a little defensively. 'God. How could I forget that?'

'I've tried to,' Rosalind admitted. 'I watched the whole thing unfold on the television in my rented apartment. First the search, after she was reported missing. Then when they found the body . . . Filming was on hold, of course. It seemed like the whole of Hollywood was holding its breath.'

'But Dominic wouldn't have forgotten,' Posy said, thoughtfully. 'Nor would Brigette.'

'Why?' God, this was frustrating. *She* was the one who knew all the celebrity gossip. She hated playing catch-up like this. But that had not been a good year, and she'd been in the UK while the other two were in Hollywood where, presumably, the media had been far more interested.

'It was their party she walked out of, the night she disappeared,' Rosalind explained. 'I wasn't there that night, so I only know what was in the news. But there wasn't any suggestion of foul play, as far as I know. Evie was . . . troubled. The verdict was accidental death, I think, but everyone suspected suicide.'

Caro tapped her nail on the side of her glass. 'Hmm. So they weren't suspects, then? Dominic and Brigette?' Rosalind shook her head. 'Should they have been?'

'You think someone believes the official verdict was wrong?' Rosalind guessed. 'I'm sure they were questioned, but that was all. There was talk – but there's always talk. And even if someone did suspect anything . . .'

'Dominic would have paid to hush it all up,' Caro finished for her. 'You're right. Still. It's the best lead we've had so far.'

'Is it, though?' Posy looked out across the water, her forehead creased with thought. 'I mean, yes, I can see someone threatening Dominic and Brigette if they thought they were responsible, perhaps. But why Rosalind? She wasn't even at the party. And more than that—'

'Why Keira?' Caro interrupted. 'You're right. What's the link between her and the film?'

'And even if there *is* a link, why would she be a more important target than Dominic?' Posy straightened up to look at both of them. 'I don't think we can just assume that Dominic is right about this.'

'*Amateurs should never get involved in police work . . . you start with an idea of what you think happened and you'll go to any lengths to prove it*,' Rosalind murmured.

'Is that a Dahlia Lively quote?' Posy asked. 'I don't recognise it.'

Rosalind gave a small, lopsided smile. 'No. It's something Jack said to me the other day. I was just thinking . . . what if that's what Dominic is doing?'

'Making this all about him?' Caro said.

'Picking a theory and going out of his way to prove it, even when the evidence says otherwise,' Rosalind replied, which was basically what Caro had said anyway.

'You're right,' Rosalind told Posy, which made her beam. Posy always did look for approval from the eldest Dahlia. 'It's too tenuous.'

'But we can't completely rule it out, either,' Caro pointed out. 'It's basically the only link we've found so far between all the things that are happening here.'

'*Is* there a link between Keira and *The Castle on the Hill*?' Posy asked.

'Keira Reynolds-Yang.' Rosalind sounded out the name slowly. 'Patrick Reynolds was the executive producer on the movie.'

'Her father,' Posy said. 'Right.'

'There it is, then.' Caro drained the last of her gin and tonic. ' "There's always a link, Bess." '

She lapsed into her best Dahlia voice as she spoke, which made the others smile, like she'd hoped. Dahlia had said that often enough, over the years. But Caro knew that finding links in fiction was one thing – all those carefully laid threads that Lettice Davenport had woven together until the joins were invisible. In real life, did the theory still hold?

Was it possible that Keira's death, and everything else, weren't actually linked at all?

'We need to know more about what happened at that party, the night Evie disappeared,' Rosalind said.

Caro had already pulled up a search on her phone, and waved it at her to show she was way ahead of her. 'Nothing obviously iffy,' she said, scrolling through the results, the words blurring a little as she moved at speed. 'Just what you've already told me. But then, if there was something Dominic had buried, it's not going to show up on a Google search. The only way to find out is if we can get him to tell us.'

'Which he's unlikely to do,' Rosalind admitted. 'If it's a secret worth killing for, we have to assume it's one that would destroy his career, too.'

Posy pulled a pained expression, as if she needed to say something but really didn't want to. Caro knew that look.

'Posy?' she pressed. 'Any thoughts on how we can find out?'

'My Uncle Sol . . . he's a film critic in Hollywood,' she said, with a reluctant sigh. 'But he's written some books too. One about, well, me.'

'Right.' Caro didn't imagine that had been a particularly bonding experience for either of them, knowing the tone of most articles written about Posy's fall from grace.

'But he almost wrote another one, too. About *The Castle on the Hill*. That's how I remembered it – I remember Uncle Sol and Dad talking about it, and how it wasn't going to be published because *somebody* had pulled strings at the publishing company.'

'You think Dominic?' Rosalind guessed.

Posy shrugged, and pulled another face. 'It could be. I could . . . I could call his PA, see what I can find out.'

Not the man himself, Caro noted, but his assistant. Well, she couldn't say she really blamed her.

And she wouldn't push her, either. Not yet, anyway. 'That sounds like a good idea. So, we have a plan. Now, who wants another drink?'

Rosalind

The party went on late, and Rosalind went to bed still listening to strains of music from downstairs, and the sound of partygoers splashing about in the heated pool below her bedroom window. She dreamed of drownings, and woke with a start far earlier than she'd have liked. Her heart in her throat, she crossed to the window and looked down at the infinity pool, barely willing to admit to herself what she expected to see.

But all she saw was the glittering surface of the water in the early morning sun, and a staff member collecting glasses and bottles from the surrounding tables.

Everything was fine.

It stayed fine all that day, too. With most of the cast nursing sore heads, it was a quiet day, which concluded with an elaborately catered dinner for just the group who'd travelled over from Wales.

'Is it me,' Caro asked in a whisper, leaning closer to Rosalind at the dinner table, 'or is Dominic getting more depressed with every course?'

'It's not you,' Rosalind murmured back. Was it the realisation that tomorrow they'd all be back in Wales, ready to resume filming, that was bringing him down? She assumed so. He genuinely seemed to believe he was safe here in France.

A point that was confirmed when she overheard him talking to Anton, in the shadow of a large bronze sculpture in the entrance hall, later that night.

'I mean, I'm practically done, aren't I?' Dominic was saying. 'Two more scenes and I'm out of there anyway. Why not just put them off until later – or better still, cut them altogether? Save us both some time and money, since you're so behind already. Besides, the forecast for Wales is horrendous for the next few days – probably won't even get to film, with that storm closing in.'

But Anton was having none of it. Rosalind didn't linger to eavesdrop on Anton's entire response, but she could hear most of it clearly as she climbed the stairs anyway. And the next day, when they all trooped down to climb into the cars back to the airport – earlier than planned, because of the approaching storm system – Dominic was there, looking resentful and afraid.

'Did you have a chance to call your Uncle Sol yet?' Caro asked Posy, as they settled into the luxuriously padded seats of Dominic's private plane.

'I've left messages with his assistant,' Posy replied. 'But nothing yet.'

Rosalind stretched out her legs, sending up a silent prayer of thanks for decent leg space, folded her hands in her lap and closed her eyes. The flight wasn't a long one, but perhaps it would give her the time she needed to work through the twists and turns of their investigation, and provide some insight.

Like why Keira was killed, if it wasn't because she was threatening people. Or why, if the murderer was among the cast, they hadn't struck there in France, where Dominic was clearly vulnerable – and so was she. Or why—

She was asleep in moments.

It wasn't until they were back on set at Tŷ Gwyn the next day that another possible connection occurred to Rosalind. She watched Rhian hurry across the main hallway to secure a window that was rattling in the rising wind and suddenly remembered. Keira had been the last person to talk to Brigette before she disappeared. She'd been there when Brigette answered her phone.

What if she had overheard something she shouldn't? Something that made Brigette run away and hide. Was *that* why she'd had to die?

Outside, the wind and rain howled around the solid stone walls of the house. Inside, the lighting team were doing their best, and hoping it would be enough.

The main order of business for the day was filming Dominic's final scenes. As was typical, nothing was being filmed in order on this shoot, so his last scheduled scene was actually one of the earlier ones in the film. A family dinner with Dahlia, Bertie and Rose – plus Charles, who only *wanted* to be family.

Even though they weren't in the scene, the rest of the cast had hung around on set anyway to clap Dominic off when he finished filming. Rosalind suspected he'd be so relieved to get out of Tŷ Gwyn, and away from Wales again, Dominic wouldn't be lingering once Anton called cut on the scene. A suspicion that was reinforced when Dominic, still reeking stale alcohol from his pores despite the make-up department's best efforts, lumbered in and said, 'Right, let's get this over with.'

Fortunately it was a straightforward, sitting-around-drinking-cocktails scene – one that even Anton hadn't tried to imbue with cinematic magic by adding a sword fight or a hike or anything. The only complications were Scarlett trying to play a record on the gramophone, despite having no idea how the thing worked, and Nina almost dropping the tray of drinks she was serving until Tristan dived in to save them.

As they reset for what would hopefully be the final take, an hour or so later, the front doors crashed open and Caro appeared, wrapped up in a waterproof and dripping all over the stone floor. She'd hung out in Rosalind's trailer that morning to do some more internet research, since most of the cast had opted to stay inside the house itself, out of the weather, and the rooms upstairs were all already occupied.

'Still raining, then?' Kit asked from behind Rosalind, as Caro shook raindrops from her hood like a stray dog.

'Just a bit. Posy still filming?' Caro glanced towards the door of the dining room.

Kit shook his head. 'They're resetting. Wouldn't have let any of us in here if they were live.'

'Shouldn't be long.' Anton's third assistant director, Harriet, appeared from the dining room, closing the door behind her. 'We just got word that the river is rising – fast. They want us out of here in case the road floods. Apparently it's prone to it.'

'Which puts us another few hours behind schedule on this movie,' Rosalind guessed. 'Possibly days if it's not clear tomorrow.'

'And we thought we were cursed *last* summer,' Kit murmured.

'Last chance to get this right,' Anton declared, before directing them to start again.

Perhaps the added pressure of the rising river spurred them on, but this time, they nailed it. And the moment Anton called cut, everyone went into action to get people out of there. There was a smattering of applause for Dominic, who ignored it all and staggered towards the stairs, his hangover apparently catching up with him.

The priority, unusually, was the crew, since they needed to get across the river and out of the village to return to their hotels.

'Everyone get out of costume and out of here post haste, please,' Harriet called, as the cast started to scatter. 'We want to get out before the storm gets any worse.'

It wasn't just the rain now, Rosalind realised, when the heavy front doors caught in the wind as someone passed through, crashing into the stone walls. The forecast had been right; there was a proper storm brewing.

Getting a cast out of costume and off set was never a speedy endeavour. And it could only be worse for the crew, who had to dismantle things and make safe before they could head out. But they were used to working fast. Trailers were locked up and secured, and the crew bus departed just as the first crack of lightning cut across the sky.

But the cast shuttle was nowhere to be seen.

'What do you mean we'll have to walk?' Anton was yelling into the phone clamped against his ear. Then he pulled it away and stared at it. 'He hung up on me!'

Rhian winced and held up her own phone. 'No, I think the signal's completely down. The storm must have hit one of the towers.'

'Like phone reception in this place isn't lousy enough as it is,' Caro murmured.

One by one, the cast gathered in the hallway, back in their normal clothes, but still made up for the most part.

'Where the *bloody hell* is Dominic?' Anton bellowed as he stormed through the entrance hall for the fourth time. 'And Gabriel for that matter. And is that bloody bus here yet?'

The small gathering of actors who were lingering in the hallway all looked at each other, but nobody answered. Rosalind was pretty sure Anton didn't actually want an answer to his second question, anyway, only the first.

'I heard him talking to someone upstairs before,' Scarlett said after a moment. 'In one of the front bedrooms.'

'I just came down from there,' Anton yelled, making Scarlett recoil. 'There's no sign of him.'

'I'll go look,' Kit said. 'I think Gabriel might still be up there, too.' He jogged to the stairs before Anton could yell about not seeing him, either.

'Oh! And I've forgotten my charger,' Nina added, dashing after him, and soon cast members were scattered all over Tŷ Gwyn again searching for co-stars and phone chargers, and Anton was sitting on the bottom step with his head in his hands muttering something about never working with kids, animals or *bloody actors*.

An uneasy feeling settled in Rosalind's stomach, as the wind howled down the chimney in the next room. 'I don't like this. Something's wrong.'

'Agreed.' Caro's gaze was darting all over the entrance hall, probably cataloguing exactly who was where. Just in case.

'You think something's happened to Dominic?' Posy's nose scrunched up at the idea.

'Or is about to,' Rosalind said. He'd been afraid. And desperate to get out of there as fast as he could. So where was he now? Why wasn't he the first out of the door?

Tristan appeared next to them. 'You three want me to hold the giant umbrella while we walk back to Saith Seren? I really don't think the bus is coming.'

'I don't think the umbrella will last the journey, either,' Posy pointed out. 'It's pretty wild out there.'

For a moment, they waited in silence, listening to the storm rage outside. But then even the sound of the wind and the rain was eclipsed by a shrill, ear-splitting scream.

'Nina? What is . . . Oh God,' Kit said, standing beside her at the top of the stairs. 'It's Dominic.'

Rosalind was at the foot of the stairs before she even realised she'd taken a step, moving towards the sound.

There were no bright lamps highlighting all the details for the camera, but they didn't need them. The chandelier hanging from the ceiling above the double-height entrance hall barely lit the balcony at all, but someone hit the switch for the wall lights up there, and suddenly everything was illuminated.

Dominic was sitting slumped in the doorway of the first bedroom off the balcony at the top of the stairs, his head lolling to one side. And standing over him, blood covering her outstretched hands, stood Nina, flanked by Kit, Gabriel and Rhian.

'Somebody call for an ambulance,' Rosalind said, as she climbed the stairs, already knowing that it was too late, even if the phone lines were working again.

Rosalind gripped tightly onto the banister, Posy holding her other arm, and Caro beside her, punching the same three digits on her phone over and over again.

Buried in Dominic's chest, glinting in the reflected lights of the crystal chandelier, was the same dagger that had almost stabbed Rosalind on set.

There was no ambiguity this time. No chance of an accident.

This was murder.

And she could be next.

Chapter Twenty

'You found another *body?' Johnnie shook his head. 'How do these things keep happening to you, Dahlia?'*

Dahlia Lively *in* Look Lively, Dahlia!
***By* Lettice Davenport, 1936**

Posy

Nina's hands were covered in blood, and Posy couldn't look away as the actress sobbed into Kit's chest.

'She's getting blood all over his shirt,' she murmured. Luckily, no one was listening. That probably wasn't the sort of thing she was supposed to be concentrating on right now. She focused back in on Dominic – on the body – again, but that wasn't much better. Nina had knocked the knife in his chest, and a sluggish flow of blood escaped around the blade, down the front of his white shirt.

The costume department will be so annoyed. She brought a hand to her mouth to muffle a wildly inappropriate laugh. Or sob. She wasn't sure.

'Did she stab him or just find him?' Caro whispered, a little too loudly, into Posy's ear.

From the way Nina had reacted, Posy was assuming she'd stumbled on the grisly sight, rather than caused it herself. But then, how could they be sure? Was she now just acting shocked and horrified to cover up for her actions?

'That's one for the police,' Posy murmured back, even though she knew none of them would be happy leaving Jack and his friends to solve it alone. Rosalind was already at the top of the stairs, her sharp gaze darting across the scene, probably mentally cataloguing everything.

Posy moved a little closer, another few steps up, to get a better look for herself. Tucked away in the doorway off the balcony, Dominic was only just visible from the stairs until she reached the top, and forced herself to turn and study him.

Dominic's hair – the thick head of salt and pepper hair he'd prided himself on – was in disarray, above his wide, staring eyes and slackened pink mouth. His hands lay limply at his sides, his fingers pale under reddened wrists. His legs were coiled under him, as he slumped in the doorway.

Posy looked away, unable to watch any longer.

Time froze, except for Nina's silent tears and shuddering shoulders, as they all waited. For direction. For answers. For *something*.

Someone to call 'Cut!' perhaps, and allow them to step back into the real world from this hideous fiction.

But the only person who could do that was Anton. And he stood behind her, hands twisting in front of his stomach, paler than she'd ever seen him.

'He's definitely dead?' Halfway between a question and a statement.

At the top of the stairs, Rosalind removed her fingers from Dominic's throat. 'Yes.'

'I can't get through to the police, or the ambulance service.' Caro glared at her phone. 'Signal is still out.'

'So what do we do?' Anton's gaze jerked between them, and Posy realised.

He was waiting for the three Dahlias to take charge.

Because this was murder, and if they couldn't get in touch with the police, or the police couldn't get to them . . . the Dahlias were the best they had.

'We need to make sure the body – the crime scene – isn't disturbed any more than it already has been,' Posy said.

'The crime scene?' Gabriel asked, incredulous. 'Somebody stabbed him! Some lunatic murderer is running around this house and you're worried about the crime scene?'

Kit looked up from the top of Nina's head, still pressed against his chest. 'He's right. They might still be here. We need to search the place.'

'And do what if we find them?' Tristan asked from the stairs. 'Dominic is already dead. And personally, I'm not in a hurry to face off with whoever did this to him.'

'They've probably already made their getaway anyway,' Rhian added, surprisingly calm. 'There are so many ways in and out of this house . . .'

'Probably escaped with the crew,' Anton agreed, causing the others to nod sagely. 'It was chaos. Would have been easy.'

Posy shared an uneasy look with the other Dahlias. None of the others seemed to realise that the killer was probably not only still in Tŷ Gwyn, but one of them. But if that ignorance was keeping them calm . . .

Rosalind nodded, stepping away from the body to clear the stairs for the others to descend. 'Let's get everybody downstairs. Into the dining room – it's large enough for all of us. As long as we stick together we should be safe.'

'We might even be able to light the fire in there.' Caro slipped her phone in her pocket.

'Why can't we go back to the Seven Stars?' Scarlett asked, her eyes wide as she clung on to Tristan's arm on the stairs. 'I don't want to stay here with a dead body!'

'It's too dangerous out there, with the storm.' Rhian's soft voice floated down from the balcony.

'I'd rather take my chances with a storm than a murderer,' Gabriel snapped.

'You won't if the river breaks its banks.' Rhian turned to Posy. 'They were warning . . . if the storm got bad . . . there might be power cuts.'

Power cuts. Just what they needed. 'Okay. Do you have candles, torches, that sort of thing?'

Rhian nodded. 'In the kitchens. I'll fetch them and bring them to the dining room?' She, at least, didn't seem worried about a murderer lurking in the shadows of Tŷ Gwyn. Because she really believed they'd escaped, or because she knew, like Posy, that it was more likely to be someone here now? Or was there another reason?

'Yes, please.' Posy looked out at the rest of the cast, all of them ashen and uncertain. 'Everyone else, let's get into the dining room, light the fire and shut the door. We'll wait out the storm and get the police here as soon as we can.'

Kit put his arm around Nina's shoulders, leading her down the stairs, saying something about a having a change of clothes in his bag. The police would want the bloodstained ones for evidence, Posy supposed. They should keep them safe.

They were followed by Rhian and then Gabriel, both silent, neither of them looking back. Posy gave the corpse in the doorway one last glance. It felt so wrong to leave him there alone, but what else could they do? The police wouldn't look kindly on them moving him to a more comfortable position, just because they felt bad.

And none of it mattered to Dominic now, anyway.

'We really *should* search the rooms up here,' Posy said, reluctantly. 'On the off chance that it wasn't one of us, the murderer might still be hiding out.' Except three women going up against a proven murderer didn't sound like a great idea. Tristan was right. What would they even do if they found them? Dominic was already dead.

'Let's leave that for the police, when they get here,' Rosalind suggested. 'Nobody is going anywhere tonight. And honestly, I think it's unlikely our murderer isn't already downstairs in the dining room waiting for us.'

'The thing I don't understand is,' Caro said, as they trailed after the others down the stairs, 'why didn't they see him?'

'Who?' Posy gripped onto the banister as she descended, feeling a little wobbly. 'Dominic?'

'Yes. Anton had just been upstairs to look for him. The others went right up there too without seeing anything odd. How could they miss his dead body just lying there in the doorway?'

'Sitting,' Rosalind said, from the back. 'He was sitting.' Her voice sounded weak. Scared, Posy realised. Because with Dominic gone . . .

No. They weren't going to let it come to that. They were going to solve this case, and they'd keep every damn suspect in the dining room at Tŷ Gwyn until they did, if that's what it took.

Posy pulled out her notebook, leaning it against the railing as she clicked her biro. The only way she knew to conquer her fear, and her horror, was with facts. 'Okay, quick. Before we forget, and before the others are watching. Who was where? I think that's going to matter here, don't you?'

'Anton came downstairs last, saying he couldn't find Dominic,' Caro said. 'Then Kit and Nina both went up too, to look for Gabriel and a phone charger, right?'

Posy nodded. 'Rhian went up there as well, didn't she?'

'She must have already been up there,' Rosalind said. 'Before, I mean. She didn't go up with the others. And I remembered something else today, too. Rhian said she saw Brigette, just before she headed into the study and disappeared. She was talking to Keira when she answered her phone.'

Posy's eyebrows furrowed as she noted it down. 'Didn't we already know that?' She flipped back through the pages, looking for evidence.

'Yes. But I was thinking . . . it means they were close enough that Keira might have seen who was calling. Or Brigette might have told her. Or she might have overheard something on that call that she shouldn't.' Rosalind twisted a handkerchief in her hands as Posy and Caro absorbed that information. Had she been drying her eyes with it? Dominic *had* been an old friend.

'You think this was all a chain reaction that started with Brigette?' Caro asked. 'But there were weeks between Brigette disappearing and Keira's death.'

Rosalind gave a tired shrug. 'I don't know. I don't think we have enough of the pieces yet to put it all together.'

We'd better find them quick, then, Posy thought.

'Back to Dominic,' Caro said. 'Scarlett said she heard him talking to someone in one of the bedrooms, but Anton said he wasn't there when he checked.'

'Did he *actually* check all the rooms, though?' Posy put in. 'Or was he just being Anton?' Their director had a flair for the dramatic, and Posy wouldn't put it past him to have just been exaggerating to get at Scarlett.

'We'll need to ask,' Rosalind said. 'But for now, let's assume he did.'

'Dominic could have been in one of the bathrooms, perhaps? I doubt Anton would have checked in there.' Caro screwed up her face a little. 'Do they all have en suites? Maybe we need a floor plan . . .'

'The point is, Dominic was alive when Scarlett came down, missing when Anton went up, and when Kit and Nina did too, but dead when they came back down. And Gabriel and Rhian were both up there the whole time.' Posy had scribbled a very rough timeline on her notepad, but looking at it, it didn't make any sense. 'How does this fit together?'

Rosalind stared out the front windows of Tŷ Gwyn, frowning, and Posy knew she wasn't seeing the wet, Welsh weather raging. She was seeing paths and plots and possible acts. Caro, too, had her arms folded tightly across her chest, her eyebrows furrowed, as she tried to make sense of it.

And as for Posy . . . she only had more questions.

'Why didn't we hear him scream? I imagine getting stabbed in the chest is quite painful. If he'd been stabbed there at the top of the stairs while we were all in the entrance hall, we'd have heard him. But if he was stabbed somewhere else, moving him couldn't have been easy . . . and there'd be a trail of blood, wouldn't there?'

'The knife was still in the wound,' Rosalind said, absently. 'So there wasn't much blood. But as for the rest of it . . . I just don't know.'

'Yet,' Caro added. 'We don't know *yet*.'

'Then let's go find out.' Posy flipped her notepad shut and tucked it into her bag, her heart still pounding in her chest. 'One of those people sitting in that room knows what happened. Let's go see if we can get us some answers.'

And hope a cornered killer wouldn't turn on them.

Caro

Rhian was already setting out candles along the length of the table in the dining room, while Kit and Tristan worked together to light the fire with wood from the log basket beside it. They seemed relieved to have something to do – something other than dealing with the emotions of others, Caro imagined.

Scarlett sat at the head of the table, her knees pulled up under her chin, her arms wrapped around them, and her feet resting on the chair. She looked like a child who'd accidentally watched an unsuitable horror movie, Caro decided – which she supposed wasn't that far from the truth.

Anton paced back and forth in front of the picture window, where Gabriel was sitting speaking to him in a low voice. Nina was collapsed into an occasional chair in the corner, so still and silent it took Caro a long moment to realise she was there at all.

Outside the windows of the long dining room, Caro could just make out the blur of the lights of the Seven Stars in the distance, and the village beyond, but it was hard to see anything else past the branches, leaves and rain that battered the glass. Then, as she was watching, the lights on the horizon winked out.

And then so did the ones in the room.

Caro's heart leaped in her chest, racing faster than her mind could keep up with.

Scarlett gave a startled shriek, but Rhian had the first candle lit in seconds, and the fireplace was beginning to give off a warming glow, too.

'Power cuts,' Rhian said. 'They're common here in the winter.'

Once the candles were all lit, everyone took a seat around the dining table, staring across at their cast mates. The shadows cast by the firelight and candlelight made everyone look sinister.

She collared Rhian quickly. 'Is there anything to eat or drink here? I know the craft services truck is still outside, but I don't think any of us want to make a run for that.'

'There's wine in the cellar,' Rhian said, promptly. 'Maybe brandy. And the kitchen is usually stocked with snacks of some sort. Shall I fetch some bits?'

'Please. Do you need someone to go with you?'

Rhian shook her head and flicked on the torch she was carrying. 'I know my way.'

It only occurred to Caro once she'd gone that she should have sent someone anyway. If not to protect Rhian in case the murderer *was* a stranger hidden somewhere in the house, then to make sure she didn't detour to tamper with the scene of the crime. But then she realised that Posy was staring after the house manager, following her every move through the open doorway by tracking that torch beam. If she went up the stairs at all, they'd know it.

Before long, she was back, wheeling a kitchen trolley with glasses and bottles and nibbles still in their packets. Posy and Rosalind sprang into action, placing them all on the table, and the cast soon fell upon them.

Caro didn't blame them. They could all do with a drink to steady the nerves after that. She just hoped there was something non-alcoholic for Posy.

'Rhian, how are you doing?' Caro asked, compassion in her voice, as the house manager tucked the trolley away in the corner of the room, where no one would fall over it in the gloom.

'Okay,' Rhian replied, her voice wan and her smile unconvincing. 'I thought I'd be fine going out there alone . . . but I have to admit, I feel better being in here with you all again.'

Caro wondered if she'd still feel so much better if she realised the murderer was probably one of them.

'That's good.' Rosalind's voice was crisper than Caro's as she came up behind them, with a lot less nonsense about it. 'In that case, you won't mind if we ask you a few questions? Good.'

Posy, Caro saw, was hiding her smile with her hand. But she also pulled out her notepad with the other, and then found her pen, so at least she was ready.

'Is this going to be about that secret passageway thing again?' Rhian asked, suspiciously, as they led her to the occasional chair in the corner that Nina had vacated.

'Not at all,' Caro assured her. 'We're just trying to figure out exactly what happened here today. So that when we *can* get hold of the police, we've got a clear record of events. Before people start forgetting, or embellishing. You know what actors are like.'

'But why you three?'

It was a valid question, Caro supposed, but she exchanged a rueful glance with her fellow Dahlias all the same. 'Because someone has to. And we've been here before.'

Rhian didn't ask what she meant by that, which was probably just as well.

'I also have a connection with the local police,' Rosalind said. 'Jack . . . I mean, ex-Chief Detective Inspector Jonathan Hughes, will want to hear everything as soon as the phone lines are back up.'

That seemed to convince her. 'What do you want to know?'

'You were up on the balcony when they found the body, weren't you?' Caro said. 'Can you tell us why?'

'Oh, um, well . . . it's my job?' Rhian looked over at Posy or Rosalind for some support.

'You mean, you were up there because of something to do with the filming? Or the venue?' Posy asked.

'Well, tangentially, I suppose.' Rhian shrugged. 'I, ah, always check over all the rooms before you guys go for the night.'

Caro shot a quick look at Rosalind. 'So, had you checked the rooms before the body was found? All of them?'

'Uh, yes? I think so?'

'And there was no sign of Dominic then?' Rosalind pressed.

Rhian's eyes widened. 'No. No there wasn't. I checked all the rooms, but I didn't see him. And then Anton came up and checked too, then the others and then . . .' She broke off, but they didn't need her to finish the sentence, anyway. Caro was pretty sure that none of them would ever forget what happened next. Nina's scream, the thundering feet, the blood on her hands.

'Did you check the bathrooms?' Caro asked, and Rhian shook her head.

'I called out, though, and nobody answered.' She looked between them anxiously. 'Is that where you think he was? But then who moved him? Or do you think he staggered there after he was stabbed?'

'That's what we're trying to figure out.' If Dominic *had* been able to move to the doorway from inside the room by himself, it explained how they hadn't seen anyone up there. Would the post-mortem tell them that? She'd have to get Rosalind to ask Jack. But if he hadn't . . . 'And you didn't see anything unusual?'

'You mean, did I see the killer?' Rhian shook her head. 'I was standing on the landing the whole time. And I hardly imagine any of us who were up there would have missed someone stabbing Dominic then manhandling him into the doorway, do you?'

And that was the crux of it, Caro thought. Dominic wasn't there, and then he was. He was alive, and then he wasn't. And every one of them had missed the whole damn thing.

Well, every one of them except the one who killed him.

'No.' Rosalind tapped a finger against her chin. 'But it seems like it happened anyway. Doesn't it?'

They let Rhian join the others at the table, following more slowly behind her.

The atmosphere around the table was ... well, tense was an understatement. Caro didn't blame any of them for the nervous looks the assembled cast shot at each other, or the way Nina was looking longingly towards the door. It felt like they were all settling in for a seance at the start of a horror movie. Except the horror had already happened.

Gabriel circled the table, pouring drinks for everyone. Once they all had a drink, he stood by the last seat, at the far end of the table, and raised his glass.

'Under the circumstances ... to Dominic.' He gave a smile that seemed both ironic and pained at the same time, then tipped his head back to down a good half of his wine.

Chairs scraped across the floor as everyone got to their feet and lifted their own glasses – everyone except Anton, at least – and echoed the toast. 'To Dominic.'

Caro let her gaze land on the face of each of the people around the table as they toasted, and sat back down again. She was sure Rosalind and Posy were doing the same, looking for something – anything – that seemed out of place.

Someone around this table was a murderer. And Caro was determined to figure out who – before anyone else fell victim to them.

But whatever it was she hoped to see, she didn't find it. Or perhaps she found too much of it for it to mean anything.

Across from her, Kit was studying the wine in his glass with a strange intensity. Next to him, Scarlett was working her way through a large bag of nuts. Tristan was helping Nina to the crackers she couldn't reach at the other end of the table, but her thank-you smile didn't reach her eyes, and she was rubbing her palms against her jeans like a less dramatic Lady Macbeth. Beside her, at the head of the table, Gabriel topped up his wine glass, and gave Caro a sad smile when she met his eye.

'It's quieter without him here, isn't it?' Gabriel said, and Posy, sitting on his other side, nodded in helpless agreement.

'I didn't know him well,' Posy admitted. 'But he was certainly a force of nature.'

Such a cliché. A thing people said about divisive or offensive characters when they couldn't find anything actually good to say. But Gabriel nodded as if she'd said something wonderfully insightful. Men often did when young, beautiful women spoke, in Caro's experience.

'He certainly was that,' Gabriel said, sagely.

'Did you know him well?' Caro asked. 'Before this movie, I mean.'

Gabriel looked up at her, surprised. 'More knew *of* him, if you know what I mean. We had people in common, and had even been in a couple of movies together, but he was in a different sphere from me, really.'

Nearby, Kit chuckled. 'I think Dominic was in a different sphere to most of us, wasn't he? He was old-school famous, with his mansion in the Hollywood Hills and executive producer credits on everything he starred in.'

'Had *you* worked with him before?' Posy asked Kit, leaning across the table and resting her chin on her hand.

'God, no.' Kit gave a self-deprecating smile. 'If Gabriel wasn't in that sphere, I *definitely* wasn't. I met Dominic for the first time on set here at Tŷ Gwyn.'

'Me too,' said Tristan, and Nina and Scarlett both nodded in agreement.

So much for finding a previously hidden motive there, if none of them had even met him before this week.

At the other end of the table, Anton drained what had to be at least his second glass of wine and staggered to his feet. 'If we're going to toast Dominic, we should at least do it properly.'

'Anton,' Gabriel said, a slight warning tone in his voice, one that surprised Caro to hear. But the director shook it off with an insistent shake of the head.

'No, Gabriel. You're all sitting there pretending you didn't know the man, but you *did*. We all did. Even if we hadn't met him, we knew him. There's no such thing as secrets in this business, is there? You'd all heard the stories, even if you weren't there to see them first-hand. Everyone knew who he was. And you know that he's not worth mourning.' He sloshed more wine into his glass and raised it. 'So here's to Dominic. May he rot in peace. And to whichever of you lot killed him . . .'

He broke off then, slumping abruptly back into his chair as Scarlett gasped.

The penny had dropped, then. It was the first time, though, that any of them had said it out loud. That someone around this table was a murderer.

And none of them could leave.

Caro reached for the wine bottle. It was going to be a long night.

Chapter Twenty-One

'There is very little about a situation that cannot be improved by a judiciously applied cup of tea.' Dahlia reached out to pick up the teapot by its delicate china handle, and smiled across the table at the woman she was certain, now, was a murderer. 'And perhaps just a smidgen of really good cake. Don't you think?'

Dahlia Lively *in* Alibis and Afternoon Tea
By Lettice Davenport, 1950

Rosalind

It was morning before the storm finally died down. Rosalind stood by the window as the rising sun revealed the extent of the damage caused; there was a tree down near the gates, the lawns were covered with debris, and she could see the river had flooded parts of the road back down to the Seven Stars.

Some of the others were dozing, sat upright in the uncomfortable dining chairs, for the most part. There were beds upstairs, but nobody had suggested separating to use them – especially since it would involve passing Dominic's body again. Anton had his head buried in his arms on the table, as if he could block out the entire world if he tried hard enough. Beside him, Scarlett was curled into a ball in her chair, leaning against Gabriel, who had one arm around her and his head tipped back, snoring.

Rosalind was amazed that any of them could sleep at all, after the events of the previous day. But she supposed that eventually even terror was overpowered by biological needs.

Caro had snagged one of the slightly less uncomfortable cocktail chairs by the window, and she stirred as Rosalind moved closer.

'Are the phones working again yet?' Her voice was heavy with sleep, and she rubbed at her eyes, smearing mascara under them. 'God, I'm too old for all-nighters like these.'

Rosalind returned a faint smile. If Caro was too old, what did that make her?

'Still down as far as I can tell.' She nodded across the room towards where Rhian was wearily holding her phone to her ear again. 'She's been trying every half an hour.'

'So what do we do now it's light?' Posy joined them, looking far too beautiful and alert for the circumstances, Kit at her side.

'I think a few of us should try and get down to the Seven Stars,' Kit said. 'See if we can make contact with the police from there.'

'I'll come.' Tristan rubbed a hand across his face and got to his feet. 'I need to get out of here anyway.'

Posy nodded. 'Me too. Okay, the three of us, then?'

'Wait, I want to come too.' Nina stood up, wrapping her arms tightly around her middle. 'I'm not staying here a moment longer than I need to.'

Rosalind scanned the room. The others had woken up now, and it seemed they all felt much the same.

'Can we just leave the body here, though?' Caro asked. 'Shouldn't someone stay with it?'

'I'll stay,' Rhian said, after only a brief pause. 'This place is my responsibility, after all.'

'I don't like the idea of you staying here alone,' Rosalind admitted. Not that she particularly wanted to stay with her.

She wanted to talk to Jack.

'I'll stay too.' Anton sat back, wearily. 'Until the police get here. It's my movie set. I'm responsible too.'

It wasn't a perfect solution, but it seemed the best that they had.

It didn't take long to gather their things together, and nobody was in the mood to linger, so just fifteen minutes later the bulk of the cast was outside Tŷ Gwyn, surveying the path back to the inn.

Tristan sucked in a deep breath of fresh and icy air. 'I feel like I can breathe again for the first time since last night.'

'Me too.' Nina tucked her hand through his arm and, together, they began to pick their way through the storm debris to the gate.

Rosalind could feel the mood lifting, too. Yes, there was still a dead body back in the house. And yes, one of them was still a murderer. But at least here, in the daylight and the open, she felt like they all had a fighting chance.

The road back to the Seven Stars had flooded during the night, but the waters were already receding. Tristan and Kit bashed a hole through a hedgerow to allow them all to walk on the other side of the hedge from the river, protecting them from slipping into the water, and they made their way through the marshy fields back to the Seven Stars.

'Oh, thank goodness you're all okay!' Rebecca met them at the door and ushered them inside, taking Nina's hand and pulling her towards a chair while the others followed. 'It's chaos in the village! The river rose so much that, with the wind too, the bridge collapsed! The road's blocked by fallen trees, so we're totally cut off, the power's still out, and there are houses missing tiles and trees down all over the place. And you lot must be in need of a good strong cup of tea!' She looked around them with a harried smile that sank into a frown. 'Where's Anton? And Dominic?'

Rosalind exchanged a look with Caro and Posy. 'Rebecca, are the phones working here? We need to call the police.'

With the bridge out, roads closed and the police force stretched across the local area dealing with the results of the storm, getting officers out to Tŷ Gwyn wasn't straightforward. But they were at least able to make the required 999 call from the Seven Stars, and promise to all stay where they were until the police arrived.

And Rosalind was able to call Jack.

She left Caro and Posy in the bar, and headed back to her suite, tempted by both the bed and the shower, but knowing if she didn't do this now she'd lose the little courage she had. She shivered a little at the chill in the air; she hoped the power was back on before tonight, or they were going to need a lot more candles, and blankets.

And now she was procrastinating again.

With a sigh, she dropped to the edge of the bed, held her phone tight in her hand, and called.

His first question, on snatching up the phone, was whether she was okay.

'I'm fine,' she promised. 'Tired and shaken and a little scared, but fine.' It felt strange to even admit that much to anybody who wasn't Caro or Posy.

'Good.' The relief in Jack's voice made her smile. 'I was worried.'

'I can tell.' Rosalind's smile faded as she realised what came next. 'Jack, I'm calling because I've got some things I need to tell you.'

'All right. Is this in my capacity as an ex-police officer, or as a friend? Just so I know what hat to wear.'

She considered. 'Honestly? Both.'

'Then talk.'

She did.

She told him everything. About the letters, the threats, the conspiracy theory, the accidents on set and the dagger, their thoughts about Keira's death – and what had happened to Dominic the night before.

She couldn't see him – the signal definitely wasn't strong enough to try for a video call – but she could imagine his face growing more pinched with every line, every threat to her life. By the time she'd finished, his voice was tight with anger.

But anger at her or the perpetrator?

'And is there a reason you didn't tell me any of this before?'

There was, of course. Many a reason. Mostly having to do with fear, pride or denial. But Rosalind didn't want to get into them.

'I'm telling you now. That's what matters.'

He let out a sharp breath. 'I'll have to talk to the team assigned to the case, tell them all this. They'll want to talk to you.'

'I'm sure they will.' A prospect she was not relishing. But with Dominic dead, it was only fair that they shared all the information they'd gathered with the police. 'You'll let me know how that goes.'

'Of course.' He paused, and Rosalind waited, sensing he had something more to say. 'I want you to understand, I'm . . . concerned. For your wellbeing.'

'For everyone's, I'd imagine, under the circumstances.' This investigation wasn't supposed to fall on him, Rosalind reminded herself. He was retired. He was only here to ask a few questions about a simple hit-and-run, take a few statements, then hand it all over to the people in charge.

Except the people in charge were stuck on the other side of a broken bridge, or behind a closed road covered in tree debris, and she had called him.

'For everyone, of course,' Jack agreed. 'But more than that, I'm worried about *you*. I want to keep you . . . safe.'

And suddenly, Rosalind realised this wasn't just a 'stay out of my way and don't endanger my investigation' talk from another angle.

This was Jack, telling her something.

She wished she could see his face.

There was a light rap on the door, then it opened to reveal Caro and Posy, both looking anxious.

'Rosalind?' Caro held up her lit phone screen and Rosalind moved closer to read it. *Ashok calling*.

What excellent timing that boy had.

'Right. Sorry, Jack, I need to . . . I'll talk to you later.' She hung up.

She needed to run. She needed to find out what Ashok had to tell them.

And she definitely needed to solve this murder before she could consider working through all the feelings the softness in Jack's voice had kicked up inside her.

Caro

'You'd better talk fast, kiddo,' Caro told Ashok, as Posy shut the door to Rosalind's suite behind them. 'My phone's getting low on battery and until the power comes back on I've got no way to charge it.'

'Right. Okay. Fast. So I've been looking into this movie of yours – *The Castle on the Hill*.' Ashok's voice was tinny over the speakerphone, sitting on the coffee table in Rosalind's room.

'And?' Rosalind prompted. Caro wondered what Jack had said that had left her so pale. Maybe she'd tell her, after.

'And I keep coming up against a brick wall. Everyone talks about the script, the cast, the auditions – then they clam up when I ask why it didn't get made.'

'What did you find out about the girl who died?' Posy asked.

'A grieving family, a promising career cut short, lots of so-called friends who'd probably met her once crying on social media. Some talk about mental health issues in her teens, but nothing concrete. Story goes she just walked out of that party one night and disappeared. It's unclear how many people even realised she was missing until her body showed up on the shoreline below the Laugharnes' beach house two days later. But there's nothing to suggest it was anything other than a tragic accident, or that it was linked to anyone else.' Ashok's frustration was clear in his voice.

'Nothing else about that night?' Caro pressed. She might not have been to many of those Hollywood parties – certainly not as many as Posy or Rosalind – but she knew how this industry worked. There were *always* stories. It was almost more suspicious for there not to be.

'Not. A. Thing.' From the way he articulated it, she suspected Ashok found that dubious, too. 'But I'll keep asking.'

Something or someone had made Evie Groves disappear. Something had happened to her next, for her to end up dead.

And someone knew what both those things were.

'If there's nothing to find, there's nothing to find,' Caro said, moving them on before her phone died. 'Or at least, nobody talking. And we need you on something else, Ashok. There's been another murder.'

Silence on the other end of the phone, followed by a sharp breath. 'Who?'

'Dominic Laugharne,' Rosalind said. 'Stabbed on the balcony at Tŷ Gwyn yesterday afternoon, although the police would probably prefer that news didn't get out just yet. They're still trying to get across to the scene of the crime right now.'

'The ex-husband of the missing Brigette, and the owner of the beach house where Evie Groves disappeared.' Ashok gave a low whistle. 'Well, now you've really got a story, ladies.'

'That's what we're hoping,' Posy said. 'But we need a way to tie it up with Keira's death, and the death threats, to really make sense of it all.'

Caro leaned in closer to the phone. 'There were four people up on the balcony. Nina Novak, Gabriel Perez, Kit Lewis and the house manager for Tŷ Gwyn, Rhian Hassan.' She thought about Anton's toast to Dominic in the dining room. 'And Anton was up there just before, although it's unclear if he could have done it. We need to know which of them has links to Dominic, Keira or Evie Groves, and the movie that never got made, for that matter.'

'We already know that Gabriel and Dominic had issues – I heard them arguing on the night Keira died – but the rest are pleading ignorance to even knowing him before this movie,' Posy went on.

'See what you can dig up, hey, kiddo?' Caro finished.

'Will do,' Ashok agreed. 'And I'll keep looking for Brigette, too. See if she's got any answers.'

'Thank you, Ashok,' Rosalind said.

'I'm just sorry I can't be more help with the Evie Groves thread,' Ashok said. 'But it's like Hollywood as a whole has pulled up walls around the whole thing. Pretended it never happened.'

Caro shared a look with Rosalind, then Posy. They'd all been around long enough to know what that meant.

No story at all meant there had to be a *big* story hidden in there somewhere. One that was so damaging to someone that 'mattered' that it could never be told – even if it meant that the less important people got trampled on in the hiding.

And the issue of who mattered or not wasn't based on things that normal people would consider right. It all came down to money, influence and power. And, too often, all three of those things lay with the men who made decisions in the film industry, the money men and the stars, not the smaller actors and actresses who did most of the work.

Twenty-something starlet Evie Groves would not have been someone who mattered. Dominic would.

If something was hidden here, Caro would bet money – lots of it – that it was for Dominic's benefit. But now Dominic was dead . . . maybe there would be *somebody* who'd be willing to talk.

'Leave it with us, Ashok,' Posy said, calmly, even though her expression was strained. 'We'll see what we can find at this end.'

Caro hung up the call, and turned to Posy. 'What are you thinking?'

Posy swallowed so hard Caro could see her throat move. 'I've been playing phone tag with Uncle Sol's assistant for the past few days. Maybe it's time for me to speak to the man himself.'

Posy

Posy retired to her own room to make the call. Contacting Uncle Sol was going to be difficult enough without Caro and Rosalind listening in and, if she knew them, offering less than helpful suggestions as she spoke.

No, this was something she needed to do alone. And not just for the sake of the case.

She needed to do this for her.

Perched on the end of the bed, she took a deep breath and tried to ready herself. The mirror over the dressing table opposite showed her shadowy reflection in the glow of her phone – too pale, too haunted. Was that the fault of the murders or the Welsh weather? She wasn't entirely sure.

And now she was procrastinating.

She glanced down at the dressing table and saw, among her lotions and potions, the shiny blue badge that Seren had given her. *WWDD. What would Dahlia do? She'd make the damn call.*

Posy held the phone in her hands, her finger hovering over the number she'd never quite managed to delete, and forced herself to remember the last time she'd seen her Uncle Sol. The less than godfatherly advice he'd given her. The dismissive look in his eye.

You know how this works, Posy – or you should. You've been in this business long enough.

He'd been right. She *should* have known. She should have known better than to trust the people around her, even her own parents, when it came to matters of money and influence. She should have known that even her own godfather wouldn't stand by her when the man she thought was the love of her life hadn't either.

She should have known she'd be on her own if she screwed up too badly. That there were no second chances in this game. At least, not for girls like her.

Men like Dominic, though, they always got their second chances – and third, and fourth, for that matter. Even when stories came out, when they got 'cancelled' by the media or the latest round of starlets, it was never the end of their road. There were still plenty of opportunities for them to tell their side of the story, to show a little contrition. And always enough people ready to talk about how the world had changed, and so had expectations. As if the fact that lots of people were behaving badly at the time made it okay.

All it had taken was a little time, and a great new project, and Dominic had been back on the stage, then on camera, and everyone had forgotten any indiscretions that got him into trouble in the first place. Maybe he hadn't been the worst of them, but he hadn't been the best, either.

Anton had been right. They *had* all heard the stories, the rumours. And yet none of them had spoken up. A fact that left an uneasy, squirming feeling in her stomach.

Had *Keira* been planning to speak?

Posy shook her head. This speculation was all well and good, but it wasn't getting her any actual answers. For that, she needed to make this call.

One last sip of water from the carafe on her bedside table, and another couple of deep breaths, and Posy pressed the call button.

She'd bypassed his assistant's number, this time, and gone straight for his private mobile, hoping he wouldn't have changed the number. It seemed she was in luck, as it rang a few times before she heard a familiar, gravelly voice on the other end.

'Who's this?' The snap in the words wasn't as sharp as she remembered, but it was, unmistakably, Uncle Sol.

'It's Posy, Sol.' While he might maintain the honorary Uncle title in her head, she'd be damned if she was giving it to him in person.

'Posy? My Posy-pie! How you doing? I heard you landed a great role . . . need a little guidance on how to make the most of your comeback? You know I'm always good for that.'

His enthusiasm made her stomach roll even more. Because of course he cared *now*. Of course he wanted to help *now*. When she'd already done the work, found her own way back into the business all on her own. When she'd battled her demons and won, and she didn't need him anymore.

Well, except for information about her investigation. She kind of did need him for that.

But none of the rest of it.

If you couldn't be there for me at rock bottom, I'll be damned if I'm letting you in now I'm on the rise again.

WWDD? She'd say 'not in this lifetime or the next', wouldn't she?

'I'm doing fine on my own, thanks, Sol. This isn't really a business call.'

There was a heavy sigh on the other end of the line. 'So you've heard, then. Who did you speak to? Your parents?'

'No, of course not.' Like she'd call them. Ever. 'What do you mean, heard?'

'It got me in the end, Posy. The Big C. Docs are doing their best, but . . . well. We'll see.'

'You're sick.' It was hard to imagine *anything* taking out Uncle Sol, but a standard, run-of-the-mill illness, even one as horrific as cancer, seemed impossible. It would take a tank, or maybe aliens, to get rid of Sol.

'But that's not why you called.' His voice was a little sharper now. 'So if it wasn't because of my fading health, and you don't want career advice . . . you must want something else. What is it? Money?'

Was that disappointment she heard in his voice? Had Sol honestly thought she might be calling to rekindle their professional or personal connections?

Except . . . wasn't she? In a way?

'Not money,' she said, shortly.

'Really? That's what all my other godkids seem to want. Figure that's why so many of their parents pick me. I mean, it ain't because of my religiosity, right?' He laughed, a croaky sound that led to a bout of coughing.

Posy held the phone a little further from her ear, and tried to ignore the feelings gnawing on her stomach. Not guilt, not exactly. Loss? Maybe.

'Sol, I need some information.' *And then I need to get the hell off this line.* 'Information I think only you might be able to give me. It's about a movie that never got made. *The Castle on the Hill.* I remember you started writing a book about it . . .'

There was no laughter left in Sol's voice as he answered. 'Are you sure? Because, Posy, you can't unknow something once you know it. And a lot of people went to a lot of effort to make sure nobody was talking about that stuff.'

'People like Dominic Laugharne, right?'

'Him, and his team. The people he mattered to,' Sol confirmed. People like Brigette, perhaps.

Posy stared at her reflection in the mirror, and considered what to say next.

What Would Dahlia Do?

She'd ask the questions, even if she didn't like the answers. And she'd keep asking, until she got to the truth.

So that's what Posy would do, too.

'Dominic Laugharne is dead, Sol. Stabbed to death on set yesterday.' She kept talking over his shocked intake of breath. 'And we think it might have something to do with that movie. So whatever you know, whatever got that book of yours pulled, I need to know it too. Okay?'

'Why?' Sol asked. 'Why *you*?'

'Because . . .' *Because I'm Dahlia* probably wasn't a good enough answer for Sol, even if it was the truth. So Posy dug for a better one. 'Because someone has got to make sure people are held accountable for a change. And nobody else seems to be doing it.'

There was a long silence on the other end of the line. And then a rustle, like she could hear him shrug, and the banging of a drawer and papers being flipped through.

'Fine. It won't make no difference to Dom now, and it won't make any to me for much longer either. You want to know? I'll tell you everything. But grab a pen, Posy-pie. You won't want to miss any of this. It's quite the ride.'

Chapter Twenty-Two

*'Honestly, Johnnie. All it takes is a little whisper in the right ear, and
soon everybody knows just what you want them to know.'*

Dahlia Lively *in* A Lively Take on Life
***By* Lettice Davenport, 1931**

Rosalind

Rosalind and Caro sat in silence as they waited for Posy to report
back. Silence was unusual for Caro, but Rosalind appreciated it,
under the circumstances. She had too many thoughts to work
through, thoughts she couldn't even articulate just yet.

Maybe Caro was the same.

Or maybe, she thought, as a light snore came from the daybed,
Caro was asleep.

Eventually, the door opened again, and Posy returned, phone in
hand.

'I think this thing is dead now,' she said, but the stiff set of her
shoulders and the tightness of her jaw belied her easy words. 'Are the
police here yet?'

'If they're not, they will be soon,' Rosalind replied.

'That phone call did take a while,' Caro observed, sitting up
suddenly alert. Rosalind envied her ability to do that. Every year it
seemed to take longer for her to go from sleep to wakefulness.

'Uncle Sol's a storyteller. Never uses one sentence when a paragraph will do. Plus he likes to set the scene and go off on tangents.' Posy threw herself into the empty chair by the coffee table.

'And did he tell you a story worth hearing?' Rosalind asked.

Posy nodded. 'I think so. Evie Groves really did die from an accidental drowning, as far as anyone can tell. Whether she meant to walk out into the water or she got swept away is unknown. But the reason she left the party . . . that I got a better lead on.'

'Oh?' Caro leaned forward towards Posy, and Rosalind realised she'd done the same.

'There was a witness – a friend of Evie's, I think – who said she saw Evie drunk and possibly drugged at the party, with Dominic. He took her upstairs. When the friend tried to find her, the bedroom door was locked. And when Evie finally came down . . . she was a mess. She claimed she couldn't remember what had happened, that she hadn't wanted it, that she had to get out. The friend tried to follow, but Brigette told her to leave Evie to her. She never saw her alive again.'

Caro swore, her expression filled with horror. Rosalind knew how she felt.

'Did Sol know the name of the friend?' She had to focus on the facts. Otherwise she might lose it.

She'd been involved in that film. On set with Evie, and probably her friend. She'd been friends with Brigette and Dominic for years. She could have been at that party.

What would she have done if she had been?

'Just that they'd met on the set for the movie.' Posy looked down at her hands. 'There's more. Sol said there was a rumour of a voicemail Evie left before she died. He couldn't say for sure if it was true. But if it existed . . . it was buried. Either Dominic's team bribed whoever had it to delete it, or the police discarded it.'

'Evidence,' Caro said. 'Evidence that Dominic had raped Evie Groves and driven her to drown herself.'

'Yeah.' Posy gave a hollow chuckle. 'Maybe that would have been the thing to finally bring him down.'

'This has to be what you overheard Gabriel talking to him about, right?' Caro bounced a little on the daybed with excitement, sending a cascade of throw pillows onto the floor. 'The secrets he said Keira knew?'

'Could be.' Rosalind considered the evidence. 'Gabriel wasn't involved in the movie, as far as I can recall, but he could have been an extra, uncredited, if he doesn't show on the main cast lists. Or he might just have been there that night at the party. We need to talk to him.'

'I think we need to talk to Anton, too,' Posy said, frowning. 'There was something about his toast back at Tŷ Gwyn . . . I think he knows something about Dominic and Gabriel, too.'

Rosalind glanced at Caro, then nodded. Posy wasn't the only one who'd noticed that. 'Anton first, then.'

The police finally made it through the blocked roads and across the river and up to Tŷ Gwyn, where they sealed off the house and sent Rhian and Anton down to the Seven Stars with instructions to stay put until officers had been able to take everyone's first accounts of what had happened.

Hearing this, Rosalind, Caro and Posy headed out to meet them.

Owain had a small camping stove running off gas in the kitchen, and he handed them travel mugs of coffee for Anton and Rhian, before they left. 'To help them keep warm on the walk.'

Rhian spotted them first, and darted forward towards them. 'The police have closed up the house!' She sounded distraught, Rosalind thought. Maybe the horror of the night before was finally catching up with her.

Caro handed her the coffee, and Rhian took it gratefully.

'How are you coping?' Rosalind asked. 'Did the police say anything?'

Rhian gave her a fragile smile. 'I feel like I could sleep for a week – but at the same time like I never want to sleep again. You know?'

'I know.' Posy stepped forward and put an arm around her, Caro backing her up on the other side. 'Come on. Let's get you back to the inn. I'm sure Rebecca and Owain can put you up somewhere until we're allowed to go.'

Anton joined Rosalind, laptop bag slung over his shoulder. 'I assume that's what you came here to tell us?'

'And to bring you coffee.' Rosalind passed it to him, and he eyed her suspiciously.

'That's all?'

The others were already a good few metres ahead, out of earshot. Rosalind *could* catch them up easily, but this seemed like the perfect opportunity to play the older lady card.

She slipped her hand through Anton's arm to keep him at her pace. 'I am glad I got the chance to speak with you alone, actually,' she said. 'I wanted to ask you about something you said last night.'

'Last night was very stressful,' Anton replied. 'For all of us. And since I've now been locked up in that house with a dead body for the last twenty-four hours, I don't much feel like answering your questions.'

Rosalind ignored that. 'You said that everyone knew what Dominic was like. Were you talking about the rumours around the death of Evie Groves?'

Anton barked a laugh, and hitched his bag higher on his other shoulder. 'Oh, you heard that one too, huh? Looks like a lot of secrets might come crawling out of the woodwork now he's gone. Dominic liked to clutch all those threads of rumours close to his chest, but without him to hold that web together, well . . . maybe there'll be a change.'

'Were you there? That night at the party?' Rosalind asked. 'I wasn't, even though I was in the film.'

'I was in London,' Anton said, shooting her a look. 'Don't you go trying to pin anything on me, Miss Dahlia Lively. Different continent. But there are always rumours, like I said.'

'And yet you hired him for this movie anyway.'

He swung around and faced her then, a finger raised and pointing. 'Because he put the money in! Do you know how hard it has been to get this movie off the ground after everything that happened last summer? Dominic wanted in on the film because he thought it would put him back in that "family favourite" box again, get him more parts in bigger films.'

'I'm sure he did.'

'I wasn't certain it was a good idea,' Anton went on. 'But Gabriel said it wouldn't be a problem, and it wasn't like anyone else was biting my hand off to invest, so I said yes because I wanted to make this damn film!'

'Gabriel?' Rosalind's spine straightened at the mention of his name. Maybe there was a link between Gabriel and the movie after all. 'Why did you ask *Gabriel* if it would be a problem? We know they've worked together before . . .'

'But not in the last eight years.' Anton started walking again, pointedly not looking at her now.

'Not since *The Castle on the Hill*,' Rosalind said, the maths falling into place easily in her head. 'Why?'

For a moment, she thought he wasn't going to tell her. Then he sucked in a deep breath, let it out, his breath misting in the cold air, and said, 'Because Gabriel Perez was dating Evie Groves when she died.'

Posy

It was too late, and too dark, to talk to anyone else that night, so after Rosalind had filled them in on her conversation with Anton, the Dahlias retired to their rooms by candlelight, and agreed to meet for breakfast to develop their plan for what happened next. Posy, alone in her room, lay in the dark staring at the ceiling for far too long, her brain spinning with snippets of conversations and secrets, Uncle Sol's voice calling her Posy-Pie under it all. And when she slept, she dreamed of the rising river, sweeping her away while around her everyone screamed.

But when she woke, at least it was to the discovery that the power had returned, and she could charge her phone and dry her hair.

The police had set up in one of the private dining rooms, and were speaking to each of the cast and the director individually about the events around Dominic's death. Just knowing they were there seemed to put everybody on edge, and the atmosphere in Saith Seren over breakfast that morning was silent and tense.

At least, until Caro arrived.

Caro, it seemed, slept far better on murder investigations than Posy did, as she positively bounded into the bar, eager for breakfast after the day of cold cuts and pre-packaged snacks they'd had the day before.

'Now we know about the movie, and Gabriel's link to Evie, we need to speak to each of the other three people who were on the balcony around the time Dominic died,' Caro said, without preamble, as she sat down at their table by the fire. 'As soon as they're done with the police, anyway. We've already spoken to Rhian and Anton, so that leaves—'

'Nina, Kit and Gabriel,' Rosalind said, ticking them each off on her fingers. 'We take one each, then?'

Caro nodded. 'I'll take Gabriel. After what Anton told you, he has to be our best suspect, right?'

Posy wasn't sure why Gabriel being their best suspect meant that Caro got to talk to him, but she was too tired to fight it.

'I'll take Kit.' The certainty in Rosalind's voice surprised Posy, and she shot her a questioning look over her coffee cup. 'Well, *you* can't do it, can you?'

Posy thought about making a comment about Jack interrogating Rosalind, but he hadn't called back yet, as far as she knew, and she didn't want to make things worse.

'I guess that leaves me with Nina, then.' The Bess to her Dahlia. And the person who found the body – or pretended to, if she was responsible. 'Any ideas what approach to take with her?'

Caro sat back in her chair, arms folded over her chest, and clicked her tongue as she thought. 'Well, she's already told us about Dominic and Keira, so we know she had some idea what the guy was like.'

'Except she was hinting that *Dominic* had a motive to kill Keira,' Posy pointed out.

Caro shrugged. 'I guess you'll just have to play it by ear.'

Filming had been cancelled, of course. Indefinitely. The whole of Tŷ Gwyn was closed off to them, the public and probably the owners too. Rebecca and Owain had put Rhian up in one of the almost finished suites out back.

Anton, in an even worse mood than ever before, had stomped through long enough to grab breakfast, his phone clamped to his ear, muttering something about reworking the schedule *again*. How he intended to do that when, as far as Posy knew, the police hadn't given them a timescale for allowing them back into the crime scene, she had no idea. But she did understand his need to do *something*.

Sitting around waiting for a murderer to reveal themselves – possibly by attempting to kill Rosalind, or whoever else was next on their hit list – did not seem like a valid plan.

Which was how, after she'd taken her own turn talking to the police, Posy found herself trailing Nina as the other actress walked into the village later that morning.

The police had asked them to stay close to the Seven Stars, and Anton seemed so determined to get the film wrapped despite everything that she couldn't imagine him letting them leave even if the police did, but they weren't under house arrest or anything. And with the village cut off from the outside world by the fallen bridge and closed roads, it wasn't like they could go far, anyway. It meant she didn't have to worry about being swamped by paparazzi, either.

She wasn't in a hurry to catch up to Nina, particularly. Partly that was because she was still trying to order the questions she wanted to ask her in her head. But also because she'd seen Nina's expression as she slipped out of the back door of the Seven Stars that morning.

She'd looked . . . furtive. That was the only word for it.

Posy was pretty sure she didn't want to be followed to wherever she was going. Which was exactly why she was following her.

The storm that had ravaged the area had passed, leaving behind fast-moving clouds in a blue-grey sky. The air was crisp and fresh, and just breathing it helped Posy start to wake up at last. She did wish she'd remembered a scarf, though.

Nina took the shortcut through the woods, barely pausing as she passed the spot where Keira had died. Posy waited, just behind a bush on the bend, until she was sure she wasn't going to look back, then followed – and stopped as she spotted the shiny red postbox on the corner.

Scarlett had told Caro that Nina had gone into the village with Kit, the afternoon before Keira's death, to post a letter. Except she could have done that right here. So why go into Glan y Wern at all? And she'd been very, very late to the Hollywood fundraiser that night. What had she really been doing?

As she hurried to catch up, her questions to ask Nina morphed into wondering what on earth she could be so secretive about that involved a trip to the village. It wasn't as if Glan y Wern offered many opportunities for covert behaviours. She wondered briefly if this had something to do with the mechanics of the murders – disposing of evidence. Except there was no murder weapon to hide – Kit's car was still impounded by the police checking the forensics, and the dagger that had killed Dominic was last seen in his chest. Gloves, perhaps? But Nina had blood all over her hands when she screamed. She'd obviously reached out to touch Dominic before spotting the knife, so any bloodstained clothes were easily explainable.

And besides, she didn't believe Nina was stupid enough to be trying to get rid of evidence in the middle of the day. No, this was something else.

She broke through the last of the trees, onto the Glan y Wern village green, near the war memorial, and scanned the high street for Nina. The river was still perilously high, rendering the lowest banks of the green little more than a few blades of grass poking through the water, but at least the rain had stopped for now, and the banks remained mostly intact, unlike further downstream by Tŷ Gwyn.

Signs of the storm were still evident everywhere – in torn bunting that had hung across the high street, and missing tiles from the slate roofs. Past the Drunken Dragon, she could see where the bridge had been. Evidence of it still remained, in splintered wooden slats and empty brick columns holding up nothing but air. On the other side, she saw men in hi-vis talking, but no vehicles, which she took to mean the road further up was still blocked by trees, too.

Looked like they were going to be on their own for a little longer.

She wondered how the police had got across. And what they had done with Dominic's body. Had they moved it to one of the bedrooms, or was he still sitting there, slumped in the doorway?

She shook the thought away, and looked for Nina, finding her leaving the pharmacy. She hurried across the street, head bowed and keeping out of Nina's sightline, to watch where she went next.

Nina seemed more relaxed, now, Posy realised. Despite the horrors of the past week, she was even smiling as she paused outside a local crafts shop. Whatever she'd been worried about doing here, she'd already done, and Posy had missed it.

Which meant it was probably time to talk to her instead.

She approached the window Nina was staring into slowly, cautiously, not wanted to spook her target. Then she blinked as she realised what Nina was looking at, one hand lovingly clasped against her middle.

Baby clothes. Hand-crocheted, tiny and delicate, baby clothes.

It could have been coincidental, or just an idle daydream, but put together with the pharmacy visit, Posy began to wonder.

What really cinched it, though, was the horrified, terror-filled look on Nina's face when Posy spoke her name, and she spotted her reflection in the window.

Chapter Twenty-Three

'I love this part.' Dahlia smiled the crooked grin she knew he couldn't resist, and Johnnie rolled his eyes.

'Which part? I thought you loved all of it.'

'I do,' she admitted. 'But this part is the best. When everyone's secrets come tumbling out like acrobats at the circus, all confusion and chaos until suddenly they stand on each other's shoulders to make a perfect pyramid.'

'And an answer to our mystery,' Johnnie said. 'Yes, I love this part, too.'

Dahlia Lively *in* **All That's Hidden**
By Lettice Davenport, 1947

Caro

Caro stumbled across Gabriel out by the river, staring at the still partially flooded road between them and Tŷ Gwyn.

'I don't think we're going to be going back there for a while,' she said, and waited, as Gabriel turned to face her.

The storm might have blown away, but it had left them with a fresh breeze and water everywhere, sticks and leaves and whole damn branches jutting out of places they shouldn't be.

'I guess not.' Gabriel kicked out at a branch in his way and moved towards her. 'Anton came to see me last night. So I have a pretty good idea why you're looking for me.'

Well, that made things easier. 'I wanted to ask you about Evie Groves.'

His hands stuffed deep into the pockets of his coat, Gabriel nodded. 'Come on, then. I talk better when I'm walking.'

Many people did, Caro had found. Something to do with not having to look the other person in the eye as they spoke. She and Annie had had some of their most profound and useful conversations out walking, even if they were just wandering the streets around their London home.

'You were dating Evie when she died?' Caro also put her hands in her pockets and followed him, as he trailed a path along the too-high river.

'For a few months before, yes. She was . . .' He looked up towards the sky. 'She was like those clouds. Moving too fast, and impossible to hold onto. She lit up every room she passed through just with her fire for life.'

'She was troubled, too, though?' Posy had said something about mental health concerns, she remembered.

'Isn't everyone?' Gabriel shrugged. 'I mean . . . yes. She had her issues, but they weren't . . . after her death, the press, everyone, they made out that it was inevitable. Part of who she was. That burning bright and dying young Hollywood legend thing. But Evie wasn't *like* that. She used to say she wanted to live to a grand old age and live in a house on the beach with her cats.'

'With you?'

Gabriel huffed an uncertain laugh. 'I don't know. Who *can* know? But . . . she wasn't the person they painted her as. Afterwards.'

'Were you in LA when she disappeared?' Caro asked.

'No. I was overseas, filming. I came back as soon as I realised she was missing, though. I tried to get a search party going, or something, but . . .' He trailed away, staring down at where his boots were squelching through the mud.

'They found her body.'

He shook his head, but didn't look up. '*I* found her body. I'd gone to the beach house to speak to Dominic and Brigette, to try and find out what happened that night at the party. And I went down to the beach afterwards and . . . there she was.'

Caro bit the inside of her cheek as she decided how to proceed. He was obviously genuinely upset by the recollections, she wasn't going to doubt that. But she couldn't shake the feeling there was something else he wasn't telling her.

Beside them, the river rushed through, racing over stones and flying over loose branches, sweeping leaves and debris along with it. Caro thought back over everything they'd learned from Sol, Ashok and Anton the night before, and tried to find it – the chink in Gabriel's story. The tiny hole that would let the truth trickle through until the dam broke.

There.

'I heard that there was a cover-up, afterwards, to keep Dominic and Brigette's names out of things.' She waited, and Gabriel gave a small nod of acceptance. 'I also heard that there was a voicemail from Evie, the night she died. One that either never made it to the police or was destroyed by them.' No response this time. But in a way, that was an answer enough. 'It was a message she left for you, wasn't it?'

If she'd been Evie Groves, and had a traumatic experience at a party with powerful and influential people, if she'd been distraught and not known what to do . . . and if her boyfriend had been overseas filming . . . Caro knew who she'd have called.

The noise that came from the back of Gabriel's throat was halfway between a sob and a groan. He stopped walking, placing a hand on the nearest tree and resting his forehead against the bark, his feet just inches away from the rushing river. Everything about his posture begged her to stop.

She didn't.

'What happened to the voicemail, Gabriel? And what did Evie say?'

'She was sobbing.' Gabriel spoke more to the tree than to her, and Caro had to move closer to hear him. She eyed the river carefully, and stayed on the far side of the tree, within grabbing distance of a decent branch. 'She said she thought she'd been drugged. That she'd woken up in a room and didn't know how she'd got there. That she was naked. She thought . . . she thought she'd been raped.'

'Did she say who by?'

Gabriel nodded against the tree. 'The last person she remembered talking to was Dominic Laugharne.'

Of course it was.

Caro wished the bastard wasn't dead, so she could do something to get *real* justice against him.

'What did you do?'

'With the time difference, and I was filming . . . I didn't get the message for hours. And when I tried to call back there was no answer. So I . . . I walked off set. Flew straight home and went to Dominic and Brigette's house to demand some answers.'

'What did they tell you?'

'That she had been drunk, or high, at the party. That she'd gone off with some guy, and they'd found her later. That they'd tried to put her to bed but she'd disappeared in the night, and they didn't know where.' Gabriel pushed away from the tree, turning around to slump against it instead. His grey face and shadowed eyes showed his guilt as clearly as his words.

'Did you believe them?'

'I . . . I wanted to.' Gabriel swallowed so hard she saw his throat move. 'I played them the voicemail, but they told me she'd been confused, under the influence. That there were plenty of witnesses at the party who'd swear by their story.'

'I'm sure there were,' Caro muttered. Dominic and Brigette types could always find people to agree with them, even if they were arguing that up was down.

'They were so persuasive. So convincing. I started to doubt what I'd heard in that message.' He looked up, meeting Caro's gaze with desperate eyes, like he was looking for her absolution. But that wasn't hers to give.

'They told you to delete the voicemail,' she guessed.

Gabriel nodded, and his chin stayed against his chest. 'Dominic . . . he hinted that if I made trouble, things would go badly for me. But if I worked with him on this . . . there'd be opportunities for me, down the road.'

A sick feeling rose up in Caro's gut. Gabriel had sold out his dead girlfriend for the chance of a movie role, somewhere in the never-never. God, what kind of an industry was this, where things like this could occur?

'I walked out of there in a daze,' Gabriel went on. 'I still thought that Evie was out there somewhere. That I'd find her and everything would be okay. But then I walked down to the beach and—'

He broke. Sobbing, he covered his face with his hands and sank down onto the muddy tree roots, his head against his knees.

'You found her body,' Caro finished for him. 'And that's why you never worked with Dominic again, until now. Why Anton had to check with you that you'd be okay working with him on *The Lady Detective*. But what I still don't know, Gabriel, is whether it was enough for you to kill him.'

Gabriel looked up in horror, his face streaked with tears and grime. 'No! I swear, I didn't. I hated him, yes. But it was too late for me to do anything for Evie. And anything I did do . . . it could only harm my reputation, too.'

Which was why he wouldn't speak out against Dominic when Keira asked. Why he'd given Dominic a heads up that she was gunning for him, the night she died. He hadn't been blackmailing Dominic – he'd been trying to protect both of them from a story that could ruin their reputations.

Her phone buzzed in her pocket, and Caro pulled it out to find a text message from Ashok. No, not a message, a photo.

Caro opened the image and stared at it for a moment.

Then she looked back at Gabriel's broken form, and decided to leave him to his misery.

She wasn't wasting any more investigative time on him.

Posy

'So. You're pregnant.' Posy put the two orange juices on the table between them, and took her seat. The Drunken Dragon was blissfully quiet at this time in the morning, and nobody thought anything of two women stopping by a pub to *not* drink pre-midday.

Nina shot her a scowl. 'In case you hadn't guessed, I'm trying not to let that news get out just yet.'

'Then I'd stop looking lovingly at baby clothes, if I were you.'

'I know.' Nina sighed, her shoulders rounding as she hunched over her drink. 'It's just . . . it's hard to think about anything else, to be honest.' There was a tiny smile, hovering around the corner of Nina's lips, and Posy couldn't help but return it.

'So I take it you're . . . happy about this?'

293

Nina nodded, and took a sip of her orange juice. 'Oliver and I – that's my boyfriend – we weren't trying, or anything, but when it happened . . . it felt right. You know how that goes?'

'I didn't even know you had a boyfriend.' They'd been trying to investigate all the cast, and yet it turned out they didn't even know the basics. Posy supposed that, being a fresher face and better known for stage than screen work, Nina's love life flew rather more under the radar than her own.

Nina dipped her chin, and her dark hair fell in front of her face, hiding her from view. 'I like to keep my private life private, as far as I can. Oliver understands that.'

'Not to mention if people knew you were pregnant it would affect your chances of getting parts.'

It wasn't supposed to, of course, but it did. Even if said role was due to film *after* the baby was born. Just another way the industry tipped those scales against women.

Nina acknowledged the point with a tilt of the head, and her silky hair fell aside again, so Posy could see her troubled expression. 'I had to tell Chrissie, in wardrobe. I'm only three months, but already my shape seems to be changing. Not enough to notice normally, but in a maid's costume tailored exactly for me?'

'You needed it letting out,' Posy realised. 'That's why you were in wardrobe that morning we spoke to you about Keira.'

'That's right.'

Posy mentally kicked herself. She should have spotted that. The costumes had been ready for weeks, and Nina had already been wearing hers for filming. Maybe there might have been a small repair or adjustment needed, but nothing to the extent Chrissie was doing that morning.

'So I assume your trip to the pharmacy this morning was pregnancy-related too?' she asked.

'Anti-nausea meds.' She gave Posy a pained smile. 'I've been suffering badly, and just run out. Luckily my doctor was able to give me a repeat prescription over the phone. We'd been hoping it would have run its course by now, but apparently not.'

Something else in the 'con' column for ever having kids. 'That's why you came into the village the afternoon before Keira's death, isn't it? To talk to the pharmacist?'

'Obviously not something I wanted to tell *everyone*.' The look Nina gave her seemed to question whether Posy intended to do just that.

'Understood.' Posy gazed across the table at her, and wondered if she was sitting with a murderer. Only one way to find out. 'Nina, can I ask you some questions about something else?'

'The murder?' Nina guessed. 'Sure. I mean, I've already told you my biggest secret. I guess I can tell you about that, too.' After that horrific, terrifying night at Tŷ Gwyn, after Dominic's murder, it seemed that the cast had resigned themselves to the fact that the Dahlias were in charge of questions.

'You found the body first. But it wasn't there when you first went up the stairs?'

'No. I'm certain it wasn't. I'd have noticed.' Hard to miss a body bleeding out, Posy agreed.

'And you went up to get your phone charger?'

Nina pulled a face. 'That's what I said. Actually, I was just looking for a bathroom to throw up in – away from everyone else. So I might not have been paying the best attention – but I'd definitely have noticed if he was there.'

That made more sense. Posy updated her notes on who was where when and why in her notebook. The charger thing had been bothering her, mostly because Nina had been on set with her most of the day, not upstairs, so when would she have left her charger?

'So you went up after Anton had come down, following Kit. Gabriel and Rhian were already up there, we think. Did you see anything strange? Can you talk me through what happened?'

'Nothing strange,' Nina said, slowly, as if she were running the events through her mind like a movie. 'I was kind of focused on making it to the nearest toilet bowl on my way up, so I didn't really see where everyone else went. But we weren't up there very long, were we?'

'Maybe ten minutes? I wasn't timing, but Anton was losing his mind.'

'Anton is always losing his mind these days.' Nina sighed. 'Anyway, I came back out and that's when I saw Dominic in the doorway. I thought he'd collapsed or something, I guess. I don't know – I wasn't really thinking much. But he was on my way to the stairs, so I stopped and bent down to shake his arm, check if he was asleep, or okay, or whatever. And then his jacket moved, and I looked down and saw the knife, and my hands were covered in blood and—' She reached out for her orange juice with shaking hands.

'You screamed.' Posy didn't think anybody there that day would forget that sound in a hurry.

'Yeah. And that's all I know for sure.'

Something about Nina's words, the way she looked over Posy's left shoulder rather than directly at her, gave her pause. 'All you know for *sure*. But what else do you suspect?'

Nina gave her a wry smile. 'I told you about what happened here, with Keira and Dominic. But I didn't tell you I heard him begging her not to talk, the day afterwards. She didn't seem to be listening.'

'Why *didn't* you tell us that?' Posy asked, frustrated.

'Because . . . because I don't want to be in the middle of whatever is happening here. I pointed you in Dominic's direction and figured I'd done enough. That you – or the police, or whoever – could figure it out from there.'

'You think Dominic killed Keira.'

'Don't you?' Nina raised her eyebrows with surprise. 'Not because she interrupted him with Scarlett, but because of who she was. The influence she had. Dominic had already had to fight his way back from allegations like this before, remember. He wouldn't have wanted to do it again.'

'That makes sense.' They needed Ashok to look up more about the other accusations Dominic had faced over the years. But added to the fact he was getting death threats over the death of Evie Groves, and his ex-wife had just disappeared . . . she could buy the idea that he'd have done anything to stop Keira talking. Like planning to meet her at the Drunken Dragon to talk, then mowing her down with a borrowed car instead, just in case. 'The night she died, Keira said something to Dominic in the bar. I wish I could remember what it was.'

'She said, "I can watch you fail anytime I like."' Nina shrugged. 'I was standing behind you.'

'Right.' Suddenly the pieces were starting to fall into place. She gave Nina a crooked smile. 'You know, you're a pretty good Bess to my Dahlia today.'

Nina laughed. 'Maybe. But, can I ask . . . why are you so keen to investigate this?'

'Because . . .' There were so many answers she could give, all of them real. But only one felt true. 'Because I'm Dahlia. And it's what Dahlia would do.'

'Right.' The crease between Nina's eyebrows and her puzzled smile told Posy that she didn't get it. But that didn't matter. Posy *did*. Finally.

So, back to business.

'But this theory about Dominic and Keira does leave us with one obvious problem,' Posy pointed out.

'Who killed Dominic? Yeah. I know.'

'We'd been assuming it was someone with a grudge for more historical reasons,' Posy said, thinking aloud. 'But what if it was because someone knew he killed Keira?'

'Revenge, you mean?' Nina nodded. 'That makes sense.'

'Who was Keira closest to on the cast? Tristan and Scarlett, Kit, and maybe Gabriel,' she said, finishing her own question. She watched Nina closely as she spoke, and saw her flinch at the first name. 'You think Tristan? He wasn't even upstairs when Dominic died.'

'No. But . . . he and Keira had been friends for years, and she always said it was nothing more. I mean, Tristan was friendly with everyone, right? But I'd seen them together over the years, and they definitely seemed to be growing closer this movie. Whispering in corners together. And . . .'

'And?'

Nina sighed. 'The afternoon before Keira died, when Kit gave Tristan, Dominic and me a lift into town . . . I saw Tristan's phone in the car. He was texting someone – I couldn't see who. But it was a . . . certain kind of text . . .'

Posy's eyebrows rose. 'Go on.'

Nina sighed. 'He was saying how he couldn't wait to get whoever he was sending the message to alone later. And, well, naked. And then I stopped looking because I *really* don't like to think of Tristan that way, you know?'

'You two have been friends a long time.' Posy's mind was whirring. 'Did he tell you he was seeing anyone?'

'No. Normally he would, but . . . well. I haven't told him about the baby, either, although I know I need to – especially now you know. The point is, if he was with someone who wanted to keep it secret . . .'

Keira Reynolds-Yang might want that. Her love life was even more likely to be spread across the newspapers than Posy's. She could see how she might want to keep it quiet, especially while they were filming together and the paparazzi were everywhere.

And Keira had been waiting for someone, the night she was killed. They'd assumed the murderer, but now Posy wasn't so sure. If Tristan had been held up, unable to meet her . . . or even gone out later and seen Dominic getting into Kit's car . . .

'You think he and Keira were together? Like a couple?' She needed to be sure.

Nina pulled an uncertain face. 'Maybe? I don't know for sure. But . . . I wondered.'

'Yeah.' And now Posy was wondering too. About a lot of things.

Chapter Twenty-Four

'It's just like this orange, Bess.' Dahlia peeled the dimpled skin away
from the fruit in her hands. 'Once we strip away the first layer of
lies, we get to the juicy flesh of truth that we've been looking for.
And inside that—' She dug a nail into one of the segments and
flicked out a pip, straight into the fire. 'That's where the solution is
hiding.'

Dahlia Lively *in* Carols and Crimes
***By* Lettice Davenport, 1939**

Rosalind

Rosalind found Kit sitting in the empty beer garden, his feet propped up on a still frost-covered table.

'I suppose you'd like to ask me a few questions,' he said, when he saw her approaching. 'You three are doing your Dahlia thing again, aren't you?'

She inclined her head in a slight nod. Kit dropped his feet to the ground, the front legs of his chair hitting the stone slabs underneath with a thump, then gestured to the chair opposite him.

'I wanted to ask if you saw anything unusual on the balcony, the day Dominic died.'

'Other than his dead body, you mean?'

'Well, yes.'

'Nothing,' he said, succinctly. 'Trust me, I've been over that afternoon again and again in my head, but I didn't see *anything* out of the ordinary up there on the balcony, or in the rooms I went into. Not until Nina screamed and I saw the body.'

'Did you check the room where Dominic was found?' Rosalind asked. 'You were up there looking for Gabriel, right?'

Kit nodded. 'No, I didn't, actually.'

'Why not?'

He frowned with the effort of remembering. 'Because . . . because the door was open, and I could see the room was empty. So I didn't bother going in.'

'You're sure?' Rosalind pressed. 'The room was empty?'

'Yeah. I'm sure.' He looked up and met her gaze for the first time since they'd been talking. 'But then how did the body get there? We weren't up there that long. How did nobody see?'

'That's the question we're trying to answer.' Rosalind wished Posy was there with her notebook, so they could run over the sequence of events again. But she was certain that Scarlett had heard Dominic, earlier that afternoon, in that front bedroom where he was found. If she'd only *heard* him, presumably that meant the door was then closed. But it was open when Kit went upstairs, and the room empty. Then, ten minutes or so later, Dominic was dying in that open doorway.

What happened in between to make it all fit?

'I suppose he could have been in the bathroom?' Kit said, after a long, silent minute. 'I wouldn't have seen him then, so it would seem like the room was empty.'

'Mmm.' It was the only logical answer. But then who had gone in there, without being seen by the others, and stabbed him?

Nobody had been watching Anton when he went up, and Gabriel and Rhian had already been up there. Could one of them have stabbed Dominic in the bathroom, only for him to stagger out and finally die in the doorway some minutes later? Or had someone else been hiding in there with him, and remained hidden until they all left the scene, before they escaped into the storm? Rosalind didn't know.

The police, when they finally finished their post-mortems and scene-of-crime checks, might be able to tell her. Not that she thought they would.

She and her fellow Dahlias didn't have the luxury of science and forensics to answer their questions. She'd leave the police searching for evidence and proof.

She'd stick to ferreting out motives.

'Kit, where were you the night of the Hollywood fundraiser? The night Keira was killed?'

He bristled at the question. 'You know I was back here drinking with Anton before she died. You *proved* that.'

'We did,' Rosalind said. 'But you never told us where you'd been *before* that. Were you meeting someone?' Not Keira, as far as they could tell – she'd been alone in the Drunken Dragon. But someone.

'I didn't tell you because it was none of your business.' Kit got to his feet, then stopped, staring across the beer garden at the archway that led into it.

Rosalind turned, and saw Posy and Caro standing there.

'I just got sent the most interesting photograph,' Caro said.

Posy gave Kit a sympathetic smile. 'I told you that you wouldn't be able to keep it a secret from them, if they decided they wanted to know.'

'But you didn't tell them.' Kit sank back down into his chair, and the others came to join them.

'Of course not,' Posy replied. 'I promised, didn't I?'

Rosalind wrapped her coat tighter around her against the chilly breeze, and decided she had no patience for cryptic conversations today. 'If *somebody* would like to tell me what is going on?'

Kit sighed. 'I only told Posy because I needed her to cover for me if Anton noticed I wasn't there that night.'

'When he asked me, I said that you'd had to get something checked on your car and weren't back yet,' Posy admitted. 'Which, with hindsight, might not have been the best possible lie.'

'Is there such a thing?' Rosalind asked, in a murmur. In her experience, no lies ever ended well.

'But this photo shows you with a young woman at a cheap hotel two towns over.' Caro waved her phone across the table, and Rosalind grabbed her wrist to look at it properly.

'Ashok sent this?' she guessed, and Caro nodded.

Kit looked between them in disbelief. 'You were having me *tailed*?'

'Of course not,' Posy said, soothingly. 'I mean, this was taken before Keira's death, so what reason would we have had then anyway?'

'So where did he get the photo?' Kit demanded, his arms folded tight across his chest as he stared them down.

'From one of your fans' Instagram pages,' Caro replied with a shrug. 'You're a recognisable face and someone recognised you. You're just lucky that it hasn't been spotted by the media yet.'

Rosalind considered the photo on Caro's phone again. In it, Kit was embracing the young woman – she looked a few years younger than him, as far as she could tell, and they were both smiling. As she swiped through the sequence of photos Ashok had sent, Rosalind watched the pair walk inside the hotel, side by side.

'Who is she?' Rosalind asked, handing the phone back to Caro.

'My half-sister. According to the DNA tests.' Kit sighed. 'I didn't want anyone to know until *I* knew for sure. She contacted me out of the blue a month or so ago, claiming to be my dad's daughter, but I didn't know whether to trust it or not, so I wouldn't agree to see her. When she suggested we get tested . . . I figured at least I'd know for sure. We got the test results the day before the fundraiser and she travelled up to Wales to meet me for the first time. I wasn't going to miss it.'

'Of course not.' Rosalind smiled gently at him. 'And I understand not wanting to air your private business, too. Thank you for sharing it with us.'

'And, uh, sorry about the private investigator thing,' Caro said, wincing a little. 'We hadn't asked him to look into you particularly or anything. He's just keeping an eye on all the cast's secrets for us right now. Just in case.'

Kit didn't look particularly mollified by that information, and Posy had her arms wrapped around her middle as if trying to make herself small enough to disappear from the centre of this conflict.

It seemed that nobody knew quite what to say next – until the sound of the Dahlia TV theme tune broke the tension.

Caro stabbed at her phone to stop it. 'Hello? Ashok?'

'You were supposed to call me back!' Ashok's voice was quiet but still audible, even though he wasn't on speakerphone. 'Did you get the photos?'

'Yes, I got them. Was that all you wanted to talk about?'

'Not. By. Half.' Ashok sounded very pleased with himself – which Rosalind hoped meant he'd found something useful. 'Can you talk privately?'

'Hang on.' Caro stood up, looking meaningfully at Rosalind and Posy. 'We need to go inside. Beer gardens aren't meant for February, anyway.'

Caro

'Put him on speakerphone,' Rosalind instructed Caro as they returned to their room. 'We all want to hear.'

Caro obliged, placing the phone on top of the books on the coffee table.

'What have you got for us, Ashok?' Caro asked.

'Not as much as I'd like,' the PI grumbled. 'In addition to those pictures of Kit, I've discovered that Gabriel has gambling debts and Tristan's flatmate hung himself five years ago. Oh, and I think I've found Brigette—' They interrupted him with impressed gasps and a whoop of delight from Posy, but he kept talking. 'Don't get too excited. I *think* I've found her, but I can't get close and I get the impression that, even if I could, she wouldn't talk to me.'

'Where is she?' Rosalind asked.

'Staying at her son's here in London, I think. Grayson.'

'You think? Have you *actually* seen her?' Posy's delight at the news seemed to have downgraded fast into a frown.

'I've seen him, looking ridiculously shifty whenever he opens his front door, taking in food that's clearly for two people, not one – I mean, M&S meal deals, for a start – and the curtains in the front bedroom haven't been open all week. Plus I traced the email she sent, to his IP address.'

'I'd have led with that one, if I were you, Ashok,' Rosalind said, drily.

'But the other stuff's so much more classic private investigator,' Ashok replied.

'All the same,' Caro said, 'the email's the clincher. She's there, and in hiding. But why?'

'Same death threats as the others?' Ashok suggested. 'I tried knocking on the door when the son was out, posing as a delivery driver, but there was no answer. And when I went back when he *was* there, with a parcel for the wrong address and needing help finding it, he came out onto the doorstep to talk to me and shut the door behind him.'

'Maybe she'd talk to me,' Rosalind mused. 'I mean, maybe not. But it depends on whether the news about Dominic is out yet, I suppose.'

'It is,' Posy confirmed. 'It hit the socials last night, and the police confirmed it this morning. She'll have heard, for sure.' The moment the bridge was replaced and the roads surrounding the area were cleared, Caro was sure they'd be swamped with reporters again.

'The police would have spoken to the son as the next of kin, apart from anything else,' she said.

'They did,' Ashok told them. 'I saw them last night. He let *them* into the house, but I don't suppose he really had much choice.'

'So the police might know Brigette is there?' Caro wondered if Jack knew, and if he was still friendly enough with Rosalind to tell them.

'Not necessarily,' Ashok said. 'They didn't go upstairs. There's a window in the stairwell, you see, so I'd have seen them.'

Caro paused for a moment. 'Ashok, are you still sitting outside Brigette's son's house right now?'

'Well, yes. I can't leave until I actually see her for myself, can I?' He sounded like he thought she was an idiot for even asking. 'Besides, this job is loads more interesting than the usual cheating-spouses work I do. And with my laptop tethered to my phone I can do pretty much all my other stuff from the car anyway.'

Caro wondered how much he was going to be charging them for all this, then remembered he was sending the invoices Rosalind's way. Just as well. She was probably the only one of the three of them who could afford it.

'We need to talk to her,' Caro said. 'Leave it with us and we'll see what we can figure out.'

'And what do I do in the meantime?' Ashok asked.

'Stick with it, I guess,' Rosalind replied. 'And let us know if anything changes.'

'Will do.' Ashok hung up.

The three Dahlias looked at each other in silence for a moment. They'd found Brigette – or Ashok had. Another piece of the puzzle. Now they needed to figure out how it all fitted together.

Posy pulled out her notebook. 'Okay, so we have Brigette. We all know what Kit was hiding. I need to tell you what I found out from Nina – and Caro, what did Gabriel have to say?'

'We need tea for this.' Getting up from the bed, Rosalind crossed to the mini kitchenette and clicked on the kettle, setting out three china cups and saucers.

Caro filled them in on her conversation with Gabriel as succinctly as possible, hoping they'd be able to move on quickly to how they were going to get Brigette to talk to them. But Posy got hung up on Gabriel's actions.

'He just abandoned her,' she said. 'For the sake of his own career.'

'She was already dead. It's not like he could have changed anything,' Rosalind pointed out.

'He didn't know that, though.' Posy's hands were clenched on her lap. 'I know you think I'm taking this too personally, but I just can't help imagining how easily that could have been me.'

'We all know how fickle friendships and allegiances can be in Hollywood,' Rosalind agreed.

'I think the guilt has weighed heavily on him, over the years,' Caro said. 'If that's any consolation.'

'It's not.' No, Caro hadn't really imagined it would be. But it was the sort of thing a person had to say, wasn't it?

'He was slime,' Rosalind said. 'Even if I can . . . understand his reasons, while not agreeing with them. I didn't speak up either, remember.'

'You weren't at that party,' Posy countered. 'You didn't have that phone message.'

'No. But I knew not to leave a younger actress alone in a room with Dominic. We all did. And not one of us said anything to anyone outside the business. We just told those girls to stay in pairs.' Rosalind tossed a teabag in the bin with unnecessary force. 'We were no better. *I* was no better.'

She was right, Caro knew. But she also knew that she'd been in rooms like that too. Where someone had all the power and everyone knew they had to work around them, if they wanted to work at all.

'What about you?' she asked Posy. 'Did you get anything good from Nina?'

Posy took her cup of tea from Rosalind, and settled cross-legged on the bed. 'Lots.'

By the time she reached the part about Tristan and Keira, Caro's mind was already skipping forward to the new avenues of investigation it opened up.

'So Nina thinks Tristan was sleeping with Keira, and killed Dominic in revenge because he was behind the hit-and-run,' Caro summarised. 'Wow.'

'That's the working theory,' Posy confirmed. 'But it has a few holes.'

'Not least the fact that Tristan wasn't up there when Dominic was killed, or found. He was in the hall with us,' Caro said, thoughtfully.

'Like I said. Holes.' Posy sighed. 'But it's a theory.'

'And it might be our next best lead to follow,' Rosalind agreed. 'But what about Brigette?'

'We need to talk to her,' Caro said, firmly. 'I can't shake the feeling that, whatever made her leave Tŷ Gwyn that day, it's the key to everything that's happened since. Rosalind, you were friends, weren't you? Do you think she'd speak to you?'

Rosalind gave a helpless shrug. 'I don't know. I can't imagine she's taking many calls right now.'

An idea sparked in Caro's brain. 'What if you went to London in person?' When the others stared at her with disbelief, she continued. 'Think about it! If you're in London, you can't be at risk from whatever madman stabbed Dominic – and don't think I didn't hear you tossing and turning all last night, I *know* you're not sleeping.' Rosalind didn't argue that point. '*And* you might be our only way of getting the information we need to solve this case.'

'The roads are opening up again after the storm,' Posy added thoughtfully. 'So the trains are probably running too. And Rebecca said they were putting in a temporary bridge. If you left tonight you could be back tomorrow afternoon – no one would even need to know you were gone.'

'Like the police, who might find my sudden flight rather suspicious.' Rosalind sighed, and Caro suspected she was worrying about what *Jack* might think, rather than the police at large. 'Okay. I'll go. But you two will have to cover for me.'

Chapter Twenty-Five

'Don't you think this will make us look rather suspicious?' Johnnie
pulled a dubious expression as he adjusted his hat in the mirror.

Dahlia gave him a fond look. 'My dear, that's entirely the point of
the exercise.'

Dahlia Lively *in* Diamonds for Dahlia
***By* Lettice Davenport, 1958**

Posy

Rosalind left for London that evening, surreptitiously packed off in a
taxi from the village, hopefully unseen. Posy and Caro watched the
tail lights disappear over the temporary bridge that had been levered
into place next to the old site of the bridge, until it could be rebuilt.

'You know, we still don't know for sure who Keira was out there
waiting to meet that night,' Posy said, as they turned to make their
way back to Saith Seren. 'Tristan seems the most likely, I suppose.
But I don't understand why he didn't show up.'

'Could technically still be Kit, if he'd arranged to see her on his
way back from his little rendezvous,' Caro mused. 'Or even Dominic,
if she was threatening to expose him and he'd asked for a chance to
convince her otherwise.'

'Or somebody else entirely,' Posy said with a sigh. 'Someone we
haven't even considered in this case and completely unconnected to

her death. But I still think we need to talk to Tristan next. If he and Keira *were* together, and hiding it, I want to know.'

'Agreed,' Caro said.

Posy had hoped to find Tristan in the bar at the inn, or at least in his room, so they could talk. But as they passed the children's playground just off the village green, she spotted a familiar figure sitting on one of the swings.

'Is that Tristan?' she whispered to Caro.

'Looks like it,' Caro replied. 'Well, no time like the present. Shall we talk to him together?'

Posy considered. Tristan's arms were looped around the chains of the swings, while his head was dropped to stare at the brightly coloured play surface under his feet. He looked . . . despondent, was the only word she could think of.

'I'll go. You head back to the inn and keep an eye on things there.'

Posy didn't make it a full step forward before Caro grabbed her arm and pulled her back. 'You do remember that he's a suspect in our murder inquiry, right? I'm not leaving you here alone with him!'

She had a point, although it was hard for Posy truly to imagine Tristan – flirtatious, fun Tristan – as a murderer. But if it had been in revenge for the murder of the woman he loved . . .

She also knew it was impossible to predict what a person would do when cornered.

'Okay. You stay hidden here and watch,' Posy suggested. 'Keep your phone out and call the police at the first sign of anything.'

'And when it takes them forever to get here?' Caro replied.

'We're in the middle of the village.' A slight exaggeration; the playground was on the edge, nearer the woods, but there were still plenty of people around and lights on in the buildings. 'We'll scream, people will come to help us, and he'll run.' At least, that was the theory.

After a moment's thought, Caro nodded and released her arm.

The village green was still squelchy underfoot from the recent rain as Posy crossed towards the playground. The sun setting over the mountains in the distance, behind Tŷ Gwyn, was so beautiful, though, that she could almost forget that a storm had raged here just a couple of days ago.

Even if she wouldn't ever forget the events of that night.

Really, Wales was a very beautiful country, but she'd prefer to visit it in a season with rather less weather – and murder.

Of course, with two of the principal cast dead, and the set closed for a murder investigation, it was entirely possible that she wouldn't be here very much longer anyway. Perhaps *The Lady Detective* would end up like *The Castle on the Hill*. A movie that never got made, thanks to scandal, death and disaster.

And Posy would have to find another way to forge her comeback from the fame wilderness.

Would she even still get to call herself a Dahlia if the movie never got finished?

She approached the swings as stealthily as she could, taking a moment to study Tristan when he didn't know he was being watched. Frown lines marred his forehead, and his usual smile was nowhere to be seen.

Tristan looked up in surprise as she took a seat on the swing next to him. 'Posy! This is a pleasant surprise. Come to play?'

His voice was warm with its usual flirtatious tone, and she wondered if Tristan had ever met a woman he *didn't* flirt with. He reminded her of Kit that way. Except, his way of doing it felt different to Kit's. Less . . . targeted, somehow. And maybe less like he expected anyone to take him up on it.

Perhaps it was all a cover, to hide the fact that he was actually in a secret relationship he didn't want anyone to get wind of. Or Keira didn't. After all, she was the big, famous name with the family connections. Tristan was the local boy, a bit-part actor even here in Britain, mostly known for teen TV shows and a part in a *Doctor Who* Christmas special a few years back. He had everything to gain from the connection with Keira, if there was one. But he'd kept it silent.

Because he loved her? And if all that guesswork proved true, the next question had to be – did he love her enough to kill?

'You might not think it's quite so pleasant when I tell you what I've come over here to talk about.'

Tristan twisted his swing to face hers. 'Oh?'

'I need to talk to you about Keira.'

'What about Keira?'

'Were you two together? Lovers, I mean?' Better to just rip off that sticking plaster and ask, right? The Caro approach to investigation, rather than the Rosalind.

Tristan's mouth formed into a O shape, then he shook his head with a laugh that sounded far more like he was mocking himself than Posy. 'What on earth could give you that idea?'

'You two were friends, right?' Had Nina really got this so wrong? Had she?

'Old friends, yes,' Tristan admitted. 'We met through a mutual friend – my old flatmate, actually, when they dated briefly – years ago. But we've never been more than that. I thought, once . . . but no. We were always better as friends.'

'Oh.' Was he lying? She couldn't tell. Posy leaned back against the chain of her swing, wondering how long it had been since she'd sat on one. Even as a child, she was more often on set than at a playground.

'Why . . . why did you think Keira and I were together?' Tristan's eyebrows were knotted in a frown, like he was trying to make sense of the impossible.

Posy sighed again. 'Nina told me you were.'

That sent his eyebrows flying into his hairline. 'Nina? Where did she get *that* idea?'

'She saw you sending a text in the car – about meeting someone that night and, um, hopefully seeing them naked. And, well, you and Keira seemed close. She said she'd seen you guys together a lot more on this movie than ever before.' Posy shrugged. 'I guess she took two and two and made five.'

'More like forty-seven.' Tristan laughed, but it sounded forced. 'I assure you, Keira and I were just friends.'

He *wasn't* lying, she was almost sure – she had developed a pretty good sense of when people were lying to her since discovering the truth about her parents. And, well, every single one of her ex-boyfriends. Okay, fine, she wasn't *always* good at telling when someone was lying, but she was pretty sure Tristan wasn't.

Which didn't mean he wasn't still hiding something . . .

'In that case, I have to ask.' Posy leaned closer, until the chains of their swings almost tangled together, and lowered her voice. 'Who *were* you meeting?' She waggled her eyebrows just a little, trying to make it sound more like she was an overcurious friend than someone investigating a murder. But Tristan turned white at the question all the same.

'They were . . . well, you know, just . . . someone. An old friend I hook up with sometimes. But I changed my mind, obviously, because I was at Saith Seren all night, wasn't I?'

Even if he hadn't stammered his way through the explanation, she'd have known he was lying. Which meant the truth was worse. But worse how? A more embarrassing relationship – or something that would put him in the police's line of inquiry for one or more murders?

314

She needed to find out.

'You were in the hall with me and the others when Dominic was found,' she said, tapping the chain with her nail as she mentally worked her way through all the things she knew about Tristan's movements that night, and when Dominic died. 'And you were at the fundraiser with us all the night Keira died.'

'That's right.' He sounded confused at the sudden change of conversational flow.

'And we know you didn't slip out to steal Kit's car that night because . . .' And suddenly, four different puzzle pieces slipped into place. 'Because you were with Rebecca in the bar. And she sent her husband to bed early because he had a headache.'

'Posy—'

'But Owain couldn't sleep. And the moon was bright and full that night, so he got up to close the curtains better, or because he thought he heard something, and he saw a light on inside one of the unfinished suites.'

'*Posy*—'

'And when he told Caro that, Rebecca dropped a whole tray of glasses. Because *she* was in that suite, wasn't she? She was who you were meeting that night. You were having sex with *Rebecca* when Keira was killed.'

No outcry of her name this time. Instead, Tristan winced, sank down in his swing and looked at his feet.

'You got me.'

'You're having a fling – an affair, even – with our landlady.' Posy tried to get her head around this. 'Tristan, you know this can't end well.'

'I know, I know.' He scrubbed a hand over his fair hair. 'I'm going to end it. I am. It just . . . it just happened. You know?'

'Not really.'

'Well, it did. But don't worry.' He jumped to his feet, the swing still moving behind him. 'I'm going to sort it. Okay?'

He pressed a friendly kiss against her hair and strode away. Posy watched him go, wondering if she'd just, somehow, made things a lot worse.

Rosalind

It was, Rosalind had to admit, nice to spend a night in her own bed, in her own flat, in London for a change. Even when they'd come down for the morning shows she'd stayed in a hotel because it was closer to the studios and the station.

But since she wasn't supposed to be in London, nobody would mind if she stayed at her own damn home for a change.

It was quiet, though, without the others around. So she called in to Caro and Posy once she was settled, to find out what they'd learned from Tristan.

'So, scandalous but not helpful,' she summarised, when they'd finished.

'Basically,' Posy agreed. 'Hopefully you'll get something more useful from Brigette tomorrow, when you speak with her.'

'*If* I speak with her,' Rosalind corrected. 'Or rather, if she'll speak with me.' They'd been friends once, yes. But that was many years ago. And if Brigette was scared . . . why would she trust Rosalind when she clearly wasn't trusting anyone else?

Still, she had to try.

'There was . . . one other thing,' Caro said, tentatively, into the gap in the conversation.

That was a red flag in itself. Caro was *never* tentative.

'What?'

'Jack was here, when we got back to Saith Seren,' Posy said. 'He was looking for you.'

Perfect. The one person who might actually notice she was missing. 'What did you tell him?'

'We put him off with some line about a headache and an early night,' Caro replied. 'But he'll be back tomorrow. Hopefully not until after you are.'

After she rung off with the Dahlias, she checked her messages to see that Ashok had agreed a time to meet her, just around the corner from the house of Brigette's son the next morning. Then she ran herself a leisurely bath, and tried not to think about murders at all.

It almost worked.

The following morning, Ashok was waiting for her as she walked down the leafy, south London street in the early spring sunshine. Cold enough to need a coat and gloves, it was still the sort of bright-skied day that gave her hope for better weather to come. She wondered how long it would take this sort of day to reach the north of Wales.

'Ready?' Ashok asked her, and she nodded.

Grayson's house was a stately looking townhouse in a row of identical ones, with a front door painted a deep forest green, and a bay tree in a pot either side of it. Rosalind rang the bell, then waited at the bottom of the two stone steps that led up to the door.

Grayson answered, and she watched his face turn ashen as he realised who was there.

'I know your mother is here, Grayson,' Rosalind said, not unkindly. 'And I'm hoping she might be willing to speak with me. I assure you, I only want to help.'

'I . . . my mother's in California,' Grayson lied.

'No,' Ashok said. 'She's really not. And we have proof.'

'Let them in, Grayson.' Brigette's voice came from the top of the stairs. 'I suppose I can't hide out here forever.'

Grayson showed them into a cream and gold sitting room before tactfully leaving to make coffee. Rosalind hoped there would be some biscuits, too.

'It's good to see you, Rosa.' Brigette's voice was whispery, and she'd wrapped a gigantic woven shawl around her shoulders.

'I'm sorry I have to visit under such circumstances.' Brigette and Dominic might have been divorced, but they'd stayed close. Rosalind wondered now how much of that had to do with the secrets they'd shared.

'The police came yesterday and spoke to Grayson.' Brigette tugged her shawl closer. Her eyes were rimmed with red, and her dark red hair frizzed around her face. 'They said you were there, Rosalind, when Dom . . .'

She broke off, and Rosalind reached out to take her hand. 'I was. I was just downstairs. Did they tell you anything else?'

'That he was stabbed – just sitting there in the doorway!' Brigette shuddered.

'They're certain?' Rosalind asked, frowning. 'He was killed where we found him?' Why hadn't they heard him scream?

'Oh, I don't know.' Brigette flapped her hand to make Rosalind let go.

'They said they thought he might have been drugged first.' Grayson reappeared in the doorway with a tray, and Ashok jumped up to help him. 'Because nobody heard him scream, I suppose.'

'It would have to be something fast-acting, then,' Rosalind mused. Scarlett had heard him talking in the room where he was killed. Practising lines, perhaps – or had she actually heard him speaking to his murderer? 'He was on set until just beforehand, drinking fake cocktails.'

Could someone have slipped something in his drink on set without any of them noticing? Perhaps the same person who had swapped the fake knife for the real one when they'd been filming her murder.

'His wrists were red,' Rosalind remembered suddenly. 'Like he'd been tied up.'

'They said something about that, too.' Grayson pushed down the plunger on the cafetière, and poured the coffee. 'They weren't sure what it meant.'

Or when it could have happened. The timings just didn't make any sense.

'Could the killer have tied him up in the bathroom?' Ashok asked. 'Then dragged him out unconscious to the doorway and stabbed him?'

'If it was very carefully planned. Or if more than one person was responsible, perhaps.' Rosalind considered the scene again, picturing that moment in her mind. 'The lights on the balcony are dim, it would be easy to stick to the shadows up there, I think.'

The more she thought about it, the more certain she was that was how it must have been done.

But this wasn't what she'd come all this way to talk to Brigette about – not really.

'When you left Tŷ Gwyn,' Rosalind chose her words carefully, 'what was it that made you make that decision?'

Brigette sighed. 'It was a number of things, really. Small things that added up until I was just . . . I couldn't stay. I couldn't.'

'What sort of things?' Rosalind thought of black-edged threats and a prop knife that wasn't.

'Mum, you don't have to talk to them.' Grayson jumped up from his armchair and perched beside his mother on the sofa. 'Not if it's going to upset you.'

But Brigette shook her head. 'I do. I have to talk to somebody. Dominic is dead, and that means . . . I don't know yet what it means. But I do know I can't live the rest of my life in fear like this.'

'What happened, Brigette?' Rosalind asked again, softly.

'It started with a note,' she said. 'A black-edged note telling me the writer knew what I had done. It was left in my car. Next, I started getting phone calls – just silence, and breathing, on my voicemails. Then that day at Tŷ Gwyn, I'd left my handbag on the table in the hall for a few minutes, and when I picked it up again there was a bottle of pills in it, with a tag saying "take them all".'

'Someone wanted you to kill yourself?' Ashok said, in disbelief.

Brigette nodded. 'I was so shaken. And then Anton started on about something, and then Keira was trying to talk to me, and all I could think about was that bottle in my bag. So I took out my phone and pretended I had a call, but really I was just checking my voice-mail messages. I expected another silent one, but this time . . . this time they spoke.'

'Could you tell if it was a man or a woman?' Rosalind asked.

'No.' Brigette's fingers were white where they clutched the edge of her shawl. 'They'd used some sort of voice disguiser, I think? They just said that it was time for me to pay, and that I knew what I had to do. So I ran into that study and locked the door and it was only when I was standing there trembling that I remembered about the secret passage.'

So Caro had been right about that all along. 'And you escaped and hid out here.'

'That's right. But I should have known . . . if I was being threat-ened, Dom must have been too.'

'He was,' Rosalind confirmed. 'Do you know what the threats were about?'

'I . . . honestly, I didn't know. Not for certain.' A hint of a lie there for the first time, Rosalind suspected. Perhaps she just didn't want to acknowledge to herself – or them – what she'd enabled in her ex-husband.

'Dominic thought it was to do with *The Castle on the Hill*.'

Brigette's eyes widened, and a thread on her shawl snapped. 'Evie Groves.'

'That's right.' Rosalind wondered how much Brigette had really known about what happened that night. Or whether defending Dominic had just been second nature. 'We've been looking into the cast, and who might have had connections to that movie. We know Keira's father was the producer, and that Gabriel was dating Evie when she died. Was there anyone else?'

'Apart from you, you mean? No. I can't think of anyone. Except . . .' Her brows lowered into a frown. 'I was looking through some old photos last night, after the police left. And I found one from that film. There was someone who looked familiar . . .'

She got to her feet and crossed to a box of photos that lay open on the desk. After a few moments of rifling through, she pulled one out and handed it to Rosalind. Ashok crowded over her shoulder to get a look, too.

'I might be wrong,' Brigette said. 'But do you see it?'

Rosalind frowned. 'No. I . . .' And then she did.

The edges of the photograph crumpled under her fingers. 'We need to get back to Wales. Now.'

Chapter Twenty-Six

'How do I love thee? Let me count the ways,' Dahlia quoted, read-
ing from the letter they'd found in Celia Hughes's dressing table.
Then she tossed it across to Johnnie. 'Well, not very many ways
given that he killed her. Murder is not a sign of a well-functioning
relationship.'

Dahlia Lively *in* Love Her to Death
***By* Lettice Davenport, 1961**

Caro

Caro and Posy opted to stay close to the Seven Stars the next day,
waiting for Rosalind to report in or for Jack to return. The police
were still talking to people in the private dining room, and there were
reports that the paparazzi had returned to the village, so they were
staying out of their way.

Everyone else seemed to have somewhere else to be, though – even
Owain and Rebecca.

Posy sat at a table near the fire, sipping on a coffee she'd helped
herself to from behind the bar, and looking over her investigation
notes. Caro had tried to join her, but sitting still had never been her
forte. Especially when her whole body seemed to be vibrating with
the need for action. For something that would crack open the case
and let them catch a murderer.

So instead she roamed around the bar examining the pictures on the walls, the hipster decorations and other details. The photo wall near the bar showed images of the Seven Stars as it had been through the years, and she studied them carefully, unsure what she was even looking for. But there was something . . .

'Did you know there used to be a coffin in that alcove over there?' Caro pointed across at the recess in the wall that was currently painted white and filled with a weird sculpture made from old cutlery. 'Probably the one that's now shelves over there.'

'That's interesting,' Posy said, in a way that suggested it really wasn't.

Caro drifted over to the coffin shelves and considered the contents. Owain had called it their heritage display, she recalled. She hadn't paid it much attention at the time, but it wasn't as if she had much of anything else to do right now.

Several shelves were taken up with letters, propped up by the envelopes, and covered in intricate cursive writing.

'*Cariad*,' she read from the envelopes. 'What do you suppose that means?'

'It means "Sweetheart",' Posy replied, absently. 'It's stitched on half the items in the craft shops around here.'

'Love letters, then.' Caro peered more closely at the letters themselves. 'Or not. *You belong to me. Whatever anybody says, I know you're mine. I must have you.* And "must" is underlined three times.'

'It *could* be romantic,' Posy said, dubiously. 'I mean, if they were fighting against the people keeping them apart. If they both felt the same. Does it say who they're from or to?'

Seren appeared on the stairs from the family quarters upstairs. 'They're letters from John Spencer-Mills to a girl called Eluned. He was the son of the guy who owned Tŷ Gwyn a hundred years ago or whatever. And she was the daughter of the owner of this place.'

'They're the fabled star-crossed lovers who used the secret passage between here and Tŷ Gwyn to meet up in secret?' Caro asked, excitedly.

'Guess so.' Seren shrugged, and headed down towards the bar, ducking down to open one of the fridges and grab a can of Coke.

Caro had just turned back to reading the letters when the back door crashed open, slamming into the stone wall, and Tristan scampered in backwards – followed swiftly by Owain, his face red with rage, and Rebecca, who tugged on his arm to try and keep him back, without obvious success.

Tristan, ducking behind the long table at the front of the bar, held his hands out and looked apologetic. 'Owain. Owain, we can talk about this.'

Caro couldn't understand the words Owain shouted in return, since they were in Welsh, but she was pretty sure most of them were unrepeatable in front of small children. She checked for where Seren was, and found her staring, wide-eyed, at her parents from behind the bar.

Scarlett and Gabriel sidled in behind the chaos, so Caro joined them. 'Did you see what happened?'

'So, Tristan and Rebecca were talking in the courtyard,' Scarlett said. 'And then when we came out they disappeared into one of the unfinished suites. But then Owain arrived and asked where Rebecca was, and idiot here told him.' She elbowed Gabriel in the ribs.

'Ow!' He rolled his eyes. 'How was I supposed to know he'd walk in on them kissing?'

Scarlett shot him a disbelieving look. 'Have you been paying *any* attention to what's been going on around here the last few weeks?'

'Honestly, I was more concerned about the deaths than the romances on this movie,' Gabriel replied.

Caro considered Scarlett's words. 'You knew about them already?' Maybe they should have spent more time questioning Scarlett . . .

'You didn't?' Scarlett sounded honestly surprised. 'I thought everybody knew. They were kind of obvious.'

What else had she been oblivious to, focusing on the murders and the death threats?

Owain broke free from his wife's grip, and vaulted across the nearest table, fists up as he closed in on Tristan, who shuffled backwards into a wooden windowsill.

'Owain!' Rebecca followed him, eyes wide with terror. 'You can't do this.'

'Watch me,' Owain growled, in English this time.

Grabbing Tristan's upper arms, he yanked him away from his corner and swung him into the main pub. 'You pretty boys, coming here, taking whatever you want and expecting us to kowtow to you all just because you're *famous*. Narcissists, the lot of you. Well, you know what? Ordinary people are worth something too. We deserve love and money and the ability to make a living, without you lot storming in here and *screwing everything up*.' As he yelled the last words, he threw Tristan against the opposite wall, barely letting him cry out before he'd grabbed him again to repeat the action. 'She's *my wife*, you bastard.'

This time, Tristan hit the wall at a different angle, his shoulder cracking against the edge of the recess in the wall, sending the cutlery sculpture flying. He slumped down against the stone floor, Owain reaching for him again, his fist pulled back this time.

Which was when the police finally emerged from the dining room to break things up, before Owain broke Tristan's nose. As things calmed down, Caro turned to Posy – only to find that she was gone.

And so was Seren.

'Why's Dad beating up Tristan? What's going on in there?' Seren asked, her voice wobbling a little as Posy manhandled her into the courtyard outside. 'Posy, tell me what's happening? Please?'

It wasn't her place to tell a fourteen-year-old girl that her mother had been having an affair, and she wasn't going to try. The best she could hope for now was some distraction. She just hoped she'd got her out of there before she'd heard too much.

'I think everyone's a little . . . fraught in there right now. With everything that's going on.'

Seren didn't look entirely convinced, but she didn't press it either, which Posy took as a win. 'Then what did you drag me out of there for?'

Ah. Posy's ulterior motive.

It had struck her, as she'd looked at Seren behind the bar as her parents barrelled in, unaware that their daughter was watching, that Seren seemed to have a knack of being places at the right time.

Even places she shouldn't be able to get to.

'That first day Caro arrived, you were waiting outside the gates of Tŷ Gwyn because you weren't allowed in, right?' Seren nodded. 'And then we put you on the list on Tuesday to come in with us, but we had to be there and sign you in, yes?' Another nod. 'But I've seen you up at Tŷ Gwyn since then, on days when none of us were there to vouch for you, and your name wasn't on the list.'

Seren stared down at the toes of her trainers. 'Yes.'

'So my question is, how did you get there?' Posy leaned against the wall behind her, and waited, while Seren winced, glanced around her and prepared to lie.

'Well, I guess once I'd been allowed in once, they decided it was okay? The security guard on the gate, I mean?' Seren said, hopefully.

Posy shook her head. 'Nope. I had to sign Caro in every day. So either you had someone other than me or Rosalind willing to sign you in, or . . .'

'Or?' Seren asked, somewhat fearfully.

'Or you found the secret passage between this pub and Tŷ Gwyn, and have been using it all week.'

Posy knew from Seren's face that she'd guessed right, so she carried on before the teenager could grab for another excuse or admit it.

'I'm not going to turn you in or anything,' she reassured her. 'I just want you to show me where it is. And tell me how you found it, and who else knows about it.'

Seren's eyes were wider than ever. 'It's . . . it's down in the cellar, under the bar. But you can get to it from the outside door, where they load in the barrels, see?' She pointed to a pair of galvanised steel doors set into the paving-slab path around the building. 'But I have to open the doors from inside . . . the other entrance to the cellar is behind the bar.'

'Think you can do it without anyone spotting you?' Posy asked, and Seren flashed her a grin.

'No problem.' She darted away back into the Seven Stars, and Posy waited anxiously, hoping that the rest of them were still too preoccupied to pay any notice to what she and Seren were up to.

A few minutes later, she heard a mechanical grinding sound, and the cellar doors started to swing open, revealing Seren at the top of a small ladder, waiting for her. 'Come on then!'

Posy eased herself carefully down the ladder into the meticulously tidy cellar, the cool air even colder than the outside world. 'Okay. Where's this passageway?' she asked, as the cellar doors closed behind her.

The police had locked Tŷ Gwyn up tight, until they could get the experts in to process the scene of the crime, probably in a few days' time. But they didn't have to actually go *into* the house, Posy reasoned, so they wouldn't really be contaminating a crime scene. She just wanted to know if it was possible. And to see the fabled secret passage for herself.

'Over here.' Seren led her behind a wall of barrels to where an old pub sign had been propped against the aging brick of the wall. When they shifted the sign to the side, a tunnel opened up behind it. 'I saw Dad carrying bricks out of the cellar and dumping them in the skip, weeks ago, but I didn't think anything of it until I came down here to find him one day and he was shifting that sign. He tried to distract me with something else, and I forgot about it – until I heard Caro mention the secret passage one day. I snuck down here to check, and there it was!'

'Your dad found it? And he didn't say anything to anyone?' Owain had said something about someone messing around with the barrels, hadn't he? So maybe he wasn't the only person who'd discovered it.

Seren shook her head. 'Not as far as I know.'

Posy stared into the darkness of the tunnel. 'Well. Want to show me where it goes?'

Seren used the torch on her phone to light their way. The tunnel was, as Posy had half expected, damp and a little smelly, but fortunately it also wasn't too long – which made sense, she supposed, since the distance between the inn and Tŷ Gwyn wasn't far – it was only the way the road twisted around to the fancy front gates that made it seem further.

Eventually, they reached a small set of steps that led up into what appeared to be a basement at Tŷ Gwyn. A musty, unused basement, with another staircase, and a door halfway up the stairs.

'It comes out into the study.' Seren skipped up the steps and wrapped her fingers around the door handle.

A shiver struck Posy's spine as a sense of foreboding flooded through her. 'No, wait!'

Too late.

Seren opened the door. And screamed.

Posy raced up the stairs behind Seren, grabbing the teen around the waist to pull her back out of harm's way, hopefully without also losing her footing on the steps . . . Her eyes widened as she looked through the open doorway into the study from which Brigette had disappeared.

There, holding a cricket bat high above her head, was Rhian Hassan.

Chapter Twenty-Seven

'A secret passageway?' Dahlia felt positively betrayed by this turn of events. 'Really?'

Johnnie laughed. 'Apparently they were once more common than you'd think. The local vicar in the village next to mine growing up actually had one that went from the church catacombs to the pub across the road, so his wife wouldn't find out what he was really doing with his evenings.'

Dahlia Lively *in* Impossible Crimes for Impossible Times
***By* Lettice Davenport, 1972**

Posy

'You?' Posy shoved Seren behind her, keeping hold of her arm until she was sure she was balanced on her own. 'What . . . ?' She trailed off, unsure exactly what she wanted to ask.

Rhian lowered the cricket bat. 'What are *you* doing here?' Which should probably have been Posy's question. Except Rhian was the manager of Tŷ Gwyn. If anyone had a right to be here it was her. But the police had sent her away . . .

'I thought the police had sealed off the whole house,' Posy said, stalling for time while she tried to get a handle on what was going on.

'So you thought you'd just break in?' Rhian asked, the sarcasm strong in her voice. 'If you're looking to hide evidence I'd say you're probably too late.'

'We're just here because Posy wanted to see the secret passageway,' Seren piped up from behind her. 'That's all.'

Rhian peered around her at Seren. 'And you already knew where it was. How?'

'Her dad,' Posy said, shortly. 'I assume this means you were lying to Rosalind when you told her you didn't know its location?'

Rhian scoffed. 'Of course I was.' She put the cricket bat down on the desk. 'Are you two coming in here, or not?'

Posy shuffled through the door, Seren behind her, then turned around, confused. 'The whole bookcase is the door?' No wonder she hadn't spotted it. 'How does it open from this side?' She knew for a fact that Caro had tried every book she could, just in case.

Rhian pushed the bookcase back into position, then reached under the desk to press a button Posy couldn't see, even now she was looking for it. The bookcase swung obligingly open again.

'Simple, really,' Rhian said. 'Of course, the whole thing was bricked up until recently. Owain and I were talking about offering a special Secret Tŷ Gwyn tour – a whole guided tour of the house and its secrets, then a trip through the tunnel to the Seven Stars for afternoon tea. We put the plans on hold when you guys hired the place for the film, but I'd already had the mechanism for the bookcase cleaned and oiled at this end, and I guessed that Owain must have kept up the work at his end, too.'

'You guessed? You hadn't talked to him about it?' Posy asked.

'Not recently.' Rhian dropped to sit in the desk chair, one hand still hovering near the cricket bat. 'But I suspected that someone had been using the tunnel.'

'Brigette,' Posy breathed. 'That *was* how she got out of here without anyone seeing her. But how did she know about it?'

Rhian looked a little uncomfortable at that question. 'I showed her,' she admitted. 'On one of the site visits. Anton had stormed off to make a call somewhere, and he'd dragged the location scout with him. He'd been rude all morning. Brigette had apologised for him, even though it wasn't her place – it was her first time even visiting, and Anton had been rude on *all* the visits. But she was nice. Sweet. And she made a joke about a house like this needing a secret room behind a bookcase, and, well.' She shrugged.

She'd covered for her too, Posy realised. She'd unlocked that door and claimed that sometimes they locked themselves – but she'd bent over to pick something up off the floor, first. Posy would bet anything it was the other key, the one Brigette had used to lock herself in.

'You didn't tell anybody about it, though,' Posy pointed out. 'When she disappeared, I mean.'

Rhian's expression turned stony. 'I saw her face before she went into the room that day. She was terrified. I don't know who called her, but from the way she was looking around her . . . she was afraid of somebody *here*. Not on the phone. And if she needed to run from them, I wasn't going to give anybody any hints where she might have gone. I've been that woman – scared, and needing to escape. So I kept quiet and let her do the same thing.'

'I still don't get the cricket bat, though,' Seren piped up from over by the bookcase.

With a slow smile, Rhian wrapped her hand around the handle of it again. 'It's my insurance. I've been guarding this tunnel entrance, see. Making sure that no one else uses it. The police just locked this place up and left a guard outside, but they don't know the house like I do. They don't care about it. I don't know what's going on with your film, or who is behind all these awful things that keep happening. But I'll be damned if they'll use my house to keep doing it.'

Rhian didn't think this was over, either, Posy realised. Even if Rosalind got Brigette to talk – to her or to the police – she might not know enough to catch the murderer. And if she did . . . it would still take time.

Meanwhile, a murderer was still on the loose here at Tŷ Gwyn and the Seven Stars.

One with Rosalind in their sights.

Wait. 'Your house?'

Rhian shrugged. 'Tŷ Gwyn belongs to my grandparents. I hadn't been back here since I was a child, until . . . well. Let's just say something happened in my life, and I needed a fresh start. You know? A place where no one knew who I was. Grandpa offered me this job here, and I took it, on the condition that it wasn't just a family favour, a way to keep me out of trouble. I wanted to do the work for real, and make this house a success.'

'You didn't want anyone to know you were family, in case they thought that was the only reason you had the job,' Posy said. 'I can understand that.'

Rhian nodded. 'Grandpa and Nan are hardly ever here anyway, so it was easy enough to just start working. But you understand now, don't you, why I was so determined to keep watch over the house? I couldn't just *leave* when the police said. So I snuck back through the tunnel and stayed in there until the police were done with searching the house. I needed to keep an eye on things here.'

'That's why you were on the balcony, the day Dominic died,' Posy realised. 'You were watching for a murderer.'

'I missed them, though,' Rhian said sadly. 'I still don't understand . . .' She broke off.

'Neither do we,' Posy said. 'But we're going to figure it out.'

Rhian was frowning, looking beyond them to the bookcase. 'I think I'd leave it to the police, if I were you.'

'Perhaps.' Posy turned to Seren. 'Come on. We'd better get back, before your mum starts wondering where you are.'

And before the murderer turned their sights on their next victim.

Back at the Seven Stars, things seemed to have calmed down, at least for the time being. Seren and Posy climbed out through the outdoor cellar door, then entered the pub from the courtyard entrance, as if they'd just been for a walk in the woods or to Posy's room. Owain, Tristan and Rebecca were nowhere to be seen, so Posy hoped they were all somewhere calming down and sorting things out. Nobody seemed to have missed them much, anyway.

Except for Caro, who was waiting impatiently for them in the bar, the letters from the glass cabinet now laid out in front of her.

'You found the secret passage and you didn't take me with you?' She narrowed her eyes accusingly at the pair of them as Posy related where they'd been.

'It was a spur of the moment thing,' Posy replied. 'Any news from Rosalind yet?'

'Not yet.' Caro pulled out her phone and squinted at the screen. 'Reception has been rubbish today, though. You know what it's like.'

'You're still reading those?' Posy nodded at the letters.

'Yeah. Listen to this one. *I don't believe you when you say you don't love me. I know better. Our love is timeless, immortal. Even death cannot stop it. And I am going to prove it to you.*'

Posy shuddered. '*Not* a love story. Definitely not a love story.'

'Agreed.' Caro gathered the letters up into a pile.

Seren had just disappeared up to her room when the front door crashed open again – this time to reveal Rosalind and, to Posy's surprise, Ashok.

She got to her feet. 'You've found something?'

Rosalind gave a sharp nod. 'My room. Now.'

Luxurious as the suites at Saith Seren were, they were still a tight fit for four people. Posy perched on the edge of the coffee table, while Ashok got the chair and Rosalind and Caro sat on the daybed.

'You spoke to Brigette?' Caro said. 'What did she say?'

Rosalind filled them in quickly and succinctly, with only the odd interjection from Ashok.

'But what really matters is what we found out afterwards,' Rosalind explained.

'We've been working on it all the way on the train.' Ashok pulled out his laptop. 'And we think we've got it. The link we've been look-ing for.' He checked over his shoulder before logging on. 'Might want to close those curtains.'

Posy resisted the urge to roll her eyes, just, as she hopped down to shut the curtains on the window looking out on the courtyard, while Caro pulled together the ones behind the daybed.

'First, take a look at this.' Ashok pulled up a photo and turned the screen for Caro to see. Posy knelt on the edge of the bed to get a look at it, too.

Smiling up at her were two middle-aged, red-faced men, arms around each other's shoulders, surrounded by people and drinks and a sunset behind them. One of them she recognised, the other she didn't.

'Who is that with Dominic?' she asked.

'Patrick Reynolds,' Rosalind said, frowning down at the photo. 'Keira's father.'

Caro turned the screen back. 'So they were friends. What does that prove?'

'On its own, not much. But this photo was taken around the same time as Evie Groves died, and all the reports and gossip I can find from back then suggest they were particularly tight. In fact, Dominic was involved in the next three movies that Patrick produced.'

'You think Patrick Reynolds helped cover up for Dominic?' Posy asked, and Ashok nodded.

'But that's not all. Turns out that Evie wasn't the only young actress involved in *The Castle on the Hill* to disappear that night,' Rosalind said. 'Brigette showed us another photo.'

She nodded to Ashok, and he pulled up an image, this time of the whole cast of the movie that never got made. Then he zoomed in on one face in particular – a beautiful young woman, beaming at the camera, her arm around the shoulders of Evie Groves.

'This is Marija Marić, an up-and-coming actress born in Croatia but who grew up here in the UK. She'd done some British TV – small parts – but not much else, before she got her big break with a part in *The Castle on the Hill*. But after the film was canned it seems like she never worked again. In fact, I can't find any record of her anywhere. Look familiar?'

Posy took the laptop and peered at it carefully. It took a moment, but then the features swam into focus, a decade or so older but still beautiful. 'That's Nina. Nina Novak.'

Ashok grinned widely, as Caro took the computer. 'Exactly. From what I can find out, she and Evie were big friends on set. After Evie's death she moved back to Britain, changed her name, and started her career all over again, working on the stage instead of film or TV.'

'Why? What would make her do that?' Caro asked.

'She was the witness,' Posy said. 'The friend Sol told me about. The one who tried to follow Evie, but Brigette stopped her. The one who kept asking questions. What would have happened to her if she kicked up too much of a fuss, if she wouldn't stay quiet?'

'I'd imagine she'd have been left with no choice but to disappear,' Rosalind said, staring down at the photo. 'If she spoke out against Dominic, maybe even talked to the police . . . if he even thought she could expose him, he'd have ruined her.'

'Blacklisted her, you mean?' Posy had heard of it happening before. Actors who behaved so badly on set, or offended the wrong person, and suddenly found they couldn't even get an audition when before they'd been hot property. Hell, it had pretty much happened to her, before the audition for *The Lady Detective* came up.

'If that's true . . . it would give her one hell of a motive,' Caro said. 'Two even – justice for Evie, and revenge against the people who blacklisted her.'

'Brigette was being threatened,' Rosalind said. 'Like we said. And if Nina was afraid Brigette might recognise her, she'd want to get her away from the set. Even getting through casting would have been nerve-racking. Dominic probably wouldn't recognise her – you heard him the other night, saying that one young actress was much like another to him. But I bet Brigette would have eventually. In fact, she did, when she found this photo.'

'And Keira might have too.' Ashok pulled up another photo. 'Look. Keira and Marija both appeared in an episode of the same kids' TV show.'

'What if Keira realised what Nina was up to – recognised her voice on Brigette's voicemail and put it together? What if it was *Nina* she was supposed to meet at the Drunken Dragon that night?' Finally the pieces were falling into place in Posy's head.

'It's just like in *The Lady Detective*!' Caro crowed. 'The first death wasn't the point – the second one was. She killed Keira so nobody could stop what she had planned for Dominic!'

'Because Nina was up on the balcony when Dominic died. And

when she pretended to find the body . . . she was actually stabbing Dominic. He was so drugged up on sleeping tablets, he wouldn't even have cried out.'

'*This* is why I had to come to Wales with you!' Ashok beamed at Rosalind, and rubbed his hands together. 'I couldn't miss this part.'

'If she's going after everyone connected with Evie's death, that could still mean you, Rosalind,' Caro said. 'She sent you death threats, after all. And she was right there on set the day you almost got stabbed, even though she wasn't in that scene at all.'

'Not just Rosalind,' Posy realised, suddenly. 'Gabriel. He was dating Evie and *his* career wasn't ruined.'

'Wouldn't *he* have recognised Nina?' Rosalind asked.

Caro shook her head. 'He was overseas filming, remember? He probably never met her. But she'd know about him. Maybe even guess that he did a deal with Dominic. 'Yeah, if I was Nina, and I found that out, I'd definitely be going after Gabriel next.'

'Then we need to find Nina,' Rosalind said. 'Now.'

Caro

The blood pumped hard through Caro's veins as they raced across the courtyard to Nina's suite. She hammered on the door, but there was no answer, so she tried the handle instead. It was locked, of course, but Posy made short work of that with her hairpins, for all the good it did them.

The room was empty. A bottle of tablets sat on the bedside table – sleeping pills, Caro assumed, not that Nina was probably taking them herself in her condition – but otherwise, the room gave them no clues at all to where Nina might have gone.

'Gabriel's suite,' Posy said, sweeping back out into the darkened courtyard without waiting to see if they followed.

When his room turned up empty too, Caro really started to worry. 'No signs of a struggle,' she said, but mostly to reassure herself. After all, Nina wasn't big, and Gabriel had put on muscle for his previous movie. Chances were, if she was after him, she had a plan more cunning than just hoping to overpower him physically. No wonder she'd picked a car to do the dirty work for her first murder, and drugged Dominic before stabbing him at Tŷ Gwyn. She didn't have the power to kill either man without increasing her advantage.

What had she used to persuade Gabriel to go with her, though? It could be anything from playing the damsel in distress to acting the seductress. She might not have the muscle, but Nina would have other powers she could use.

'Let's check the bar,' Rosalind suggested, as they all gazed around the empty room. 'See if anyone saw where they went. Someone must have seen something.'

As they headed to the back door, Owain emerged from the side of the inn, looking rather calmer than the last time Caro had seen him.

'Owain! Have you seen Nina anywhere?' she called out to him.

Owain looked up in surprise, as he held the door open for them all. 'Nina? No. Why? Is she not in her room?'

Caro didn't answer, pushing past into the bar to try and find someone else who might be able to help. But the bar was empty too – or so it seemed.

Owain followed them inside, and headed behind the counter – and cried out. 'Becca!'

The three Dahlias rushed to his side. Rebecca lay slumped against the fridges, blood drying on her temple. Owain grabbed her and clasped her against his chest, rocking slightly as he murmured to her in Welsh.

Posy darted in and put her fingers to Rebecca's throat, looking for a pulse. 'She's alive. Ashok, call an ambulance.'

But Caro was preoccupied by another thought. Why would Nina attack Rebecca? What did she have to do with things? Unless she'd just got in the way . . .

Suddenly things started to make sense – although Caro almost wished they wouldn't. She knew which part of the story they were in, now.

In almost every Dahlia Lively mystery, as the Lady Detective closed in on her suspect, there was a moment when the murderer realised there was no good way out, not anymore. That they were going to be caught, come what may. And all that remained was to leave as much damage and distraction in their wake as possible.

Was that where Nina was now? Did she know they were on to her? Had she seen Rosalind arrive with Ashok, perhaps? Overheard them talking? Or had someone else figured it out – Gabriel perhaps?

Whatever had changed, Caro suspected Nina had no fear now. And there was no telling what she might do next.

Rosalind crouched in front of Rebecca too. 'Rebecca. Rebecca!'

Rebecca's eyes fluttered open, her face bloodless. They didn't have time to coddle her, though. They all knew that.

'Where is she?' Rosalind demanded.

Rebecca stuttered her answer. 'They went to the cellar.'

They. She already had him. They had to hurry.

'The secret passage.' Posy was already on her feet, heading for the hatch behind the bar. 'Come on.'

Caro squeezed Rebecca's arm in a desultory attempt at comfort, then turned to Ashok. 'Stay with her. Call the police. You need to get cars with sirens up to Tŷ Gwyn. Fast.' Nina had to know it was all over already, but hearing the sirens might be enough to shock her into giving up.

Caro hoped. One way or another. Because three unarmed women going up against a killer wasn't a great plan. She wanted backup.

They should stay and wait for that backup. Except that could cost Gabriel his life, and so they'd go anyway. Because they were Dahlias.

What else could they do?

Ashok nodded, his expression stunned – and a little disappointed. He'd wanted to be here for the big ending, she knew. The *J'Accuse*, such as it would be. But he was a good guy; he'd do what mattered, even if it meant missing out on the excitement.

Rosalind tossed him her mobile phone. 'Call Jack Hughes too; the number's in there. Tell him what happened.'

The stairs down from the bar to the cellar were rickety, but it was the tunnel itself that Caro hated the most. Damp stone walls, threatening to constrict and trap her at any moment. She shuddered, and kept close to the others as they hurried through.

Finally, the steps Posy had told them about came into view, carrying them up into the hidden room behind the bookcase in the study at Tŷ Gwyn.

'Thank God,' Caro muttered, pushing past the others to get to the last few steps. She frowned as she realised the stairs continued up to the left, after the study door, and wondered briefly where they led. *Focus, Caro.*

They had a murderer to catch.

'Ready?' She didn't pause for an answer, or even really register Posy's uncertain, '*Wait.*' Caro pulled the lever that swung the bookcase out of the way, and stepped straight into the study, thankful Rhian wasn't waiting for them with a cricket bat this time.

Hang on. Where *was* Rhian? Wasn't she supposed to be guarding this place with her life, or something?

'Look,' Rosalind said, and Posy darted across to Rhian's prone body, lying beside the window seat, cricket bat abandoned beside it. The end of the wooden bat was stained red, and now she looked, Caro could see blood trickling out from under Rhian's hijab.

'Is she still breathing?' Rosalind asked.

Posy gave a shaky nod. 'I think so. I should call an ambulance.'

'Ashok's already on it,' Caro reminded her. 'They'll be here any minute.'

'Then should we . . . wait?' The uncertainty in Posy's voice gave Caro pause, just for a moment. But they'd come this far. And she had to know.

Besides, the police weren't here *yet*. And Gabriel could be running out of time.

Caro strode across to the door to the hall, Rosalind and Posy close behind. This door opened easily and Caro stepped through – and stopped.

There, in the centre of the balcony, in the small circle of light from the chandelier, stood Nina, leaning out. Her hands bound, her mouth gagged by a cloth, her dark eyes wide with fear.

They'd got this wrong.

But if it wasn't Nina . . .

Behind her, Posy whispered a name, and all the puzzle pieces started to rearrange themselves in Caro's head, the picture they made this time a very different one altogether.

Chapter Twenty-Eight

'Dahlia! Slow down!' Johnnie's pleas blew away with the snowflakes
on the wind as she raced across the frozen field. 'What if it's a trap?'
'Then I'm going to spring it.' She kept running.

Dahlia Lively *in* A Very Lively Christmas
***By* Lettice Davenport, 1943**

Rosalind

The image before her didn't make any sense. They'd been so sure it
had to be Nina. Except there she was, bound and gagged and terrified, and suddenly Rosalind's mind was filled with all the questions
she should have asked before. Questions that had been pushed aside
in the chaos of realising that Nina Novak was really Marija Marić.

Like how she'd moved Dominic's drugged body from where she'd
hidden it without help. Or why she'd waited until now, this movie, to
take her revenge. Why she'd sent death threats to Rosalind, when she
must have known she hadn't even been at the party the night Evie
died. Why she'd gone back to the pharmacy for sleeping tablets *after*
Dominic was dead – if that was what she'd really been there for at all.
How she'd got Gabriel to follow her down the tunnel to Tŷ Gwyn,
and how she'd overpowered Rhian and Rebecca.

Why Gabriel was nowhere to be seen.

'It was him,' Posy whispered behind her, and Rosalind blinked.

'What?' she said. 'Who?'

'I finally figured it out.' Pushing past her and Caro, Posy moved into the hallway, stepping closer to Nina but not actually approaching the stairs.

Good girl, Rosalind thought. *Keep your distance.*

'You can come out now,' Posy called. 'I think I understand.'

It felt like the whole room held its breath, waiting to see if Posy was right.

And then, out of the darkness of the balcony, Tristan stepped into the narrow wedge of light beside Nina, and held a knife to her throat.

Rosalind swallowed her instinct to gasp. She wouldn't give him the satisfaction.

Tristan. How could it be Tristan? He hadn't even been on the balcony when Dominic was killed. And he'd been with Rebecca the night of Keira's accident.

But however he'd done it, Posy seemed to have figured it out. And Rosalind had to trust her.

She manoeuvred herself to the side, where she could see both Posy and Tristan, as well as keep an eye on Nina. Caro took the other side of the hall. Rosalind gave her an approving nod. She'd be able to see any approaching vehicles through the front window from there, if they didn't hear the sirens first.

One of them should be doing something for Rhian, but under the circumstances Rosalind felt rather more duty bound to keep an eye on Posy, if she was determined to take on a killer.

This wasn't like Aldermere, when they'd held all the cards and a spare ace or queen up their sleeves. This wasn't a big *J'Accuse* scene, with everyone gathered genteelly around for tea and confessions. The murderer didn't look like he planned to go quietly, led off in hand-cuffs by the handily waiting policeman.

Just stall him, she thought hard at Posy, and hoped she somehow heard. *Stall him until Jack and the police get here. That's all we have to do. Just keep him talking.*

'You understand?' Tristan scoffed down at them, never loosening his hold on Nina for a moment. 'I highly doubt that, Posy Starling. But go on, tell me what you think you understand.'

He didn't even look like Tristan, Rosalind thought. It wasn't that he was suddenly ugly, now his murderous tendencies had been revealed. More that he stood there now with a confidence she'd never seen in him before. A certainty in his God-given right to be there. To do as he pleased.

Even if it meant taking a life.

'You did it for Nina, didn't you?' Posy didn't look quite like herself, either. She looked up at Tristan, one hand on her hip, one foot stretched out, so sure in her understanding of what had gone on here – and Rosalind realised.

She looked like Dahlia Lively.

Because she was.

'I did *everything* for her,' Tristan growled. 'I loved her, right from the start. I looked after her when we were just kids, starting out, working on that awful show. She left me for Hollywood, just after Keira joined the cast, you know. But I forgave her!'

Tristan hadn't been in that photo with Marija and Keira, Rosalind was almost sure. But they should have realised. He'd known both of them, been friends with both of them. He had to know Nina's secret too.

'She came back to London after everything that happened, and I was her shoulder to cry on,' he went on. 'I helped her rebuild her career on stage as Nina instead of Marija. For years, I listened to her, I was always there, and all she ever told me was what a good friend I was. How lucky she was to have me. Never that she loved me. That she *saw* me the way I saw her.'

'So you knew you had to do something more,' Caro said, from by the window. 'Right? Something to prove yourself to her.'

'Prove myself?' Tristan shook his head. 'I'd already done that. I needed to give her what she'd always wanted, to do something so big that she'd *have* to love me back.'

'She'd owe you,' Posy whispered.

'Exactly!' His arm tightened around Nina, making her whimper, and Rosalind sucked in a breath. 'I did everything you wanted. Everything you talked about. You came back from LA so angry, didn't you, darling? They'd made you small and afraid. They'd taken your friend, and everything you worked for. You wanted them to make them feel the same way, but you couldn't. So I did it for you. I made Dominic and all those other old-timers feel that same fear you felt on that movie. I *terrified* them for you. But it *still* wasn't enough, was it?'

Fear. Rosalind assumed she must have been one of those old-timers, too, then. Because she'd been scared half to death ever since she stepped on the set of this movie. Was that what all this had been about? Fear?

'The death threats. The conspiracy theory about me online. The switched knife prop that you almost stabbed me with . . . you were behind it all,' she said, her voice whispery soft in the echoing hall. He'd wanted her afraid, not dead. That was the only reason she was still there.

Tristan turned his sneering smile on her. 'Of course I was. And it worked, didn't it? You were afraid.' He laughed. 'Poor old Brigette was so terrified by that anonymous voicemail and those pills in her bag that she actually disappeared before I could even get to any of the good stuff! I wonder if anyone's found her yet, or if she's still too scared to come out from under the covers.'

Rosalind decided not to enlighten him on that one.

'I half hoped she'd kill herself in that study,' Tristan said, easily, as if he were talking about a scene in a film. 'That we'd walk in and find a body. *That* would have scared you all, wouldn't it? And I'd done it before – influenced someone into taking their own life. The flatmate who introduced me to Keira, as it happened. He was always talking about being so depressed he should end it all, especially after I persuaded Keira to break up with him. All it took was a few careful nudges and he was all the way there . . . and I was so hoping I'd manage it again, here at Tŷ Gwyn.'

He was gone, Rosalind realised. The Tristan they thought they'd known no longer existed – if he ever had at all. Everything about him had been an act.

'Brigette didn't matter anyway,' he said. 'She needed to suffer, for Nina. For covering for Dominic for all those years, hiding what he really was. But she wasn't needed for the film. Dominic . . . I had to wait. Move too soon and they'd shut down filming, you see. I couldn't actually *kill* anyone here on set until I was ready for the grand finale – to show my love everything I'd done for her.'

'That's why you made Keira's death look like an accident. A hit-and-run. But why kill her at all?' Caro asked. 'She wasn't involved with the movie. Her father was. Why did she have to die?' She was right, Rosalind realised. They'd assumed Nina had done it to protect her identity. But Keira already knew who Tristan was.

Maybe that was why, after all.

'You want all my secrets for free, do you?' Tristan twisted to look down at Caro. 'Why not ask Posy? Since she *understands* me.'

And suddenly all attention was on the youngest Dahlia, and there was nothing Rosalind could do to help. No advice to give, no quirk to teach.

It was Posy's turn to be Dahlia. It was time.

All Rosalind and Caro could do was watch. And hope.

Posy

Posy swallowed, hard. Her scattered thoughts seemed to flash like the reflections of light in the chandelier overhead, unable to focus their beam in one place. But she had to, didn't she?

She had to be Dahlia. For all of them.

At least, until Jack arrived with the police.

So she forced herself to think about the question – and the answer. Why had Tristan killed Keira?

'I think Keira got too close. She was too good at exposing secrets, wasn't she?' Posy said. 'I think she overheard Brigette's voicemail and recognised something about it, even though you'd disguised your voice. Or maybe she saw you switch the knives? Maybe both. I don't know. Whatever she'd noticed, I bet she'd wanted to talk to you about it, hadn't she? So you'd arranged to meet her in the Drunken Dragon the night she died. But you never showed.'

'Very good.' He pointed the knife down at Posy in acknowledgement, and she felt Rosalind flinch behind her, as if ready to jump out of the way if he threw it. But Nina took the opportunity to try and wriggle free, and he quickly shoved the blade back against her throat. 'I don't know if she recognised something from the voicemail – it's possible, I always practised all my voices with her.'

His voices. Another piece of the puzzle came into focus. Scarlett had heard Dominic speaking in the room before he died. But he'd have already been drugged by then. It had to have been Tristan, pretending to be him.

'But she *did* say she was "worried about me" and my "obsession" with Nina.' He scoffed. 'She was another one. Took everything I ever did for her – every break-up I comforted her through, every argument with her family, every Twitter storm she was in the middle of – and stuck me in the friendzone. Not that it mattered, in the end. She wasn't the one for me, and she knew it. That's why she got so worked up about Nina, I think. She realised what she'd passed up on.'

He was unhinged – as if the murders hadn't given that away already. Posy forced herself to keep her gaze on Tristan, and not glance towards the window to search for flashing blue lights. Where was Jack?

'So you took Kit's car and knocked her down on her way back to the Seven Stars,' she said, instead. 'So she couldn't expose what she thought you were doing.'

Tristan gave a high-pitched giggle. 'Two birds with one stone, so to speak! That find-a-friend function on phones is *very* useful. I think she hoped I'd use it to make sure she got home okay from nights out, but as a bonus, I could track exactly when Keira got bored of waiting for me and nip out to smash into her on the side of the road. And using Kit's car . . . well, I never met a man I wanted to frame more. You know what I mean? He always got everything so easily. Any woman he wanted. Even Keira, until I turned her against him.'

'Her phone. It would have shown your messages, I suppose?' Rosalind said. 'So you took it from her body and, what? Threw it in the river?'

He nodded. 'Easy as anything. I'd been using a burner since I got here anyway, just in case. Told her I needed a new number because some fans had got hold of my old one. She never even questioned it. That sort of thing would happen to her, so she believed it might happen to me.'

The bitterness in his voice rang out, loud and strong, until he cast it aside and grinned manically at them again.

'Then it was back to the pub and the clueless Rebecca in no time. I slipped the keys back into Kit's pocket as she kissed me by the bar. She barely noticed I was gone and, even if she did, she was so star-struck she'd *still* have given me my alibi.'

Alibis. They'd written Tristan off as a suspect early on because of Rebecca's alibi for him when Keira died, but also because he'd been in the hallway with them when Dominic's body was found. How had he done it?

One hand on her hip, Posy centred herself and ran through things again like a storyboard for a movie, seeing not just everything Tristan had *wanted* them to see, but what happened behind the scenes, too.

And then she had it. Posy smiled.

'So, you'd done what Nina wanted. You'd terrified Dominic and everyone else connected to the film or Evie's death. But it still wasn't enough, was it?'

Tristan shook his head. 'I knew it wouldn't be. Not until Dominic had suffered the way he made those girls suffer. Well, maybe not *quite* the same way. But I knew that if I killed Dominic for her, Marija would *have* to love me.'

'So you laced his cocktail on set with sleeping tablets, right? I bet you did it when Nina almost dropped the tray and you steadied her.'

'Very good. I rumpled the rug a little to help her trip, but if that hadn't worked I'd have found another way. You took so many takes to get it right, Posy, I had plenty of opportunity. And I used to do sleight-of-hand magic in college, you know. It was easy.'

'So then you lured him upstairs to that front bedroom, the one above the study, after we finished filming?' Posy guessed. 'He hurried up there fast enough. You'd told him there was something there, perhaps? Or that you needed to talk to him? Then when he passed out, you hid him in the bathroom and pretended to be him until you were sure you'd been heard.'

Another sly smile. 'That's right. But I bet you can't tell me how I was in two places at once, though, little miss detective, can you? Because I was right there in the hallway with you when Nina found Dominic's body, and I've got plenty of witnesses to say I never went up those stairs.' He nodded towards the main staircase.

He thought he was so clever. But Dahlia always saw through clever plans, didn't she?

'You didn't need to,' Posy said, one eyebrow arched, Dahlia style. She couldn't see her reflection, but she knew it was right at last. She felt it. 'You pretended to be looking for Dominic downstairs, like the rest of us, and used the second set of stairs in the secret passage Rebecca had told you about. The one that leads from the study to the Seven Stars – or upstairs, to where I assume they let out in the front bedroom? From there, it was only a few steps to drag him out into the darkness of the doorway and plunge that dagger into his heart, then disappear back the way you came and be ready to comfort Scarlett in the hallway when Nina found him.'

He didn't look quite so smug now, Posy thought. And in the distance she heard the very faint sound of sirens. *Finally.*

'But *none* of it was enough, was it, Tristan?' She just had to keep him talking a little longer. 'She still didn't love you. And worse than that, she was pregnant by another man. She told you at last, I take it?' That had to be what sent him over the edge tonight.

Tristan's face distorted into a twisted, ugly parody of his usual handsome expression, and he adjusted his grip on the knife. 'That was when I knew. It would *never* be enough. Because if this *slut* would open her legs for the likes of him, why would I want her anyway?'

He seemed to see no irony in the fact he'd been sleeping with Rebecca the whole time. Perhaps he was past that kind of reason. Or perhaps he truly believed in those double standards. 'Then why bring her here? Why not let her go now?' The sirens were growing louder, surely he must hear them too. Must know that there was no way out of this, not anymore.

But Tristan didn't loosen his hold on Nina for a second. And then she got it.

'Because you don't want anyone else to have her either, do you?' Posy whispered, her heart plummeting as her head spun at all the sounds assaulting her ears.

The crunch of tyres on gravel. The slamming of car doors. The sirens – over everything else, the sirens. Police hammering on the front door, calling for them to open it.

Tristan dropping the knife so it bounced towards the stairs.

His rasping voice, beyond reason. 'We're going to be together forever!'

And then Nina's scream as he threw them both over the edge of the balcony rail, hurtling towards the stone floor below.

Epilogue

'I still don't get it,' Johnnie said, shaking his head. 'How did you know?'
Dahlia smiled. 'Let me explain. You see, it started with a brooch,
and a dog, and, later, a letter.'

Dahlia Lively *in* Flowers and Feuds
***By* Lettice Davenport, 1965**

Caro

'How did you know?' Caro asked Posy later, as they all sat back at the
Seven Stars drinking cups of hot beverages and waiting for word
from the hospital. 'You said his name. But you couldn't have seen
him, standing on the balcony. How did you work it out?'

Posy swirled her peppermint tea around in her china cup, and
Caro joined her in watching the tiny escaped flakes of mint dance
and writhe in the water, letting her think.

She'd been Dahlia, in there. Properly. And for the first time, Caro
had felt the mantle truly pass on.

Across the table, Rosalind sat pressed close against Jack. Caro
wondered if she'd felt it, too.

They were all gathered together at that long table, everyone
staying at the Seven Stars, except for Tristan, of course, and
Anton, who was fielding endless calls in his room. Rebecca had
been taken into hospital overnight as a precaution. Owain was

back behind the bar, while Seren had been sent to Auntie Bethan's for the night.

'It was a number of things,' Posy said, slowly, finally answering the question. 'But I think it started with Gabriel.'

'Me?' Gabriel looked almost as shaken as those of them that had been at Tŷ Gwyn that night. Older, even. She supposed eight years of keeping a secret that had led to multiple deaths would do that to a person.

Caro thought she'd aged a few months at least in the moments between Tristan dropping the knife, and the few seconds later when Nina elbowed him in the chest as he jumped, buying herself just enough space to grab hold of the railing and hang on until she and Posy and Rosalind could race up the stairs to haul her back over and to safety.

But recalling that made her remember how they'd all stood and looked down at Tristan's broken body on the stones below, the blood and other things oozing out from his skull. And Caro really didn't want to think about that anymore.

Posy took another swallow of peppermint tea, perhaps to try and calm her rolling stomach, if hers felt anything like Caro's. She took a sip of her own brandy to compensate.

'I realised that if the murderer was going after everyone connected to Evie Groves and her death, they'd have sent you a death threat too,' Posy told Gabriel. 'Unless they didn't know about you and Evie – and Nina must have done. But when I overheard you and Dominic arguing, he asked if she'd got to you too, and you didn't know what he was talking about.'

Nina hadn't really reacted to the news they'd thought she was a murderer, except to say, 'Oh.' One too many shocks for one night, Caro supposed. Although it turned out the bottle of sleeping tablets in her room really were only prenatal sickness medication.

'I knew Gabriel and Evie were together,' Nina said, eyebrows furrowed. 'But he was out of the country when it happened. He didn't have anything to do with it.'

Caro gave Gabriel a meaningful look. Maybe tonight wasn't the time to bombard Nina with more horrible home truths, but she suspected he'd be coming clean and paying penance soon enough.

'That can't have been enough to get you to Tristan, though.' Rosalind frowned at Posy. Caro had a feeling that the eldest Dahlia might be just a little bit miffed she didn't solve this one first.

'No. It wasn't just that,' Posy admitted. 'I remembered Dahlia once saying that murders were almost always committed for money, revenge or love. And if we'd ruled out revenge, and there wasn't any money . . . that left me with love.

'I thought about how Rebecca had been the one knocked out, and how she'd never been far from Tristan, this whole time. And then I was thinking about the secret passage – and that made me think of the letters Caro was reading me earlier and . . .' She shrugged. 'I don't know. It all just fell into place.'

'Except Tristan was in the hallway with us when Dominic died,' Caro pointed out. That's why they'd excluded him from their suspicions.

Posy nodded. 'I know. I couldn't make sense of that, but I knew he must have had a way around it. Then, when he was taunting me about being in two places at once, I remembered the second staircase, and how good Tristan was with voices.'

Another memory came cascading back, too late now, of course. 'The first day I was on set,' Caro said. 'I heard Dominic practising his lines, before I heard Keira and Gabriel arguing in the other room. But then the crew member who came to fetch Keira and Gabriel said that everyone was waiting downstairs, ready to film the scene. But it didn't click at the time. Dominic never left the room. It must have been Tristan in there, practising his voices – and he must have used the secret passage to get downstairs.'

It wouldn't have been enough to solve things on its own, but it still galled Caro that she'd missed it. Next time. Next time, she'd get there first.

The shrill tone of Jack's phone sounded, and he fumbled to answer it, standing and moving apart from Rosalind to listen to what the person on the other end had to say. Caro tried to listen in, but she could only hear his end of the conversation – and he wasn't giving anything away.

'Okay. Thanks.' He hung up, and headed back over. Caro offered up silent prayers to any deity listening as she waited for his words.

A smile broke out over Jack's face. 'Rhian's awake. She's going to be okay.'

A small cheer went up at that, and Gabriel stood up, teacup raised, at the head of the table. 'It's been a horrible night, but at last some good news. And at least . . . at least it's over now.' He sat down abruptly, as if the lacklustre toast had been too much for him.

Kit took over where he'd broken off, his own teacup in the air. 'To the Three Dahlias.'

'The Three Dahlias,' the others mumbled. But there was no real celebration to be had that night.

Caro was *almost* glad. Nothing about this was worth celebrating, save perhaps that they'd all survived the night.

All of them except Tristan. And Dominic. And Keira.

Still, it was hard not to feel some satisfaction that they'd saved at least one life. Two, if she counted Rhian – three if she included Nina's baby. It had been worth it. It would always be worth it.

Across the table, Jack had sat back down, closer than ever to Rosalind. Caro hid her smile and tried to at least look as if she wasn't eavesdropping on their conversation – although, really, if they didn't want her to hear they shouldn't talk with her in the room.

'You're not the same woman I used to have supper with in London, are you?' Jack was saying, smiling fondly at Rosalind. 'Not Frank's wife anymore.'

'Frank's been dead a long time,' Rosalind pointed out, with a small shrug of her elegant shoulders. 'And I like to think . . . I think I've only ever been becoming more me, all these years. More real, perhaps.'

'More you,' Jack echoed. 'Yes. I like that.'

Whatever Rosalind said next, she lowered her voice for, and Caro gave up trying to listen, turning her attention instead to another Dahlia, a little further along the table, oblivious to the man staring at her from his seat catty-corner to hers.

Posy caught her eye, and gave a small frown. *What?*

Caro tipped her head in Kit's direction, and saw Posy's gaze follow.

'What?' Posy asked, aloud this time. Apparently Kit couldn't follow her unspoken conversation the way her fellow Dahlias could.

Kit gave her a lopsided sort of smile. 'That's two murderers you've caught now, Starling. If the acting thing doesn't work out for you, at least you've got a viable career as a private investigator.'

'I think I'd just like to get this movie made,' Posy said. 'If we can.'

Kit placed a hand over hers, and Caro was sure that neither of them even realised there was anyone else in the room. 'If anyone can make this film happen, it's you, Posy. I have faith in you.'

Posy's smile spread slow but true across her face, matching Kit's. 'You know what? So do I.'

This time, Caro looked away, not because she couldn't hear, but because she didn't want to. This was their moment, if they chose to take it, and she wouldn't intrude.

Well, not any more than she already had.

Besides, someone had slid into the chair next to hers, and she looked up to find Ashok there beside her, looking contemplatively at her.

'What?' she asked.

'You know, I've been thinking about hiring an assistant,' he said, stretching his arms behind his head. 'Someone who knows what really matters in an investigation.'

'That would have to be someone pretty special,' Caro said, her mind already spinning with possibilities. 'Probably someone worthy of being a partner, rather than an assistant.'

'Perhaps you're right.' He tilted his head as he looked at her. 'What do you think? Interested?'

'Well, I have been looking for a new challenge.' She wondered what Annie would say about the idea. Knowing her wife, if it made Caro happy, the idea would be met with enthusiastic approval. 'I've got this book to write first . . .'

'Whenever you're ready,' Ashok said.

Ready. Ready to move on. To find her next thing. To let Posy be Dahlia. To be *Caro* again, fully.

She ran a finger over the WWDD badge on her jacket.

Never mind Dahlia. What Would *Caro* Do?

Put like that, the decision was easy. There'd be time to write in between solving mysteries, anyway.

'Do you know,' she said, beaming. 'I think I might be.'

Eighteen Months Later

Posy

Camera bulbs flashed around Leicester Square, as Posy Starling took her first step onto the red carpet, her co-star on her arm. Her sparkling silver gown shimmered as it fell to her metallic high-heeled sandals, and her neck felt weighed down by her borrowed diamonds.

'Oh, she's loving this, isn't she?' Rosalind, elegant in a russet velvet gown, murmured the words in Posy's ear. She nudged their linked arms forward to gesture to where Caro was waving to the crowd from her place next to Kit.

Caro hadn't been formally invited to the premiere, but since Kit had invited her as his date, nobody could really object – not even Anton. So here she was, dressed in green silk, and with her dark hair in perfect Dahlia waves.

'I just can't believe we're really here,' Posy replied, still smiling for the gathered Dahlia fans. 'That we even managed to make the film.'

Filming of *The Lady Detective* had, of course, been stalled while the investigation around the events of Dominic and Keira's deaths had been conducted. And of course, their existing footage had needed to be junked – not even Anton could promote a movie on which one cast member had killed two others.

None of them had wanted to go back to Tŷ Gwyn, either, so another location had needed to be found. Filming had taken place with a revised cast over an intense few months at a castle in the Scottish Highlands, owned by a delightful – and handsome – young laird, who had taken quite a shine to Libby when she visited the set. And this time there had been no threats, no accidents, and absolutely no murders.

Posy hadn't really believed it could happen until this moment, though. At the back of her mind she'd just assumed that something else would go wrong.

But here they were, at the premiere of *The Lady Detective*, and soon the whole world would be able to watch her starring as Dahlia

Lively.

'You're really a Dahlia now,' Rosalind said, as they reached the end of the carpet. 'Not that you weren't before, to us.'

A warm feeling filled Posy's chest at the words.

She belonged here. She was Dahlia.

It was almost enough to make her wish for another mystery to solve.

'Posy! Posy!' Someone was calling her name from the crowd, and so she turned to smile and wave one last time before heading in to watch the movie.

'*Dahlia!*' The same voice, but more desperate. Posy paused. 'Please! I need your help.'

She scanned the crowd, knowing Rosalind was doing the same at her side. There: a woman, holding up a photo of someone – a man she didn't recognise.

'He didn't do it!' The woman yelled. 'You have to help me prove it.'

Posy glanced at Rosalind, unsure what to do now. Was this just some prank, someone playing with the idea of them really being Dahlia Lively? Or was this something real?

'Ms Starling, Ms King.' A burly security guard tried to usher them inside.

Posy craned her neck back to try and find the woman in the crowd again, before she lost sight of her completely. She couldn't see her. But she heard her parting words.

'The real murderer is still out there. You have to help me find them!'

Acknowledgements

When I wrote my acknowledgements for *The Three Dahlias* last year, the number of people who had heard of Rosalind King, Caro Hooper and Posy Starling was tiny. This time around, that number has grown wonderfully – and so have the number of people I need to mention here!

Firstly, a huge, huge thank you to every reader who took a chance on my Dahlias – and especially to those of you who wrote reviews, posted on social media, recommended the book to friends, or got in touch to say you'd enjoyed it. The response from readers to the world of the Dahlias has been beyond my wildest dreams. (And I love chatting with you all, so please do come find me on social media, or sign up to my Dahlia Diaries newsletter on my website, www.katywatson. co.uk)

Massive thanks, too, to the booksellers and librarians around Britain – and across the world – who championed the book and got it into the hands of those readers. Truly, we writers just don't deserve you and everything you do. Please get in touch and I'll send you all *What Would Dahlia Do?* badges as a small token of my appreciation.

And thank you to the fabulous crime writing community, the CWA, and all the fellow authors who've supported me along the way – especially Janice Hallett, S J Bennett, Clare Mackintosh and Frances Brody. It's such a lovely, warm community to be a part of (even if we're all secretly plotting murder in our heads).

Some of the biggest thank yous must go to the whole team at Constable – for getting my Dahlias out into the world in the first place.

To my editor, Krystyna Green, for knowing what this book needed to be, even when I couldn't quite see it. To Howard Watson, for the nicest copy-edit I've ever had. To Amanda Keats for shepherding it to print. To Beth Wright and Brionee Fenlon for all their hard work on the publicity and marketing front. To Hannah Wood for the gorgeous covers that really encompass the feel of my books. And to Christopher Sturtivant and Caitriona Row, and everyone else behind the scenes, for everything they've done – and keep doing – to support these books.

Thank you, too, to super-agent Gemma Cooper, for always being my biggest cheerleader, my first call, and the only person to have ever taken me to for coffee and cake in a prison cell. But most especially for reading this book more times than anyone could reasonably be expected to read it, and still managing to sound excited about it by the end.

I owe a huge thank you (and probably a few drinks) to the four people who advised me on all things murder and police: Dave Carter (MBE – congrats, Dave!), Karen Hutchinson, Laurie Rush and Rich Smears. Thank you for putting up with all my hypothetical questions (even when you were about to get on a plane for your holidays – sorry Rich!), talking me through your work day and hooking me up with the right contacts (thanks Karen!), showing me around your patch and telling me your best stories (thanks Laurie!), and not only correcting my errors and misconceptions in the manuscript (thanks Dave!), but also helping me to understand how much I don't know I don't know (all of you!).

It goes without saying that all mistakes or misrepresentations of police procedure, unintentional or otherwise, are my own.

My final thank you is, as always, to my family. To Simon, my own Dr Watson, and to Holly and Sam, for traipsing around the country with me – from Agatha Christie's Greenway to Harrogate Crime Festival – while I promoted *The Three Dahlias* and bringing me cups of tea – or just giving me cuddles – when I was grumbling about this book. And thank you to my parents, my brothers, my cousins, my aunts and uncles, and many friends, for making *The Three Dahlias* the default birthday and Christmas gift for basically anyone over the age of thirteen!

I'm so grateful that my three Dahlias have found a place in people's hearts – and on their bookshelves. Thank you all xxx

NEW IN 2024

Keep reading for a sneak peek at Katy Watson's third book
in the Dahlia Lively series,
Seven Lively Suspects . . .

Chapter One

'We could go see a movie,' Johnnie suggested. 'One of the new talkies, even. If you wanted.'

Dahlia sighed. 'Oh, all right. But only because there aren't any good murders that need solving right at this minute.'

Dahlia Lively *in* Murder Looks Lively
***By* Lettice Davenport, 1933**

Caro

Caro Hooper took her date's hand and stepped out of the car onto the red carpet. 'Anton must be positively seething somewhere, watching this.' Her words were almost lost in the noise of the crowd gathered in Leicester Square, but Kit was close enough to hear them.

He chuckled. 'If you attending this premiere as my date is the only thing our esteemed director is worrying about tonight, then I reckon we're doing okay. Don't you?'

Given the long road it had taken to get them there – metaphorically, rather than the journey from the London townhouse she shared with her wife, Annie – Caro had to agree.

Against all odds, the movie reboot of *The Lady Detective* had been completed, and very soon the world would be able to watch it. Posy Starling had officially taken her place in the detective pantheon by starring as the lady detective herself, Dahlia Lively. And the *original*

Dahlia, Rosalind King, had also managed to not only appear in the latest movie, but also survive the experience – which hadn't seemed such a sure thing eighteen months earlier.

They'd had to recast and relocate after the murderous events of the original film shoot in Wales, but filming up in Scotland instead hadn't been such a bad thing. For instance, the handsome young laird whose family owned the estate they'd filmed at had taken a considerable shine to their script writer, Libby McKinley. Caro smiled as she watched Libby and Duncan make their way along the carpet ahead of them.

'Our turn.' Kit tugged her hand through the crook of his arm, and they stepped forward together. He really was an old-fashioned gentleman – even though Caro knew she wasn't the Dahlia he *actually* wanted on his arm tonight.

Annie had laughed when Caro told her that Kit had invited her to the premiere as his date.

'Which one of them do you suppose put him up to that?' she'd asked. 'Posy or Rosalind?'

'Probably both,' Caro admitted. 'But Anton can't really complain if it's Kit taking me, not them.'

Kit Lewis was a rising star whose brightness was starting to eclipse the rest of them. If Anton wanted him back on set for the sequel, starring as DI Johnnie Swain once more, he couldn't afford to offend him. Which worked out nicely for Caro.

Anton hadn't wanted her on set in Wales, and he *certainly* hadn't wanted her on set in Scotland, but in the end he hadn't had much choice in the matter. Caro wasn't about to start letting men – or anyone – tell her where she could and couldn't go at this point in her life. And besides, Anton knew she was writing a novel based on their first murder investigation at Aldermere – the investigation that had turned Rosalind, Caro and Posy into the Three Dahlias, each of them as famous now for solving murders as for playing fictional detective, Dahlia Lively, on screen. Given his part in the events that transpired at Aldermere . . . Anton really did need to stay on her good side.

Which didn't mean he had to like it. Caro glanced around the gathered celebrities and film people on the red carpet to try and spot him, intending to give him a rather smug smile, but he must have already headed inside as he was nowhere to be seen.

It had been a long time since Caro had been on display like this. Ever since her TV series, *The Dahlia Lively Mysteries* had been cancelled, she'd not exactly been in high demand for premieres and parties – or for parts, either, as it happened. The lack of roles for forty-something women in TV and film was just one of the reasons she'd turned author.

But she hadn't forgotten how this all worked. She smoothed down her green silk dress, smiled her brightest smile, and raised a hand to wave to the crowd as they walked towards the cinema entrance, and the photographers and reporters waiting for them. Tomorrow, her photo would be in the papers beside Kit's, forever connected with Dahlia Lively and this movie – and there was nothing that Anton could do about it.

Revenge really was best served cold.

'Not that I don't appreciate you inviting me,' she said to Kit as they walked. 'But can I assume that you'll be going home with a different Dahlia tonight?'

Posy had been frustratingly cagey about her relationship with Kit – whether it was on, off, serious or imaginary was the subject of much gossip online *and* on the film set. The fact that Kit had spent so much time out of the country filming new projects over the last year couldn't have helped matters, though.

Posy was very protective of her privacy – and for good reason – but *really*. She could at least put Rosalind and Caro out of their misery and give them the details. Even Rosalind shared the basics of her developing relationship with her old friend, ex-detective inspector Jack Hughes – although she'd just smiled beatifically when Caro had asked her how the sex was.

If Posy would give her the same, Caro wouldn't have to interrogate Kit for the gossip.

As it was, he just shook his head. 'That's entirely up to her.'

'Hmm.' Caro cast a glance back over her shoulder to where Rosalind and Posy were making their way along the red carpet, both looking utterly stunning in their own ways, as usual. 'Well, if she doesn't, she's a fool.'

Kit squeezed her hand in gratitude for her support. 'Not a fool. Just . . . cautious.'

It would do Posy no harm at all to throw caution to the wind every now and then, in Caro's opinion. But then, she hadn't been around for the period of Posy's life where she'd had no caution – or common sense – at all, so what did she know?

Still, the most rebellious thing Posy had done in a while was to buy a flat in an area of London that may – or may not – be on the cusp of regeneration. Caro hadn't had the opportunity to visit yet, but she was bracing herself, all the same. Rosalind, she knew, had continued sending Posy listings for flats long after the sale went through.

Kit stopped for photos and to sign autographs for many of the fans who'd waited probably hours to see him. They waved their phones and notebooks, and Kit just smiled and posed, camera flashes brightening the summer evening around them. One or two of the fans wanted to catch Caro's eye, too, which was gratifying.

They'd barely made it halfway along the red carpet when she heard another voice calling her name – this one with rather more insistence than the others.

'Caro! Caro Hooper!'

Best smile in place, Caro turned to try and find the fan, scanning the crowd.

When she saw her, Caro knew in an instant that the woman wasn't there for an autograph, or a selfie. She wasn't even there for the movie.

She was there for Caro. Her own past coming back to haunt her.

'Caro!' the woman called again, waving wildly.

It was the eyes she recognised first. The pale blue eyes so like her brother's. She was older now, of course – it had been over four years since Caro had seen her, across the courtroom, staring accusingly at her.

Her fluffy blonde hair hung around her shoulders, the summer evening sunlight making it glow like a halo. She'd pushed her way to the front of the rope line, so Caro could see she wore a long, embroidered dress with flowers on it. And this time, there wasn't accusation in her gaze.

There was hope.

Caro turned away.

'Everything okay?' Kit murmured, as he took her arm again. At the front of the cinema, the security team were starting to beckon them in.

'Fine,' Caro lied. 'Your fans done with you?'

'For now.' Kit gave her a wink. 'What about yours?'

'Oh, this is your crowd, not mine,' she said, as casually as she could. 'I'm saving my hand strength for all the books I'll need to sign at festivals and such this summer, now *The Three Dahlias* is published.' The release had been cunningly timed by her publisher to coincide

5

with the premiere of the new movie, and she'd held her launch event the night before.

'Probably a good idea. From what I've heard, it's going to be a huge hit.'

'That's the idea.'

As they stepped towards the foyer, Caro comforted herself with that thought. Soon her name would be back on everyone's lips, not because of a film she didn't even appear in, but because of something of her own. A book she'd written, herself, and a murder she'd solved – with a little help from her friends.

This was going to be her year, and no face from the past was going to change that.

Behind her, she heard the desperate voice call again.

'Posy! *Dahlia!* Please! I need your help.'

A chill settled in Caro's chest, despite the summer evening, and her steps slowed. She didn't turn, though. Just listened.

'He didn't do it! You have to help me prove it.'

Of course he did it. Who else could have?

'Caro?' Kit asked, frowning.

She waved a hand to shush him. 'One moment.'

Reluctantly, she twisted halfway round. Behind them, her fellow Dahlias had almost reached the doors, too – Posy sparkling in the silver dress from some up-and-coming London designer, and Rosalind elegant in a russet gown that looked too warm for the British summer but perfectly fit her classic brand.

They'd stopped on the red carpet, staring out into the crowd at the rope line. And Caro knew exactly who they were looking at.

Sarah Baker.

The security team were ushering Rosalind and Posy inside now. But Sarah's last words echoed in behind them.

'The real murderer is still out there. You have to help me find them!'

Caro grabbed Kit's arm and started walking again.

She might be a part-time private detective and part-time crime author now, but the case Sarah Baker was talking about wasn't one she had any interest in revisiting.

Ever.

Rosalind

The movie was good.

No, it was better than good. It was everything Rosalind had hoped it would be.

She'd seen snippets before the premiere, of course. But she hadn't wanted to watch anything much until it was the finished article, complete with the music score and credits and everything. The way audiences would watch it, around the world.

And they were going to love it.

She smiled as she considered the individual performances. For herself, her turn as Aunt Hermione came across well – at least well enough to forestall having to move into voicing funeral plan adverts any time in the near future, she hoped.

But more importantly, Posy's performance as Dahlia Lively *shone*. Oh, she wasn't the Dahlia Rosalind had been, or even the Dahlia that Caro had embodied. She was her own Dahlia, a Dahlia for *now*, and she was perfect.

Which, Rosalind had to admit, was a relief. Not least because it meant Posy might stop squeezing her hand so hard now the credits had rolled.

'It was good,' Rosalind murmured to her, while around them the theatre burst into cheers and applause. 'You were perfect.'

Posy let out a long breath, as if she'd been holding it for the entire one hundred and ten minutes. 'Thank God for that.' She looked up at Rosalind with a shaky smile. 'Now we just have to make it through the after party.'

Because, of course, the film was only the start of it.

Rosalind hadn't planned to attend the premiere alone, but Jack had little to no interest in being photographed on the red carpet and, besides, he had some sort of plumbing or guttering emergency to deal with back at his cottage in the hills of Llangollen. Rosalind might have finally learned to say the name of the town where he lived, but she drew the line at assisting with home maintenance when Jack could easily have paid someone else to fix it. But he liked to believe he was still a jack of all trades, so she ignored the fact it was clearly an excuse to avoid the cameras and went without him.

It did occur to her, as she travelled home from Wales, that there were rather a lot of things they were ignoring in their fledgeling relationship – like the two hundred miles that separated them most of the time, and kept the relationship perpetually in those early stages, even more than a year after their first official date.

Posy probably would have come with Kit, Rosalind assumed, if he hadn't been bringing Caro. It was fun to see Caro on the arm of the hottest young actor on the block, though. Rosalind imagined Annie was in stitches, watching at home.

They were led out of the cinema, past more fans and more cameras, to the cars waiting to take them to the after party. Rosalind had hoped to catch up with Caro, to see what she'd made of it, but she and Kit were too far ahead, and there were more autographs to sign, anyway.

She saw Posy scanning the crowd, and guessed what she was looking for – the woman who'd called out for Dahlia's help before the movie started. Heaven only knew what that was all about. These days, the three of them were almost synonymous with amateur murder investigations – although whether that was because they'd solved two genuine murder cases together, or because they were famous for playing Dahlia Lively, Rosalind wasn't entirely sure. Either way, the papers had enjoyed coming up with pun-filled headlines for both.

'Any sign?' she asked.

Posy shook her head, without Rosalind needing to elaborate. 'She must have gone.'

'Perhaps.' Except, why would she leave after so desperately calling for their help, when she knew they'd be coming back out this way again?

Probably just a crank, Rosalind decided. Or a ploy to get their attention for a photo or autograph. Nothing to waste time worrying about.

She ignored the strange feeling in the pit of her stomach that suggested otherwise.

The after party was being held at a museum space not far away, and sprawled over several floors and rooms, all well stocked with champagne and canapés. The museum itself seemed to specialise in crime memorabilia, which was presumably why it had been chosen, but Rosalind wasn't entirely sure that *all* of the rooms really fit with the Dahlia Lively vibe.

Almost as soon as she was through the door she was collared by an old acquaintance for a chat, and lost Posy in the melee. It was a very boring five minutes before she was able to escape and explore the rest of the party.

She spotted Posy looking cosy with Kit in a far corner as she passed through one of the side rooms, and the sight made her smile. She was about to move on through the archway to the next exhibit space when Posy looked up and noticed her. She placed a hand on Kit's arm, murmured something to him, then broke away to head towards Rosalind – only to recoil at the exhibit she had to pass close by to reach her.

Looking at it even from a greater distance, Rosalind didn't blame her.

'Okay, I could have lived without ever seeing that,' Posy said, as she stepped around the display of a murder victim's severed head rendered in alarming – and hopefully not authentic – detail. Really, the death and gore theme didn't go so well with the designer dresses and diamonds filling the rooms.

Rosalind tugged on her arm and led her back through to the main atrium, where the displays were less, well, niche. 'Come on. I want to find Caro.'

'Me too.' Posy worried at her lower lip with her teeth. Rosalind had a fairly good idea what was bothering her.

'Stop worrying. She'll have loved you, too.'

'Then where is she?' Posy murmured, as they moved through the crowd.

Rosalind didn't have an answer to that. She'd expected Caro to be waiting at the door, ready to congratulate their Dahlia protégée on a stunning performance – just like they'd both been there at Caro's book launch the night before, to celebrate with her. But so far, their third Dahlia was nowhere to be seen.

The problem with a party like this one, especially when in the company of the star of the movie, was that it was almost impossible to get anywhere quickly. There were too many people who wanted to stop and chat – to pay compliments or, more often, fish for opportunities. Several women stopped Posy under the pretence of asking who had designed her dress, when they had to know that information would be on the gossip sites the next morning. Still, Posy took the chance to promote the work of Kit's up-and-coming designer friend, and Rosalind kept a fixed smile on her face as they made their way around the gathered horde.

Ignoring the waffling of a film critic who was apparently trying to suck up to Posy with some barbed backwards compliments about other actresses, and occasionally Posy herself, Rosalind scanned the crowd again. She didn't find Caro, but she did spot someone who put a real smile on her face this time.

Across the marble hall, Libby McKinley waved from the sweeping staircase, and her companion gently grabbed her arm to stop her from slipping.

'Sorry, you must excuse us,' Rosalind said, not really caring she'd cut the critic off in the middle of a sentence. She slipped a hand through Posy's arm and led her towards the stairs.

'Libby! And Duncan. It's so good to see you both!' Posy leaned in to hug both Libby and her Laird-of-the-Manor boyfriend, and seemed genuinely relaxed and happy for the first time that evening.

Rosalind gave them her own embrace, then stood back. 'So, how did it feel, Libby? Seeing your story up there?'

Libby laughed. 'It's hardly my story, Rosalind. It will always be Lettice's.'

'Your interpretation, then.' Rosalind thought that the script writer wasn't giving herself enough credit. Yes, she might have adapted the story from Lettice's original novel, but she'd certainly made it her own, adding touches and twists that brought it up to date for a modern audience. And that was before she got started on Anton's request for five possible endings.

In the end, Rosalind suspected that everyone would be satisfied with the one he'd chosen for the final cut. Libby certainly seemed to be; she was glowing as she gushed about how good they'd both looked up on the screen, how beautiful the cinematography was, and how the cast had brought her script to life.

Or maybe that glow had to do with something else.

Rosalind reached out to grab Libby's left hand as she waved it around for emphasis as she talked. 'Never mind the film – tell us about this!'

'This' being the giant diamond sitting on Libby's ring finger. Posy gasped and wiggled closer for a look, while Libby blushed a delightful shade of pink.

'Oh, well, yes. I wasn't going to steal anyone's thunder by announcing it tonight but . . . invitations will be in the post!' Libby smiled up at Duncan soppily, and even Rosalind's creaky old heart was warmed by the look they shared.

'We're thinking of a Christmas wedding, up home in Scotland,' Duncan added.

'It sounds perfect,' Rosalind said, approvingly, wondering how Jack would feel about spending Christmas in Scotland. 'And I want to hear all about it later. But first . . .'

'Have you seen Caro yet this evening?' Posy finished for her.

'Oh, she was just upstairs in the detective fiction display room,' Libby said, waving a hand in the general direction of where she'd last seen Caro.

'Of course she was,' Rosalind muttered. 'Probably looking for an exhibit about her personally. We'd better go find her before she starts giving tours to the guests. Congratulations again, you two. Come on, Posy.'

From the balcony level at the top of the main staircase, Rosalind could see out over the whole party. Camera flashes sparkled off champagne glasses, and the volume of the conversation rose well over whatever music was being played over the speakers. But the buzz was good. The buzz spoke of a successful movie, one everyone had enjoyed. Even the producers and the investors were looking relaxed.

Only Posy still looked tense. And Rosalind was sure that as soon as they found Caro, and the other Dahlia told her she'd done a good job, Posy would unclench.

'*There* you are!' Caro emerged from a side room, glass of champagne clutched in one hand, beaming as she leaned in to kiss Posy's cheek. 'Kiddo, you were amazing.'

Rosalind bit back a laugh as she watched Posy's shoulders visibly relax at her words.

'You weren't bad either,' Caro continued, as she embraced Rosalind.

'For an ageing relic?' Rosalind asked, pointedly, one eyebrow raised.

'For a national treasure,' Caro countered.

'What are you doing up here, anyway?' Posy asked, looking around them at the mostly empty balcony.

Rosalind frowned as she followed suit. There were a few small clusters of people up there talking more quietly than the raucous conversations downstairs, but this definitely wasn't where the party was.

And Caro was always where the party was.

'Oh, just checking out the amateur detective display, to see if we're mentioned,' Caro replied, too casually.

Posy clocked it, too, if Rosalind read her look right.

Something was going on with Caro. But finding out what it was would have to wait until after the party, she decided, as Anton was moving purposefully in their direction.

'And here they are. Our three Dahlias.' Posy and Caro both turned as one at the sound of Anton's voice behind them. He gripped hold of the banister as he took the last two steps, followed by three women – one Rosalind recognised, and two she didn't. 'I've got some people who'd like to talk to you three.'

Rosalind glanced across at her friends, and saw all the colour drain from Caro's face.

Maybe they wouldn't have to wait, after all.